D0816202

Also by Kait Ballenger

Seven Range Shifters
Cowboy Wolf Trouble
Cowboy in Wolf's Clothing

WICKED
COWBOY WOLF

KAIT BALLENGER

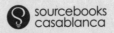

sourcebooks
casablanca

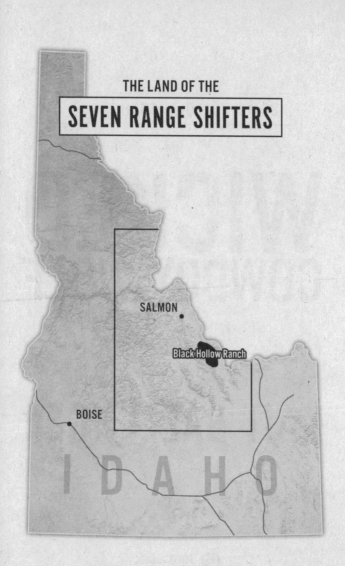

THE LAND OF THE

SEVEN RANGE SHIFTERS

SALMON

Black Hollow Ranch

BOISE

I D A H O

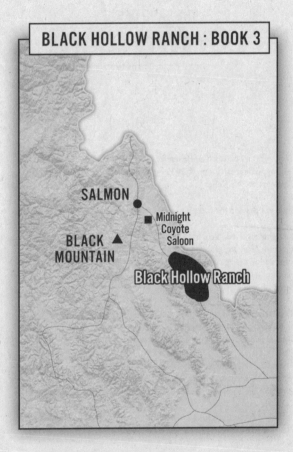

BLACK HOLLOW RANCH : BOOK 3

SALMON

Midnight
Coyote
Saloon

BLACK ▲
MOUNTAIN

Black Hollow Ranch

Published by Sourcebooks Casablanca, an imprint of Sourcebooks
P.O. Box 4410, Naperville, Illinois 60567-4410
(630) 961-3900
sourcebooks.com

Printed and bound in Canada.
MBP 10 9 8 7 6 5 4 3 2 1

Chapter 1

THE RANCH WAS CRAWLING WITH GREY WOLVES.

The Rogue lingered on the outskirts of the forest, watching the activity in the distance as he leaned against the trunk of a mountain pine. He surveyed the vast ranchlands before him as he tipped his Stetson lower, adding an extra layer of shadow to his face. The old cowboy hat was only a precaution. He knew none of the pack wolves would recognize him. Aside from his scars, it was one of the key advantages to having the identity of a ghost, and a good thing too…

…since he didn't trust anyone else to deliver the target.

He shot a glance over his shoulder toward Bee. The brown mustang gave an angry flick of his tail, the black hair smacking against the pine where he was tied. Bee wasn't mighty pleased with this arrangement.

That made two of them.

"Behave," Rogue warned the horse. "It won't be long."

He strode onto the ranch, ignoring Bee's frustrated huffs. It was easy enough to blend in among the Grey Wolf cowboys. With the Seven Range Shifter clans all meeting at Wolf Pack Run today, there was a plethora of unfamiliar shifters on the ranch. None of the guards so much as raised their heads at him. Not that a rogue werewolf would be their top safety priority. Their focus would be protecting the Pact from vampires—a heightened level of security that would be forgotten once the Pact members left the ranch this evening.

That would be their mistake.

It only took him a handful of minutes to locate his target. An entrance to the kitchens connected to the private conference room where the Pact members were meeting. Rogue was patient, slowly making his way inside, slipping among the shadows. Once near the room, he watched a server enter, allowing him a quick glance inside.

Immediately, he spotted her. He couldn't have missed her if he'd tried. Not with the way his heart was pounding.

Standing in the conference room next to her beast of a brother, talking with animated movements as she pointed toward a massive chart behind her, she was breathtaking. Everything he remembered and more.

He shook his head. The pain in his chest was all the reminder he needed. She wasn't his, and she never would be. She'd stopped being a possibility for him long ago.

He watched her, patiently lingering in the shadows of the kitchen as he formulated a plan. She wouldn't recognize him, though his heart knew her better than the back of his own hand. He would have known those gorgeous green eyes anywhere. The ache in his chest grew.

It's better this way, he told himself.

He'd repeat those words until he was convinced they were true.

He didn't care what it took, or how it hurt him. Her life and the lives of so many others depended on his sacrifice. It didn't matter that she didn't recognize him or that he died a little more inside whenever he looked at her. He would keep his promise to her, to his family. No matter the personal consequences.

And come hell or high water, Rogue would survive losing Maeve Grey again…

"Mae, Alexander is headed this way *again*." Maverick's voice held more than a hint of disapproval. He'd hated her "little backup plan" from the start. Her brother loved her, and as such, he'd always been fiercely protective of her, but pack-master or not, this was *her* choice to make, and she'd do whatever it took to save her pack.

Maeve finished scribbling on her napkin as she ignored her brother's protests. The quick sketch had been a nec-essary release of tension. The image of a running horse was more cartoonish than her normal work, but it'd been enough to ease her anxiety for now. It was better than rip-ping her hair out. She'd been trapped at the Seven Range Pact's annual reception listening to Maverick negotiate for nearly two hours now, yet *still* none of the other packmas-ters had made a firm commitment, and with every passing second, the vampires drew closer to destroying everything she cared for.

And all while she was forced to wear a pair of heels. Her cowgirl boots would have been infinitely more comfortable, but beauty knew no pain when it came to saving her pack, so she'd make do. She'd feared the other packmasters would be wary despite Maverick's best laid proposals, and she wasn't about to waste a perfectly good cocktail dress.

Every summer, the seven shifter clans that ruled over Big Sky Country and formed the Seven Range Pact met at an annual reception held at Wolf Pack Run, a formal soiree complete with suits, ties, and dress Stetsons. This year's occasion was the largest and most extravagant yet. Though typically the annual reception was only held during peacetime and was only attended by the varying shifters of the Seven Range Pact, this year, despite the heightened security concerns, Maverick had made an exception and sent invitations welcoming their usual guests along with several additional Canadian shifter clans. Extenuating circumstances, as he called them.

Mae shook her head. She'd worried this plan wouldn't pan out, but Maverick had been insistent, and while she might have formulated her own backup plans, she trusted implicitly that he'd do whatever it took to steer the pack on the correct course. He always had.

In a normal year, the official purpose of the reception was to build camaraderie among the various packs despite their differences in species. As one of the last living members of the Grey family, one of three founding families of the Grey Wolf Pack, Mae had a personal obligation to represent the pack with grace and poise—and no one was more aware of that obligation than she was. But it was the unspoken reason for this year's soiree that had made her concoct her backup plan.

Mae couldn't allow her lifeblood to be the downfall of her pack.

"Mae," Maverick grumbled again. This time, with even more urgency. "Don't offer yourself up like a lamb for slaughter."

"It's *my* choice." She shot her older brother an annoyed glare. "It's *my* blood they used."

She was tired of Maverick's protesting. On more than one occasion, he'd urged her to marry a pure-blooded alpha wolf, for tradition and all that, but to hear her brother tell it, he only wanted the best for her, and there was no way in hell he'd offer her up like this. She rolled her eyes. She failed to see how her plan was much different. At least seducing Alexander to save her pack was *her* decision.

Mae set down her pen, forcing a smile as her eyes traveled across the table and landed on the alpha wolf headed toward them. Alexander Caron was a massive, muscled wall of a Canadian packmaster from a few hours north of Wolf Pack Run, and the man who could save them all, according to her brother.

A month earlier, the Grey Wolves had discovered the vampires' plans to develop an injectable serum that would allow them to feed from shifters, and the purer the blood, the better. Feeding from humans was mere sustenance, but feeding from shifters would increase a vampire's power tenfold. The development would soon change the outcome of the war between the shifters and the vampires unless Mae's kind found a way to combat it. All their enemy had needed to complete their plan was a blood sample from a pure-blooded Grey Wolf...and they'd taken that sample from Mae.

It was only a matter of time before the serum was in wide use, and then her kind would no longer stand a chance against the bloodsuckers.

Alexander had an army full of alpha warriors that would give the Grey Wolves a fighting chance against the vampires, with or without the serum.

If only she could convince *him* of that...

Alexander joined them at their table and extended a hand toward her. "Care to dance again?" he prompted, casting her a smile. His teeth were beautifully white and his beard perfectly trimmed. He was the ideal image of a handsome cowboy.

Most she-wolves would find the powerful alpha wolf handsome, assuming a woman was into the whole clean-cut male thing, but Mae couldn't have been less attracted to this wolf if she tried. She supposed if she had to put her finger on it, it was because she preferred her men a little more on the rough and rugged side, much like the Grey Wolf cowboys—not that any of them ever gave her so much as a second glance, considering her brother was their packmaster. But even that reasoning failed to fully explain *her* lack of interest.

Still, she'd intended to charm Alexander for the sake of the pack, because they needed this alliance, and thus far, all her brother's efforts had been in vain. Not to mention, her role could pay off twofold. Pack expectation dictated she marry an alpha wolf of pure bloodline if she ever planned to settle down, and considering she didn't want any of the alphas at Wolf Pack Run, Alexander was one of her few remaining options. The pack elders hadn't started to nag her yet, but it wouldn't be long, and the way she saw it, maybe if she faked an attraction to Alexander, eventually she would come to care for him.

Maverick had suggested that if she planned to seduce a packmaster in the name of making alliances, he might as well pull out the hot iron, burn a brand on her ass, and send her off to market like all the other cattle on the ranch.

Mae hadn't been amused with that comparison, but as she'd reminded him, *she* wasn't amused by the prospect of an arranged marriage or the notion of trading herself for some alliance either. For the sake of her pack and their collective safety, she'd do anything. But that didn't mean this whole little charade didn't offend every feminist bone in her body.

Desperate times called for desperate measures.

"Mae." Maverick cleared his throat again.

Ignoring Maverick, she smiled at Alexander. "Of course," she said. "I'd be happy to dance with you."

This would be the fourth time since the start of the reception. He still hadn't offered the support of his pack to them, but apparently, dancing more than once an hour was necessary.

Maverick cast her a frustrated look from the corner of his eye as he signaled for one of the waitstaff to bring another glass of whiskey. Maverick might disapprove, but she could practically hear their father's voice in her head, so similar to Maverick's now that it was eerie.

It's a small sacrifice, Mae.

She'd been raised a Grey, which meant sacrificing herself for the greater good of the pack was expected, even if she'd begun resenting the obligation years ago. Maverick knew that struggle as well as she did. She loved her packmates and would do anything for them, but that didn't mean she always had to be pleased about what that required of her.

Mae set down her pen and accepted Alexander's hand. He guided her out onto the dance floor just as a slow country ballad began to pump through the speakers. The lights strung over the tented outdoor dance floor lit up the summer night with a soft romantic feel as a warm breeze wrapped around them. Gently, the alpha wolf pulled Mae into his arms, slowly swaying her around the floor. She forced herself to smile up at him.

"You have a lovely smile," Alexander said as she finished laughing at one of his jokes.

Mae tried not to let that smile fade. "Thank you," she

replied. The compliment was genuine and sweet, but it didn't stir so much as an iota of her interest.

She fought back a heavy sigh. What was wrong with her? She wanted love, marriage, a family, and there was nothing wrong with Alexander—or any of the other alpha wolves the pack elders had suggested over the years. They just weren't...

They just weren't for her...

Because they're not him, her inner self whispered.

The thought made her chest ache. She could think of only one person who'd ever captured her heart, and she hadn't seen him in over twenty years.

"What's on your mind, darlin'?" Alexander asked. He must have sensed her thoughts were elsewhere rather than on the dance floor with him where they *should* have been, had she not been pining for a dead man.

Now was as good a time as ever. Each passing minute gave the vampires more time to put the serum into wide use. She needed to get this show on the road—fast.

"Alexander, dancing with you all evening has been lovely, but why don't we head back to my—"

The alpha wolf shook his head, the brim of his Stetson lowering slightly as he stopped Mae short. "Save your breath, darlin'. I'm not interested."

Mae nearly tripped over one of his cowboy boots. *Stupid high heels.* "E-excuse me?" she sputtered. She couldn't have heard him correctly.

Alexander chuckled. "I've known the game, darlin'."

Mae's brow wrinkled in confusion. "And yet you've gone along with it anyway?"

Alexander nodded. "I have." He spun her outward

before pulling her back and catching her in his arms again. The move was so smooth and belied a gentility that would have made a more receptive woman swoon.

"Because even though you're attracted to me, you think I'm better than that?" she asked.

Man, did he have to go and be so sweet and make her feel like even more of a tool?

"You *are* better than that, but you're wrong on one part." Alexander let out another bemused chuckle. "No offense, darlin', but I'm not attracted to you."

It was all Mae could do not to stop dancing right then and there. "You're not?"

He shook his head as he lowered his voice. A playful grin crossed his lips. "I'm more of a *Brokeback Mountain* kind of cowboy, if you catch my drift."

Mae's eyes widened. "Oh. I wouldn't have thought…" She struggled to find the words.

"Not every gay man has a feminine side," Alexander said. "It's no secret, but I don't make a habit of advertising my sex life to my fellow packmasters."

"Of course." Mae nodded. Maybe that explained the lack of attraction on her end. Perhaps she'd sensed she would have been barking up the wrong tree? Though if she was honest with herself, she knew deep down the problem wasn't Alexander—it was her. She glanced up at the massive alpha wolf. "So why keep asking me to dance? Why bring your pack here?"

Alexander shrugged. "I like to dance, and you're as good a partner as any. Not to mention, I have a profound respect for your brother. He's one of the fiercest and fairest packmasters I've ever known, and I like to examine my options.

This serum thing leaves me with some questions for my own pack and some questions for you."

"Alexander, we're desperate, and if you don't get on board in time, your pack will be too. Last month when the vampires took me captive, their intent was clear. The serum they've created allows—"

"I know. My question isn't about what the serum can do or cause."

Mae raised a brow. "What exactly *is* your question then?"

"I've been listening to your story all night, and I'm still unclear about one part," Alexander said.

Mae swayed along with him, allowing him to lead. "I'd be happy to clarify," she said.

That she could do. Even if her backup plan had failed miserably.

Alexander stared down at her, his dark-brown eyes searing into hers as if he were trying to see through her. "How *exactly* did you escape the vampires' cells?"

Mae nearly choked on her own inhalation of breath. It was the one question she *didn't* want the Canadian pack-master to ask, because if the truth was ever revealed to her brother, to Alexander, to anyone here at this reception, their chances of ever claiming more allies would be shot. The consequences for her pack would be deadly.

"That's a good question," she said.

While she struggled to formulate an explanation for Alexander—one that hid the dark truth—the alpha wolf twirled her around again. But as she faced away from him, she let go of his hand, stopping midspin, because at that moment, any hope she had of an explanation was lost.

Mae froze. Slowly, she blinked, standing there like

a deer in the headlights. She couldn't possibly be seeing straight.

It was *him*. The answer to Alexander's question and one of her darkest secrets was standing right there on the other side of the dance floor. As if it were normal, as if *he* were normal.

Nothing about this moment—nothing about *him*—was normal.

Her heart began to pound.

The Rogue. The Dark Devil. The King of the Misfit Wolves. She'd heard the nicknames more than once. And yet he lingered there in the shadows, toasting her with a champagne flute as he cast her an amused smirk. Then he drew a long sip from the glass. Mae blinked, hoping, *praying* the wolf before her was only a memory, a figment of her imagination, caused by the stress of Alexander's questioning and that would suddenly disappear.

But he didn't.

She gaped. The Rogue was one of their most wanted enemies, a criminal wolf who was foe to all and friend to none. He was considered a leader among the packless rogues of their kind, a violent vigilante. His true identity was known to none, and even now, few had seen his face and lived to tell about it. Mae wasn't certain how the leaders of the Seven Range Pact didn't notice him.

From the heels of his leather cowboy boots all the way to the smirk across his face, this devil with a too-charming grin was a man not to be crossed.

And yet she'd struck a bargain with him when she'd been trapped in the vampires' cells, still bleeding from where they'd drawn her blood for the serum. Her freedom and safe release from the cell in exchange for the tool he'd used to make their escape—along with her silence about him and his identity.

In her mind, she was back there again. Inside the vampires' cell as he peered at her from the shadows of the next cell over. She could still hear the deep rumble of his voice as it wrapped around her.

Even from the corner of the dance floor, he commanded the room, towering over the Pact members in both height and hard-earned muscle. Only a handful of the Grey Wolf's elite warriors compared, and yet he was watching *her*. His ice-blue eyes met hers, and a devious grin curled his lips. He was taunting her, daring her to out his identity.

But she couldn't.

Not unless she wanted to negate the deal they'd made, and not unless she wanted to ruin the Grey Wolves' chances with Alexander. If anyone knew she'd partnered with an infamous criminal to escape the vampires, they'd never believe a word she said about the serum. Any chance of them gaining more allies would fly out the window. It would be a death sentence for her pack.

Whatever the Rogue was here for, she needed him to leave.

Now.

The feeling of Alexander's hand squeezing her shoulder in concern wrenched her back into the moment. "Maeve?"

Mae blinked several times, glancing to where Maverick sat at the head table, then over her shoulder to Alexander and then back to where the Rogue had stood. Already, he was gone, the racing thrum of her pulse the only trace he'd been there in the first place.

"Maeve, are you all right?" Alexander asked.

"Y-yes," she stuttered as she tried to recover. "I'm not sure what came over me."

———————————

The pink summer sunset had long since faded to nightfall by the time Mae returned to her cottage on the other side of the Grey Wolf compound. As she approached home, she cringed at the thought of the poor excuse she'd given Alexander. There was no way he'd bought her lie. Sure, she and Maverick had scheduled Alexander for a meeting with the Pact, which was a small step forward, but if they didn't get him on board and fast, their prospects were limited.

But Mae was determined. She would find a way to save her pack. She had to.

Feeling more than a little defeated, she shuffled up to her door, scanning the other nearby pack cabins. Hers was one of many adjacent to the dining hall and the main compound building, which housed the elite warriors and the main pack offices. She grabbed her keys from her purse. As she did so, she glanced over her shoulder, as if she might find the Rogue lingering there in the darkness. But she didn't. He'd disappeared without a trace.

She released a long sigh. From what she knew of his dangerous reputation, it was just like the arrogant bastard to trod right into a pack of alphas that would just as soon see him torn apart. He really was a rogue with a devil-may-care attitude to match his title. She gripped her keys tighter in her hand.

After unlocking her front door, she slipped inside.

Immediately, the sound of tiny hooves clopping against tile sounded from the darkness. She flicked on the dim entryway light. Tucker, her teacup pig, stared up at her from the white tiled floor, his beady black eyes sparkling with pleasure at her arrival. He let out a pleased oink. Mae grinned.

Bending down, she scooped him into her arms, coddling him like a baby as she cooed at him. Still a piglet, Tucker was no bigger than a small dog, and according to the breeder, he'd been the runt of the teacup litter and would likely stay small.

With Tucker cradled against her, Mae made quick work of feeding him a bottle of milk replacer before snuggling him into his fluffy, pink dog bed in her living room. Once the piglet was rocked to sleep, she showered before she changed into her nightgown and settled into the comfort of her bedsheets. The day had left her worn out, but her mind refused to calm.

Had she really seen the Rogue, or had it all been in her head?

That question still plagued her. She wasn't sure how he would have gotten onto the ranch without detection, especially considering the heightened security for the reception.

She shook her head. It must have been her imagination, a memory triggered by the stress of Alexander's questions. The Rogue couldn't possibly have shown up at Wolf Pack Run only to disappear again.

Though it had felt so real…

She sighed, sinking deeper into her mattress. It wouldn't be the first time she'd thought of him since their encounter in the vampire coven.

Heat rose in her cheeks. She'd dreamed of him almost

every night since—and not in the way she *should* have. The memory of the night when her life had been threatened by bloodsuckers was a dark one, but when she dreamed of that night, of him, her dream often took a completely different course from reality. Instead of dreaming of the danger she'd faced, she'd woken more than once to the thought of his uncharacteristic heroism as he whisked her from the vampires' cells, only to find her own hand exploring between her legs.

It was sick. She knew it. She shouldn't be attracted to a dangerous criminal like him. Despite that, he stirred something primitive inside her. She knew what sort of dark circles he traveled in, yet she couldn't seem to help it. A wolf like the Rogue was everything forbidden to her: a non–Grey Wolf, a vigilante.

Not to mention one of her brother's enemies, and the antithesis of every criterion she should consider for a mate.

Somehow, that only made him more appealing.

By her birthright, she was destined for a Grey Wolf alpha warrior. She shuddered at the thought. The Grey Wolf warriors were all fine men, handsome cowboys, but they were practically her *brothers*.

Mae tossed and turned in her bed as she tried to put the Rogue from her mind, but still his face taunted her. Eventually, her hand trailed beneath her nightgown. Maybe if she eased this ache, the desire would go away. Maybe then, sleep would claim her. Slowly, her fingers probed the folds between her legs, locating her own clit. She knew her body, what she liked.

Gently, she massaged and probed as she remembered how it had felt when the warmth of his breath had brushed against her ear, the deep timbre of his voice thrumming through her.

You won't regret this, he'd whispered.

She imagined his lips trailing downward.

What would it be like to be with a criminal like him? Something told her every touch, every caress would be more powerful, more sinful…just *more*. Soon, she was moaning in climax, the walls of her core tightening in a delicious wave that sent a rush of moisture straight to her center. She cried out, arching her back against the pillows.

As the last throes of her orgasm shook her, she relaxed into her sheets, sated, though it was little more than a fantasy. At that thought, a pang of sorrow thrummed through her. That was all her dreams would ever be—fantasy. Not just him, but *all* her heart's desires. She wanted more than she could have. She always had. She loved her pack, but the duties that bound her to them had never been her choice. She may have been a Grey by birth, but if she were braver, she'd live her own life. She'd make her own choices.

If she were free…

Mae lay there, the weight of the things she'd never have pressing down on her, constraining her chest so much that she struggled to breathe.

If only…

At least she could dream. Her dreams and desires were hers alone. She released a long sigh, switching on the light of her bedside table as she reached for a book to read. Until the sound of a familiar voice came from the darkness.

"Evenin', Princess."

Chapter 2

THE DIM LIGHT OF A TABLE LAMP CUT THROUGH THE shadows. Rogue leaned against the bedroom doorway, his Stetson hiding the scarred half of his face as he raked his gaze over her. As soon as Maeve Grey had flicked the light on, she'd scrambled to her feet. She stood at her bedside, wearing little more than a thin, pink nightgown and clutching a large hardcover book from her nightstand like a weapon.

He shook his head.

Despite her pure Grey Wolf bloodline, by both wolf and human standards she was petite, which meant physically armed with knowledge or not, she wouldn't hold her own in a fight against an alpha like him.

But if looks could kill…

She snarled at him. "What the hell are you doing here?"

As if he hadn't made a habit of sneaking into her room hundreds of times before. He shook his head. He'd known when they'd met in the vampires' cells that she didn't recognize him. Twenty years and a half-deformed face changed a man, but still, that didn't make her lack of recognition sting any less.

He crossed his arms, leaning harder against the doorframe as he took in the sight of her.

She gaped at him as if she'd seen a ghost. She *had*, though *she* was none the wiser.

"You're in *my* bedroom," she snapped.

He shrugged a single shoulder. "I gave you fair warning."

She blinked. "I didn't expect you to show up in my *bedroom*."

"And where else do you suggest I find you alone? I couldn't have announced my plans in the middle of that fancy soiree of yours. It would have scandalized the Pact, and then where would that have left you?"

Her lips tightened into an enraged pucker, and she glared at him.

He grinned. Even when they were kids, he'd always had an appreciation for her hot temper. Some things didn't change.

He shoved off the doorframe, straightening to his full height. "You were never taught to check the shadows of your apartment? Seems like something that beast you call your brother wouldn't overlook."

"I must have missed that lesson," she said.

"Pity."

Maverick had been remiss in his brotherly duties then. Hence, the reason she was here, unprotected and alone with *him*, one of the most dangerous wolves in North America. His eyes narrowed as he watched her. Clearly, she didn't recognize the danger he posed.

That was a mistake.

He didn't intend to harm her, but *she* didn't know that.

She'd made his plans easy for him, far too easy for his liking. The spare key to her apartment had been hidden directly under the sunflower doormat. Not that he couldn't have picked the lock, but that trusting inclination of hers would make his job more difficult, get her into trouble. At the very least, if the fire blazing in her green eyes was any indication, he could lead a she-wolf to water, but he couldn't make her drink.

Good girl, Mae-day.

"What are you doing here?" she asked.

"At the moment?" He grinned. "Observing."

Her eyes widened in realization. From the way her shoulders tensed, she was painfully aware of exactly what he'd just observed.

That made two of them.

"How long have you been there?" She sounded breathless, throaty. All too similar to the noises she'd made.

"Long enough." A smirk crossed his lips as he raked his gaze over her. "Don't worry, Princess. I only arrived during the grand finale."

She blushed, and his cock gave an eager jerk. *No.* Maeve Grey was no longer meant for the likes of him, but after that little display, he was still as hard as a damn diamond. Old habits died hard, he supposed. At fifteen, he'd been so crazy in love with her that he could scarcely see straight. But that had been when he was young, naive, before he'd learned the hard way that love was for fools who enjoyed tragedy and that she'd never be his. They lived in different worlds now, universes apart, and it'd been so long since he'd cared for anyone that Rogue wasn't even sure his black heart remembered how.

Even if he wanted to love her, he'd never be worthy of her.

But fuck, if he didn't still want her.

He gave her another once-over. Despite her large green eyes and spritely features, many a Montana cowboy would overlook her. With her thin frame and dark-brown hair so short, a lesser man would have said she wasn't feminine enough—boyish even. But only a blind man could miss the plumpness of her pink mouth, the delicate curve of her hips, and the perky breasts hidden beneath her nightgown. They were no more than a handful, but enough to taste, to lick, to tease, and that was all before the scent of her sex had filled his nose. Now that he knew the delicious sounds she made when she came…

That was even more dangerous.

He stepped toward her, and she growled, raising the book higher.

He nearly chuckled. "If I wanted to hurt you, I could have done so while you were…"

"I thought I was alone." Beneath his gaze, the crimson on her cheeks grew deeper by the second until there wasn't an inch of pink in sight. "S-sometimes I need help sleeping," she stammered.

He quirked a brow in amusement. As if she needed an excuse to want pleasure…

Slowly, he prowled toward her, closing the distance between them. She shouldn't feel ashamed. She was fucking beautiful. He plucked the book from her hands, disarming her. "And what keeps you up at night, Maeve Grey?" He leaned in close, his breath a whisper against her ear. "Whose face do you think of as you pleasure yourself? Some valiant Grey Wolf Prince Charming?"

Perhaps the clean-cut packmaster she'd danced with all evening.

Her eyes flashed to the golden color of her wolf, and she snarled at him.

Confirmation enough, as far as he was concerned. The predictability in that annoyed him.

Immediately, she changed the subject. "If it's my brother you're here for, your timing couldn't be worse," she said.

Of course she'd think he was here for her beast of a brother. Her whole life would have centered around living in his shadow.

Maverick Grey was a massive warrior-sized thorn in Rogue's side. Bloodshed between the rogue wolves and the packmasters who treated them as second-class citizens wasn't Rogue's goal, particularly when it came to Maverick Grey. The Grey Wolf packmaster was one of Rogue's fiercer and more formidable opponents, rivaled on the battlefield by only a select few, himself included. In that regard, he had a healthy respect for the self-righteous bastard. He and Maverick had squared off indirectly more than once, battling like a heated game of chess. Rogue was more a thief than a murderer, procuring resources and securing backroom deals for his kind, but if he could screw the Grey Wolves over in the process, all the better.

Not that there wasn't a fair share of blood on his hands.

"It's not your brother I'm interested in, Princess."

Had she been in wolf form, Rogue had no doubt her fur would have bristled. "I'm no princess," she growled.

Clearly, he'd struck a nerve.

"You aren't going to hurt me," he said.

"You say that as if you know me."

"I do know you, Mae." Those words were truer than she'd realize. "I knew you the moment you made a deal with me in the vampires' cells. The only thing I didn't know was how soon we'd meet again." He retreated on that enigmatic statement and sank into a nearby recliner, draping his legs across the arm, his old, black leather cowboy boots crossed at the ankles. "Are you not Maeve, daughter of Thomas and Sharla Grey? Younger sister to Maverick, the current pack-master of the Grey Wolves?"

She didn't respond. They both knew the answer to that.

"Have you not lived a life full of privilege and leisure, sitting atop your pedestal in the Versailles that is Wolf Pack Run? Protected, cared for, safe…"

He'd given everything, nearly lost his own life to ensure she had those comforts and yet…

"All while you turned down your nose at the rest of us."

At all rogues, the packless wolves among their kind.

Wolves like him.

The benefits of pack life were plentiful: a built-in support network, a safe home base, a guaranteed income, bountiful monetary and educational resources, and most importantly, protection from outsiders. Whether they were threatened by other shifter clans, vampires, the hunters of the Execution Underground, or even human law enforcement, pack wolves held a distinct advantage in survival.

It was a sheer numbers game. Rogue knew that firsthand. Rogue wolves were loners by either birth or circumstance, and the numbers weren't on their side. They were outcasts, misfits, the vagabonds of their world. Pack wolves like Mae would never understand. She would never know what it was like to go hungry, to not have a home, to be a pariah among both wolves and humanity.

"I've never done *anything* to the rogues," she said.

"Exactly." He sneered. "Let them eat cake."

Just like the rest of them. He'd do well to remember that. She'd done nothing, said nothing, while those without a pack lived a life harder than she'd ever know. He'd come to expect it by now. They all did, yet she disappointed him more than most.

Because he'd once thought her better than that.

He scowled. They were the ignorant dreams of a silly boy. *She's not for you, and she never will be...*

Mae's hands balled into fists. "My cage may be different from yours, but it's still a cage."

He tilted his head. That's what she thought of the privileged life he'd given her?

He shouldn't have been surprised. They both had something the other wanted. She had the protection of the Seven Range Pact for her family. He had true freedom, what she'd wanted ever since they were children all those years ago. Freedom she'd never known, and from the desire in her eyes, freedom she still wanted—badly.

What he wouldn't give to see her enjoy just a taste of it.

"And what about you? What saint are you to point out my flaws?" she asked. "How are my sins any worse than yours?" She counted off his crimes on her fingers. "Thievery, bribery, extortion, breaking and entering... I'm sure I'm missing some."

"You forgot grand larceny, but I'll excuse it this time." He grinned. Her list only touched the tip of the iceberg, but the challenge in her eyes stirred something low in his belly. He rose to his feet. "But there's one key difference between you and me, Princess."

She bristled at the nickname again.

Slowly, he stepped toward her, lowering his voice into a conspiratorial whisper. "I don't pretend to be the good guy."

Her eyes flashed to her wolf. She was a spitfire, and he liked that more than he cared to admit.

"If you didn't come for my brother, then who? What shifter of the Seven Range Pact are you here to extort, or do you just enjoy taunting me?" Her words were spit like venom, but he'd been bitten by worse vipers.

"I have no interest in the Seven Range Pact."

Her eyes narrowed as if she didn't believe him. "But why the risk then? I could have exposed you."

"We both knew you wouldn't. I walked straight into that reception and practically served myself up on a platter for your brother and the Pact, yet you didn't so much as utter a word."

"Of course I didn't," she snapped. "We had a deal."

"You're a woman of your word, Maeve Grey. I knew that from the start. But even for an honest woman like you, a promise to an enemy is fool's gold in the face of protecting your pack. It's not the deal we struck that made me trust in your silence. It's more than that."

"I kept my word. That's all."

"Don't lie, Mae. Not to me."

"You need to leave." Her mouth drew into that angry, delicious pucker that made him envision what would happen if he pressed his lips against hers. He'd make her melt against him, part those tightened lips with ease.

"Tell me the true reason you didn't expose me, and I'm gone."

And there it was, the challenge sparked in her eyes, and before she could think better of it, she was squaring off with him. "I didn't tell them because I didn't want to." She said the words as if she hated it, as if the truth angered her. "I wanted to keep it my secret. Make my own choice for once."

So Maeve Grey wanted to emerge from beneath the

pressure of her brother's thumb, and he was her means to do it.

"That, I believe," he purred. This was the Maeve he knew. She might not have recognized who he truly was, but she was still intrigued...by him, by the darkness, by everything that was forbidden to her. She always had been. He'd known that from the start.

"Now go," she said, pointing toward the door again. "I won't let you ruin our chances with Alexander. My packmates depend on it." From the fire in her eyes, she'd do anything to protect those she cared for.

Their goals were more alike than she knew.

"Don't worry, Princess. I already have what I need."

She frowned. "And what is that exactly?"

A devious grin crossed his lips. "You."

"Me?" Slowly, she backed away. "You said you would leave."

He grinned. "Fool's gold, remember?"

A look of panic came over her. She hadn't been afraid before, but she was now. Good. Let her see the real him. Nothing deserving her intrigue. He was the monster in the darkness, the wolf hidden in the shadows. Everything she should stay away from.

Without warning, she darted past him, but he didn't try to stop her. She wouldn't go far. She ran to the kitchen and grabbed a massive butcher knife from the knife block, wielding it like a weapon. At least it was better than a book.

He sauntered in after her. "Does brandishing cutlery make you feel better?"

Her gaze darted between him and the blade. "Yes."

"Then by all means." He leaned against her granite

countertop, ignoring the knife. He knew she wouldn't dare use it. Not this time. "Don't worry, Princess. I'm not going to hurt you."

That wasn't a part of the plan. Even he didn't prey on the vulnerable. He'd caused trouble for the Grey Wolves more than once, but he had every intention of protecting Mae, even with his life if necessary. It was a shame she had no idea what she was worth or the power she held. Any of the leaders at that reception earlier would have fought any battle, shed any amount of blood, if they knew her true value like he did. But they didn't. Not yet.

A life as a criminal had its perks.

He slid his hand over the granite countertop as he moved toward her. The onyx rings on his fingers flashed in the dim glow. "You wanted to make your own choices, and I'm offering you your first one."

He watched with a grin as she lowered the knife ever so slightly. He saw right through her. She'd made her choice the moment she'd chosen not to expose him to the Pact.

If she knew what was good for her, she'd never make a deal with a wolf like him, but Mae had never been afraid, even when they'd been children and he'd been a scared, mean little boy without a friend in the world.

He was no longer that scared little boy who could save her from the darkness, because he *was* the darkness. And if Maeve Grey wanted the freedom of life lived in the shadows…well, then he'd give it to her.

Chapter 3

MAE HELD THE BLADE STEADY. "WHAT ARE YOU OFFERING?" she asked.

Apparently, she hadn't learned her lesson after making a deal with him the first time. She watched the Rogue with wary eyes, careful of any sudden movement he made. She didn't think he was here to hurt her, but she was smart enough not to fully trust him either.

She wasn't about to underestimate a wolf like him.

He straightened from where he leaned against the counter to his full height until he towered over her. All long limbs corded with muscle. He moved with the languid grace of a predator. She'd only seen that kind of movement from a handful of the strongest Grey Wolf alpha warriors. The warriors with the darkest pasts and the most enemy deaths to their name.

"The kind of deal that gets you allies far more powerful than Alexander," he answered.

He stepped into the dim glow of the moonlight streaming through the kitchen window and Mae gasped. Up close in the vampire cells, she'd noticed his scars, a sharp contrast to the intact side of his face, which revealed a chiseled chin, sharp cheekbones, and a regal blade of a nose. But in the cells, his scars had been cast in fiery dungeon shadows. Now, as he prowled closer, his full features emerged. The moonlight highlighted his past wounds in stark relief. Several large scars marred the right side, stretching from above his brow all the way to his chin. They gnarled and puckered the smooth skin, showing clear evidence of the dark life he lived.

For a wolf not to heal, even from a wound like that, the blade that cut him had to have been drenched in liquid silver. Once the metal particles entered the bloodstream, a shifter's healing ability was stunted and functioned little better than that of a human. It was a cruel, vile technique meant to maim and destroy, practiced only among the worst of their kind.

Whoever had done that to him had intended to kill him and failed...

Mae's heart pounded in her chest as she struggled to draw breath. He was as intimidating as he was beautiful. The scars were horrifying, and they should have made him alarming to look at, terrifying even, but they only made him breathtaking somehow. Powerful. She couldn't bring herself to look away.

What she wouldn't give to be able to capture his likeness. To have him sit for her as she replicated the challenging planes of his face in graphite. He'd be a difficult but worthwhile subject. Carefully, she studied his face, the sharp caverns of his cheekbones and the coldness of his icy blue eyes. There was something so familiar about that wicked gaze that stopped her breath short.

A dark smirk crossed his lips, the one that both irked her and did unimaginable things between her legs. To think he'd just watched as she'd...

Another blush flooded her cheeks.

His mischievous grin widened as if he caught her thoughts.

"Do you know anything about snake venom, Mae?" he asked, catching her off guard.

She gave him a once-over. "No, but I imagine you do." She'd never met another wolf who reminded her more of a coiled viper prepared to strike. It was as intriguing as it was unnerving.

"You can't make antivenom without the original source. The venom is the base of the antidote." Those cold eyes raked over her. "And right now, you're the vampires' perfect kind of poison."

Mae stiffened. "What do you mean?"

"There's a bloodsucker, one of the vampires' scientists. He was one of the key developers in creating the vampires' serum."

"The serum from my blood?"

"None other. Ever since I learned what those bloodsuckers were up to, I've been tracking him, but he's gone off the grid. Vanished. Likely on his coven leader's orders. To protect their secrets."

"And how do you know this?"

"I'm a dealer in secrets and favors, Mae. You know that well, and when you're a wolf like me, you know the right questions to ask from the right sources."

His answer was more cryptic than she cared for, but she didn't press further. "And what does that have to do with me?" she asked.

"Everything." He eased closer. "Before he vanished, this bloodsucker was tasked with finding a way to make the serum he'd created from your blood foolproof, perfect for widespread use against shifters, but word on the street is he found a way to counteract the serum. There's only one antidote, a counterinjection that reverses the effects of the serum..."

Mae's breath caught. An antidote to the vampires' serum would be the Grey Wolves' saving grace. Everything they'd needed from Alexander and more.

"And the bloodsucker scientist who created it can only create an antidote injection for widespread use by obtaining further blood samples from the original source of the serum," Rogue finished.

From the original source...

"Me." It was a statement, not a question.

"None other."

Mae gaped. Her blood had been used to create the injectable serum that could be the downfall of her species, but it could also be used as a cure for that same injection.

Her mouth went dry. "But the vampires don't want an antidote for widespread use," she breathed.

The Rogue gave a single tilt of his head. "Precisely."

"Which means..." Her voice trailed off.

Something darkened in his icy blue eyes, sending a chill down her spine. "Which means the vampires want you dead," he finished.

Mae was shaking her head. This couldn't be happening. It couldn't. "No, they already took what they needed from me. They created their serum injection. They got what they wanted."

He quirked a single brow. His Stetson dipped low over his eyes, covering his scars. Even with them, he was entirely too handsome. Why did the devil come in such an appealing package? "And you think that'll stop them?" he asked. "Their serum injection means nothing so long as there is the possibility of counteracting it by creating an antidote. So long as you live and breathe, you're a threat to their plan. Whoever has both their scientist and you could stop them in their tracks."

Mae didn't respond. If what he said was true, she needed to confess everything to Maverick, and fast. Maverick would be angry—furious even—but he would be fair and forgiving. Even on his worst days, he was a model older brother. He'd always found a way to make time for her as his little sister, and she knew he had always cared deeply for her well-being, starting long before their parents had passed years ago, leaving only the two of them behind. He would be angry with her, but this was bigger than her. She could trust Maverick to handle the situation, and while the Rogue might have saved her life once before, she couldn't trust him. He was a known criminal. Hell, she didn't even know his real name.

His predatory gaze followed her every move, waiting for her reaction. His stare made her feel naked, laid bare. And that was saying something, considering he'd already seen her do...*that*.

She cleared her throat, putting on her sternest secretary voice, the one she reserved for when one of their ranching business associates was giving her flak or trying to undercut them on a deal. "This has all been very intriguing, but you need to go."

He chuckled as he eased closer, forcing her to step back. "I'm not leaving until you hear my offer."

"What could you possibly have to offer me?"

"Everything you wish," he countered.

Mae laughed. She didn't believe him for a second. "Sure you can."

"What makes you think I can't?" he asked.

She hesitated as her laughter cut short. She supposed that was a good question. She knew how powerful he was. In some ways, not even her brother could rival him. Not when it came to navigating the supernatural underworld. Maverick had to make the honorable choice—always—to play by the pack's rules and traditions.

She shook her head. Something still wasn't adding up. "Why me? Why bring this to me and not Maverick?"

From the quirk of his lips, that question seemed to amuse him. "Why not you?"

Mae blinked. His answer caught her off guard. She served this pack every day, cared about them as her family. She'd sacrificed so many choices for them, no less than Maverick, and yet she didn't even have the title or the power of being packmaster in return. All because he'd been born first? Because he was an alpha *male*? She would never begrudge her brother his role as packmaster—he'd more than earned her and the pack's respect over the years—but the pack's inheritance traditions weren't exactly progressive.

This concerned her directly, so hell, Rogue was right. Why *not* her? Why wasn't it her place to make a deal with this devil if it would save her pack?

"Once word spreads, not even your brother will be able to protect you, Maeve. Not only will the vampires want to destroy you, but you think none of the Seven Range Pact will double-cross the Grey Wolves to get the antidote first? Think again."

The hairs on the back of Mae's neck prickled. Of course. If further blood samples from her were the key to creating an antidote for widespread use, she'd become sought after like a commodity. A tool used for power. It would be a race to the proverbial finish line. Whatever pack had access to blood samples from her would need only find the scientist who knew how to re-create the antidote for mass production—and having the solution to counteract the vampire's serum would give any pack unprecedented power.

"The only way you get out of this alive is if you disappear," he continued. "If *no one* is able to find you." His implication was clear.

Who better to help her disappear than him?

"But what do you get out of this?" she asked. "Rogue wolves don't have a side in this war."

"Think again, Princess. When the vampires wanted test subjects, who do you think they targeted? A missing pack member draws far too much notice. Involved or not, they'll make *us* their victims again. We need that antidote as much as you do. Our lives depend on it."

He drew closer.

She tried to move, but he blocked her path.

He wouldn't let her walk away that easily. And he'd already tipped his hand when he said he'd come for *her*.

She brandished the knife again, but he suddenly had hold of her wrist, disarming her within seconds. He slammed the blade onto the granite countertop. She had nowhere to go. No escape.

This close to him, she should have been scared, but she wasn't.

She felt the heat radiating from him. He didn't touch her, but somehow he didn't have to. Her nipples tightened in anticipation, betraying her, and her breath quickened. She'd never reacted this way to another male before. Having him close like this was visceral, primal.

"We're the unwilling guinea pigs in the Grey Wolves war, and the Pact continues to turn a blind eye." His voice was low. "I won't sit by as they kill another of mine. Help me, and I'll help you and your pack."

It was crazy. He made it sound so easy.

"And that's all you expect in return? For the antidote to be given to the rogues as well?" she asked.

"I told you I deal in secrets, favors." He smiled. "I'll collect further payment when it's due," he answered cryptically.

She sucked in a harsh breath.

"Time is what you need, Mae," he said. His voice was coaxing, an alluring velvety growl. "I can buy you time."

Deep down, she knew he was right. This would be new information for Maverick. It would take weeks to find the right intel to move forward, but the Rogue likely already had leads and plans for how to find the scientist, and the clock was ticking. Each moment that passed without the antidote endangered the lives of her pack members, her family.

"I'll find the bloodsucker that can create the antidote from your blood sample to save your pack, and in the meantime, you'll have the ability to disappear, to remain safe under my protection, and whatever else you wish. It's a generous offer." The Rogue leaned in toward her. He was so close she saw flecks of gray in the deep blue of his irises, like ice floating in a freezing ocean. The warmth of his breath brushed her ear, sending a delicious chill down her spine. "There're things I can give you that others can't," he whispered.

She wasn't so certain he was talking about the vampires anymore.

"Tell me what you want, Princess, and it's yours." His words vibrated through her like a gentle, thrumming purr.

"I just want to save my pack," she murmured. "I want the antidote for them. That's all." Without her, they wouldn't be in their current position. Not if she hadn't been taken captive by the vampires. Sure, if not her, it could have easily been someone else in the pack, but that failed to matter. *She* was the sister of the packmaster, the pure-blooded wolf whose blood had been pivotal to the vampires' plans. She couldn't let her pack down.

Rogue's hand fell away from her cheek, and she was suddenly all too aware of the loss of his touch. "Done." He stepped away from her. His absence left a void of heat in its wake. "You shouldn't have agreed."

Mae's mouth went dry. "Why not?" she asked.

A dark grin crossed his lips. It was part warning, part amusement. "Because nothing good ever comes from deals with a devil like me."

She opened her mouth to respond, but in the lull of silence, she heard the quiet snick of the lock on her door turning. The noise broke the spell between them. Had her wolf senses not been attuned due to Rogue's presence, she wouldn't have even heard it. Mae froze. Fear gripped her. She glanced toward the Rogue.

The mischief in his eyes was gone, replaced instead with intense focus. "Do as I say," he hissed. Without warning, he was beside her again. He gripped her by the waist and lifted her, throwing her over his shoulder as if she weighed little more than a bale of hay.

Sweeping her into her pantry, he lowered her from his shoulder, pinning her against the shelving as her legs dangled over his hips. He drew the door against him until they were wedged in the corner. Anyone looking inside would see only canned goods and other nonperishables, but if one of the vamps were to actually come in or look behind the door…

Silently, they waited, their ears pricked to the slightest movement. Several minutes passed as he and Mae lingered there, their bodies pressed together. When no further sound came, the tension in her body eased.

"Maybe it was just my brother or one of my packmates?" she suggested. More than one of them had a key to her place, for safety protocol.

Rogue shook his head, drawing her attention toward him as he silently raised a finger to his lips again. His message was clear.

They could still be out there, waiting, watching. She and the Rogue weren't in the clear just yet.

She nodded as she stared up into his face.

In the darkness, her wolf eyes traced his features. He was all sharp angles and hollows. With the threat of the vampires lessened, she was suddenly aware of how close they were. The heavy bulk of his muscled frame pressed into her, and the spiced scent of his aftershave filled her nose.

Through her nightgown, the rough fly of his jeans rubbed her center. Whether from their nearness or the adrenaline of battle she wasn't certain, but she could feel the rock-hard length of him, pressing against her. She bit her lower lip, trying to hide her desire as damp heat pooled between her legs. Her clit was still sensitive from where she'd pleasured herself, and every slight movement he made massaged her, teased her.

He glanced down at her again as his eyes flashed to the gold of his wolf's eyes. A dark emotion she couldn't place reflected there, and a wicked grin crossed his lips. He smelled her desire, her arousal. He had to, which meant he knew *exactly* what this was doing to her. He leaned in until they were nearly nose to nose. Even in the darkness, she could see the hunger in his eyes.

"You're playing with fire," he warned. His whisper shivered through her. His lips were so close they almost brushed against hers.

She wasn't certain what he meant by that. But for a moment, it didn't matter that they were strangers. She inched closer, pure instinct taking over. "I've never been afraid of fire," she whispered back.

Something dark flared in his eyes, and her breath caught. If he drew any closer, his mouth would be on hers. Her lips parted, anticipating. Mae wasn't certain who leaned toward whom. All she knew was that his lips were on hers, his mouth claiming hers in a kiss that was as dark and tempting as the man himself.

She melted into him.

Being kissed by the Rogue was like being kissed by sin. Temptation. Desire. Need. Those words held meaning now. And she couldn't get enough.

His mouth pressed against hers, opening the seam of her lips with ease as his tongue stroked against hers in fierce, powerful swipes. He tasted like Tennessee whiskey, a delicious mixture of malt and rye. He was everywhere, one of his hands massaging through her hair. The other gripped her waist as he pulled her closer.

He ground his length against her. She felt herself slicken,

and a familiar pressure built between her legs. As if her body had a mind of its own, she rocked her hips against him, bucking and moving until she moaned against his mouth. His cock stiffened.

Just when she thought he might take her right there against the pantry wall, he froze. He broke the kiss between them, though his lips lingered near hers. If she didn't know any better, she would have said there was pain in his eyes when he looked at her.

His whole body tensed in a way that cut the tension between them.

At his alert, she sensed the presence too. There was movement in her living room.

Lowering her to the floor, he turned toward the door, using his large frame to shield her. His hand fell to his blade.

From where they stood behind the pantry door, through the thin space between the door and frame, she had a sliver of view across her kitchen and living room. The light from her bedside lamp cast shadows of movement on the kitchen floor. Gnarled tree branches and another form. A chill ran down her spine as a shadow approached. She gripped Rogue's arm, pointing toward the movement.

A deep, guttural grunt sounded. Mae's heart kicked into overdrive as she realized the source of the noise. It wasn't the vampires that had found them.

It was a teacup pig.

She caught Rogue's arm just as he drew his dagger. "It's only Tucker," she whispered. "My pig."

Rogue quirked a brow. "You keep a pig in your *house*?" He looked at her as if she'd grown two heads. She supposed a cowboy like him would think that was insane. Her brother certainly did.

"He's a pet," she shot back.

At the sound of Mae's whispers, Tucker wandered into the pantry with a pleased grunt.

Rogue glanced down toward the offending piglet. Tucker grunted again, his beady black eyes gazing up at Rogue as if to say *I found you,* before he wandered back out of the pantry, likely back toward his fluffy, pink dog bed.

In response, Rogue's lip curled into a snarl. "Damn pig."

Mae frowned. She was about to tell him, Rogue or not, that no one snarled at Tucker…

But that was when she heard her front door slowly creak open.

"Tuck—!"

Rogue clapped a hand over her mouth, muffling her shriek of terror in the nick of time. "Scream and you'll be dead before sunrise," he hissed against her ear.

The sickly sweet smell of death wafted beneath the door of the pantry. Instantly, she stilled. Her wolf had only choked on that scent once before.

Inside the vampires' coven.

Her eyes widened in realization. He'd told the truth. The vampires *were* after her. Silently, he lifted a single finger to his lips.

She didn't protest. Faced with vampires, even a criminal shifter like him was an ally, and at the very least, he'd offered to save her, to help her save her pack.

She stiffened as the nearly silent footfalls continued. With her on alert like this, her wolf senses came alive. Even from inside the pantry, she heard every creak of the floorboards. Each second stretched for hours as the vampires circled the inside of her home like sharks hunting for a single drop of blood. Mae watched in horror as adrenaline pumped through her veins. More than one vamp was tearing her home apart, searching for something.

Searching for me…

A chill ran down her spine as the truth of the Rogue's warning sank in.

He'd been right. The vampires were after her, and with their keen sense of smell, they *would* find them, sniff them out. It was only a matter of time.

Rogue eased a blade from his belt as he turned so she was positioned behind his back as they lay in wait. The element of surprise might be his only advantage.

"She's not here," a deep voice sounded from inside her bedroom. "They must have been tipped off and moved her."

"No," another answered. This voice even more chilling than the first. "We'll find her. She's here. I can smell it."

At that dark promise, Mae shivered, gulping down her urge to cry out, but Rogue gripped her hand—hard. The feel of his large palm engulfing hers caused her to calm instantly. As he released her, his grip on his blade tightened. From the intense look in his gaze, all he needed was for one of the vamps to draw near the pantry, and then he planned to attack.

The sound of boots shuffling over her carpet followed as one of the vampires emerged from her bedroom. Through the crack of the doorframe, she watched as the vampire sniffed the air. Its brow furrowed as its glowing red eyes fell on the pantry door. Slowly, its dark silhouette approached. Rogue's eyes flashed to his wolf. Only a few more feet and the vampire would be on the wrong end of his blade.

"Hey, what's this?" the other vamp in her bedroom called out, laughing darkly. The bloodsucker approaching the pantry paused, his attention drawn toward his comrade. He was only a few steps out of Rogue's reach.

Rogue mouthed a silent curse.

The vamp inside her bedroom stepped out, bending down to the floor outside her line of vision. Several grunts sounded as Tucker started to oink. Mae's eyes widened in horror.

No, Tucker, she silently pleaded.

Suddenly, a second shadow blocked the bedroom light, followed by a screaming pig squeal that pierced her ears.

"Tucker!" Mae shouted.

"Shit!" Rogue kicked open the pantry door. The wooden frame smashed as he charged through with all the power of a bull. Both vamps were on Rogue within seconds, meeting him in hand-to-hand combat.

Mae didn't think. Scrambling from the closet, she searched for Tucker. As she dashed toward the bedroom, the grunts and thumps of Rogue fighting off the vampires mixed with the unmistakable sound of gunshots in the distance. Violence erupted throughout the compound. The howls of the Grey Wolf warriors sounded in a chilling chorus, alerting the pack. A shiver ran down Mae's spine. This wasn't just an assault on her—it was a full-on attack against her pack.

Tucker was huddled in the corner of her bedroom, trembling like a terrified, abused animal. Scooping the piglet into her arms, she ran for the front door.

She needed to get out of here, to the underground bunker with the other women and children.

She wrenched open her front door, only to find herself face-to-face with her enemies. Red eyes stared at her. So many glowing red eyes. Mae stumbled back inside with a shriek, dropping Tucker, who darted through the open door into the melee with a terrified squeal.

Instinct took over. She had no choice but to fight.

Shifting into her wolf, Mae lunged for the vampire closest to her and sank her teeth into the flesh of its arm. The taste of iron and death coated her tongue, disgusting and foul, but she was no match for several at once. A second vamp ripped her from its friend. Mae's head bashed against the drywall. Pain split through her skull and a yelp tore from her throat before she fell to the floor, her temple throbbing.

She tried to stand, but the second vampire gripped her by her scruff, lifting her until her neck was exposed. She winced, bracing herself for the pain of its bite.

But it never came.

Suddenly, she fell to the floor, free of the vampire's grasp. When Mae opened her eyes again, Rogue was standing over the vampire's corpse, a lacquered stake clutched in his hand. Vampire blood was spattered across his face. Mixed with his scars and the golden glow of his wolf eyes, he looked lethal, feral. She'd expected Rogue to leave her for dead like the criminal he was, to abandon her. But he hadn't.

For a fleeting moment, it didn't matter that he was a criminal. The dark emotion in his gaze told her everything she needed to know.

I'll protect you. You have my word.

Two more vampires burst in through the door, drawing Rogue's attention back to the fight. A roaring battle cry ripped from his throat as he met the oncoming bloodsuckers blow for blow. Though it was two against one, he held his own. He shifted into his wolf—a massive grey alpha, at least twice her size. He was gorgeous and wild, fighting as if he regularly faced danger and death. Considering his reputation, she had no doubt that was true, but this wasn't for his own interests.

This was for her.

When the last bloodsucker fell, Rogue stood over them in wolf form. His chest heaved in and out as his haunches lowered. Black tufts peppered his steely-gray fur, and a gnarled scar marred his left eye, mirroring his human form.

Fighting still raged in the distance, the echo of automatic weapons carrying loudly in the still night air. But here, inside her home, for the moment, all was calm.

Slowly, the air around him bent and twisted as he shifted. Mae shifted into human form again and lowered her gaze. She retrieved her nightgown and tugged it on. When she turned around, he was clothed, the only signs of the fight a few small spatters of blood on his face and hands.

"Thank you," she whispered. "That was"—she searched for the right word—"heroic," she breathed.

"Make no mistake, Princess. I'm no hero."

She wasn't sure she believed him. He was every bit her savior, as much as the devil darkening her doorstep.

Another round of shouts sounded from outside her house.

"More will come," he snarled. "Run."

Mae fled for the door, Rogue right at her heels. Outside, the sounds of clashing metal weapons and gunfire rang in the distance. The damp night grass moistened her bare feet.

As she turned to run, Rogue's sharp whistle drew her

attention, and seconds later, a large, brown mustang gal-
loped into sight. Rogue vaulted into the saddle. The horse's
brutal black eyes flared as the horse let out a furious whinny.
But the dark cowboy who rode the beast was the true
intimidator.

The sounds of the Grey Wolf warriors' howls echoed
again. A chill ran down Mae's spine. Her friends, her family.

"I have to help them," she murmured.

She started to run toward the main compound. She
had to help, to try to save them. But Rogue and his horse
blocked her path. "Easy," he warned. "If you value your life,
you'll come with me." He extended a hand toward her. His
dark gaze pierced hers. "This is the only way you can save
them."

Another round of gunfire rang out, confirming her worst
fears. Each shot shook her as if the bullet had landed in her
own chest. Everything in her called out to go to them, to find
some way to protect them. But if what he'd said about the
antidote was true—and she doubted many things about the
Rogue, but not what he'd said about *that*—then he was right.

This was the only way.

Her eyes darted to where the sounds of the melee originated. "And what about Tuck—?"

"Get on the damn horse, woman," he growled.

Her heart thumped hard against her chest as adrenaline coursed through her. She glanced between him and
the expanse of pasture where the sounds of battle raged in
the distance. What was the word of a criminal worth? She
wasn't sure she knew the answer, but as she stared into his
ice-blue eyes, some instinct told her *this* wolf's word was
worth more than most.

Tentatively, she placed her hand in his.

He tugged her up into the saddle in front of him before he gave the horse a sharp kick. The mustang raced toward the surrounding forest.

As they rode into the darkness, uncertainty shook her and the hairs on the back of her neck rose on end. Mae would go to any length to save her pack. Leaning forward, she gripped the saddle horn. She didn't allow herself to look back as the last sight of Wolf Pack Run and the vampires faded into the distance. She only glanced over her shoulder toward the wicked wolf at her back.

Chapter 4

WHAT HAD SHE GOTTEN HERSELF INTO? MAE swallowed—hard—as Rogue tugged on the reins. His deep voice wrapped around her, smooth as velvet.

"Almost there now," he said.

Those were the first words he'd spoken to her since they'd escaped Wolf Pack Run. For the past several hours, they'd ridden in silence, only the late-night sounds of the forest and the bright summer moonlight guiding their way. Cradled in the darkness and with the gentle sway of the horse beneath her, she'd lost herself in the passing of the trees, so much so that she'd almost allowed herself to forget the mysterious wolf at her back.

She had no such comfort now.

As his horse slowed, Rogue dismounted, making quick work of removing his remaining weaponry from the leather saddlebag. Mae watched as he retrieved three extra blades. He slipped one into each boot before he passed the third to her. "For protection," he grumbled. "Helluva a lot better than a kitchen knife."

"You say that like a chef's knife is useless for stabbing someone."

He pegged her with a hard look. "In untrained hands, it is."

Mae averted her gaze. Somehow, she got the impression he knew that from experience. She turned the knife over in her hands. She was still perched in the saddle.

"You gonna dismount?" he drawled.

"We're stopping *here*?" Mae arched her brows as she looked around them. "We're less than a mile from the border of the packlands."

"I'm aware of that." He drew a flask from the back pocket of his jeans. "We'll walk from here."

"Why?"

He swirled the whiskey inside his flask. The smoky scent drifted to Mae's wolf senses on the summer breeze. He didn't answer. Instead, he drew a long swig from the flask. "Are you incapable of walking?" he asked. "I offered you protection, not pampering, Princess."

She scowled. "If you're implying I'm high maintenance, save it." With one quick swoop of her leg, she dismounted, landing in the dirt with a graceful thud. A layer of grime covered her bare feet and her nightgown hem, and she clutched his blade in her hand. She knew she looked every bit the stubborn country girl. "For your information, I figured we'd at least find a rogue house."

The cottages—which, from Mae's understanding, were scattered throughout the country—provided a safe haven for packless wolves.

A bemused grin crossed his lips. "How's a pack wolf like you know anything about that?"

She shrugged. "My cousin, Belle. The one you met in the vampires' cells. She's told me plenty about rogues."

A once-rogue wolf and physician who'd been coerced into a nefarious pack called the Wild Eight, Belle Beaumont was now as Grey Wolf as they came, considering she was mated to the Grey Wolf high commander, Colt Cavanaugh.

Rogue cast Mae a dark glance. "If you've got a problem roughing it, you can thank your brute of a brother. There're no rogue houses within a hundred-mile radius of Wolf Pack Run, thanks to him."

She bristled. "Maverick is fearsome to his enemies, but he's not a criminal."

"I might be a criminal, but you can trust in that."

"I do." Her hand rested on the leather of his mustang's saddle. Her features tightened and her eyes flashed to those of her wolf, drawing into a look that was meant to be threatening. "You knew about that attack," she accused. "Are you in league with the vampires?"

He smirked. From his display of amusement, he thought she was no more a threat to a wolf like him than a fly. If she was honest with herself, she likely wasn't. He held the upper hand between them, whether she liked it or not.

"If you truly believed that, you wouldn't have come with me. You wouldn't be trusting me to find the bloodsucker to create the antidote for you and your packmates." He pocketed his flask. "I've done a lot of things, but colluding with vampires isn't one of them."

"How can I be certain?"

"Says the woman who alerted them to our hiding place."

She gaped at him. "What was I supposed to do? Let them kill Tucker?"

"Last I checked, you could have chosen *not* to endanger our lives for the sake of a hog."

She wrinkled her nose in disgust. "Tucker's not a hog. He's a *teacup pig*."

His brow furrowed. "There's a difference?"

She placed her hands on her hips. "Of course there is."

Rogue adjusted his Stetson. "A hog by any other name still rolls in sh—"

"Hush your mouth," she hissed. "He takes buttermilk baths, you monster."

He chuckled again as he stepped away from her. "Is that to make the bacon more flavorful?"

Her jaw dropped. "Tucker will *never* be bacon," she growled.

"You work on a ranch," he countered.

She knew as well as he did that the Grey Wolves sold their livestock to make a living. It was the way most people—werewolves or not—made their living around these parts. But that didn't mean she had to consume the product the pack produced.

"Yes, but I'm a vegetarian," she said.

"Of course you are. A vegetarian rancher who names their livestock," he gently mocked.

"I can respect the work of my pack without endorsing it." She placed her hands on her hips. "And I don't see how naming Tucker is any different from you naming your horse."

"Bee is not food."

"Neither is Tucker." She crossed her arms over her chest. "What kind of a name is B anyway? It's a letter. Not a name."

"Like Tucker is so much better. It rhymes with fuc—"

She growled again, interrupting him. "It's because he loves to *tuck* his blankets into a pile with his snout."

"He's a pig. It's called rooting, like when they look for acorns in the wild, and Bee is a nickname. His full name is Beelzebub."

She wrinkled her nose. "What a horrible name for such a gentle giant."

"You've never seen him backed into a corner."

As if in response, the horse in question stomped one of his front legs and started biting at his reins to get free. Rogue reached into the horse's mouth and removed its bit, only for the beast to snap at his hand in response. He cursed at it beneath his breath as Mae examined the forest around them.

Still on edge from the vampire attack, every sound, every movement alerted her.

"If we slow our pace, they could find us," she warned.

From the dark grin on Rogue's lips, her response amused him. "So worried Big Brother will come after you?" He cleared his throat. "Don't worry, Princess. Your brother and his minions won't notice you're missing yet."

She scowled. She'd meant the vampires, not her pack-mates, but he'd meant to irk her and he'd succeeded. "Those *minions* are the Grey Wolf elite warriors," she grumbled. "And *my* packmates. The same packmates I want to *protect* from the vampires and their serum." She paused and drew in a deep breath. What sort of damage had been done to her home, her family and friends?

Rogue seemed to read the concern on her face, and the harshness in his features softened. "Forget about your pack and the vampires for now. Come sunrise, we'll be long gone." He stepped forward, pegging her with a dark stare. Even in the moonlight, his eyes were stunningly blue, chilling and as cool as ice. "And *you* will be safe."

It was a brutal reminder of all that was at stake—the antidote, her pack, her *life*—and everything he'd done to save her.

He'd been so heroic. Nothing like the criminal character his reputation painted.

Mae was about to say as much, but Rogue froze. His

eyes flashed golden. Had he been in wolf form, his haunches would have risen in fierce warning. Mae stiffened. She heard it too. A rustle in the bushes.

Slowly, as the rustling grew louder, Rogue reached to his boot, grabbing the dagger he'd secured there. He eased it from its sheath, crouching in preparation for a fight as Mae clutched the blade he'd given her until her fingers turned white. Her heart raced.

But instead of a threat, a small pink-and-black-spotted piglet emerged from the bushes.

"Tucker!" Mae squealed, instantly dropping the knife.

"Shit," Rogue swore.

Mae raced toward the piglet, scooping him into her arms and cradling him against her as she cooed. "Oh, you sweet, sweet baby."

Rogue quirked a brow. "How the hell did he get all the way out here?"

"Maybe he hid in one of our bags?" Mae shrugged. "What does it matter? He's here now." She tickled under the pig's chin. "You found us, you smart little piggy."

"Intelligent bacon," Rogue grumbled. "Who knew?"

The horse gave a huff of acknowledgment.

"Pigs are incredibly smart," she shot back.

Rogue was shaking his head. "Pigs aren't smart. They're easy to train. They're gluttons motivated by food."

"Hush," she hissed at him, drawing closer to where he and Bee stood. But as she did so, Tucker let out an angry grunt, snapping and biting at the air as they neared Bee.

In response, Bee growled. Actually *growled*. The horse bared its teeth, snapping its jaws at Tucker as his dark eyes flashed in anger. Mae was certain she'd never heard a horse *growl* before, except for Black Jack, a hellion of a beast belonging to Wes, the Grey Wolf second-in-command. In an instant, Rogue's typically sweet horse suddenly looked as if he'd been possessed by a demon. Hell, it put even ornery old Black Jack to shame.

Mae blanched, scurrying back with Tucker still grunting angrily in her arms.

"Easy. Easy." Rogue tugged on Bee's reins, fighting to calm the mustang.

"Apparently, Beelzebub *is* a fitting name," Mae muttered.

Rogue shot her a look of *I told you so*. "That was nothing. I suggest you keep that monstrous little *hog* away from him."

She stroked Tucker's smooth hide in an attempt to calm him. "It isn't Tucker's fault. It's his instincts. Pigs are very territorial."

"He's no match for Bee's temper when he lets loose, and unlike your pig, Bee isn't destined to be food."

"No, but if he comes after Tucker again, he may be glue when I'm through with him."

Rogue ignored her comment. Gripping the reins of his horse, he led the mustang alongside him, heading into the shadows.

"Where are you going?" Mae asked.

"To the river."

She quirked a brow. "The river?"

The river ran just along the outskirts of Grey Wolf territory. It was the marker the pack recognized as the end of their lands. She and her closest childhood friend, Jared, had ventured there once when they were children. It'd taken them all day to make the trip, and they'd returned so late after dark that the Grey Wolf soldiers patrolling the packlands had needed to escort them back home. Their parents had nearly skinned both their hides. But the adventure had been worth it.

Rogue sauntered into the darkness, leading his horse behind him.

The shadows swallowed them both, leaving Mae standing there alone.

She hesitated, staring at the spot where Rogue had disappeared. Despite the fact that she was alone and rarely trekked this far from the ranch, this part of the forest felt familiar, safe. She was still within the reach of her packmates. But just up ahead, near the river, the shadows looming over her might as well have been screaming.

This way lies danger.

But if she stayed…

She thought of her brother, her packmates. The Grey Wolves wouldn't surrender. The vampires might have caught the pack off guard this time, but she knew the fierce warrior wolves among her pack wouldn't allow the vampires to overrun them. Even as she and Rogue had made their escape, it was clear from the sounds and the few glimpses she caught that the wolves were winning. She hadn't been able to take in the full scale of the attack, but she suspected there were some casualties. Her heart broke at the thought. Innocent wolves, her friends and distant relatives, had been taken unaware by those bloodsuckers.

And if Rogue was right, they'd come to Wolf Pack Run for *her.*

And they would keep coming, keep hurting more innocents…

Unless *she* put a stop to it.

She set Tucker down before she finally charged after Rogue. Immediately, Tucker began rooting for acorns under a nearby tree. The piglet would follow her eventually. Using her wolf senses, she tracked Rogue's scent until the roaring river rush sounded in the distance. She rounded a large pine, pushing its needles aside. The riverbed glittered as the moonlight slowly faded and daylight drew nearer. Each ray of the rising sun lessened the threat of vampires following them—for now. They were upwind, so if the vampires were still coming, they'd notice the bloodsuckers' scent. Rogue's horse stood at the edge of the water, enjoying a long drink as his dark rider lingered next to him. He seemed to be searching for something.

With careful footing, Mae made her way to the river. When she reached Rogue's side, she glanced toward him, only to instantly regret it. In the time it'd taken her to scuffle down to the riverbed, he'd stripped off his shirt and cast it onto a large rock nearby. Every muscled ridge of his abdomen was visible. His was a body of a cowboy, a testament to working long, hard hours on the ranch, and his core reaped the benefits.

Mae gaped. "What are you doing?"

He reached for his belt buckle. "Making use of my time."

Her eyes widened as he unbuttoned his jeans. "By stripping naked?"

"Last I checked, even pack wolves didn't shy away from nudity."

She gaped at him.

"I'm covered in vampire blood. The river is as good a place to bathe as any, Princess, or are you too good for a bath in open water?" He cast a glance over his shoulder.

The now-open material of his jeans rode so low on his hips that Mae could see a thin trail of dark hair that led down to...

Her cheeks flamed.

His eyes transitioned to his wolf's. He gave her a once-over, his gaze lingering at her bare, dirty feet and the muddied hem of her nightgown. "You may be a pack wolf, Princess, but you strike me as a woman who doesn't mind getting her hands dirty—or her feet, as it were." One side of his mouth kicked up.

She frowned. "Says the man who sneaks into women's bedrooms."

"We've been through this, Princess. You had fair warning. There was no *sneaking* involved. But I'll take it you're not joining me?"

If she'd been a braver woman, she would have joined him just to spite him.

And to fulfill her own fantasies...

"Not a chance." She turned away, refusing to watch him for another second. No matter how curious she was.

A moment later, a gentle splash told her he'd waded into the water. When she turned, he was submerged in the river, the moonlight shining down on him. She watched him disappear into the depths to wet his hair and then resurface. Beneath his Stetson, it had looked like he sported a close-shaved military buzz, but his Stetson had hidden an undercut, the top of which revealed a patch of jet-black hair. The deep ebony reminded her of the streaks of black that were in his coat while in wolf form. He may not have been Grey Wolf Pack, but that coloring was still rare among their species. She'd only seen it once before.

The thought immediately soured in her stomach. No. She wouldn't sully the memory of her dearest friend by comparing him to *this* wicked wolf. Handsome as sin or not.

"Are you certain you can really protect me, make me disappear, and retrieve the vampire we need to create the antidote?" she called out to him. She needed to distract herself. She wouldn't dare let him think that she was standing here out of curiosity or for the sake of watching him bathe.

Because she *wasn't*.

"Having second thoughts?" He scrubbed a hand over the planes of his chest.

She tried not to notice the ample muscle there. But she was failing—miserably. "No. But you're only one wolf."

For some reason, she got the impression that amused him.

He slicked back his hair, the damp coils tamping down to his head. "Leave the details to me."

She crossed her arms. "And what comes next? We find the vampire and force him to create the antidote for widespread use before the bloodsuckers find me?"

He washed his face as he nodded. "I have several associates searching for information through the back channels, the underground. Sources your brother and packmates can't even begin to tap into. We'll find someone who's seen something. We always do, and once we negotiate the intel, we'll have the scientist's location and the antidote will follow."

"And what if someone else finds the scientist before we do? You said yourself that the other shifter clans would soon be after the antidote, too, that Seven Range Pact or not, they wouldn't hesitate to double-cross my brother."

"We're several steps ahead already. Time is on our side, and even if they did, it wouldn't matter. Your blood is the key to the antidote. In this chess game, you're the queen, the most valuable player on the board, and *that's* why our highest priority is for you to stay off the radar. You need to disappear."

"You make it sound so easy."

"Our key advantage is that no one will know where you are. That gives us time." Even in the moonlight, his gaze darkened as his eyes sparked gold again. "And for a wolf like me, it *is* that easy." He faced away from her and stood.

Mae's eyes grew wide as he rose naked from the river depths. The bare muscles of his back moved with such grace and fluidity that his tanned skin glistened with water droplets in the moonlight. A black tattoo of a dragon snaked over his spine. Wide shoulders tapered down into a lean waist. She followed the lines of the ink on his back, which only brought her sight lower to the two delectable dimples just above his perfectly muscled…

He started to face her again. She gasped, tearing her gaze away. Heat flooded her cheeks, but she kept her eyes averted, focusing instead on Bee's hooves. She would *not* give him the satisfaction of knowing she'd been watching him. Not even if he had the most perfect muscled ass she'd *ever* laid eyes on. Not even though he'd kissed her senseless in a way so memorable that it felt like all the times she'd been kissed before didn't matter. She was here to save her pack. Nothing more.

She heard his dark chuckle beneath the rushing sounds of the river.

"Enjoying your view?" he called out.

"I don't know what you're talking about," she called back.

A moment later, water sloshed near the river edge. She didn't look up. All she could see were his bare feet, and she intended to keep it that way.

He stepped beside her, grabbing his clothing. "Don't act like you've never seen a naked cowboy before, Princess."

"That doesn't mean I want to see *you* naked, and if you keep teasing me, considering that kiss, I might think you have other motives than the antidote."

"You're not unattractive, Mae."

Not unattractive?

"Watch it," she scoffed. "Those superb compliments will cloud my head with silly delusions of romance."

"I don't do romance." He leaned toward her with a conspiratorial smirk. "So don't make something as little as a kiss more than it is."

Hurt seared through her, but she didn't dare show it. "You say that like I want it to mean something."

"You wouldn't have brought it up if you didn't." Slowly, he eased closer until she felt him lingering behind her. A drop of water from his hair dripped onto her shoulder, and the chill of the river water radiated from his bare skin. "I smelled your desire," he purred.

A shiver ran through her. And from his dark laugh, he'd noticed.

"I know the sounds you make when you come," he challenged. "Saw the way you arch your back as you moan."

"It was dark in my bedroom," she shot back.

"I'm a wolf, Mae. All the better to see you."

Her jaw tightened. "I'm not loud."

She heard the amusement in his voice. "All the better to hear you."

Her hands clenched into fists. "It was a mistake."

"That doesn't mean you've learned your lesson."

"And what's that exactly?"

"Never trust a wolf like me, Mae." He leaned in toward her, the heat of his breath tickling the sensitive skin of her neck. "Because once he sees you, hears you"—he inhaled a sharp breath, and for a moment, she thought his lips might brush the delicate skin of her throat—"he just might want a taste…"

He stepped away from her. When he returned a moment later, a wry grin crossed his lips. He was holding his flask again. He extended it toward her. "Drink," he insisted. "To our newfound alliance."

"What is it?"

"Something to make the travel to my ranch smoother," he said.

She stared at his offering.

The longer she hesitated, the more amused he seemed. "You don't trust me, little lamb?"

Little lamb?

He was challenging her, taunting her. Again.

And she'd be damned if she would let him win.

Mae snatched the flask from his hand. "I'm no lamb." She lifted it to her lips, chugging several long swigs. The fiery whiskey burned down her throat, but she didn't dare allow herself to cough. As the burn subsided, she pegged him with a hard stare. "You forget I'm just as much of a wolf as you are." She allowed her wolf eyes to flash.

He grinned. That devilish smile was becoming all too familiar. "We'll see about that."

Stepping around her, he grabbed his shirt from the rock and pulled it on. He glanced behind her. For a moment, she thought he was watching the skyline, where the stars were just beginning to fade into the early light of morning, until he said, "You're late."

Mae glanced behind her. Several wolves in human form emerged from the shadows, slowly closing in on them. The hair on the back of Mae's neck rose on end, and goose bumps prickled across her skin. But Rogue seemed unfazed by the wolves' presence. Were these his men? Her gaze darted between the advancing wolves.

"What's going on?" she asked. "I thought you said we were going to your ranch."

"And we are." He stepped away from her. "But you didn't think I'd let a Grey Wolf be privy to its location, did you?"

Her eyes darted to the black sack and rope in one of his men's hands. Realization dawned on her. With the promise of her pack's safety dangled in front of her and the vampire's attack, it'd been all too easy to forget this man was still her brother's enemy. He wouldn't want a Grey Wolf like her knowing where his ranch was…and he had no intention of taking her there as a partner.

He intended to take her as a prisoner.

"We had a deal," she breathed. "You said you'd protect me."

"And I intend to keep my end of the bargain. No harm will come to you. You'll be perfectly safe, as promised."

"You misled me. If you think threatening to put a bag over my head and tying me up counts as safe, you're delusional!"

"I said I would protect you from the vampires and find the antidote. Nothing more."

"You bastard," she growled as his men eased closer.

Her words didn't seem to faze him. "I've been called far worse and deserved it."

As his men drew closer, Mae snarled. She crouched low, preparing to shift.

"Don't make this harder than it has to be, Mae. I promise

to be a gentleman. Rogue's honor. I'll even have one of my men retrieve that damn pig of yours," he said. A dark grin crossed his lips. "But you really should be more discerning when making deals with the devil."

Mae stepped backward, preparing to make a run for it. She was about to tell him that for all she cared, he could take his damn deal and shove it, but at that moment, her foot caught on one of the river rocks. Suddenly, the world tilted on its axis as she stumbled.

The next thing she knew she was lying on her back, a searing pain throbbing through the base of her skull. Off in the distance, someone was swearing like a sailor, but his voice became garbled as her vision blurred. The colors of the early-morning sunrise blended into a kaleidoscope as she blinked up at the sky.

Her eyes grew heavy as a pair of strong arms lifted her. Rogue held her in his arms, clutching her to his chest as if she weighed nothing.

Mae fought to keep her eyes open, to focus on the sharp lines of his face, but it was no use. The darkness encroached on her faster than a striking viper. And she was suddenly tired. Too tired to fight.

"You'll go to hell for this," she slurred.

"You forget, Princess"—he brushed his thumb over her cheek—"I'm already on the list of permanent residents." He stared down at her. The blue of his eyes filled her with cold as her eyelids grew heavy, so heavy she couldn't keep them open any longer. The last thing she heard before she slipped into darkness was his deep voice whispering to her.

"I'll take care of you, Mae. You won't regret this."

Chapter 5

MAE HAD NEVER BEEN TO THE OCEAN BEFORE, YET SHE felt the waves beneath her in a gentle, swaying movement. The water was warm, and the waves wrapped around her like a pair of powerful arms. An unfamiliar voice echoed from beneath the surface, bubbling from within the deep, muffled and distant.

Jared.

At the name, she instantly stiffened. She was twelve again, barely a woman, and the sharp hands of her mother were pulling her, tearing her away. She was screaming, pleading, yet her cries fell on deaf ears. She needed to find him, to save him, to tell him she loved him, but she couldn't move.

He's dead, her conscience answered.

The water around her grew cold with her guilt. The ocean stilled like the eerie calm in the eye of a storm. Mae struggled to breathe as the water pressed in around her, threatening to swallow her as she drowned in its depths.

Jared was dead, which meant she might as well be too. The waves whispered in a crashing chorus as they closed in around her, crushing her, claiming her.

Your fault.

Mae woke with a start, sitting up as a jolt of energy thundered through her. Her heart pounded against her breastbone as she struggled to catch her breath. She was lying in a massive four-poster bed in an unfamiliar room, and…

She wasn't alone.

She startled, scrambling back toward the headboard.

"Easy there, lass." The warning tone was strangely familiar.

Mae's eyes darted to where the voice originated.

The Scottish brogue belonged to a large wolf of a man. A thick beard obscured most of his face, save for a pair of hawkish brown eyes that watched her every move. He was perched at the edge of the bed. If the sheer size of him wasn't enough to intimidate, coupled with the full sleeves of elaborate tattoos covering his arms, the eyes that watched her would have been. From the scent and size of him, he was an alpha, and if the grimace on his lips was any indication, a man not to be crossed.

"Who the hell are you?"

He didn't answer.

She gripped the sheets beside her. "Where am I?"

Behind him, a large picture window revealed the early sunrise. The streams of light it allowed in illuminated the room. Outside, sprawling ranchlands were in view with cattle grazing and blue-ridged mountains in the distance. They weren't Montana mountains; she recognized that much, but with those lands, they couldn't be far from her home state.

"Black Hollow," he answered, drawing her attention back toward him.

"Which is where exactly?" she asked.

He watched her with those hawklike eyes. "'Tis a well-kept secret where the Rogue keeps his home."

The Rogue.

She touched a hand to the back of her head. A small amount of blood had dried and matted the back of her hair.

Though she'd passed out, the wound was small and superficial enough that with her true nature, it was already well on
its way to healing. Only the occasional throb in her temple
served as a reminder.

She fought down a snarl. It was all coming back to her
now. The attack on her packmates. The promise of the antidote. That handsome, scarred face beneath his Stetson hat.
That devious grin. The whiskey she'd drank to their deal,
and then the sunrise blurring before her eyes. The last thing
she remembered was staring up into his face as she'd faded
into darkness…

And yet she'd been enough of a fool to kiss him.

She growled, her wolf eyes flashing as she moved to
the edge of the bed. All she could think of were his men,
standing there with those horrible black bags and ropes. It
didn't matter that it hadn't come to that. She'd throttle him
for ever considering manhandling her like a prisoner. She
didn't care that he was an alpha wolf. She'd strangle the bastard within an inch of his life.

As soon as her feet hit the ground, she headed for the
door.

Wrenching it open, Mae charged out into the hall. From
the vantage point of the windows, she was on a large second
floor, lines of rooms filling the halls of the mansion ranch
home. She rounded on the nearest door and ripped it open.

"What in the bloody hell are you doin', lass?" The
Scottish wolf leaned against the doorframe. His massive
arms crossed over his chest as he watched her.

She didn't pay any attention to him. She was too busy
seething. To think, for a moment, she'd thought him a hero
for saving her, for helping her save her packmates.

I'm no hero, he'd warned her.

She scowled. He didn't earn points for honesty as far as she was concerned.

When the first room was empty, she wrenched open a second door.

The Scot watched her, not bothering to stop her.

Mae ignored him. She searched several rooms until finally, she rounded on the other wolf. "Where is he?"

"Rogue?" He quirked a brow.

"No," she spat back. "Tucker."

"Tucker?"

"The teacup pig," she specified.

He looked at her as if she'd grown two heads. "Ach, of course. He said ye'd be askin' after the hog. He's in the pen with the other wee piggies."

In a pen?

Mae snarled.

That rat bastard. Tucker was a *house* pig.

Turning away, she barreled down the hall. This time, in search of Rogue. The hall led to an open landing with a rustic wooden balcony that looked down over the first floor. Once at its edge, she scanned the area below. An open floor plan revealed a massive kitchen with an adjacent dining room large enough to feed a small army. A sprawling den and several other larger rooms and halls led deeper into the mansion.

Even the main compound at Wolf Pack Run—which housed all the apartments of the pack's elite warriors—wasn't as immaculate as this. The Grey Wolves ran one of the largest ranches in the state of Montana. It was a multimillion-dollar business. But that profit supported well over one hundred Grey Wolf families who made their home at Wolf Pack Run. Not to mention that the pack sent significant income to the subpacks and used funds from that same income as part of their operation costs.

Mae kept the Grey Wolves' books. She knew the cost and profit margins of every item on that ranch. She could recite the numbers in her sleep, she spent so much time poring over them. They lived well, but not extravagantly.

This was extravagant, a mansion fit for a ranching king.

She scowled. Of course, Rogue would have considerable wealth to back up all that power. She should have realized. Somehow, that only fueled her anger.

Mae barreled down the stairs in search of him. Within seconds, she was at the door. Her hand clasped the handle, giving it a mighty tug.

But it didn't move.

"You'll find it locked, ye ken?" the Scot called down to her. "Ye dinna think we'd be lettin' ye make a run for it now? Not with the vampires searching for ye." Her attempt had been so futile, he hadn't even moved from the top of the stairs where he stood.

Which meant…

She was essentially the Rogue's prisoner, and she'd been foolish enough to agree to it.

His words played in her head. *Our highest priority is for you to stay off the radar. You need to disappear.*

And he intended to do that by keeping her locked away.

Her hands clenched into fists as she seethed with anger.

Fine. If that was the way he wanted to play his hand, so be it. That didn't change the end result. She'd subject herself to a few days locked in his mansion if it meant saving her pack.

Her thoughts turned to Maverick and the other Grey Wolf cowboys, and her chest constricted. Though it'd appeared the Grey Wolves had been winning the battle, she worried the carnage could still have been brutal. Who could have been hurt? And were they worried about her? Searching for her? Since the start of the war, the vampires hadn't been brazen enough to directly attack Wolf Pack Run, only the outer edges of their ranch and the Grey Wolf subpack lands. The fighting had been the sole burden of the Grey Wolf warriors.

Until now…

"I need to speak with Rogue," she said. He'd have knowledge of the state of her pack after the vampire attack—who had been hurt, if there were any casualties. She may have agreed to let him lock her away in his mansion, but she had a right to know that her family and friends were all right.

"Doona fash yerself. He'll be back soon." Rogue's watchdog looked as if he expected this answer to placate her.

It didn't.

Rogue's guard eyed her warily before he said, "Ye've stunning emerald eyes. Curiously green…" He said this as if it confused him.

The observation was so unexpected from this towering beast of an alpha wolf—who looked more likely to eat nails for breakfast than to utter a kind word—that Mae wasn't certain what to make of it. She chose to ignore the comment. "When is 'soon'?" she asked.

"Not long before sundown." He tore his gaze away from her. She was thankful to no longer be under his hawklike scrutiny.

"Does my brother know I'm here?" she asked.

"Best save yer questions fer Rogue, lass."

"Just answer me that. I'll save the rest for Rogue." When the Scot didn't answer, she softened her tone. "Please," she pleaded.

The Scot shook his head. "No. It wouldna be wise, lass. It'd only make them further target for the vampires. The bloodsuckers'll do whatever it takes to get to ye, including hurt yer friends and family if they think yer pack knows where ye are. The bloodsuckers will want answers, and they'll do whatever it takes to get those answers, ye ken?"

Mae's stomach churned at the thought of her friends and family being further targeted, thanks to her. That was the last thing she wanted, but she loathed the idea of them being worried about her. "But if they don't know where I am, they'll be wasting resources searching for me."

"We need them searchin' fer ye. It'll make the vampires direct their attention elsewhere if they know yer pack doesn't have ye. Better ta waste resources than risk yer safety and yer pack's. The vampires'll be watching. 'Tis fer the greater good." He beckoned her upstairs. "Come along, lass," the Scot said again. His tone was gruffer now, tinged with warning.

She caught the subtext. That was enough questions for now. She was trapped here in the mansion for the duration of her stay, and this goliath of a Scottish wolf was her keeper...until *he* returned. She scowled.

With a frustrated huff, she climbed the stairs until she reached the second-floor landing again. Silently, her captor led her back to the room where she'd woken. When they reached the door, he gestured her inside.

Mae sighed. "I suppose I have no choice but to wait here for Rogue then."

She stepped inside. He made to follow her, but she pushed the door back against him, barring him from entering.

"*Alone*." Her eyes flashed to her wolf's.

The Scot grumbled, but she was too used to dealing with the Grey Wolf alphas to be scared immobile. She slammed the door in his face, locking it behind her. He likely had a key, but that didn't stop her. Some muttered Gaelic curses were muffled by the door, followed by a few colorful expletives in English, but the swearing soon quieted. Whoever he was, the Rogue's watchman must have decided she wasn't worth the fight, because a few moments later, Mae heard his weighted footsteps padding back down the hall.

Mae sat by the window, lost in thought, as the sun finally dipped low into the western sky. An hour later, her head was still throbbing occasionally from the nearly healed wound, but she would manage. If Rogue wasn't back yet, he was sure to be soon, and she wasn't about to sit here waiting on him any longer. She was more than eager for word about her packmates.

Tentatively, she peeked out into the hall. Empty. No sign of Rogue, his Scottish watchdog, or anyone else. Slipping from her room, she ventured down the corridor. When she reached the staircase overlooking the first floor, she found it equally empty.

"Hello?" she called.

No one answered.

She let out a frustrated huff.

Using her wolf senses, she homed in on the sounds of the house. There were muffled voices, somewhere the next floor up.

"Hello?" she called out again. "Is anyone there?"

Still no answer.

The voices grew louder as she ascended the staircase to the third floor. She glanced down one of the halls. A door at the end was open, barely cracked, as though someone had tried to close it and it hadn't latched. The voices became more distinct, coupled with a harsh static sound crackling through a heavy speaker—perhaps an intercom—that had apparently drowned out her approach. The unnatural noise was even harsher to her wolf senses.

The crack between the door and the frame revealed a large control room. Mae peeked inside. Rogue and the Scottish wolf from earlier stood in front of the adjacent wall, both their backs facing her as Rogue fiddled with the intercom's dial. The wall they watched sported a large map of the United States. Small multicolored lights were scattered across the map's surface, some lit, others not.

But the two rogue wolves seemed to be focused on one particular unlit bulb in Montana. Not far from Wolf Pack Run.

The bulb flickered on.

The Scot tapped it with his finger. "Electricity's on in the rogue house. He'll 'ave reached it then." He raised his voice over the intercom's static.

"Good." Rogue nodded. "Use the underground call-out system to get ahold of him. The sooner we have the intel, the better."

Intel.

Adrenaline coursed through Mae.

Silently she slipped back out into the hall, lingering just outside the door. She was out of their view but close enough to hear their exchange. She knew it was sneaky, but if Rogue intended to keep her locked away like a prisoner in the name of their protection agreement, he might not be as forthcoming with information as she wished. She might learn more if she kept her presence hidden—for now.

A brief lull of quiet passed, followed by the sound of the intercom connecting, then rasping static.

"Are ye there, lad?" she heard the Scot ask.

"I am," an unidentified voice answered back. "But there's not much time. They expect me within minutes."

Mae quirked a brow. The voice was strangely familiar, but she couldn't place it. Who was on the other end of the line? It couldn't possibly be...

Mae's eyes widened. No, she wouldn't even allow herself to speculate. Rogue couldn't have a mole inside her pack...

Could he?

"Get on with it then," the Scot ordered over the intercom. "When's the next vampire attack?"

"Wolf Pack Run. Four moons from now," the unidentified voice answered.

No.

Her family. Her friends. They'd all be at risk. They would barely have time to recover from the first attack, let alone prepare for a second.

"Should I warn them?" the static-filled voice asked.

Mae's heart pounded as she waited for the response.

"No," Rogue finally answered. "Don't warn them. We'll be in touch soon."

At those words, Mae's stomach churned.

A click sounded, followed by disconnected static. The line had gone dead.

The gravity of exactly how mistaken she'd been hit her.

Rogue wasn't going to warn them, to do the noble thing.

Of course he wasn't. He was her brother's sworn enemy.

It didn't matter that he'd saved her or offered to help her and her packmates; he had no intention of being a hero. He was a criminal after all. He'd said as much, yet deep down, she hadn't believed him.

Until now.

The weight of her mistakes hit her with enough force that her breath caught. It all made sense now. Why a criminal like the Rogue would offer to help her, why he hadn't taken this deal to Maverick instead, all of it. He'd been lying to her from the start. It didn't matter that she'd agreed to come here. She wasn't simply being treated like a prisoner.

She *was* a prisoner.

And her pack was in danger…

She had to warn them.

Fleeing down the hall, Mae rushed back to her room, slamming the door shut behind her. She needed to get out of here, to find a way to tell Maverick about the attack. Forget Rogue and his plan for the antidote. Now that she knew he'd let her packmates be attacked in cold blood, she wasn't even certain his offer for the antidote was legitimate. He'd likely been misleading her all along. She needed to find a way to escape, to warn her packmates. If she told Maverick everything, he'd find a way. Her brother was the most capable warrior she knew.

An hour later, she'd paced the length of the bedroom floor so many times, Mae was surprised she hadn't worn a hole in the marble. She needed to find a way out of here. With a defeated snarl, she flopped onto the bed, gripping the linens and pulling them over her head until she was tangled beneath them. But the feel of the sheets clenched in her hand did the trick. Immediately, a memory of when she was a child gripped her. Jared had been grounded for fighting, even though he'd only been defending himself from the other boys again. His father had locked him in his room, telling him he couldn't come out for the evening, but that hadn't stopped him.

"How did you escape?" she'd whispered to him when he'd shown up outside her windowsill.

Pushing herself to her feet, Mae crossed the room to the massive paneled window and looked out over the ranchlands. She was only two stories up. It was too high to jump, even for a wolf, unless she wanted to break a leg, but she had another idea. Carefully, she flipped the latch, testing it. When an alarm didn't sound, she grinned, her eyes darting back to the four-poster bed and the knotted sheets that lay atop the mattress.

Jared's voice, no more than thirteen at the time, echoed in her head.

"There's always a way to escape, Mae-day. Always."

Mae smiled wide. The only person she'd ever gifted with her heart might be long since dead, but that didn't mean his memory had to be.

Chapter 6

ROGUE TIPPED OFF HIS STETSON AND SWIPED THE sweat from his brow. Damn, it was hotter than Hades. It was dusk, and the summer sun had long since begun to set. Bright tinges of pink and orange clouded the western sky over the blue-ridged Idaho mountains in the distance. Normally, he and the crew would have turned in by now, but they'd lengthened their work hours during the summer, using the extra daylight to their advantage, and even though it had been close to day's end after his and Murtagh's security meeting, he'd come back out to the pasture.

He never felt right turning in before his ranch hands did.

"You headed in?" Boone, his young work companion for the day, asked as he sauntered out of the barn and toward the waiting truck.

Frenchie would already have dinner ready, and since the classically trained chef had joined their ragtag band of misfits, Boone, a young rogue who wasn't a day over nineteen, never missed dinner while it was hot. But there was still daylight, which meant there was still time to work.

With the start of June and the days growing hotter, they'd already run the hay tedder over the pastures, but tomorrow would be Rogue's first day hooking the square baler up to the tractor. He needed to check both pieces of machinery over to ensure they were well oiled and in good repair so he wouldn't find himself stuck out in the middle of the pasture tomorrow.

There was nothing that wasted a workday faster than a piece of broken equipment.

Not to mention, he was trying to avoid a certain she-wolf.

Mae wouldn't be pleased to hear about the impending vampire attack on Wolf Pack Run, even if he intended to warn the Grey Wolves directly beforehand. She'd want him to warn them straightaway, but he needed time to get his man on the inside out of there, or else their intel surrounding the vampires' movements—and thus their leads in securing the antidote—would be compromised. She was bound to be angry with him.

But it wasn't her anger he feared. *That* he could withstand.

It was the hurt he would cause her. Not now, but in due time. He tried to push the thought aside as his shoulders tensed, but he couldn't. The kiss they'd shared haunted him. The look of longing in her emerald-green eyes when his lips pulled away from hers had torn him to shreds, more than he cared to admit. He didn't want to consider what that meant for his end goal.

His role was to protect her, then betray her. Nothing more. *She's not for you*, he reminded himself.

Rogue nodded toward Bee before he crouched next to the hay baler again. "You go ahead, Boone. I'll ride back soon. We have security measures to discuss."

Regardless of his conflicted feelings, with Mae under their protection and the vampires after her—and potentially her packmates as well—he and his men needed to be prepared, even though no one likely knew her location. Already, he'd put his men working detail duty on high alert, but they'd need to go further. Discuss their plans, strategize their next steps to find the vanished bloodsucker who'd created the antidote.

He'd only be a half hour behind Boone, but if he didn't get this done before nightfall and any afternoon rain set in tomorrow, the square bales would act like sponges to the moisture. Come morning, he'd need to cover a good amount of ground, so the tractor had to be ready before he ran out of light.

And Mae was safe from the vampire, from her pack, from *him*—for now.

"Yes, sir," Boone mumbled. He climbed into the truck, closing the door behind him before the engine roared to life.

As Boone rode off in the pickup, Rogue grabbed his toolbox and set to work.

A half hour later, the last rays of sun hid in a thin line over the mountains, casting the ranch in darkened twilight. Rogue was fixing to pack up his tools and call it a night, when out of the corner of his eye, he spotted movement on the other side of the pasture. He froze. The fine hairs on the back of his neck rose in alert.

Carefully, his wolf eyes scanned the darkness, finding nothing. But he knew better than to deny his instincts. His property might be guarded by a small army of rogue wolves whom he compensated well for their loyalty, but his men weren't infallible.

Still, this close to the house, if they had an intruder, he usually would have been alerted by now. Maybe an animal? If it was an animal, from the size, it was likely a bear. Slowly, he eased from where he crouched, coming to stand as he cleaned off one of his wrenches with a handkerchief. With tentative movements, he returned it to the toolbox and headed toward Bee. He gave the horse a firm, alerting pat as he surveyed the darkness.

He'd seen movement near the trees. He was certain.

He mounted Bee within seconds.

Gripping the reins, he gave the mustang a hearty kick. Bee reared up with a sharp whinny before they shot into the dusk. The summer wind whipped across Rogue's face, and the sound of the crickets chorused against the clopping of Bee's hooves. He rode until he reached the forest, scanning through the trees for any sign of life, but only the ghostly shadows of the trees followed him.

He was alone.

By the time Rogue returned to the house, night had fallen over the pasture. He headed straight to the dining room, his thoughts swirling with concerns about Maeve, their kiss, and all that had passed between them, but when he arrived, all thoughts of her were lost. As Rogue entered the dining room, he wasn't certain he was seeing straight. The hall-length table, which normally boasted a handful of modest dishes, was covered from end to end with an elaborate feast. Several plates of beef tenderloin and prime rib roast sat at the center, surrounded by bone-marrow gravies and a cornucopia of side dishes—the best the ranch had to offer. Everything from homegrown Idaho potatoes to fresh seasonal vegetables and fruit.

Four of his most senior warriors already appeared to be sitting down to the feast, with more of his men quickly filtering in.

He quirked a brow in confusion as he joined them. Usually Frenchie used their resources more appropriately, saving spreads like this for celebrations only, but apparently, the chef had decided to go all out tonight.

Rogue sat down across from the warriors, only reaching

for his silverware as an indication that his men should go ahead and eat their fill. He had little appetite.

"What's the status report on the initial attack at Wolf Pack Run?" he asked. He'd need to know in order to take necessary measures to protect his man on the inside and get him out, if needed, before he found a way to send word of the forthcoming attack to the Grey Wolves.

The door to the dining hall swung open as one of Frenchie's kitchen hands delivered more plates.

"A handful of casualties. Mostly lower-level warriors. Foot soldiers," Sterling answered.

"That's not good enough. I want names. I don't care what tier they are."

She'll want to know.

He shook his head. He shouldn't be considering what Mae would want. Not considering his long-term plans for her. Rogue hesitated before he asked his next question. "And her brother?" He couldn't even bring himself to utter his enemy's name.

It didn't matter how he felt about Mae, how the feel of her lips and lithe body pressed against him haunted him, her brother would always remain his enemy. He respected Maverick as a warrior and knew that he was the only man on this green earth whose feelings for Mae would ever rival his own, but there had been too much blood spilled between them. So much it had once stained the mountain snow red.

It'd been mostly his and barely any of Maverick's, only because they'd both restrained themselves for *her*.

Always for her. Everything Rogue did was for her. It always had been.

He pushed the memories aside.

Sterling frowned with disappointment. "Unscathed," he answered.

A small favor for Maeve, Rogue supposed. "Good. We need him alive. At least for now." Rogue reached for his napkin. "And the vampires' entry point?" He had more than a passing curiosity about how the vampires had managed to penetrate Wolf Pack Run.

The door to the dining hall swung open again. Rogue quirked a brow in that kitchen hand's direction but quickly refocused as Yuri gave his report.

The Japanese cowboy removed his Stetson. "A traitor, like you suspected. Our source says it was a member of the other shifter packs. The vampires stormed when the cougars took their turn on patrol after the gala."

Rogue nodded. "Not surprising. We've known for some time that the Grey Wolves' alliance with that particular branch of the Seven Range Pact has been tenuous at best."

Which meant there would likely be further discord between them. No matter. It didn't affect their kind. Rogue opened his mouth to give the warriors the rundown on his heightened security plans and request a status update on their intel about the vanished bloodsucking scientist's where-abouts when the door swung open again, interrupting him to reveal *yet another* elaborate dish.

Rogue growled. "What in the blazing hell is going on with all the damn food?"

The group of men in front of him exchanged nervous glances. When none of the four most senior responded, Rogue stood, leaning over the table, resting the weight of his torso on his hands as he scanned the faces of the handful of others who'd joined them.

"Well…?" he prompted.

Finally, Boone's eyes fell to the empty seat beside him, where the table had been set for one extra. "Murtagh just—"

Rogue growled, cutting Boone short. Damn it all to hell. That Scottish bastard had sworn to stop treating their *prisoners* as *house guests*.

The door to the dining room opened again, and this time, Murtagh and Frenchie shuffled in, working together to carry a very large tray of… Was that a whole Iberico ham?

Rogue stabbed an accusing finger toward Murtagh. "We had an agreement. You swore there would be no more taking in every stray wolf off the street, *especially* not her." He could tell by the smug look on the Scot's face that Murtagh had never had any intention of keeping his word. "You're a goddamn liar."

Murtagh nodded, not an ounce of shame in his eyes. "Aye, guilty as charged, but you're one to talk." Without missing a beat, he turned toward Frenchie. "Best bring in the champagne now."

Rogue snarled. "There will be no champagne. Not on my watch."

Murtagh addressed Rogue while assessing what appeared to be some kind of carved Sunday roast atop a silver platter. "Do ye have something against champagne?" he asked, as if they were having a polite conversation about the merits of various drink.

Rogue drew closer, forcing the Scottish cowboy to meet his gaze as they came nearly nose to nose. Rogue's voice was a low, grumbling growl. "You know very well I have nothing against champagne." He couldn't believe he was having this fucking conversation. "She's not staying here. She's going back to Wolf Pack Run with her fellow Grey Wolves as soon as we have the antidote."

Murtagh glanced up from the roast. A dark twinkle filled his hawklike eyes, and the edge of his lips twisted into a smug grin. "Easy there, brother," Murtagh warned. "Why not let her have a little fun while she's here? There's no harm to it."

Rogue growled again. Had Murtagh been any other wolf, Rogue would have gutted him years ago. But that was the problem, wasn't it? Murtagh wasn't just any other rogue wolf in his charge. It had been Murtagh who'd found him beaten within an inch of his life after the night he'd been cast out and become a rogue; Murtagh who'd nursed him to health, who'd seen him through the years of blood, sweat, and broken limbs at the Midnight Coyote during the dark times before he'd become *the* Rogue, back when he'd been nothing more than a powerless, packless wolf with nothing to his name. And it had been Murtagh who'd stood loyally by his side no matter what Rogue asked of him, no matter the cost, ever since. He was the only wolf Rogue dared to trust, to call a friend, a brother, and for that alone, Rogue owed Murtagh his life.

And the damn Scot would never allow him to forget it.

"The whole ranch is dining together tonight. I even invited the gardener and the maids." Murtagh smiled a crooked grin. "We have a *guest*, after all," he said, as if this explained everything.

"She's not a guest," Rogue shot back.

"Nae, but she isn't a prisoner either," Murtagh replied.

The Scot was insufferable. Rogue glared at him. "You know very well that treating her as anything *but* a prisoner will do more harm than good."

"I told you he would say that," Boone mumbled from

across the table. The young ranch hand shoveled a mountain of food onto his plate, enough meat to satisfy a whole pack of wolves for days—or a growing young shifter as it were.

Murtagh cast Boone a look, which said clearly *Shut yer mouth before I wallop ye around the ears, lad*.

Boone fell silent before he quickly lowered his eyes and crammed a large bite of food into his mouth. He knew better than to challenge the Highland cowboy.

Murtagh was tasked with dealing with the young rogue wolves under Rogue's command, the street urchins drawn in from the underworld of shifter society, outcasts of their world who had nowhere to go, no one to turn to. Rogue gave them a bed to sleep in, food in their bellies, and a roof over their heads. He provided them with a purpose, a cause to fight for, something to believe in, and Murtagh gave them the skills with which to wage their war. While Murtagh might have been quick to give Rogue lip himself, he only did so because over the years, he'd earned the right, but when it came to the wolves in Rogue's charge, the Scot ran a tight order.

Turning his attention back toward Rogue, Murtagh crossed his arms over his chest. The sleeves of tattoos covering his skin writhed as the muscles moved. "If not a guest, what exactly would ye call her then?" He quirked a brow. "A rutabaga?"

"Speaking of which, the roasted rutabaga is delicious by the way," Sterling added as he scooped another bite from his plate.

One of their oldest and longest acting soldiers and ranch hands, Sterling was nearly as seasoned as Rogue and Murtagh. Rogue still remembered the day they'd come across Sterling outside a bar down in Amarillo. The packless, dark-skinned cowboy had been managing to survive in the human world by working as a mule for drug traffickers across the southern Texas border. It had been a situation born of exploitation and necessity, and it hadn't taken more than a single conversation to convince Sterling to give up that life and join their cause. The rogue wolf had been all too eager to leave, to find a home and a purpose.

It wasn't easy for a rogue wolf to make a normal life among humans without the resources of a pack. Considering the wolves' nocturnal inclinations and need to shift and hunt regularly, holding a nine-to-five job proved difficult enough, let alone the risk they ran of being killed by human hunters. The Execution Underground hunted rogue wolves as if it were sport. The threat made living a normal life among humans damn near impossible. Pack wolves—the Grey Wolves specifically—had deals with the organization, protections in place that kept them safe from the murderous human bastards, but rogues had no such luxury. That forced them to live on the fringes, to exist in the rotten, dirty underworld of life, even among humans.

But they wouldn't for much longer. Not if Rogue had anything to say about it.

He scowled at Sterling's enthusiasm for Murtagh's shenanigans as he turned back toward the Scot. "This coming from the man who suggested bringing her here by any means necessary."

"That was before," Murtagh answered.

"Before what?"

"I think ye ken what I mean." Murtagh leaned in near Rogue's ear, lowering his voice so only the two of them could hear. "The fact the lass upstairs is the reason ye were cast from the Grey Wolf Pack."

Rogue stiffened. Murtagh was the keeper of many of Rogue's secrets. He alone knew Rogue's real name and that Rogue had been a Grey Wolf. Murtagh knew the motivations of Rogue's drive for revenge, but *how* the sole heir of one of the pack's three founding families had managed to be cast from the pack, the finer details of his life before he'd been a rogue wolf, and his history with Mae weren't among them. Rogue had kept those details to himself.

Murtagh eased back, one brow quirked as he challenged Rogue to contradict him.

"Out." Rogue held Murtagh's gaze, refusing to look away. "Everyone out," he ordered.

"What?" Sterling asked through a mouthful of roasted rutabaga.

"I said everyone out," Rogue repeated with quiet authority.

Sterling grumbled. "I've already begun to eat. Since when do we get the boot when we're—"

"If ye had better manners, ye'd have waited fer our *guest*," Murtagh said, emphasizing the word enough that Rogue snarled.

"It won't kill ye to wait," the Scot continued. "Ye heard the man."

Rogue's men knew better than to press him. Murtagh alone was brave enough to risk it. Boone, Sterling, and the others pushed back from their seats. The scrape of the chairs against the marble created a screeching chorus. There were several mumbles of hungry impatience about the food potentially getting cold as they exited, but the dining room doors quickly shut behind them, leaving Murtagh and Rogue alone.

Rogue broke eye contact, facing away from Murtagh and taking a sudden interest in the various dishes laid out across the table. "I don't know what you're talking about."

It was Murtagh's turn to growl. "Doona lie, ye daft ninny. Not to me." The Scottish cowboy stepped toward him, circling around the table until Rogue was forced to look at him. "Ye told me she was the target because she was the packmaster's sister," Murtagh accused.

Rogue nodded. "And she is."

"Ye lied, Jared," Murtagh hissed.

"I didn't. Not about that." Rogue grabbed a highball glass of what appeared to be moonshine that Boone had been drinking and lifted it to his lips. "And you know better than to call me by that name. That boy died years ago…"

"Like hell he did, or that lass wouldn't be upstairs now."

Rogue turned away from him again.

Murtagh growled. "Years ago, back when we were makin' our way through Durango, ye got drunk as a skunk one night and got to mutterin' all about the days before ye were a rogue wolf. Finally admitted to more than just bein' a Grey Wolf who'd been unfairly cast out. Sumthin' about a female and founding families, and bein' cast from the pack fer the love of her. Gorgeous green eyes on the lass, ye said."

So that was how Murtagh had realized. It was impossible not to notice Mae's large, emerald eyes. Not if a wolf took more than a passing glance at her…

Unfortunately, she and her beastly brother shared the stunning trait.

Murtagh was shaking his head. "Ye never did hold yer drink well."

Rogue scowled.

"She's the packmaster's sister, the key to the antidote, but that's not the only reason ye abducted her, ye mangled fud." Murtagh stepped closer. "Ye dinna think I would ken who she was the moment I set eyes on 'er?" He leaned in, resting his massive weight on the tabletop. He glanced toward the door, lowering his voice as if he feared someone might be listening on the other side. "She's the reason yer no' a Grey Wolf any longer, and she's the lass ye've been pining over all these fool years."

Rogue scoffed. "I pine over no one."

Murtagh banged his fist on the table. "Yer bum's out the window, ye bampot. Save it fer someone who believes ye."

Rogue sipped the liquor as he attempted to ignore Murtagh. The astringent taste of the moonshine coated his tongue, but he should have known better than to think the Highlander would relent.

Slowly, Murtagh pushed to standing. "Fine," he said, his temper cooling considerably. "Then I suppose ye doona care if I take to the lass then, do ye?"

Rogue stiffened.

"'Tis been a while since I've bedded a woman, and she's a pretty little thing," Murtagh continued. "Fine eyes, the emerald color of the Highland hills. A handsome face and a ripe, round pair o'—"

The glass Rogue was holding shattered from the strength of his grip. "Another word and you'll find one of these shards in your jugular."

Murtagh smiled in satisfaction. "'Tis true then?"

There was no point in trying to deny it any longer. "Yes, it's true," Rogue admitted. "But I fail to see why that matters."

Murtagh was shaking his head. "So this is yer plan then, is it? Kidnap the woman ye lost everything for and then betray her? Christ, Jared. Ye might as well take yerself out ta the stables and do yerself in." Murtagh swore under his breath in

Gaelic. "What happens when she realizes who ye are? Then what becomes of ye?"

"She won't." Rogue met his gaze. "Not until the time's right."

Not until it would already be too late. Then the deed would be done. He'd have his revenge, the better life the rogue wolves in his charge had worked for, and more importantly, he'd have kept a twenty-year-old promise.

"Are ye so certain of that?" Murtagh asked.

"She knew me as a young Grey Wolf pup. Not a deformed rogue of a wolf." Rogue gestured to the scarred side of his face. "If she was going to recognize me, it would have happened by now."

"And if yer wrong? If she does ken who ye are, ye canna tell me ye'd still want ta go through with it."

"Why wouldn't I?" Rogue faced the dining room's picture window, which looked out over the ranchlands, the sprawling mountains in the distance. "She's nothing to me now."

He felt the lie singe through him the moment he uttered the words. Maeve Grey would never be *nothing* to him. But she had to be, needed to be, and thus, he willed it to be so.

"Ye canna expect me to believe that." Murtagh saw right through him. He always did. "So that's yer plan then, is it? To betray her to seek yer revenge?"

"She'll have her pack's protection. That's all she wants. On that, I'll have kept my word. It's about more than revenge, and you know it." Rogue gestured to the door. "Their lives are at stake. *Our* lives are at stake." He lowered his voice as he met Murtagh's gaze. "And someone must pay for Cassidy's death."

A grim tension tightened Murtagh's features. "I know that, brother. Better than anyone else, but is it worth it?"

Silence passed between them, but Rogue couldn't bring himself to consider it. He couldn't. Not after everything he'd worked for.

"And your plan is so much better?" he accused. "What exactly did you have in store, now that you know who she is to me? Ask me to woo her over a feast fit for a king? Was that it? When the time comes, it will only make the sting of betrayal more painful." He knew Murtagh all too well, and as lethal and cunning as the ol' Scot could be, deep down, he was also a hopeless Highland romantic.

"It's better than yer plan, that's fer certain." Murtagh plucked an olive off one of the dishes and examined it before popping it into his mouth. "At least then, there'd be a chance she'd forgive ye when it's all said and done," he said between bites.

"She'll never forgive me. Not after this."

"How can ye be so certain?"

The question stopped Rogue short.

"Because I know Maeve." He paused to consider. "Perhaps even better than I know myself. She wouldn't willingly help betray her brother, her pack. Not even with the guarantee of their safety. When she learns the truth, she'll hate me for it."

Even if she knew what her brother had done…

"So that's it then?" Murtagh brushed off his hands on the sides of his work jeans. "What becomes of ye after the fact?"

"I don't know what you mean."

"Do ye really think ye can stand losin' her again?"

Rogue wasn't sure he knew the answer.

"Ye forget that I know ye better than most, *Jared*," Murtagh said, stressing his true name. For the past twenty years, only Murtagh had dared call him that. "Ye barely survived the first time."

"That's my concern and mine alone."

The silence that lay between them was deafening.

"Right then." Murtagh strode toward the door, likely to retrieve the other ranch hands again. "But doona say I dinna warn ye when yer but a shell of the man ye once were. I picked up the pieces the first time, but I willna be doin' it again." He paused as he reached the exit, waving a hand toward the wealthy display of food. "'Tis a waste to let it go cold."

"I should feed it all to the pigs to spite you." Rogue flicked a glance over the array of plates. Many of his men and staff had known true hunger, even starvation before he'd taken them in off the streets. He'd never deprive them of a hot meal in their bellies. "Let the men eat it."

Murtagh grinned. "Does that mean ye'll consider my suggestion? If she fancied ye, it would make dealin' with her while she's here a wee bit more pleasant, that's for certain. She was right livid when she realized ye'd locked her in."

Rogue shook his head. "I said you could eat the food, not that I'd consider your ridiculous idea. It would only hurt her more, and I'll flay the balls off you the next time you mention it."

"Well, if *you* won't put such a feast to good use"—a mischievous glint filled Murtagh's brown eyes—"and ye doona intend to charm her, what if I—"

Rogue knew Murtagh had no true interest in Mae. The Scot preferred his women—one woman, to be specific—with a few more curves and a head of hair so fiery it brightened even the grayest of the Highland fog.

His friend was only trying to get a rise out of him, but still, Rogue's eyes flashed to his wolf's. "I dare you."

"I hear Scots are mighty popular with American lassies

these days." Murtagh waggled his eyebrows suggestively. "You doona think I could woo her away from ye?"

"She's not mine to begin with." Rogue shook his head, even as a grin crossed his lips. "But if that were the case, I'd like to see you try."

"Many a lass can appreciate a grand gesture." Murtagh nodded to the feast. "Ye take note of that," he joked. "In case ye change yer mind."

"What a helpful tip." Rogue's voice dripped with sarcasm. He headed toward the dining room doors, passing Murtagh to reach the exit first. As he gripped the door handle, he paused, looking back at his friend over his shoulder. "And Murtagh?"

"Aye." Murtagh met his gaze.

"Does it help if it's a romantic gesture the lady in question would actually appreciate?"

Murtagh quirked a brow in confusion. "Aye, it does."

Rogue nodded. "I thought so." He turned to leave before he paused. "Oh, and one more thing."

Murtagh looked toward him again.

Rogue cast a glance at the meat-laden table. "For your information, Maeve Grey is a vegetarian"—his eyes fell to the expensive imported ham—"and the pig she brought with her is a pet." Rogue strode from the room, a satisfied grin on his lips as the sound of Murtagh's muttered curses followed after him.

It was roughly an hour later that Rogue found himself standing outside the guest suite, staring at the doorframe. As he stood there, his fist hovering over the lacquered wood as he prepared to knock, he hesitated.

Perhaps Murtagh was right. Perhaps he would gather more flies with honey than vinegar. It would make the whole ordeal smoother.

But would it bring her too close?

She's not for you, and she never will be.

Distance was best for both of them. She would never forgive him for using her against her brother, yet something in his chest—where the cavernous black hole resided in place of his heart—told him that maybe it was worth the risk. But where would he even begin?

He banged on the door.

When she didn't answer, he called out, "Mae."

No answer.

He knocked again—harder. "If you don't open the door, I have a key," he said.

A moment later when there was still no response, he keyed open the door.

And that was when he saw the bedsheets, tied into knots that formed a rope, dangling out the open window...

With Mae nowhere in sight.

She'd used the very trick he'd taught her as the means to make her escape.

First Murtagh and now this. Rogue snarled. *Let that be a lesson to you*, he chastised himself as he let out a frustrated curse before he barreled down the stairs and out into the dark night after her.

Nothing good ever came from him being nice.

Chapter 7

MAE RAN UNTIL HER FEET ACHED AND ALL FOUR OF HER legs threatened to give out beneath her. The nighttime summer breeze blew, ruffling the fur of her coat. It caused a chill to prickle her haunches, though she was far from cold. She paused to catch her breath and glanced up at the night sky. The stars twinkled over the vast landscape, their brightness only obscured by the light of the full moon. Even in the shadows of the towering pines, she could see everything clearly, the moonlight and her wolf senses illuminating her path. She inhaled a deep breath of mountain air. The adrenaline that coursed through her veins caused her to pant with excitement. She'd escaped. She'd actually escaped.

And courtesy of a rope made of bedsheets at that.

There was still a slight ache in her skull from the healing head injury, but what little pain remained was nearly gone. In a moment of daring, she threw back her head and howled. The release of tension felt so good that, had she been in human form, she wouldn't have been able to stop herself from laughing with elation. When calm finally settled over her, she glanced up at the moon one last time, sending out a silent prayer.

Thank you.

Jared had saved her yet again.

Mae stepped forward. She needed to put even greater distance between herself and Black Hollow. Then, once she was certain Rogue wouldn't find her, she could track her location, find the nearest town or city, and make her way home. She could survive as long as she needed in wolf form. But if she followed the scent of exhaust fumes from a nearby highway, it couldn't be more than a few days. She hadn't been able to find Tucker before she made her escape, but once she was safe, she'd do whatever it took to convince Maverick or one of the other Grey Wolf warriors to come back and retrieve him. He'd be okay until she was able to get back to him.

Prepared to make her journey, she stepped forward, only to pause as a rustle in the underbrush caught her attention. Funny. When she'd stopped here, she'd been certain she was alone. Her wolf senses hadn't detected any other shifters or animals. Slowly, she crept toward the bushes, determined to find the source of the noise before whatever it was found her. As she drew closer, she raised her haunches and bared her teeth in case she needed to fight. But when she emerged on the other side of the brush, she saw only three small grizzly cubs. The cubs wrestled with one another near the base of a mighty pine. She most likely hadn't caught the scent because they'd been in the treetops above her. They couldn't be more than a few weeks old.

Mae stepped back, prepared to make her retreat, but then her tail brushed against something…furred.

As Mae turned toward the source, she froze.

Behind her stood a towering mother grizzly bear. From the sheer size of her, she likely weighed over a thousand pounds. Slowly, the bear rose onto its hind legs. Its large, dark eyes fixated on where Mae stood in wolf form…near the mother grizzly's vulnerable cubs.

The grizzly let out a resounding roar.

Mae bolted, running through the forest with the angry grizzly at her heels. Her muscles burned and her limbs ached, but she didn't dare slow her pace. Her life depended on it. Her true nature might have made her stronger and faster than a human, but she was no match for a thousand-pound grizzly. Mae's heart pounded as she ran. She darted left and right in an attempt to throw the animal off, but it was no use.

Just when she thought she might be able to outrun the beast, an unexpected tree blocked her path. The shadows had obscured it from view. All it took was that single moment of hesitation, and the bear had her cornered.

Mae skidded and turned, just managing to stay on her feet. The grizzly swiped out, five-inch claws narrowly missing Mae's face. Mae growled and bared her teeth in an attempt to warn the bear back, but it acted as if she were nothing more than a weak pup. The grizzly roared, its sound instantly drowning out Mae's growls as it prepared to charge. Mae braced and prepared for what would surely be a fatal hit, but instead, an equally feral snarl answered.

Rogue tore from the brush in wolf form, colliding with the bear. The surprise attack caught the grizzly off guard, and it staggered, giving Mae the spare moment she needed. But the surprise attack would be Rogue's only advantage. The grizzly turned on him. Fearlessly, he positioned himself in front of Mae, placing himself in the line of fire—to save her, to protect her.

Once again. Mae's heart raced.

The bear charged.

Rogue met the grizzly head-on, biting and snapping at the large beast as he dodged its blows. Mae watched the lethal dance in horror. With each second that passed, she became more convinced that Rogue had won. Until one of the grizzly's massive paws collided with Rogue's side.

A high-pitched yelp tore from his lips as he crumpled to the ground. At the sight of him lying there, unmoving, the bear roared again before it retreated—returning to where they'd started to find the young she so fiercely protected.

Mae shifted into human form before she rushed to Rogue's side. The ebony wolf lay at the base of a tree he'd collided with, courtesy of the mother grizzly's paw. Mae knelt beside him, uncertain if he was breathing. Involuntarily, he shifted into human form, likely from succumbing to the pain.

Several gashes from the grizzly's mighty claws marred his chest. Mae's breath caught as he moaned in agony. There was blood everywhere…

Mae didn't think. He'd saved her life. Twice now. He may be a rogue, a manipulative devil who'd misled her on their deal, but he was a man. A man with a life and people who cared about him.

And she wouldn't leave him here to die.

———

There was no doubt in Rogue's mind that death lingered over him. Pain seared through his chest, the sting of torn flesh and bone intensifying with each breath he drew until he became convinced he'd rather not breathe at all. He could feel the heated rush of blood leaving his body, the intense chill its absence left behind. Every second drew him closer to the inevitable, closer to darkness, until, for a moment, he was certain he saw the face of the angel of death himself.

Hello, old friend.

He greeted death warmly, as they'd been acquainted many times before. More than once, Rogue had drawn so close to death that even in his waking hours, he could recall the sensation. First, the absence of thirst, hunger, need. The loss of his vision and voice came next, followed shortly by the absence of sound and touch until he was floating in an endless ocean of emptiness. The waves rising faster than the tide until suddenly, he was carried out to sea. His body became a black hole, void of all emotion and sensation.

He had no name, no purpose, no identity.

Then every time, just as he became certain the gravitational pull of the tide would swallow him whole, he saw her. The pain in her eyes. Her quivering lip. The single memory that would haunt him for all eternity, and then, in a rush that hit him like the force of a tidal wave, he remembered himself.

His past. His present. His future.

The promise he'd made to her.

Blood ran down Jared's throat as he struggled to breathe. He crouched near the creek, hidden in the safety of the forest, far past where the other children would look for him. He sank onto a slate rock, surveying his reflection in the creek's surface. As he touched the broken skin on his cheek, the cut throbbed. It wasn't deep, but it still hurt.

At least it wouldn't scar. Not this time.

Tears clouded his eyes. He smashed his fist through his watery reflection. He should have taken his own blade to them, shown them what it was like to hurt, to feel cruelty, but he'd been too scared, and they were so much larger than him…

A small voice broke the silence. "Are you okay?"

He shot a glance over his shoulder. Maeve Grey peeked out from among the pine trees. He knew her, of course. Everyone knew everyone on the Grey Wolf ranch. They'd probably played together when they were small, but now he was a whole ten years old and she was only seven, and he couldn't remember the last time he'd spoken to her.

"Go away," he growled.

Mae eased out from the pine needles. "Are you crying?"

Jared swiped his forearm across his eyes. "Alpha wolves don't cry."

She watched him for a moment. "You're no alpha wolf."

It was the same taunt the other boys threw at him, but when she said it, there was no cruelty, only observation. Somehow, that made it worse.

"Not yet," he snapped. "But I will be some day."

And then he'd show them...

"I don't like alphas. They're snarly and hot-tempered." She inched closer, her pink tennis shoes shuffling through the mountain dirt. "I saw what they did to you."

"I said, go away," he growled again. He plunged his hand into the cold spring water. He cupped the water in his palm to wash the blood away, but he only managed to smear it further.

"Let me help you." She reached toward him.

His eyes flashed to his wolf's. "I don't want help." He lunged toward her with a snarl.

She stumbled, falling onto her bottom with an audible thud. Mud splattered over her purple dress, leaving her covered in muck. Her lower lip quivered in a pathetic wobble before she ran off into the woods. He stared after the spot where she'd disappeared. That would teach her not to follow him.

He sat down on the rock again and curled his legs into his chest. A few minutes later, a rustling sounded from a nearby bush. Immediately, he froze. She'd likely gone and told her jerk big brother and his stupid friends, and they'd come for him. That'd be his luck. He jumped to his feet, prepared to run, but when the brush parted, only Mae emerged again, holding a broken plant in her hand.

"I thought I told you to shove off." He bared his teeth.

This time, she ignored him. She didn't say anything, just crossed the mountain rock toward him and set the plant down at his feet like an offering. Why wouldn't she leave him alone?

He picked the plant up and examined it. There was a gooey green substance oozing from the broken branch. "What's this?"

"Aloe vera."

He frowned. "I don't have any burns. They didn't get that far."

At least not this time…

"My mom told me it cleans things." She gestured to his wound. "I want to help."

"Fine," he grumbled, dropping back down onto the rock.

If only to get her to leave faster…

Kneeling beside him, she reached into the creek and cupped some water in her hands. "Friends help each other," she whispered.

He inched away from her. "I don't have any friends." He sounded pathetic, but it was true. The other boys found any excuse they could to torture him.

"You do now." She gently poured the water over his wound. The cool liquid soaked his cheek.

He frowned. "I don't want your pity."

"Good. You won't get it." She wiped the blood away before she rubbed aloe on his wound.

His grimace faded. "What will I get from you?" He glanced toward her then.

"I told you already." She extended the aloe plant to him. "Friendship."

He gripped the other half, each of them holding a side of the plant between them like a wishbone. "I don't know how to have a friend." Nor did he think he wanted one. She was a girl, and several years younger, though her smile softened him to the idea.

She grinned in a way that lit her whole face. "Then I'll teach you."

And she did. She taught him more than friendship. She taught him he could love—deeply. Sometimes so much it hurt…

Slowly, the memory gave way to another.

Jared tapped on the window, low and rhythmic. "Psst. Mae," he hissed.

When she didn't respond, he leveraged his footing on the drainpipe and used one hand to push the second-story window open. At fifteen, he had more strength than when he was only a boy, and he'd snuck through this window more times than he could count. He gripped the wooden sill, pulling himself inside. "Mae, you won't believe what my father gave me. He—" He turned toward her.

Mae sat on her bed in her pink nightgown, her knees cradled to her chest as though she wanted to disappear. Tears poured down her cheeks.

Jared lowered himself onto the bed next to her. "Mae, what's wrong?"

He wanted to hold her, protect her, but they hadn't touched like that since they were kids. Not since he'd started to grow what she called his milk mustache, and definitely not since her mother had bought her first training bra.

"It's nothing," she whispered. She swiped the back of her hand over her cheeks before she eased next to him. She leaned her head onto his shoulder. Her hair smelled of juniper and berries. His heart raced. He'd thought more than once about kissing her but had never dared.

"You missed dinner again," he said, unsure of what to say.

"I wasn't hungry."

"You're far too thin as it is," he teased. Her already small frame had grown thinner over the past few weeks. It wasn't like her not to eat. "Are you sure you're okay?"

"I am now that you're here." She leaned further in toward him as she forced a smile. "Tell me your news."

His excitement felt silly now. Reaching to his belt, he fumbled with the old leather holster and removed the blade, extending the dagger toward her.

She lifted her head from his shoulder. "What's this?"

"It's my father's battle blade. He gave it to me tonight." A swell of pride grew in his chest. The gift meant he would start his training soon. Someday, he'd assume his father's role as Grey Wolf second-in-command. If he dared to dream, there was even talk among the pack that another one of the founding families might claim the role of packmaster for a generation or two. That meant he or Colt Cavanaugh could be considered, instead of Mae's brother, Maverick.

Mae beamed at him. "Oh, Jared. I'm so happy for you." She threw her arms around his neck. He caught her, holding her against him as she drew him into a bone-crushing hug.

As she drew away, she lingered for a moment, staring up into his face until her gaze fell to his lips. His eyes flickered to his wolf's involuntarily, and he thought for a second she might kiss him, but then she turned away.

"I want to draw you." Mae reached into her bedside drawer, removing her sketch pad and graphite pencils. She was an amazing artist, full of natural talent. She'd been doodling on the sides of her paper in school for years until a few winters back when Jared had bought her a sketchbook for Christmas. She placed one of her pencils between her teeth, turning her head to the side as she looked at him. "Hold still."

He chuckled. "All right."

They sat there like that for a long time as Mae worked out the details of her sketch. Jared watched her draw as he admired the details of his father's blade. Seeing her concentration as she studied him was mesmerizing.

"There," she said finally. "It's not done yet, but that's the basic outline." She passed the sketchbook to him.

He glanced down at the thick, white paper. There he was, sitting on her bed, his father's blade in hand. With more work, the graphite image would be like a photograph.

Mae scooted over next to him. "I still need to work on the hands a bit," she said, pointing toward the image. "Those are always the hardest."

Jared shook his head. "I think it's perfect."

Mae smiled. "You always say that." For a moment, they both stared down at the image, admiring the dark lines. Mae leaned her head on Jared's shoulder again. "Have you ever thought about running away from here?" she whispered. Her words were so soft he almost didn't hear them.

He'd thought about it plenty of times before she'd come along.

When the boys used to bully him, he would think about shifting into his wolf and running until his paws bled, far past the edges of the Grey Wolf territory and deep into the Montana mountains. Sometimes he'd wanted that so badly he'd ached for it.

"Yeah, I have," he admitted. "But I haven't felt that way in a long time."

"Don't you want to make your own choices? Live your own life?" Mae asked.

Jared lifted a hand and ran it lazily through the locks of her hair. She kept it short, almost boyish, much to her mother's disappointment. But he liked it that way. It drew attention to her face, to her large green eyes. "I'm not sure what you mean, Mae-day."

He'd given her the nickname four years ago. One time when his father had been shouting for them to come to dinner. "Mae-day! Mae-day!" Jared remembered yelling as they'd leapt from a pine tree. They'd been so high up that they'd each broken a limb—his arm and Mae's ankle. Their parents had been furious.

"Do you even want to be second-in-command?" Mae asked, drawing his attention again. "Or packmaster, if it comes to that?"

The question caught him off guard. He'd been born into the Black family. The Greys, the Blacks, and the Cavanaughs: they were the three founding families of the Grey Wolf Pack, currently under the Greys' rule. There would never be anything else for him. It was his birthright.

"Of course," he said.

She sighed, sinking lower so her head was partway on his chest. "I guess I'm the misfit then."

He shook his head. "If you're a misfit, then I'm a misfit." When she didn't respond, he cupped her chin and forced her to look up at him. "What's wrong, Mae?"

"I just…" She released a long sigh. "I've realized everything's spelled out for me. I don't have any choices. I'll spend the rest of my life at Wolf Pack Run, working for the ranch. What kind of life is that?"

He wasn't sure how to answer.

She crossed her arms over her chest. "I won't even be able to marry who I choose. I have to pick an alpha wolf with a strong bloodline. 'For the sake of the pack,'" she mimicked her father's voice.

"It's not the worst fate," he offered.

"But what if I don't want to marry an alpha?"

The thought of Mae, at only twelve, worried about marrying anyone confused him. He didn't think about such things, even at fifteen. He guessed he'd always assumed when they were older, he would marry her.

She sank back onto the bed. "I want to make my own choices. I want adventure. I want to travel the world and make art. Not be stuck here on this ranch. I want…" She struggled to find the words.

"Freedom?" he offered. He lay down next to her, staring across the bed into those large green eyes, eyes that lately had been too sad. It made his chest ache. He couldn't stand the sight of her pain.

Another round of tears gathered in her eyes as she nodded.

He gently swiped them away. When he drew his hand back, one of her eyelashes was stuck to his finger. "If you want freedom, I'll give it to you," he whispered. "Someday I'll take you away from here, Mae. As far as you want to go."

Her brow scrunched. "What about being packmaster? You'd lose your chance."

His father's blade lay on the bed between them.

"I'd give it up if that would make you happy. I swear it." He extended his hand toward her, where her eyelash still clung to his finger.

She blew on it until it floated away. "I wished for it."

"There's no need to wish. I promise you."

A smile curled across her lips, and he returned it, a feeling of triumph growing in his chest. But a sudden thump from down the hall startled them both. They sat up. Heavy footsteps drew near, and the color drained from Mae's cheeks.

"Mae, what is it?" Jared asked.

"You have to go," she whispered.

Jared blinked at her. She'd never kicked him out of her room. When they'd been small, they'd stayed up half the night together, huddled under her bedsheets, laughing and playing stupid games until the dawn broke and he slipped home again.

She shoved against his shoulder. "Jared, you have to leave now. You—"

"I'm not leaving you like this, Maeve."

She looked terrified.

He'd never seen her so afraid.

The panic in her features grew. "Stay quiet then and close your eyes." Using her wolf strength, she shoved him from the bed and into her open closet before she slammed the door shut behind him. She leaned against the frame.

A moment later, he heard the door to her room open.

"What are you doing?" The voice was an adult male, but not her father.

The thin reels of light from her nightstand shone through the wooden slats of the closet door, allowing Jared to see.

"Nothing," Mae squeaked. She scurried to her bed. She sat down, moving the sheets to cover Jared's blade.

The bedroom door clicked shut, and a massive figure stepped into view. It was only her uncle Buck, who lived down the hall. So why did Mae look so terrified?

"What's this?" Buck asked, picking up Mae's sketchbook. He glanced down at the drawing. "Is this Jonathan Black's boy?"

Mae nodded.

"I told you, you need to stop fixating on him."

"He's my friend," Mae said.

"He's a weak excuse for a Grey Wolf, just like his father. He'd never be fit to be packmaster," Buck scoffed.

Jared bit his tongue to stop himself from snarling.

Mae cringed as Buck ripped the drawing from the sketchbook, tearing it in two. The pieces dropped onto the floor before Buck eased onto the bed beside Mae with a satisfied smile.

Jared froze.

"Now, where were we?" Buck purred.

Jared would never forget the terror on Mae's face as Buck lifted the hem of her nightgown. Buck's large hand slid up her bare leg as Mae whimpered. Jared saw red. He'd kill the bastard.

Bursting from the closet, Jared lunged. He caught Buck off guard, knocking the alpha wolf to the floor. Jared's fists pounded into Buck's face, but Buck acted as if Jared were little more than an annoyance.

Rolling his weight on top of Jared's, Buck gripped him by the throat. "You little fuck," he snarled. Buck's grip tightened until Jared struggled for air.

Mae was sobbing. "Leave him alone, Buck!"

Jared's face burned from lack of oxygen as the sounds of Mae's crying rang in his ears. She was yelling, pleading with Buck to stop, but Buck ignored her.

"Stop! You'll kill him!" Mae shrieked.

As Jared's vision grew dark around the edges, a tortured scream rang through the room. Suddenly, Buck seized. He released Jared, swaying slightly before he collapsed in a heap on the floor. Mae stood over Buck, shaking from head to toe as she clutched Jared's blade in her hand. The bloodied knife slipped from her fingers and clattered onto the hardwood beside Buck.

"Jared." Mae rushed to Jared's side. She held him in her arms, rocking him and crying uncontrollably as Jared regained his breath.

"It's okay, Mae. I'm okay," he rasped. Thanks to her.

Everything he had, everything he was, was thanks to her. She had to know that.

Mae's eyes darted between him and her dead abuser. "What have I done?" she breathed.

Suddenly, the door to Mae's bedroom burst open. Her father, the packmaster, stood in the doorway. His dark eyes immediately fell to his dead brother…and then to Jared.

Jared didn't think.

Forcing himself to his feet, he snatched his father's bloodied knife from where Mae had dropped it. "I did it," he said before Mae could utter a syllable.

"No," Mae whispered. She clutched his arm.

But he couldn't allow her to take the fall for this. Pack law was clear. Killing another Grey Wolf was a death sentence, or worse, an order to be cast from the pack…for good. Packmaster's daughter or not, Mae would lose everything.

Jared couldn't allow that to happen.

Mae had saved him in more ways than she knew, and now it was his chance to save her. He loved her. He had to protect her, risk everything for her.

"I did it," he repeated. "I killed him."

As his eyes met the packmaster's, he only regretted he hadn't killed Buck himself, because Jared had made a promise to Mae, to give her freedom, happiness, and that was what he would do.

No matter the cost.

He only hoped the packmaster would show him mercy, make his death quick, because if he didn't, the sight of Mae's quivering lip would haunt Jared for eternity...

As Rogue floated through his unconscious mind, despite death lingering over him as sure as the sun set in the west, he realized with stunning clarity that he could not die. Death held no power over him.

Because he had unfinished business to attend to...

Rogue jolted awake. The pain in his chest seared from the sharp movement, making him feel like he'd been torn in two. His eyes shot open as he struggled to draw breath. He was lying supine on his bed in the dark, the moonlight streaming in the window, the only light in the room. A cool summer breeze drifted in, causing the drapes to flutter along with the starched white linen canopy of the four-poster bed.

Though he was awake now, a presence still loomed, but instead of death lingering over him as he bled out on the forest floor, it was only Murtagh who sat at his side.

"Good. Yer awake finally."

"How long have I been out?" Rogue asked. His throat felt parched as though he was dehydrated.

"Two days," Murtagh answered.

Rogue let out a groan. Which meant two days gone from their lead on the vampires. They would be working to find her, catch her—and with her escape, now he would be, too—and to add insult to injury, he had two more days of ranch work to catch up on. Not to mention, there was the little matter of all his plans for his fellow rogues going to shit, considering he'd lost the woman who was the key to saving them. Why the hell had she run? Slowly, he attempted to rise up onto his elbows.

"Don't move, ye blasted numpty," Murtagh hissed. "Yer bandages were just changed. Best not soak through them again."

Rogue's eyes darted down to his bare chest, where several large bandages were wrapped around his torso. There were no dark stains beneath, which meant he wasn't still bleeding heavily, and given that he was breathing and conscious, he'd live. Lord knew he'd survived worse than a grizzly's claws. Ignoring Murtagh's warning, Rogue used his elbows to ease himself farther up on the pillow.

Murtagh grumbled his disapproval.

"I've saved your life more than once, and you're a beast to take care of, so you'd best not complain," Rogue shot back.

The movement caused a slight throb of pain, but with his true nature, it would soon be little more than a flesh wound. The scent of yarrow drifted from the linens. The plant was usually used for superficial injuries, but for a wolf, it provided assistance enough in slowing bleeding. Still, he'd been lucky. A few more hours out there in the woods with nothing to slow the blood flow, and his fate would have been questionable. Thank God, Murtagh had found him.

"Thanks, by the way," Rogue grumbled to the Scot.

Murtagh cast him an amused grin. "It's not me that saved ye and cared for ye." The Highlander nodded over his shoulder.

Rogue followed his gaze to find Mae sitting in the antique armchair by his window, looking every bit as out of place in his bedroom as she likely felt. The clothes she wore, which she appeared to have borrowed from one of the maids, were spotted with blood—his blood—and from the looks of the bags under her large green eyes, it appeared she hadn't slept in days.

Murtagh's voice lowered to a whisper. "She's hasn't left yer side in two days. But ye think she does not ken who ye are? If not in her head, at least in her heart."

Rogue's eyes widened. He wasn't certain he was seeing straight.

Mae had been trying to escape, so when he'd been attacked by the grizzly, he'd just naturally assumed…

But she was still here. With him. By his side and caring for him as Murtagh said.

Which means…

Something near the black hole in his chest stirred. He shook his head. *Which means nothing*, he chastised himself. She could have run back to her pack, told her brother everything, and let Maverick lead the charge in finding the antidote—cut out the middle man. It would have been a risk to her safety, but he knew she would have taken it after how he'd misled her. Yes, she was here, but not for him, not for Jared. She was here for the Rogue, for the dark persona he'd become over the years.

But why?

She's not for you, and she never will be. The brutal memory of a still-boyish voice echoed in his head. Yet his eyes held hers. He expected her to look away, but she didn't.

Murtagh cleared his throat before he stood and headed

toward the door. "Right, then. Best be seein' a man about a horse."

Rogue shot the Scottish cowboy a glare. "Subtlety has never been your forte, Murtagh."

The other wolf ignored him, casting him an annoying wink as he made his exit.

When the door clicked shut behind the Scot, Rogue watched Mae from his position on the bed, his eyes never leaving her. With Murtagh gone, Mae lowered her gaze and refused to look at him. Instead, she toyed with her hands, twisting them as if there were imaginary rings on her fingers as she stared out the window toward the darkened pasture. The moon cast a dim light on the ranchlands below.

Rogue could practically feel those small, delicate hands gripping his shoulders again. Her fingers had dug into his skin as he'd kissed her in a sharp and tantalizing scrape against his skin.

As a teenager, how many nights had he dreamed of having her alone in his room like this? Back then, he'd wanted little more than to kiss her, to be tender with her. It'd been a thrilling and exciting dream. Now, the thought of the two of them alone in a darkened room was almost as terrifying as it was tantalizing. Years of a life lived in the shadows had hardened him, and he no longer trusted himself to be gentle. Not in the way she deserved.

Alone in a darkened room with him was no place for a princess like her.

No matter how much he wished it.

With Murtagh no longer grumbling over his movement, Rogue eased himself out of the bed and stood. At first, his feet felt unsteady against the marble flooring, and his abdomen ached with the use of his healing muscles, but he quickly found his balance. The pain was minimal in comparison to what it'd been before, enough that he could ignore it, and he had to remind himself to take it easy for now. Come morning, he'd be as good as new.

He made his way to the open window, where Mae stared out into the night.

"Does it hurt?" Mae asked, breaking the silence. She nodded toward his chest.

She was uncomfortable with quiet, with being lost in her own thoughts, unless she had a graphite pencil in her hand. He'd always been eager to spend those silent moments with her, to watch the inner workings of her mind play out on her delicate face. He remembered that now.

He supposed some things never changed. "I've lived through worse," he answered before he paused, considering her. "But never thanks to a Grey Wolf."

The reminder that they were enemies bothered her. He read it in her face as clear as day. She lowered her eyes to her hands again.

"Why?" he asked.

"I overheard your and Murtagh's security meeting, heard you say not to warn my packmates about the vampire attack. I...I jumped to conclusions. Murtagh already told me you'd planned to warn them in time. I'm sorry I—"

"Don't apologize."

He couldn't stand her guilt. Not over the likes of him. He may have done the right thing this time, but she wasn't wrong in thinking ill of him.

Not considering all that lay ahead.

"I didn't mean why did you run." With his well-deserved reputation, he more than understood it.

She glanced up at him. "I'm not sure what you mean then."

"Why save me?" he asked.

The weighted question lingered between them. It highlighted the silent tension that crackled throughout the room.

"If you really thought me so cruel, you could have backed out, left me there on the forest floor." He turned toward the night, his eyes scanning the dark sprawling hills of his ranchlands. "But you didn't."

Had she not saved him, he would've lain there for hours before Murtagh or any of his men found him, bleeding there on the forest floor before peacefully slipping into darkness. For a man like him, it was as peaceful a death as he could hope for. Not that he wished for it. He didn't fear death, nor did he want it. He'd simply faced it so many times that he'd ceased to be afraid. In his world, it was hunt or be hunted—and he'd chosen to become the fiercest hunter of them all. While that might have made him a miserable son of a bitch, it gave him something to live for.

A purpose. A promise. And he'd sworn to himself years ago he wouldn't draw his last breath until he'd seen that promise through. Rogue was a lot of things, but he was also a man of his word.

Mae didn't answer. Instead, she stared out the window toward the stars. "A friend once told me she saved a man's life, even at risk to her own, because it was the right thing to do." She turned back toward him. "I suppose that's why."

"It's more than that." Of that, he was certain.

She shifted in the seat of the armchair until she leaned forward. "You've saved my life twice now." The hint of admiration in her eyes seared through him. "That counts for something."

He shook his head. "We've been through this. I'm no hero."

"And yet you keep playing one. At least when it suits you."

He retreated from the window, crossing the room toward his dresser. Reaching inside, he pulled an old shirt from the depths of his drawer and tossed it to her. At the very least, he wouldn't make her sit there covered in his blood.

She caught the shirt and glanced down at it before she met his gaze again. "Thank you." Her sweet voice was barely above a whisper. He wasn't certain whether it was the shirt or saving her that she was thanking him for. But in any case, it stirred something in him. Something soft and foreign.

He needed some cold water on his face—and fast. Before she made him forget himself.

He stepped inside his master bathroom, coming to stand in front of the sink. "Saving you twice before didn't seem to matter when you were making a run for it." His tone was harsh, accusatory, even to his own ears. She likely thought that was due to anger at his injuries. But it wasn't. It was hurt. Hurt that the reason she'd saved him wasn't the one he wanted to hear.

Because I know who you are, Jared, because I love you. I always have.

That was what he'd longed for her to say.

But he knew better than to hope for such things. Those words would never be spoken between them.

He'd lost that chance twenty years earlier.

From her position on the armchair, she could see straight into where he stood. She watched him with those bright-green eyes. "You kidnapped me."

He twisted the faucet handle. Water rushed from the spout, and he splashed the cool liquid over his face. Rogue snagged a nearby towel and dragged the material over his cheekbones, his scars.

A moment later, when he turned back around, she was wearing the shirt he'd given her. The baggy old work shirt bore a few small holes, but somehow, on her, it was breathtaking. It barely covered the slender curve of her thighs, and damn, if his wolf didn't notice.

Down, boy.

"Abducted," he corrected.

Her brow furrowed. "What?"

"You said I kidnapped you." He turned off the faucet before he raked his gaze over her. "Last I checked, you weren't a child, which means it's abduction, not kidnapping. If you're going to keep company with criminals, best keep your crimes straight."

"It's not like I had much choice in the matter," she snapped.

"You did have a choice, and you made it," he corrected. "You agreed to come here."

She didn't argue the point further. Instead, she crossed her arms over her chest, only causing the shirt to ride higher. His attention fell to the curve of her thighs. All it would take was a few inches higher and then...

"You're bleeding again." She pointed.

He touched his cheek. Crimson blood stained his

fingertips on the scarred side of his face. Apparently, the bear had cut him there during the melee, but with all the scar tissue already present—not to mention the worse wounds on his chest—he'd barely felt the pain on his face. But even with his true nature, the scar tissue slowed the healing. Washing away the dried blood with water and then scrubbing it with the towel must have reopened it.

"I'll be fine." With the scar tissue, it would take longer to heal than the larger wounds, but it'd be gone in a few days' time.

She pushed to her feet before she headed over to his bedside.

"What are you doing?" The sight of her standing there by his bed, wearing nothing but that old T-shirt, was doing strange things to his head.

She retrieved the medical supplies tucked near the footboard before she beckoned him to her side. "Patching you up. What does it look like? You saved me, and I don't like the idea of being in your debt."

He crossed the room again to his dresser, where a clean shirt waited for him. "I think you've already discharged that debt."

"If it weren't for me, you wouldn't have run into that bear in the first place."

He gestured to the bandages on his bare torso. "I told you, I'll be fine."

"Do you always refuse help when it's offered?"

He paused but didn't answer. The question caught him off guard. He was back there again. He was ten and she was seven. Over twenty years earlier, a broken, sad child hiding by the creek after the other boys had taunted him again.

She'd crouched beside him as she extended an aloe plant to him, for the small cuts the other children had inflicted. It'd been a sign of friendship, the first he'd ever felt. For years, she'd been his only friend, his only place of refuge.

Once upon a lifetime ago…

"I'm not taking no for an answer." She sat down on the bedside, patting the spot next to her before she busied herself with a handkerchief, a bottle of isopropyl alcohol, and some gauze.

Confined by the bedroom walls instead of out in the fresh mountain air, she was close enough that he couldn't escape the delicious scent of her and how it called to him like a siren. From those gorgeous eyes to the curve of her pink lips, everything about her was perfection. Hell, even the gentle slope of her neck, her shoulders, her collarbone was somehow erotic. What he wouldn't give to trail his lips over that sensitive skin. His cock stiffened.

He cleared his throat. "Little consequence in comparison to my chest." He wrenched a drawer open. He needed to keep her away from him. Of that, he was certain.

"Quit protesting." She removed a handkerchief from the bedside table and poured the alcohol onto it before she reached for him. When her delicate fingers gently wrapped around his wrist, he stiffened.

Twisting toward her, he growled. "No."

He didn't allow anyone to touch the scarred side of his face, especially not her. Not even when his cock was aching for her to touch him anywhere. Anywhere but *there*.

Mae shook her head. "I told you. I won't take no for an answer." She had the same determined look on her face that she'd worn years ago when she'd proclaimed herself to be his friend. She'd forced friendship on him even when he hadn't known he wanted it.

He should have expected as much. "It's not help if it's unwanted. It's coercion."

"Well, I'm learning from the best, aren't I?" A grin quirked her lips.

He wanted to devour that grin right off her gorgeous mouth. When she looked at him like that, her soft touch still holding on to his wrist, he imagined all the things he wanted to do with her, *to* her. Things far more dangerous and tempting than allowing her to touch his scars...

"Fine," he relented. If she wanted to see his deformities up close and personal, he'd let her. Maybe then she'd see the monster he was. Maybe then she'd finally realize she should be afraid, and maybe, just maybe, when he realized his scars repulsed her...

...he would no longer ache for the past.

He sat on the bed and she joined him at his side. She reached for him, but just before she touched his cheek, she hesitated. She hadn't even touched him yet, and already she was disgusted.

"I may look like a monster, but I'm not going to hurt you." Her reluctance offended him more than he cared to admit. His reputation painted him in a grim light—and for good reason—and he knew that side of his face was hideous, deformed, but he'd just risked his life for her, saved her...and with them alone in his room like this, the thought of when he'd kissed her inside that godforsaken closet haunted him. He'd kissed her so thoroughly that the feel of her against him was forever seared into him.

And then he'd told her it meant nothing to him.

What a load of horseshit.

"It's not that. I was afraid *I'll* hurt *you*." She reached for him again.

This time, she didn't shy away. With gentle movements, she cupped his cheek and used a handkerchief to wipe away the fresh blood. Her touch was gentle, tender. Some of the nerve endings on that side were damaged, making it less sensitive, yet he was aware of her every movement. Rogue could count the number of times someone had touched him there on less than one hand. The stroking movements of her palm and handkerchief as they brushed against him felt foreign, distant, as if she were touching him through a kind of veil.

A veil of time lost…

As she tended to him, he watched her, searching for her disgust, but he didn't find any. Instead, he only found kindness, maybe a hint of curiosity, but not disgust. This close to her, he could imagine what it'd be like to lean in and capture her lips again. She'd tasted sweeter than he could ever imagine. But he wouldn't. Not now. Kissing her again would be a mistake.

But he'd been a fool to never take advantage of that opportunity as a teenager, back when they had stood a chance. Back when he'd been worthy of her.

The pale green of her eyes was washed even lighter in the moonlight, and for a fleeting moment, he lost himself there. For the first time in years, he forgot who he was. Suddenly, he was no longer the Rogue, a dark, nefarious monster of a criminal who lived his life among the shadows, who'd earned his reputation through sin and blood. Instead, for a brief moment, he was Jared. Just Jared. Sitting next to the woman he'd once loved, the woman he'd sacrificed everything for.

Twenty years earlier, he would have told her everything. Back then, they would have sat on the roof of her house beneath the stars, perched there like two night owls as they exchanged whispers. Back when he'd meant something to her.

Silently, he willed her to see the truth.

But she didn't.

Mae broke eye contact, turning away.

Pain seared through him, but he pushed it down, shoving the memories and emotions into the cavernous hole in his chest, the place where the darkness of his past ate away at him, where he kept his secrets. She didn't see him, and she likely never would.

And he hated that he wanted her to so desperately.

She rubbed the handkerchief over his skin one last time, the caress leaving his cheek free of blood. She reached for more isopropyl alcohol. Unscrewing the cap, she tried to pour some onto the handkerchief material, but it spilled onto the thigh of his jeans. "Crap. I'm sorry. Let me—" She reached for his thigh.

Instantly, he caught her wrist in his. "Don't," he warned.

His eyes flashed to his wolf's. He needed to keep his distance for both their sakes, and if she stroked her hand over his thigh when they were alone like this, now that he knew how she tasted...

Her lips parted and she swallowed a gasp. He could tell she was both intimidated and intrigued, but she'd never admit it.

"You don't scare me," she whispered.

"Pity," he said. "I should." His voice was a dark, purring growl.

They lingered there, their gazes locked and neither one of them willing to relent. The tension between them grew so thick he could have cut it with his knife. Temptation thundered through him. All it would take was one tug of her wrist, and she'd topple into his arms. One little pull and he'd finally claim her. This time, there would be no interruptions to stop them. He'd have his way with her. And from the heady mixture of fear and desire in her eyes, she wouldn't protest.

Her tongue darted out to wet her pink lips as Rogue fought to keep his grip steady. He was close enough that even in the moonlight, he could count the spattering of freckles on her cheeks, the way they speckled across her nose and climbed to reach her eyes. Close enough to see the amber starburst that encircled the green of her iris. Close enough to watch the cords of her throat dance as she swallowed. Close enough to want to taste her and to know that if he dared, she would let him again. What he wouldn't give to have just another taste…

She's not for you, and she never will be.

Not with what lay in their future now.

"Draw nearer and you'll regret it," he warned.

The truth instantly broke the tension for them both.

"I'm sorry," she finally whispered again. She tore her gaze away, and he released her wrist. She quickly repoured the alcohol, this time away from his lap.

When she turned back toward him, she refused to meet his eyes. Instead, she focused just over his right shoulder, away from him. "This'll hurt," she warned. She swiped the damp handkerchief over the open wound.

He hissed in response. But the pain brought instant relief, reminding him of himself, of who he was, what he was, what remained at stake. When all was said and done, Mae would be little more than collateral damage in the game he played. Once their deal was complete, she'd hate the very earth he walked on. She'd been a fool to make a deal with a wolf like him, and she'd soon realize that, because he wasn't the hero in this story. He was the villain.

And the sooner he remembered his role, the better.

"You're tougher than I am. That would make me howl," she said.

"I don't suggest it. Not unless you want your packmates to come looking for us. They'll have put out word that you're missing by now, offered an award for information."

"I thought you said they wouldn't find us." Her eyes widened. She almost looked panicked.

"They won't, because they won't be looking for you *here*, but best not risk it."

Tucking the handkerchief away, she ripped off a piece of the gauze as he watched her.

"You seem concerned they'll find you," he said. There was something she wasn't saying. He sensed it.

"I'm just...not eager to go back yet."

He quirked a brow. "And what would make a princess want to leave her castle?" He stiffened. If anyone had hurt her again, he would bleed them dry.

"If she's been locked away..." She said it so quietly he almost didn't hear her. The words weren't intended for him, but he heard them nonetheless.

He stilled, taking in the sight of her sitting there before him. With that sad look of longing on her face, she looked too vulnerable for his liking. It brought back harsh memories he didn't care to relive. "You don't seem all that locked away to me."

They both lingered there. The sound of the cicadas outside the window echoed and screeched through the night.

"You wouldn't understand," she said.

"Try me," he urged.

She hesitated, glancing toward him as if she wasn't certain whether to trust him, but finally she answered. "It's just... I've never so much as left the state of Montana. Even after my parents died and Maverick became packmaster, I went to college for finance in downtown Billings, because that was what was *expected* of me. It was the best choice to serve the pack. Then it was back to Wolf Pack Run to work on the ranch, because that was expected of me too. But it..." Her voice trailed off.

But it wasn't what she'd wanted. She didn't need to say it. He knew that without a doubt.

"It sounds like you have everything you need," he offered.

"What's having everything when you weren't the one to choose it? I've never been in control of where I go, what I do, who I love. It's part of being a Grey. There are rules, restrictions, responsibilities to the pack." The words flowed forth as if she'd held them in far too long. She released a long sigh. "I may not be locked away, but when every choice has already been made for you, it starts to *feel* that way, like you're trapped and..."

She hesitated.

"...and you can never get out," he finished.

Her breath caught, hitching on a quick inhale. For a

moment, she watched him, scarcely breathing. "Exactly," she whispered. It was clear from her surprise that she couldn't believe he understood.

But he always had. Even when he'd been fifteen and sitting on her bed as she cried on his shoulder, he'd understood. She'd wanted so much more than life had given her, to have every door wide open before her. In the years since, he'd been so steeped in his own hell that he'd nearly forgotten how much she'd longed for the only thing he'd ever had.

Freedom…

The sadness in her eyes tore him to shreds more than he cared to admit.

She placed the gauze over his wound.

"Why not leave then?" he asked.

Her brow furrowed. "I could never leave. They're my family. I love them."

Yet she had no idea what her father had done, what her brother had hidden from her in a misguided attempt to protect her. The thought sickened him. He clenched his teeth. Gathering the supplies from her, he crossed the room, placing them on the bathroom counter as an excuse to put some distance between them.

Before the past swallowed him whole, as if he were Jonah in the belly of the whale.

"Love doesn't sound all that appealing if it puts you in a cage," he growled.

"When you love someone, you'd sacrifice anything for them, even your own happiness." There was hurt in her voice, pain so palpable he struggled to breathe beneath the weight of it. "But a man like you wouldn't know how to love, would you?" she said.

He tensed. He couldn't look at her. Not now. "No, I wouldn't," he lied.

"You have no idea what it's like to have obligations to a pack, a family, expectations, to not have a choice in the outcome of your life," she continued.

He *did* know what it was like. He knew *exactly* what it was like, but he didn't dare tell her that. He knew how it felt to have every piece of his identity, his sense of self, stripped away from him…like he was fifteen again, barely more than a child, stripped naked and so badly wounded he couldn't even shift as he struggled to find shelter in the snow. The prickling ice had gnawed at his bare feet for so long it had felt like fire, as if he were walking through the mountains on hot coals.

"You're right," he lied again, shoving the memory down. "I don't."

Not anymore…

"It's strange," she said. "I don't know why I'm telling you this. I don't even know your real name."

Rogue swallowed the lump in his throat. "It's Rogue," he ground out. "Just Rogue."

To her, that was all he ever would be. Jared was dead.

And he'd do well to remember that.

Chapter 8

WICKED—THAT WAS THE TITLE MAE WOULD GIVE THE portrait she wanted to draw of him. As Rogue turned back toward her, moonlight reflected on his face, making him all hard lines and sharp angles. Between the hollows of his cheekbones and the puckered ridges of his scars, he looked like a man who'd been through hell and back, a man who'd walked through the veil of shadows yet survived. Everything about him was testimony to power and hardened will, to wild, feral darkness. The contrast made him breathtaking.

She didn't believe that his real name was Rogue, but from the way he'd nearly growled it at her seconds ago, she wasn't going to press the issue. If he wanted to be called that, so be it.

She watched as he leaned against the window, staring out into the darkness. She'd never longed for her art supplies as much as she did now. This man knew survival, the kind most beings—human or otherwise—had never been forced to endure. She saw it in the languid way he moved, how he carried himself, in the sharp, predatory nature of his gaze. Looking at him like this, the planes of his face obscured in shadow and moonlight, his hardened jaw drawn in a tight line, most would believe him when he said he didn't know love.

But she didn't.

And she wanted to capture that on paper.

"I want to draw you," she blurted out before she could stop herself. "The chiaroscuro would be amazing."

His heavy gaze turned toward her, ice-blue eyes unlike the warm, tanned lines of his face.

"It's the contrast between light and dark," she confessed. "I like to draw, portraits mainly, and yours would have great chiaroscuro. I'd render it in black and white. Graphite only. It seems fitting for a wolf who lives his life somewhere between the light and the dark."

He watched her. The scarred side of his brow furrowed and caused a ripple effect in his face. The tissue had felt taut, almost stiff beneath her touch. His eyes narrowed, and the cold in his icy blue irises deepened. Enough to make her shiver even though it was summer.

Whatever tenderness had passed between them appeared to be over, and she could tell she'd been dismissed. She gathered the message loud and clear. Turning to leave, she gripped the door handle, then paused. There was something electric between them. Hell if she knew why, but there was. He wasn't the type of cowboy she was supposed to want, but to pretend she didn't was a lie.

Don't lie, Princess. Not to me. His words echoed in her head.

What kind of woman would she be if she just left? If she allowed the openness between them to pass? She feared she already knew the answer far too well.

She'd be a woman who accepted what was given to her, who did what was expected of her. The kind of woman she'd always been until *he'd* come into her life and she'd chosen otherwise. Making a deal with him to save her pack wasn't the ultimate rebellion, *he* was, and if she walked away now and ignored what she felt, deal or not, nothing would change. She'd still have made her decisions out of loyalty to her pack, not for herself, and after their deal was through, they'd part ways. Years later, she'd always wonder what *could* have been if only she'd been honest about the darker truth of what she was here for, with herself, with him.

With this dark, wicked cowboy who'd risked his life for her as if she meant something to him, even though they were strangers…

She didn't want to be that kind of woman.

Facing him again, she squared her shoulders, forcing herself to be brave. "I know what you're doing," she said before she could stop herself.

He crossed the room to his bedside table, where a bottle of Jack Daniel's sat.

Murtagh had insisted on leaving it there. "*Fer his pain, ye ken?*" the Scot had said.

Rogue gripped the bottle by the neck and drew in a heavy swig. When he was finished, he glanced at the black label as if he were bored with their conversation, but he wasn't fooling her.

She knew better than that.

"And what exactly am I doing, Princess?" His whiskey-graveled voice shook her.

"You're trying to scare me, push me away because you're feeling vulnerable, but it won't work. If you wanted my fear, you shouldn't have risked your life to save me." She settled her gaze on him. She'd hold those intense eyes of his, no matter how that caused goose bumps to prickle over her skin. "Art isn't about pursuing perfection. It's about embracing flaws. The scars should make you terrifying, but to me they don't. They only make you intriguing. It's beauty with depth."

He was still watching her. From the spark of fire behind

those icy eyes, she *would* have feared him, had she not known better. But she knew it was only because she was prodding his wounds, and not the visible kind. He'd done the same to her only moments before. She wasn't certain what had compelled her to confess her dreams, her fears to him, but she hadn't been able to stop herself. Her draw to him was magnetic.

She ignored his glare and continued. "The unscarred side of your face is handsome, but contrasted with the scars, you're authentic. You're—"

"Deformed," he snarled.

"I was going to say breathtaking," she shot back.

He tensed. But he didn't scare her. Despite the fire burning in his eyes, she got the impression that he was feeling as raw and vulnerable as she had moments earlier. Telling him her dreams had made her feel far too open and bare, but there'd also been a bit of freedom and power in confessing the truth to someone.

It was like standing naked in front of a lover for the first time, thrilling yet terrifying.

There was a magnetism between them, and she didn't doubt he felt it. She'd never experienced anything like it before. Her thoughts turned to the kiss they'd shared. Sure, she'd been kissed before, but never like *that*. Never in a way that had left her feeling forever changed, like the memory of it was as much a part of her as any of her limbs. She could still feel the tingling sensation on her lips, and dark criminal or not, she wanted more.

"I want to draw you, because I like looking at you," she confessed, "and because the contrast in your features would be a technical challenge, and because you saved me."

He cut her a look. "Don't mistake self-interest for heroism, Princess."

She refused to believe him. It was more than self-interest. The fury, rage, and passion she'd seen in him as he'd battled first the vampires and then the bear said it all. No one fought that way unless it was personal, intimate. And he'd fought that way to save *her*. She wasn't certain why, but she'd be damned if she'd pretend she hadn't seen it.

"You've saved my life twice now," she challenged. "Three times if you count the deal we made in the vampires' cells."

"I need you alive for the antidote as much as any other shifter." There was a sharp edge to his voice and if she hadn't been so used to dealing with alpha males like him back at Wolf Pack Run, it might have warned her off as he intended. But she wasn't buying it for a second.

She shook her head. "I don't believe you."

"And what *do* you believe, Princess? That I'm some sort of damaged hero, and when I saved you, it was an act of pure selflessness?" He set down the bottle of Jack on the table with an audible thud and prowled toward her. "That deep down, when we kissed, I had true and honest intentions?"

Slowly, he advanced on her, backing her toward the door until she was pressed flush against it. "In this fairy tale, I'm not the hero who scales the drawbridge. I'm the wolf who darkens the door." He was so close now that he was nearly pressed against her. "And when I do valiantly scale bridges to save the princess, it's only because I intend to burn those bridges down."

He pressed both hands against the doorframe just above her head. "Lust has a way of clouding judgment." He leaned in, so close that she thought he might kiss her again.

Her nipples tightened.

"Don't let it cloud yours," he whispered. He shoved off the doorframe, retreating from his onslaught.

Mae struggled to draw breath. Damn him. "It was *you* who kissed *me*," she said.

He arched a brow, and that wicked grin crossed his lips. "Was it?"

Mae gaped at him. When she opened her mouth to protest, she was about to tell him how ludicrous that was but stopped short. His question sparked a bead of clarity inside her. It was true, and she couldn't bring herself to deny it.

When they'd been there together in the dark, their bodies pressed against each other in a way that was as deliciously sinful as it was forbidden, she wasn't certain who had leaned in to whom. Maybe she *had* kissed him…

Because if she was honest with herself, she'd wanted him from the start. From the very first time they'd encountered each other in the vampires' cells. Like hell if she could explain it or understand why, but it was true and it'd colored every decision she'd made in regard to him ever since.

"Mae."

Something about the way he said her name caused a delicious chill to run down her spine. He might be a nefarious criminal, a cowboy wolf with a past darker than the midnight fur of his wolf form, but he wasn't going to hurt her. He'd made that abundantly clear.

He rounded on her, stalking toward her like a predator hunting its prey. "Is that why you came here?" He drew closer. Each step he took drew the air from the room until he loomed over her, his presence leaving her struggling for breath. "Some sort of walk on the wild side?"

With him standing over her like this, his body so close she could feel the heat radiating from his bare skin, her bravery faltered.

And he knew it. She could see it in the wicked amusement on his scarred, handsome face. He'd smelled her desire, knew she wanted him. He'd made that abundantly clear.

"Don't avoid the question, Princess." He eased closer, each word punctuated with deliciously devious intent. "Is. This. What. You. Came. For?"

He faced her, and from the fire raging behind his cerulean eyes, he understood. She'd confessed her darkest desires to him. He knew what she wanted.

Freedom.

Freedom to love, *to want* whom she chose.

Even if that meant she wanted a dark and dangerous cowboy.

His hand clamped overtop hers where she gripped the bed railing as he leaned in toward her. He didn't even have to pull her into his arms. One hand over hers, the rough callused skin of a cowboy's hands, and that was enough to draw her in.

He was the hunter, but she couldn't call herself prey.

Because she *wanted* to be captured.

The hard length of his arousal pressed against her stomach. Slowly, he trailed his knuckles over the curve of her cheek.

In a move so brazen she couldn't believe she did it, Mae reached out and cupped the fly of his jeans in her hand.

He growled, but it wasn't aggression she heard there.

It was desire. Pure and raw.

"I can feel that you want me, too, just like you did the first time."

At the feel of her touching him, his already graveled voice deepened. "When I kiss you and it means something, you'll know it."

"I wouldn't expect anything less," she admitted.

This man. This dark, dangerous cowboy was a hedonistic rebel, and if Mae had to guess, he loved those he cared for as passionately as he hated his enemies. It didn't matter that he didn't love her. She wanted that passion.

Even if it was only a taste.

"I'm not asking for romance." She released him, and from the spark of frustration on his features, he didn't want her to. "You're everything I'm not supposed to want in a mate, but there's something between us, and I…" She struggled to articulate what she was feeling. "I can't ignore it," she finally said.

She'd regret it if she did. She'd always wonder what could have been.

Rogue shook his head as his gaze raked over her. "Your brother would tell you you're being a fool."

She placed a hand on his chest. "My brother would also tell me to follow pack traditions, to listen to orders, to do what I'm supposed to." The beat of his heart thrummed beneath her fingertips. "But I refuse to behave."

His eyes flashed to the golden of his wolf's. If she'd allow them to, she knew hers would already be there.

"It was you," she continued. "That first night in my bedroom. You asked me who I thought of when I"—she struggled to say the words—"pleasured myself, and I never answered." Her eyes transitioned to her wolf. "The answer was you."

His low, rumbling growl vibrated through her chest.

"You said you could give me things others can't." Her fingers traced over one of the tattoos on his torso. "That's all I'm asking for."

Suddenly, he gripped her hips in his large, masculine hands, using his strength to seize total control over her within seconds. "Well, in that case…" His gaze darkened, and it stirred something low and primal in her belly. "I'm never one to disappoint."

If she'd thought he'd take her rough and hard, she'd been mistaken.

Instead, he moved with a gentle, lithe grace belied by all the strength she knew he possessed. Using her hips to leverage her weight, he laid her out on the bed before him. His hands ran up the length of her thighs, teasing her legs open until she lay straddled against his hips. He peeled the shirt she wore over her head, her underwear shortly following. As he stripped her of her clothes, his eyes never left her. With only his eyes, he feasted on her until she lay there bare before him.

"Is this what you want?" he whispered.

He stared down at her, taking in the sight of her nude body. She'd expected a wild hunger in his eyes, a greedy need that fit the wicked wolf she'd come to know. But instead, as he trailed a hand over her belly, his touch was so deliciously gentle and his gaze so soft, it was almost…reverent.

She nodded. She did want this. She wasn't certain she'd ever wanted anything more.

At her affirmation, something flashed in his eyes. Not the feral hunger she'd expected, but something softer. There was pleasure and desire there to be certain, but there was also something more vulnerable.

Something like sadness…

Though she couldn't begin to understand why.

But it was gone just as quickly as it came.

Slowly, his hands trailed up the length of her thigh, savoring and worshipping every inch of her skin, the pace of which built an anticipation inside her she could barely handle.

"You're beautiful," he whispered, his voice uncharacteristically soft. "Breathtaking."

Who was this man who touched her with such care and passion? Surely not the devilish rogue she'd come to know? No, whoever he was now was someone else.

Only once his hands had caressed and paid homage to every inch of her skin—her legs, her belly, her breasts, her nipples, every small curve of her—did he gently cradle her sex in his palm. The heat and pressure of his large hand warmed her, and she felt herself slicken. She was dripping in anticipation for him. Every inch of skin he'd touched ached for him.

As he used two fingers to part the lips of her pussy, his thumb drew delicious circles over her clit.

Mae cried out, bucking her hips forward.

In response, he dipped his fingers inside her as he used his free hand to grip one side of her hips, guiding her until she rode his hand.

His golden wolf eyes met hers as he massaged deep inside her. The sensation was so sinfully good and so surprisingly tender that Mae felt certain she would fall to pieces. She felt the tension building inside her. He leaned over her, curling his fingers, pressing even harder into that spot until she was crying out in pleasure. The tension inside her mounted to an apex until she was teetering on the edge.

"Don't fall in love, Mae," he growled again. "You know this isn't real." A wave of moisture coated his hand. "Because if you expect to heal my tortured soul, you're mistaken." He drove his fingers deeper into her. This time, a little harder, faster. Exactly what she needed.

It was as if he knew her body, as though he could read her every desire plain on her face.

She was teetering on the edge. "But if it's freedom from being a Grey that you're after"—he leaned over her, and that familiar wicked grin crossed his lips, softer now but just as sinful—"then I'll make you come so hard you forget your name."

On this, he was a man of his word. Rogue dropped to his knees, his head dipping between her legs until suddenly his mouth was on her. He captured the bead of her clit in his lips and sucked—hard.

Mae came apart on a wave of pleasure. The muscles of her pussy writhed and clenched as she rode him. His tongue lapped over her, greedily devouring her until she shook. The power of her climax thrummed through her.

When the last throes of her orgasm had dissipated, she lay there on the bed, still wet and open for him. He raked a hand through his hair as he licked the last of her taste from his lips. His gaze flicked over her, his irises transitioning back to his human form. Distant pools of blue. And then she saw it again. The streak of pain in his eyes she couldn't begin to understand. It was so intense and heartbreaking it tore her pieces, even though she didn't understand it.

What about this pained him?

He moved to step away from her.

But as he did, she reached for him.

"Rogue," she whispered.

He caught her hand in his. "Don't call me that." The sadness in those words cut through her. "Not now." His gaze met hers, and whatever vulnerability she'd seen there was gone in an instant. He didn't need to say anything for the message on his face to be clear. She'd pushed too hard, gotten too close. To what, she wasn't certain, but she knew without a doubt she had.

And he wouldn't allow it again.

He quickly released her hand, stepping away from her as he grabbed the bottle of Jack from the nightstand and headed toward the door. He held the door open, gesturing with the bottle for her to leave. "You've had your pleasure. You can go now."

Hurt seared through her. Mae sat up on the bed, tugging the shirt down to cover her intimate parts. She hadn't expected tenderness, but she thought they'd at least spend the night together.

"What about the antidote?" She asked the question because she couldn't think of anything else to say.

Without looking at her, he said, "We'll discuss it come morning."

"And…" Her voice trailed off.

What about us?

She was being ridiculous. There was no *them*. It was only heat and passion between them. Nothing more. There couldn't be anything more. She barely knew him.

And yet…

She felt it without a doubt.

He caught her meaning instantly. "Forget about what's between us, Princess. You'll be better off."

"I'll be better off?" She stood, crossing her arms over her chest to hold herself together. She felt more vulnerable than she'd expected. It would have been easier if he'd been what she'd anticipated. Not this. Not this quiet, powerful stranger whose gentle touch stole her breath away. "How do you know what's best for me? Now you sound like my brother."

A fire lit behind his eyes, and his nostrils flared as if he were the dragon on his back, struggling to contain his anger. His next words were harsh in their quiet rage. "I may be a monster, but never compare me to the likes of *him*." Finally, he turned toward her, the shield he used to protect himself, his secrets, back in its rightful place. "Run back to your room now, Princess. We've burned enough bridges for tonight."

Mae fled from the room without so much as a backward glance. She didn't need to be told twice. As she did, tears poured down her face, though she didn't know why. It wasn't until she reached the safety of her room that she allowed herself to admit what she was crying for.

Not the Rogue. Never for him. It was the gentle wolf who'd held her in his arms tonight. The man behind the mask. That glimpse of him had been its own kind of terrible cruelty.

Because if she knew anything about the Rogue, it was that he'd never allow her to see that wolf again.

Chapter 9

THAT NIGHT, ONCE MAE RETURNED TO THE GUEST SUITE, she fell into a deep, restful sleep where she dreamed of a pair of piercing blue eyes staring at her from the darkness. She was in human form, standing at the edge of the Custer-Gallatin National Forest, just outside Wolf Pack Run, and from beneath the pines, a pair of glowing eyes watched her. She glanced up as the wind whistled through the trees. The rolling gray clouds and thunder overhead cast an ominous threat. A storm was coming.

As she looked back toward the trees again, all sound ceased save for the rustling of the leaves in the wind. The eyes that had once been an icy cerulean blue had shifted, transitioning into the gold of a wolf's eyes. Familiar eyes.

Jared, a sharp voice whispered.

Suddenly, Jared darted deeper into the trees, disappearing among the foliage. Mae ran after him, shifting into wolf form. She chased him for what felt like miles, years. Yet instinct told her she was supposed to follow, to find him. She had to reach him, had to catch him.

Come home, the voice called.

She ran until she reached the edge of Grey Wolf territory. Their spot on the rocks by the river, where she'd found him that day so many years ago, the day they'd become friends. Ripples of movement disturbed the water's surface as if he'd run until he was fully submerged in its depths. But as she neared the edge, he never resurfaced and she found herself alone.

Mae, a familiar voice whispered on the breeze.

She turned away from the riverbank to meet the gaze of the wolf behind her, but Jared's eyes weren't what she found. Instead, a dark wolf with midnight fur and its face half-gnarled with scars stared back at her. A sharp ringing filled her ears as flashes of memory flooded over her like a tidal wave. The river. The aloe plant. The battle blade on her bed…until she was left with the singular image of a handsome scarred face beckoning her from behind cell bars.

An accusing voice inside her head hissed.

Dead.

Your fault.

"No!" she shrieked at it.

Mae startled awake to the feeling of a pair of eyes watching her—or more accurately, *three* pairs of eyes. Slowly, she blinked, the dark-cerulean gaze from her dream all but forgotten as she tried to discern if the three children peeking at her from the footboard—two young boys and a little girl—were real or if she was seeing things. She swiped a sleepy hand over her eyes and looked again.

No, they were still very much there.

She cleared her throat. "Hello?"

The heads suddenly disappeared beneath the footboard, and a harsh whisper followed—from the elder boy, if her guess was correct. "I *told* you both she would wake up."

Mae sat up, still working away sleep and confusion and trying to discern what on earth would cause three small children to be lingering at the foot of her bed, until a low, guttural grunt gave her a hint. She should have suspected as much.

Shaking away her remaining drowsiness, Mae crawled to

the foot of the mattress and leaned over the edge. The children stared up at her from their seats on the floor, eyes wide as if they'd just been caught with both hands inside the cookie jar—or feeding said cookies to a teacup pig, which considering the crumbs on the floor and the melted bits of chocolate all over their hands, appeared to be what was happening.

"Hello," Mae said.

Tucker, who was cradled in the older boy's arms, looked up at her and oinked again. From the looks of it, he was more than enjoying the food and attention.

Her eyes darted to him and then the children. They continued to stare at her.

Mae cleared her throat. "Am I…uh…interrupting something?" she asked.

The eldest one, a boy of maybe eight, puffed out his chest with confidence, the edges of his lips pulling down into a slight scowl. "Yes, you are actually."

"Oh, my apologies then." Mae smiled.

"We're sneaking food to the piggy!" The youngest cast Mae a toothy grin before promptly popping a chocolate-smeared finger into his mouth. He couldn't be more than four, and the idea of doing something secretive seemed to please him—greatly.

The middle child, a girl of likely five or six, shook her head. "We're not sneaking, Noah. We're experimenting. This is important scientific work. Our hypothesis is that pigs will eat *anything*." She turned her eyes toward Tucker's chocolate-covered snout. "Including chocolate chip cookies."

Mae raised a brow. "Hypothesis," she repeated. "That's quite an impressive word for a little girl."

"I like science and I'm not little. I'm *five*," the girl corrected. She held up five chocolate-chip-covered fingers. "And I'll learn to shift any day now."

A smile crept over Mae's face. "You don't say." She remembered all too well telling Maverick something similar when they'd been children. Since he was older, he'd reached shifting age first and had lorded it over her as any annoyingly affectionate older brother would.

"That's *factual* information," the girl added. She grinned. From the large hole in her smile, she'd recently lost her first tooth. "Murtagh says I have an *expansive* vocabulary."

"I'd say Murtagh's right," Mae noted.

The girl beamed.

The frown on the older boy's face deepened. "Murtagh only says that so she'll practice her spelling words."

His sister's face immediately flushed red. "He does not. Take it back, Will." She growled. The sound was pure wolf pup, barely threatening, but Tucker squealed anyway.

"I won't," Will challenged. He glared at his sister, despite still holding Tucker, clearly for her and his younger brother's amusement.

His sister scowled. Though as she turned toward Mae, her expression softened again. She cast Mae a conspiratorial look. "Rogue says education is important." The way she said Rogue was filled with more than a bit of admiration.

Will made a fake vomiting noise.

His sister turned red again and pointed an accusatory finger in his direction. "You didn't do your math problems last night and I'm going to tell Murtagh and he'll tell Rogue!"

The youngest, Noah, as the girl had called him, nodded in unison.

"I don't see Rogue doing long division every day," Will grumbled.

His sister produced another cookie from inside her pocket and extended it toward Tucker. "You wouldn't have to do it every day if you practiced what Murtagh taught you."

Tucker gobbled the cookie down within seconds, only to attempt to wiggle away after, but Will wrangled him tighter against his small chest. In response, Tucker cast Mae a pleading look and let out a huffy grunt.

"You and your stomach got yourself into this mess," she mumbled to him.

The children paid little attention to them.

Will hoisted Tucker further into his lap by the pig's overfull belly. Tucker's beady black eyes bulged slightly.

Serves you right, Mae mouthed silently to the pig.

She turned her attention back toward the heated debate.

"I'll be one of Rogue's men," Will said to his sister. "I'll fight vampires and work the ranch. Who needs long division for that?"

"Actually, long division is pretty important to ranch work," Mae said.

Immediately, the conversation came to a screeching halt. The two older children stared at Mae, eyes wide as if she'd just announced she intended to make Tucker into breakfast, while their little brother started to screech "Sit, piggy!" repeatedly as if Tucker were a trained dog instead of a pig. A beat of silence passed between them as Mae took in all three of their faces… Well, as silent as a room with three children would likely get anyway.

Rogue, she'd noted as Will had spoken. Not Dad, yet there'd been so much admiration in the girl's voice.

Will's nose wrinkled in disgust. "What would you need long division for on a ranch?"

Mae crossed her legs, perching at the foot of the bed. Luckily, she'd changed the night before, so she was fully clothed. "Math is one of the most important skills needed to run a ranch."

"You're lying," Will accused. "Did Murtagh put you up to this?"

"I'm not lying. Promise."

"See!" The girl stuck out her tongue at her brother.

"How would you know?" Will glanced over at Mae.

"Hold that thought." Mae quickly ducked into the restroom, changing into a fresh pair of clothes and quickly brushing her teeth before she returned to her perch on the bed.

"So?" Will prompted again at the sight of her. "How would you know? You're not a rancher." He said this as if he were certain of that truth.

"You're right. I *could* be a rancher, but I'm not. But I do work and live on a ranch, and I know math is important to a strong ranching business, because that's what I do. A ranch needs to make a profit—or at least break even. You need math to keep track of expenses and return on investment. I'm in charge of bookkeeping." Along with every other secretarial task that her brother and the elite warriors threw her way. It might not have been the life she wanted, but she'd always been good with numbers, and she took pride in her abilities. The Grey Wolves' business books were flawless.

"That's what calculators are for," Will grumbled.

"Do you not have calculators on the Grey Wolf ranch?" his sister asked.

This time, it was Mae's turn to be surprised. Bringing up pack status seemed like something untoward to do, but from the curious looks on their faces, the children didn't feel the same. She supposed to a child—rogue wolf or not—no subject was taboo.

"Well, we do, but—" Mae started.

"Are you surprised we know you're a Grey Wolf?"

The question caught Mae off guard. "'Surprised' isn't really the word I was looking for."

Confused was more like it. She was still trying to figure out who these children belonged to, why there were vulnerable children here of all places, and how they managed to know more about her than she did about them.

"You look surprised," the girl said matter-of-factly.

Mae shrugged. "You're very perceptive."

"So are you surprised?" The children stared at her, waiting for her to elaborate more.

Mae floundered. "I-I'm only surprised since we haven't been introduced."

"Oh, that's easy," the girl answered. "That's Will." She pointed to the eldest. "That's Noah." She pointed to the younger boy. "And I'm Hope."

"Nice to meet you all. I'm Maeve Grey."

Will mumbled a begrudging hello as Noah cast Mae a chocolaty-toothed grin.

Hope giggled. "We know who you are, silly. You're a princess. Rogue said so."

Mae shook her head. "Not really. I'm actually not—" She was about to say that being sister to the Grey Wolf packmaster wasn't very glamorous and the princess moniker wasn't legitimate—not to mention the word grated on her, thanks to a certain alpha-hole cowboy wolf—but Hope quickly cut her off.

"You should come to Martha and Ollie's wedding," she announced.

"Martha and Ollie?" Mae raised a brow.

Noah jumped to his feet with excitement. "The...the... they're..." he stuttered. "They're—"

"They're horses," Hope interjected, finishing his sentence for him.

Immediately, Noah's excitement deflated. He clearly didn't appreciate having his thunder stolen from him.

Mae turned her attention toward the small four-year-old. "You know, when I was your age, I used to stutter sometimes too."

Noah glanced up at her, a spark of intrigue in his large brown eyes.

"My mind was moving faster than my mouth could. I bet that's the same for you. Your mouth will catch up someday. At least that's what my mother used to—"

"We don't have a mother," Will snapped.

Mae stiffened. An immediate tension filled the room.

Hope's face became beet red again. "We do too! She's just..." Hope's voice trailed off. Noah's eyes filled with tears, and his chin began to quiver.

No one needed to finish Hope's sentence for Mae to understand. Whoever these children were, their mother was no longer living, and from the looks of pain on their grief-stricken faces, her death had been recent.

An empathetic lump formed in Mae's throat. It'd been years since her own mother had passed, and she'd been an adult at the time, much better able to handle the pain of losing a parent than a child was, but she knew all too well how crushing grief could feel for someone so small. She knew firsthand how it felt to lose someone she loved at a young age. She still felt that grief as acutely as she had then. It hadn't lessened with time. It'd only grown to be a part of her day-to-day.

"Our mother's dead," Will said as if he were challenging his siblings to say otherwise. "And why would anyone want to go to your stupid wedding, Hope? Horses can't get married. Not really." Will finally released Tucker, who let out a startled squeal before darting from the room. The sound of his tiny hooves against the dark marble flooring disappeared down the hallway.

Hope's small fists tightened, and her cheeks flushed red again. "They can!" she wailed at Will as she fought back tears.

Mae's eyes darted between where Tucker had just escaped from her room and the teary-eyed little girl. It didn't matter that she didn't know these children; they were just that: children. Children who were grieving and in desperate need of love and affection, and she could be the one to give it to them.

Escaped or not, Tucker could wait.

Mae reached out and clasped Hope's hand. "I'd love to come," she announced.

It would give her a chance to roam about and search for a certain rogue wolf to whom she had more than a few things to say. Besides, it wasn't as if she had anything better to do than continue to keep her head down as he'd instructed—except maybe find Tucker before Rogue's men made him into bacon. Murtagh had eyed Tucker a little too wolfishly for her liking, and if she didn't act fast, she might find her pet on a roasting spit.

"Our mother loved weddings." Hope sniffled. "She would have loved my ceremonies." She said this last part with just a hint of rage as she cast a glance toward her older brother.

"I'm sure she would have," Mae whispered. "Why don't you take me to meet Martha and Ollie? I've never been to a horse's wedding." She rounded the bed and extended her hand toward the girl.

No one moved and Mae thought maybe she'd misjudged until finally, with some reluctance, Hope took her hand. A moment later, Noah did the same. With tentative steps, Mae led them toward the door.

When they reached the hall, Mae glanced back at Will, who remained by the bedside, his arms crossed over his chest. The mix of pain and anger on his small face was all too familiar. She'd seen the same anger at the world on the face of another small boy. She knew the deep hurt it masked.

A hint of tears stung at the edges of her eyes. *Oh, Jared.*

Mae cleared her throat. "Will you join us, Will?" she asked.

Will hesitated, glaring at her as if she were the last person on earth he wanted to spend another moment with. She likely was, considering she'd drawn attention to his and his siblings' grief.

He let out an annoyed huff. "Who wants to go to a stupid horse's wedding anyway?"

Mae nodded. "If you want to be alone, I understand." She and the two other children turned to head toward the stables, but they were only a few feet down the hallway when she heard the sound of Will's footsteps trailing behind them.

Chapter 10

IT WAS A LONG WALK TO THE STABLES, AND BY THE TIME they'd found Tucker and made their journey out to the pasture, Mae was certain she'd been asked more questions than if she'd been interrogated by Rogue's men themselves. The latest in the line of questioning was about the merits of strawberry versus raspberry jelly, because as Hope put it, she was firmly in the nothing-is-better-than-strawberry camp, while Will and Noah preferred raspberry. Hope was convinced she could get the cook to make strawberry jelly, if only Mae sided with her, since as a "guest," Mae's word would carry more weight.

Guest wasn't exactly what Mae would call it, but all things considered, the situation was complicated.

As they reached the stable, after much reluctance to pick sides, Mae finally admitted, "Actually, I prefer raspberry jelly, because it's more ta…" Her voice trailed off as they stepped inside.

She'd expected the stable to be empty. Instead, amid the scent of hay and freshly mucked stalls, Rogue waited for them. The sunlight streamed through the window, highlighting the dust that danced through the air and reflecting the polished sheen on the brown leather of Rogue's Stetson and chaps. He stood with his back facing them, rubbing polish into a rough patch on Bee's saddle.

At the sound of approaching footsteps, he turned toward them. "You're late. I—" His words were cut short as his eyes fell on Mae. His gaze flicked between her and the children.

"Tart!" Noah suddenly proclaimed. He nearly shouted the word.

All eyes turned toward the four-year-old.

"You were going to say raspberry jelly is tart," he told Mae. This time, without a hint of a stutter. He smiled a wide grin. Finishing someone else's sentence for them, instead of someone doing so for him, appeared to be a thrill.

"You're right," Mae admitted. "I was." She grinned before she turned her attention back toward Rogue. He was wearing a worn work shirt, but from the looks of it, his bandages were gone. "I see you've recovered well," she said.

Not that she'd expected any less. Her cousin, Belle, had taught her a few medical skills, and Rogue had been nearly healed during their encounter the previous night.

He gave a tilt of his chin in acknowledgment. "Only thanks to you."

She wasn't certain what she'd expected from him after their encounter last night, but the subtle gratitude in his tone surprised her.

Rogue cleared his throat. "Noah, why don't you give Bee a snack? Be careful he doesn't nip your fingers." Retrieving an apple from his pocket, he tossed it to the small boy, who missed the wayward fruit in midair but retrieved it a moment later. Rogue patted Bee on his muscled rump, and the horse wandered down the stall block away from them as Noah eagerly followed the beast.

A beat of silence passed as Rogue turned back toward Mae and the other two children. She and he held eye contact, both of them uncertain what to say. The situation was made all the more awkward considering they had an audience.

As if to prove that point, Hope glanced between them. "Are you going to have babies?" she asked loudly.

She cast an innocent, inquisitive stare toward Rogue, but Mae found herself sputtering all the same.

"What the devil would make you think that?" Rogue asked. The gentleness in his eyes undermined the harsh tone of the question—a gentleness that looked so out of place on his hardened features that Mae wasn't certain what to make of it.

She raised a brow. Who was this enigma of a cowboy? A man who all the world thought was a dark criminal but who'd saved the life of his enemy's sister at risk to his own, who made love with passionate gentleness, and who had enough softness in his cold heart to be kind to children?

Hope released Mae's hand before stomping over to Rogue's side as if she owned the place. She settled her fists on her narrow little hips with an exasperated sigh. "You're staring at her the same way Ollie stared at Martha before they made babies."

Rogue gaped at her, his expression one of such raw surprise that Mae had to clap a hand over her own mouth to keep from laughing. Apparently, all it took to render a wicked cowboy wolf speechless was a sassy five-year-old in pink cowgirl boots.

"Of course they're not going to make babies together, Hope. That would mean they'd need to get married," Will said. His brow drew low as he looked back and forth between them. "You're not marrying her, are you?" he asked.

"No!" they both answered in unison.

At least there was one thing they could agree on…

That answer seemed to placate Will, at least for now. But Hope wasn't having it. "Rogue said Ollie needed to make Martha an honest woman since they made babies," she said to catch Mae up to speed.

Mae quirked an amused brow. "Did he now?" A grin spread across her lips. She was trying to hold in her laughter at the thought of Rogue attempting to provide excuses for horses mating to a pack of small children, but she was failing—miserably.

"That's what real men do, right, Rogue?" Will asked.

Mae's grin widened. Ever since they'd met, he'd had the upper hand between them, and if she reveled in the thought of making him squirm, now was her chance. "Is that so?" She cast Rogue a coy smirk. "I'm particularly interested to hear your answer after the events of last night."

"What happened last night?" Hope and Will asked in unison.

"Nothing that concerns you," Rogue answered.

The children's eyes turned toward him.

"Well?" Will prompted.

Rogue scowled at Mae as she held in a chuckle.

"In theory," he grumbled under his breath. "Any sort of decent man anyway."

Mae was trying her best to concoct a witty retort when a loud crash sounded from the other side of the barn. The chain of events that followed happened so fast, Mae barely had time to blink.

Tucker, who had followed them out near the stables, had rounded an entryway around the back, only to come face-to-face with Bee. The animals' rivalry from their previous

encounter and the glint in both their black beady eyes
would have been worrisome enough, but the situation was
made worse by the small four-year-old boy—and the delicious Granny Smith apple he'd just dropped between them.

Both animals dove for the apple.

Mae and Rogue ran for the boy.

Chaos ensued.

They dove toward Noah, both of them unfortunately
missing the mark as the small child wandered aimlessly
out of the line of fire, completely oblivious to the danger.
Instead, Rogue and Mae collided with each other. Mae let
out a high-pitched shriek. The shrill sound caused one of
the nearby horses to startle. The horse kicked at its stall
gate, shaking it enough that a nearby kerosene lamp fell
from the shelf. The liquid contents splashed up the length
of Rogue's jeans.

That would have been the end of it, but the resulting
noise startled the horse in the adjacent stall. The massive
beast kicked over a heat lamp that was still plugged in from
the night before. The plugged-in bulb shattered, causing a
spark that lit the hem of Rogue's jeans.

"Shit!" he swore.

He stomped his boot, trying to put out the growing
flame to no avail. Mae snatched a nearby saddle blanket
from the shelf and threw it around Rogue's lower half,
patting it in an attempt to put out the flames. The blanket
smothered the fire quickly.

A moment later, a throat cleared.

Murtagh stood at the mouth of the stable with the children beside him. Noah, who had wandered safely away as
soon as Mae and Rogue dove for him, clutched the massive

Scot's hand as Will and Hope looked on, and to Mae's surprise, Bee and Tucker weren't even fighting and had somehow managed to split the apple in two.

Which left Murtagh surveying the two of them where Mae stood, positioned behind Rogue, a blanket wrapped around his lower half as she patted... Oh, Lord.

As she patted the cowboy's muscled ass.

The smoke from the fire had all but dissipated.

Murtagh shot Rogue a chastising look. "I ken yer a man not to be tamed, but best no' be doin' that in front of the children."

"It's not what it looks—"

Rogue's snarl interrupted her.

"Bacon," he growled.

Mae released the blanket, allowing him to step away from her. "What?" she asked.

"Bacon," he repeated. "That pig of yours is going to be bacon by the time I'm through with him."

She tossed the blanket over one of the stall gates. "It's just as much Bee's fault."

Rogue shook his head at her before waving a hand at all of them in dismissal. "Out. All of you, out of my stables."

Hope let out a disappointed wail. "But what about Martha and Ollie's—"

"Tomorrow." Rogue removed his Stetson and raked his fingers through his hair.

"But you pro—"

"Tomorrow," Rogue repeated. His next words were far more gentle. "I know what I promised, Hope."

Murtagh squeezed two large hands over Hope's shoulders. "Ye heard the man, lass. Yer tutor will be arrivin' shortly. Best be off with yeh." Murtagh herded the children out the stable door. The sight was akin to watching a wolf gently herd innocent sheep.

"And take that nasty little pork chop with you," Rogue called after them.

Before Mae could protest, Noah eagerly scooped up Tucker, struggling to hold the piglet's weight. Tucker grunted at how hard Noah squeezed him, but Mae supposed it served the teacup pig right for ever getting mixed up with the group of adorable hellions. Not to mention, she had business to attend to.

The ragtag group disappeared a moment later.

Now was her chance.

Mae turned to confront Rogue, but he had already mounted Bee and was halfway out the back stable entrance. Mae released a long sigh and shook her head as she charged after him. She wouldn't be so easily avoided.

———————————

Had Rogue been a God-fearing man, he would have prayed she didn't follow him, but he knew firsthand that not even God could save him from the likes of Maeve Grey when she set her mind to something. Her steps over the grass were silent, but he felt her presence behind him as keenly as if he were looking at her.

"I have a bone to pick with you," she called after him.

He tugged on Bee's reins, slowing the mustang. "If it involves either teacup pigs as indoor pets or small children asking about horse's mating habits, then save it. It can wait." He nudged Bee again.

"It can't wait." She stepped in front of him, blocking their path. Her eyes flashed to her wolf's. She wasn't pleased and he knew it.

"Can't or won't?"

The gold in those wolf eyes flared. "Both." She placed her hands on her hips.

Rogue shook his head. He inspired fear in most men, and yet, what was it about the women in his life—whether adult she-wolves or no older than five—that facing a man like him made them braver than men twice their size? It was starting to become a nuisance.

The summer breeze blew a strong gust as the mustang moseyed out to the barn, but the sun shone down from overhead, warming the rolling green hills. The blue-peaked mountains crested the skyline.

Maeve followed after them. She and the children must have spent the better part of the morning walking out to the stables on foot, but in spite of that, she kept a brisk pace with him.

"You need to tell me everything—about the vampires, the antidote, what our next steps are. I understand my safety is important, but I'll be damned if you keep me totally in the dark like some kind of prisoner. I understand the need to lie low, but I still expected to be in on this. Working together," she continued, oblivious to his inner turmoil. "Partners."

Partners...

Like they'd been when they were children. Partners in crime, his father had called them. Only this time, Rogue's crimes were real. At that thought, he fought back a grin. He supposed there wasn't any harm in keeping her informed.

"My men have been quietly gathering intel to find who

knows the vanished bloodsucker's whereabouts. Our next step is meeting with my associate for information. In the meantime, you'll continue to lie low."

"No." She shook her head. "I want you to take me with you. I want to help my packmates, be involved in the search."

She said it as if they were discussing the strategies of a game of chess rather than talking about a dangerous search that could result in both of them being killed. This wouldn't be all fun and games. Of that, he was certain.

Leave it to Mae to be willing to risk everything, even her life, for those she loved. Years ago, she'd killed Buck to save him without so much as a thought to her own safety.

That was why he'd sacrificed everything for her—because she'd loved him then as no one else ever had, not even his distant father or his mother who'd passed years earlier. Mae had picked him up when the other boys knocked him down. Mae had cared for him despite him being weak and scared. Mae had taught him to be confident, to have enough self-esteem to one day fight back against the blows of his enemies.

Before this life, Mae had been his only real family, his only true love, and *that* was why he'd confessed to killing Buck. She'd made him stronger, taken a damaged boy and healed him until he was whole, and he'd be forever loyal to her for it.

Even now, after all this time, even knowing the pain, the havoc that singular decision continued to wreak on his life, if faced with the same situation, he'd do it again. He'd give himself up for her in a second.

All for her.

"How am I supposed to keep you safe?" he challenged.

They'd need to go more than a few miles from the safety of

Black Hollow, and every shifter and bloodsucker in the states of Montana, Idaho, and beyond would be looking for her.

She shrugged. "You're supposed to be a criminal mastermind. I'm sure you can figure it out."

"I appreciate the vote of confidence, but that's not going to happen, Princess."

"Why not?"

"Because I refuse to risk your safety, that's why. The answer is no."

"You can't make this decision for me."

"I *will* if it means you'll be safe."

She growled, her hands clenching into fists. "I expected to be partners," she accused. "*That's* what I thought I was agreeing to."

"I offered you protection," he reiterated. "Not partnership."

"You were misleading and you know it."

He shook his head. "Perhaps you should have considered that possibility when you chose to make a deal with the devil."

She stepped in front of Bee, forcing horse and rider to come to a halt. "You can't keep me locked away like a prisoner."

"The locks and guards are for your protection. I won't allow you to throw yourself to the vampires." He gestured toward the forest.

She crossed her arms over her chest. "You saw what happened when you kept me out of the loop before. I'm a smart, capable woman. I can help you, and without me there *is* no serum, no antidote." Her lips drew into an impertinent pucker.

Rogue growled, even as his cock stiffened. He wanted nothing more than to grip her by the back of the neck and claim those defiant lips for his own. He'd replace her righteous anger with moans of pleasure. She'd always been too smart, too stubborn for her own damn good. Not to mention, she had that damn longing for adventure. He'd seen that much in the way she was so eager to get away from her packmates. She'd been that way since she was a small girl—and it was dangerous.

This wouldn't be all fun and games. Of that, he was certain.

"It's *my* life at risk," she challenged. "Which means it's *my* decision."

He shook his head. *Damn it.* She always had managed to get her way from him, even when they were kids.

"Fine. If you want to risk your life, so be it." All it would take was one little scare, and she'd change her tune. "We meet him tomorrow night."

"So soon?" Mae's voice rose an octave.

Rogue chuckled. "What's the matter, Princess? Scared?"

His taunt had the effect he intended and she bristled.

"No." Her jaw drew tight, meeting his challenge. "Not in the slightest."

"You should be," he warned. But as he turned away, he couldn't help the grin that curled over his lips.

One last adventure, Mae-day. For old time's sake.

Leaving her with that final warning, he gripped Bee's reins before giving Bee a kick, and the mustang started to trot forward again.

"Wait!" Mae called after him.

Rogue pulled Bee to a halt.

"How am I supposed to get back?" She nodded toward the mansion.

It looked like little more than a pinprick off in the distance. She'd walked more than a mile to get herself out to the stables. He'd happily give her a ride back, but considering she wanted to play hardball with cowboys like him, if she wanted a ride…

She'd have to ask for it.

He waited, watching her for a long beat, but she didn't budge.

"Well…" she said, clearly waiting for him to offer.

He nodded to the nearby stables. "You're a smart, capable woman," he teased, repeating her earlier words, just as she had done to him. "You'll figure it out." He tipped his Stetson lower with a challenging grin and nudged Bee into motion again. "Welcome to Black Hollow Ranch."

Chapter 11

MAE HATED HIM RIGHT NOW. SHE ABSOLUTELY HATED HIM.

It was nearly nightfall by the time she climbed the mansion steps. She gritted her teeth as she shuffled forward. Her feet were starting to ache. Sure, she'd only been a short walk from the stables, and she'd been able to ride back to the mansion on one of his spare horses, but that'd been *after* she'd come to the rescue of one of his stable hands.

Well…maybe *rescue* was the wrong word, considering she'd been the one to accidentally knock over the stable hand's teetering wheelbarrow of manure. She'd felt it was only fair to offer to help clean the mess up. Half an hour later, it failed to matter that she'd been the one to knock the wheelbarrow over. She was still cursing Rogue for not readily offering her a ride. She hadn't mucked stalls like that since she was a wolf pup, and her arms were feeling it something fierce.

Gripping the massive door handle, she wrenched the door open and stepped inside. Immediately, she froze. Her stomach dropped and a wave of anxiety gripped her. The small dining room was no longer empty. Instead, Murtagh and four other male wolves dressed in ranch clothes sat around the table. Their Stetsons hung on pegs on a nearby wall, and they had mugs and bottles of beer in their hands as they pored over a game of poker. At the sight of her, the room fell so silent, she could have heard a piece of straw hit the marble floor.

Mae gulped. Each one of them was massive—alpha wolves comparable to Rogue or the Grey Wolf warriors. But unlike the cowboys at Wolf Pack Run who were rough around the edges, these wolves looked nearly as feral as Rogue, and if their leader's reputation was any indication, they too were criminals. They definitely looked the part. *Rough around the edges* didn't cut it—*jagged* was a better description.

Mae had never seen so many scars, tattoos, and scruffy beards in her life, and was that...? She blinked. Yes, it was. One of them was *actually* wearing an eye patch. Even beneath his Stetson, it made him look like a pirate.

Which she guessed wouldn't be that far-fetched for this crew.

With narrowed eyes, they watched her, quiet tension filling the room as they assessed her with suspicious eyes. She knew she looked the worse for wear, considering she'd just walked several miles in the evening humidity, but they weren't staring in disgust. Instead, they looked as if they would eat her for breakfast with a side of nails...

Her stomach gave another lurch. What had she gotten herself into?

Murtagh was the first to break the silence. "Ach," he swore. "He dinna so much as offer ye a ride back?"

"I rode back on one of the spare horses, but I...uh... had a little run-in with a wheelbarrow shortly before that. It was my own fault." She swallowed the nervous lump in her throat, her eyes refusing to leave the other wolves who were still staring at her as if she were about to be made into minced meat. "I didn't ask for a ride."

"Ye should no' 'ave had to." Murtagh set his beer stein

down on the tabletop with a heavy thud. Golden liquid sloshed over the edge. "I tell ye, if my da had raised that boy, he'd 'ave—"

"We know," the other wolves groaned. In unison, they faked their best Scottish accents. "He would 'ave cuffed 'im 'round the ears," they mocked before settling into a round of jesting laughs.

The tension eased slightly, and Mae finally felt as if she could breathe again.

Murtagh grumbled, easing down from the chair where he sat. "If I'd 'ave known he left ye out there, I would have come fer ye myself hours ago."

One of the younger wolves clapped him on the back with a smirk. "Always the gentleman, Murtagh." Despite his youthful features, a large red beard consumed half his face.

"Shove off, Boone," the dark-skinned cowboy with the eye patch grumbled. "You would have gone out and helped her too. Poor thing looks like the cat dragged her in."

A wolf so covered in tattoos he didn't seem to have any bare skin left raised his glass. From his features, he was clearly of East Asian descent. "Or a group of rogue wolves."

Eye Patch grinned. "But even mussed up, she's a pretty little thing."

Boone shook his head. "Of course she is. With how long a flame—"

Murtagh shot Boone a pointed look, silencing him instantly. "*Rogue* willna be keen on either of ye speakin' like that of the lass."

"I didn't mean anything by it, Murtagh. I was just saying—"

"Just nothing," Murtagh said.

"Don't be so uptight, Murtagh," Eye Patch grumbled.

"We'll play nice with her," Boone added. "We swear it."

"I'm standing right here, you know," Mae interjected. They were talking as if she couldn't hear them. Placing her hands on her hips, she used the tone she reserved for when the Grey Wolf cowboys needed to be whipped into shape. "Being a pack wolf doesn't make me deaf."

At that, the group turned their attention toward her.

"And for that matter, I might look like something the cat dragged in, but I'm no worse than any one of your motley crew," she said.

The rogue wolves exchanged silent glances. For a moment, Mae was certain they might throttle her. Apparently, she'd overstepped her bounds. All of them against her wasn't good odds. She gulped, resisting the urge to clap a hand over her big mouth, but to her surprise, the rogue wolves burst out laughing, deep belly laughs that shook the whole kitchen island. The relief that settled over her was immediate.

Eye Patch thumped the tabletop as he roared, "I like her already."

The other men raised their mugs in agreement.

Murtagh nodded. "She'll be giving 'im a run fer it, all right." He ambled over to Mae's side. From the slight sway in his step, the Scot had clearly had more than a few drinks. They likely all had. Tossing a large tattoo-covered arm around her shoulders, Murtagh nodded at each wolf as he introduced them. "This is Yuri. Our Japanese transplant." He nodded to the other tattooed wolf. "Sterling," he said, nodding to Eye Patch. As his eyes fell on the last wolf, his Scottish brogue thickened. "And ye'll 'ave to ken this is the wee lad of the bunch, Boone."

Boone looked about as pleased as a wrangled bull to be called a "wee lad."

Boone and Murtagh's conversation devolved into back-and-forth bickering, while Sterling and Yuri watched her. Sterling grinned. Beneath his Stetson, his gold tooth glinted in the light. "I heard you demanded to be Rogue's partner."

Mae gave a reluctant nod.

Sterling banged his fist on the table a few times to get Boone and Murtagh's attention. "Tell us. What did you tell the Rogue when you stopped him out in the pasture?"

Mae hesitated. "I…I told him I'd be damned if I'd be treated like his prisoner."

Sterling's grin widened. "And what did he think of that?"

Mae shrugged. "Well, he wasn't very pleased."

"He wasn't very pleased," Sterling echoed. The rogue wolves burst into another round of drunken laughter.

"I would have paid all my winnings to see his face," Yuri laughed.

Mae couldn't help her slight grin.

Murtagh was shaking his head at them. "Enough with ye now. She'll be wantin' a bath and some food in 'er belly."

At the mention of food, Mae's stomach gave a rumbling growl. She hadn't eaten since dinner yesterday evening, and a shower sounded like heaven at the moment.

Murtagh turned his attention to a hall that presumably led to the kitchen. "Daisy!" he hollered. "Daisy!" He glanced toward Mae. "Daisy's one of our ranch hands," he said.

The she-wolf who appeared a few moments later looked *nothing* like a Daisy. Large and stately, she was nearly as tall and wide-shouldered as the men—an Amazon if there ever was one. Her frizzy brown hair was swept back into a makeshift bun. "What the hell are you hollering about?" she asked. "It's supposed to be my night off."

"Can ye fetch some food?"

Daisy scowled. "Just because I'm a woman doesn't mean I'm getting your dinner for you."

"It's not because you're a woman. I meant on account of the fact that ye were in the kitchen," Murtagh said.

Daisy scowled, and Mae fought down a laugh at Murtagh's expense. That comment didn't fare much better.

Daisy placed her hands on her hips. "Fetch your own damn sandwich, you—" Her voice stopped short as Murtagh nodded toward Mae. At the sight of her, Daisy's eyes lit up before a smile crossed her lips. "Another woman on these godforsaken ranchlands," she said. "Thank goodness."

Before Mae could protest, Daisy had ushered her into the kitchen.

Mae and her companion made casual conversation as they both raided the kitchens. Daisy, who'd been born a rogue she-wolf rather than becoming one by circumstance or choice, confessed everything about life at Black Hollow Ranch. According to her, female rogues were less common than their male counterparts, particularly out in the western states, so having another woman to talk to was a treat.

By Daisy's account, only she, their male chef, and a few stable hands lived in the mansion full-time. They kept the ranch in order while Rogue and his men traveled. Apparently, Rogue owned multiple ranches throughout the west, not to mention several other "not-to-be-disclosed" underground operations.

Together, she and Daisy persuaded the cook, who the rogue wolves affectionately called Frenchie, to create a vegetarian dinner option for her. The chef assembled a fresh caprese salad, complete with cherry tomatoes and basil from the ranch's small garden peppered with fresh mozzarella from a nearby dairy farm and homemade balsamic vinaigrette.

Mae was so hungry she ate every bite.

An hour later, she felt a bit more herself again. She sat at the table in the midst of a game of poker with Daisy and Rogue's men. Though Mae had been wary of them at first, as the evening drew on, she warmed to the group considerably. Murtagh was more bark than bite. Boone was so young and green, he was relatively harmless. Yuri was a quiet, stoic type, and Sterling, bless his sweet heart, had even trudged out to the pigpen in the dark and retrieved Tucker for her.

With her belly full and satisfied, Mae cradled a sleeping Tucker in one arm. "Read 'em and weep, boys." She grinned as she laid down a straight flush before she swept all the chips on the table toward her.

"Shite!" Murtagh banged his fist on the tabletop.

"She's a damn card shark. I swear you're counting them," Boone moaned. He shoved more chips toward her.

Mae grinned. She *was* counting them, but considering they were only playing for fun, it didn't hurt anything. She'd learned the trick in a game theory class she'd taken as a math elective for her finance degree back in college. Art would have been her preferred choice of major, but considering her artistic talents wouldn't lend much help around the ranch and she was good with numbers, she'd ended up with finance.

At least it left her with a few card tricks up her sleeve.

"You just don't like to lose to a woman," Daisy cackled,

her tone full of sass. She shot Mae a mischievous grin. "Are the Grey Wolf cowboys such sore losers at poker?"

Mae laughed. "Typically." She smiled at the rogue wolves around the table. "This has been fun, and dinner and the snacks were delicious," she announced.

"'Tis all right if ye don't like meat, I s'pose," Murtagh grumbled. His mood had gone south. Oddly enough, he seemed displeased with the snacks Frenchie had brought them.

Mae smiled. "Better than all right. That's the best meal I've had in a long time."

Murtagh grumbled again, muttering something under his breath about heading to bed before he made his exit.

Mae glanced toward the other rogue wolves. "Did I say something wrong?"

Daisy shook her head. "No, it's not you. It's just…" Her voice trailed off.

"Murtagh isn't too fond of Frenchie being the new cook," Yuri finished.

Mae raised a brow. "Why not?" The cook had seemed friendly and accommodating. Not to mention his culinary skills were outstanding.

The group exchanged knowing glances.

"It's nothing personal. We all love Frenchie," Boone said. "But he replaced our old cook, and sometimes Murtagh gets…moody about the old days."

Mae's brow furrowed. "Because he liked the old cook's food better?" That didn't make a lick of sense. There was something they weren't saying.

"No. No. Cassidy was a horrible cook," Yuri said.

Sterling faked throwing up beneath the table.

"Have some respect," Daisy chastised.

Boone leaned forward, twisting his mug of beer around on the table. He was clearly underage, but none of the rogues seemed to care that he was partaking. "Murtagh would have eaten anything Cassidy made, even if it tasted like pig's ass—and not the good kind." He shot a glance toward Tucker as if imagining what he might taste like before he said, "Cassidy was Murtagh's younger brother."

Was. Mae caught the distinction there. Her heart sank. She didn't know any of them well, but Murtagh had been kind to her, and the thought of anyone losing someone they'd loved for so long pained her.

Briefly her thoughts turned to Jared…

She knew what grief was like, to have love in her heart that had no place to go.

"Murtagh's only sour about Frenchie sometimes because he's Cassidy's replacement," Sterling clarified, bringing her back to the moment.

Yuri nodded solemnly. "Cassidy crossed the rainbow bridge three months back, thanks to the vampires' serum." He growled. "Those bloodsucking fuckers."

Mae stiffened. Rogue had mentioned that his kind had been targeted in the early serum tests, but he hadn't said the victim was someone close to him. From the sounds of it, Murtagh had known Rogue for years, which likely meant his younger brother had as well.

"I'm so sorry to hear that," Mae said.

"Death is a way of life for rogues. We don't have a pack to protect us," Boone said.

"Couldn't you join a pack?" Mae asked.

Silence fell over the group. The question hung heavy

in the air, as if she'd asked if they liked to eat children for breakfast.

"I mean…that is, if you wanted to," she added, trying to amend her error.

"It's not that easy for us. Too many things to disqualify membership. Criminal background checks, previous pack history, and more," Sterling said.

Boone scowled. "The cards are stacked against rogue wolves."

"But things will be better once we have the antidote." Daisy stood and gathered several empty beer bottles off the table. "Rogue will make certain of that."

The weight of Daisy and the other wolves' optimism hung heavy on Mae's shoulders. Not only did her own pack need this, but so did these wolves. It didn't matter that she didn't know them well. It raised the stakes even higher.

Later that evening, when Mae returned to her room for the night, she found a sketchbook and a large tin box of professional graphite pencils along with a white eraser on the edge of the four-poster bed. On top sat a note, one word scrawled across its surface in elegant cursive. Somehow, the writing seemed familiar. She picked up the note.

Truce?

Of course, he'd likely heard about her incident in the stables, and a cowboy like him wouldn't apologize. A small smile crossed her lips nonetheless. She sat on the edge of the bed, running her fingers over the sketchbook as she petted Tucker. As she trailed her hand over the thick, coarse paper, her thoughts wandered toward the wicked wolf—stubborn, criminal, handsome manipulator that he was. After the abduction incident, she'd been certain she had him figured out. Maverick and the Seven Range Pact had always painted him as a dark criminal, someone who undermined the authority of packmasters everywhere for no good reason. She still didn't forgive him, but…

Mae glanced toward the door, her thoughts turning to the rogue wolves downstairs.

Now, she wasn't so certain. If not him, who else did these wolves have to protect them, to look out for their interests?

She didn't have to like it, but maybe her initial instinct had been right.

Maybe, he wasn't such a villain after all…

Chapter 12

WHEN MAE WOKE SEVERAL HOURS LATER, SHE COULDN'T get back to sleep. She lay in bed for what felt like hours, her mind replaying every scenario since the moment Rogue had first turned up in her bedroom and worrying over what lay before them the following night. Despite their newfound truce, she still wasn't certain she'd made the right decision in partnering with him, though she supposed time would tell.

After more than one unsuccessful attempt to quiet her mind and return to sleep, she finally threw back the covers and ventured out of bed. The children and Murtagh had mentioned a library in the south wing of the mansion, and she intended to find it. With any luck, she'd find an entertaining read to pass the midnight hours. With tentative steps, she crept from her room and descended the staircase to the first floor.

The mansion was quiet. Wolves were nocturnal by nature, but she'd observed that much like Wolf Pack Run, Black Hollow bustled most when the sun was high in the sky, since ranching work lent itself to daytime hours. Her footsteps pattered on the cold marble flooring as she crept through the darkness. As she ventured through the mansion, she passed several closed doors with lights shining beneath the frame. Muffled voices traveled out into the hall from inside. Apparently, she wasn't the only one burning the midnight oil.

When she reached a large pair of wooden double doors

that she felt certain must lead into the library, she paused. What if it was his private study and he didn't want her there? She pushed the thought aside as quickly as it came. No. After everything she'd been through, she at least deserved the enjoyment of a good book. He owed her that much. Mae slipped inside.

The library was illuminated only by a table lamp in the corner. Shadows lent the row of shelves an eerie, abandoned quality, but Mae didn't need an abundance of light to see the grandeur. Mahogany shelves filled with thousands upon thousands of volumes lined the towering walls. A spiral staircase led up to a second-floor landing, which revealed even more of the collection. From the looks of it, the library held everything from the latest fiction to old historical volumes. She allowed her eyes to wander, taking it all in with a keen sense of wonder.

"You like it?" The deep voice sounded from behind her.

Mae turned to find Rogue cloaked in shadow, an open book in his hand. He'd been standing not far from the table lamp, yet he blended so well into the darkness, it was as if he were born of it.

The shadows covered the scarred side of his face until the old wounds disappeared into the dimness. He was one with the dark, a phantom king who lurked among the shadows and fancied himself a devil, and she was the innocent standing at his crossroads.

"What gave you that idea?" she asked. She *did* like it. In fact, she loved it. She wished the Grey Wolves had something this grand back at Wolf Pack Run, and the thought that they didn't fueled a hint of jealousy in her, but she hadn't uttered a single word.

"You wear your emotions on your sleeve, Princess. You couldn't hide your true feelings if you tried."

She didn't bother to deny it. Perhaps it was true. For him, she was easy to read. What she didn't say was that she'd wager that wasn't the case for everyone. Yet for him, without even trying, she was as open as the book clutched in his palm.

She shrugged. "I like to read, if you couldn't tell from the massive book I nearly clocked you with when you snuck into my bedroom."

He grinned. "Funny. I don't recall you doing much reading then. I think you said you were…what did you call it?" A smirk curved his lips. "Having trouble sleeping?"

Her cheeks flushed red.

"Is that what brings you down here tonight, Princess? Trouble sleeping?" he teased.

"Yes, actually." She said it with a bit more challenge in her tone than she intended, but that only seemed to amuse him. "Though not in the way you mean."

He used the book to gesture to the rows of shelves. "I'm sure you'll be able to find something that tickles your fancy."

Mae caught the entendre as plain as day. A flush rose on her cheeks, but she didn't respond. She didn't dare bait him further.

Ever since their previous encounter had ended on such a low note, she'd attempted to distance herself emotionally. She'd had a glimpse beneath his cynical exterior, and she knew he was capable of passion fiercer than her deepest fantasies, but she wanted more, and experience with the Grey Wolf alphas had taught her better than to push a man like him. If she pushed him, he'd only retreat again.

And she wasn't willing to take that risk.

She might only have a few days with this hardened cowboy, but she intended to make the most of them and reveal the man behind the mask.

Thankfully, he dropped the subject as she turned back to survey the shelves again.

"How many of them have you read?" she asked after several moments of silence between them. She glanced in his direction.

A dark chuckle escaped his lips. "Not as many as I'd like," he said. "The life of a rogue wolf isn't so luxurious." He paused. "At least not for most."

Mae wandered over to the closest shelf and examined one of the volumes there. A resource on ranching, which, from the looks of it, dated as far back as the 1700s. "I've never thought of reading as a luxury, more of a fundamental right," she said.

"Speaks to your privilege."

"I've never thought of myself as privileged."

He shook his head. His Stetson had been cast aside on a nearby armchair. Seeing him without it still seemed strange to her. "You wouldn't. Your brother and his merry band of Grey Wolf alphas have ensured otherwise."

"You make it sound so intentional." She plucked another book down from the shelf. This one, a compilation and analysis of Greek mythology. She quirked a brow. Interesting literature choices for a cowboy. But what about this man didn't make him an enigma?

"Isn't it?" When she didn't respond, he propped his book facedown on the table beside him and stalked toward her. "Tell me, Princess. Have you ever been uncertain where you'd rest your head at night? Where your next meal would come from? Hunger, homelessness, greed… They're all connected." He stood near her now, looming over her from where he lurked in the shadows. "You have no idea what it's like to live outside your pack, because they don't want you to. That would destroy the little deal they have with the Execution Underground. The Grey Wolves get to enjoy their truce with the human hunters, their exemptions, their abundance of resources, all while the Execution Underground turns a blind eye.

"That deal is what allows the Grey Wolves to fly under the radar, unharmed and protected from the Execution Underground's human hunters, so long as the Grey Wolves help guard the human civilians the hunters are sworn to protect. Civilians who would loathe all shifters if they knew of our nature. It's a sellout of our species to humanity.

"And as if that little agreement wasn't seedy enough, catering to humans who loathe us for the sake of their protection when they're the ones who choose to hunt *us* in the first place, for good measure, why not let both groups blame every mishap between them on the rogue wolves?"

Mae struggled to draw breath. She knew about the Seven Range Pact's deal with the human hunters of the Execution Underground. They all did. But she'd never examined it in such a cynical light. The deal had been brokered by her father, long before Maverick had become packmaster, but as the heads of the Seven Range Pact, the Grey Wolves and their allies still enjoyed the fruits.

The Grey Wolves along with the other shifter clans in the Pact made regular patrols of the geographical regions they inhabited, protecting humans from the likes of their vampire enemies. They were so invested in that protection, in that vendetta against the bloodsuckers, that it was the reason for the escalation of the war they were currently in.

Had the Grey Wolves not needed to preserve their deal with the Execution Underground, the deaths the vampires had started causing among innocent humans almost a year earlier, while tragic, wouldn't have made a difference to the pack. It had only been once the Grey Wolves retaliated and the war began that the vampires had begun targeting shifters, and rogue wolves had been caught in the crossfire.

When she examined it in that light, Mae understood Rogue's distaste for her pack.

"Survival," he continued. "For most of us, that's all that matters." The cynical mask he kept in place faltered. "For me, that's all that mattered. Until I became so powerful they couldn't ignore me any longer." He eased away from her. "That's the only thing that separates me from the rest of them."

She saw that now. The way he viewed himself. The underdog. The Prince of the Downtrodden. A vigilante of justice.

Robin Hood…

"And the books?" she asked. "How do they play into that?"

He lifted a single shoulder in a half shrug as though the answer was inconsequential. But to her, it wasn't, because it was yet another piece in figuring out this complex cowboy.

"I started collecting them a few years ago when surviving no longer was a day-to-day struggle."

Around the same time the Grey Wolves had first started to hear whispers of his name. He'd amassed power and influence in their world so quickly it had nearly made Maverick's head spin. She'd eavesdropped over the stories among the Grey Wolves' elite alphas with eager interest.

"And now?" she prompted.

"I'd like to think I'll read them all—someday." His cerulean gaze circled the room. The color was so blue, like the vast Montana sky just before a storm rolled in.

Her eyes widened. "All of them?" She tracked his line of sight over the walls of books. There were thousands of them. More than she could ever hope to read in a lifetime, and she considered herself a voracious reader. "I wouldn't have pegged you as an optimist."

"Not an optimist, a pragmatist. I read at least one book a night. Couple that with a shifter's extended life span, and maybe I'll have enough time."

Her jaw dropped. "A book a night? When do you sleep?"

Those icy eyes pierced her. "Men like me often find the darkness more restful than sleep, Princess."

His words chilled her, reminding her that she'd far from seen the darkest side of this cowboy. Of course a wolf like him would know terrible horrors, things that would likely keep her awake for an eternity. His reputation wasn't built on sunshine and rainbows. A heavy tension settled between them as they lingered there together, among the books and the dark wood and the soothing scent of dust jackets perfuming the shelves.

She gestured to the book he'd propped on the table. "What are you reading?"

He lifted the thin volume and held it up for her to see.

"*The Tempest*," she said.

"A reread," he clarified.

"You like classic plays then."

"I suppose I do."

"What about *The Tempest* drew you to rereading it?"

"I suppose I identify with the main character."

"So you fancy yourself some sort of heroic Prospero?" She'd never considered Prospero to be heroic—more controlling and manipulative—but most performances of the play painted him as a hero.

Rogue lifted the book from the table side and closed it. "I didn't say that."

She considered him. "If not Prospero, that only leaves…" Her voice trailed off. He identified with Caliban, the hideous, half-human monster Prospero subjugated.

Before she could push the subject further, he nodded toward the window where the moon shone through, a bright beacon in the otherwise black mountain night. "It's late, Princess. What's causing you to lose sleep?"

She wasn't sure how to answer without revealing her anxieties. Finally, she settled on "I'm cursed with an excellent memory."

"I know that affliction well."

An unsavory man like him would. She wasn't surprised to hear that.

"Though I wouldn't imagine a good memory would cause a princess like you to lose sleep," he added.

She watched the gentle sway of the pine trees in the night breeze. "The vampires are out for my life. My pack is in danger, and the only man with answers is my brother's sworn enemy." She released a long sigh. "The better question is: how *do* I sleep at night?"

He paused to consider this. Gesturing to the array of shelves, he asked, "What are you in the mood for?"

Mae scanned the selection, not certain where to begin. "Something that will help me escape, something that will make me forget." She wrapped her arms around herself. "Or at least something that will put me to sleep." She smiled.

Without missing a beat, Rogue strode toward one of the shelves. He hooked his finger on the spine of a particularly old-looking volume and removed it, extending it toward her.

Mae gripped the book in her hands, running her palm over the old leather cover. It was a book of retellings of classic Greek myths. She opened the book to somewhere in the middle, reading the header on the brown, aged page. "'Orpheus and Eurydice,'" she read.

"A love story," he commented.

"A tragic one."

"All the memorable ones are. Orpheus and Eurydice. Romeo and Juliet. Tristan and Isolde," he listed. "They all die tragically at the end, or they may as well when they lose the love of their life. Sentient beings can't experience love and obsession so complete without tragedy and loss. When you love someone, heartbreak is inevitable."

Mae didn't subscribe to that idea. She believed in romance, in happily ever afters. She might not have experienced her own yet, but she had to believe there was a happily ever after somewhere out there, waiting for her. Otherwise, Jared would have given his life for nothing.

"That's a grim view," she replied.

"It doesn't have to be." He trailed a finger over the spine of another title.

Though his gaze was focused on the shelf, Mae had the feeling his mind was somewhere else.

"Some might call it romantic, even though it's painful."

His Adam's apple trembled, though his features were stoic, as if he were carved of ice despite the summer warmth. He stared at the hardcover beneath his fingertips. "When you love someone, you give them a piece of yourself. They walk around with your heart in their hands, careless and unprotecting, even if they love you back. They hold a part of you forever, and no matter what you do, you can't take it back. You can't reclaim yourself."

He trained his gaze on her, and the raw vulnerability there caused a lump to form in Mae's throat. "There's always a bit of loss in that," he said.

Mae struggled to speak around the empathy that shook her. Why did she gather he spoke from experience?

The moment passed as quickly as it came. The softness in his gaze dissipated. Stepping closer to her, he reached out and closed the cover of the still-open book in her hands. "It's late," he said. His voice was a low grumble, yet gentle. "And tomorrow night won't be easy. The intel about the bloodsucker's whereabouts could be muddled, and you'll have to keep a level head, regardless of what's said about your packmates and the serum. You should get some rest." He stepped away from her, crossing back to the other side of the library where his own book waited for him.

Mae clutched the large hardcover he'd given her to her chest as she headed toward the door. She'd learned better than to push him. But when she reached the exit, she hesitated. Maybe she hadn't learned her lesson after all, because try as she did to walk away from him, she couldn't allow this moment to pass.

She turned toward him. "The children," she said. "Will, Hope, Noah. Are they yours?"

To say that had been the question he'd been anticipating would be a lie. As Rogue stood there in the dark, the moonlit shadows from the forest shining through the window as passing clouds caused the gnarled limbs of the tree branches to dance across the floorboards, he could have sworn she'd recognized him. Here in the dark moonlight, meeting in secret to share hushed whispers, tucked away and protected from the cruelties of the world. This was their legacy, the nightfall that brought him back to when they were young. Back to a time when it'd been just the two of them. Together. Misfits against the world.

He released a long sigh as he stepped toward the Chippendale service bar in the corner where an old decanter of whiskey glowed amber beneath the lamplight. He uncapped the decanter and poured himself a glass, pausing only long enough to enjoy the smoky scent as he swirled the glass beneath his nose. He threw back the liquor before he set the glass on the wooden bar top with a thud.

"No," he answered as he poured himself another. "No, they're not mine."

"I'm sorry to ask. I just assumed…"

"No need to apologize, Princess. It's a reasonable assumption." He grabbed another empty glass and glanced toward her. "On the rocks?"

Clearly, she wasn't going to follow his advice and rest before their dangerous excursion tomorrow. He supposed that made two of them.

She shook her head. "Neat," she corrected.

He gave an appreciative nod. "A cowgirl's drink." He poured her a glass and extended it toward her.

"You forget I spend most of my time with ranchers. Alpha wolves at that. I can hold my own." She accepted it before taking a slow sip. "If they're not your children, whose are they?"

He raised a brow. "Do you find questions of paternity particularly interesting?"

She shook her head. "No, it's just…" She hesitated. "They mentioned their mother had passed. It sounded as if her death was fairly recent, and considering they're here, I wondered if…"

"If she meant anything to me," he finished.

He saw right through her. She wanted him, and it was dangerous. Unlike her, he was aware that he was the last man on earth an innocent Grey Wolf female like her should ever want, and he was determined to protect her from himself.

Even if the torture of that destroyed him in the process.

Her cheeks flushed red, and she rushed to explain herself. "I didn't know if maybe she was family or—"

"I have no family."

"Oh." Mae fell silent as she gazed at the glass in her hands.

He gathered the distinct impression she was trying hard not to look at him. He should have left it at that, not encouraged the subject further, but before he'd made the decision to continue, he said, "They're orphans."

Mae tore her eyes away from her drink to look at him, the sadness and pity there evident.

"Their mother was a rogue she-wolf. She was a single mom, without an alpha or a mate to protect her. In our world, much like in the human world, women and children are the most vulnerable to predators. They live like the rest of us. No pack to keep them protected. Since they're smaller, weaker physically, and more prone to streaks of senseless alpha male violence, when they live off the grid like the rest of us and there's no one to come searching for them, they make unfortunately easy targets. She was a casualty of the vampires' early trials of the serum. Easy prey. I know her kind. They're the most frequent victims I find, despite my efforts to protect them."

"Efforts to protect them?" Mae muttered as she considered his words. "That's why you created the rogue houses, as refuges to care for rogue women and children?"

"Exactly. It's the only thing I knew how to give them. Rogue wolves aren't known for freely giving trust, especially not to someone as powerful as me, and even if they did, I'm not an easy man to find. But word eventually gets around. That's how Daisy found us, among others who've sought refuge with me and my men at Black Hollow until they've gathered what they need and have gone." He shook his head. "But I didn't know the children's mother. Not personally."

Mae pressed onward. "If you didn't know their mother, how'd they end up in your care?"

"Contrary to the belief of pack wolves, my role as the Rogue isn't all mischief and mayhem. To them, I'm a leader, someone to turn to when things go wrong."

"Like a packmaster?" That was the same role her brother took among the Grey Wolves.

"No," he answered. "Packmasters make decisions for the greater good of the majority, the minority and underdogs be damned. I *care* about the underdog, the mistreated, the left behind."

"The misfits?" she asked.

The memory connected to that word didn't escape him. *If you're a misfit, I'm a misfit*, he'd once whispered to her. The words he'd spoken to her so many years ago came to him as easily as if he'd uttered them to her only moments ago.

He closed his eyes. No. Not him. Not the Rogue. He'd spoken those words as Jared, a fellow Grey Wolf with a life, a family, a future. Not a monster. Not an outcast. Not her brother's enemy. At least not that he'd known at the time.

"Precisely," he answered her. He turned to stare out the window. The moon shone bright.

"So when their mother died, it was your responsibility to ensure their well-being?" she asked.

"It's my responsibility to ensure rogue wolves aren't taken advantage of, and had those children been left to fend for themselves, they would have been." He knew all too well what happened to packless shifter children. He might have been older than Will, Hope, and Noah when he'd been cast out of the Grey Wolf Pack; at the time, he might have thought himself nearly a man, but he'd been a child all the same. In retrospect, he saw that with clarity.

But being a child hadn't afforded him any mercy. Not from the likes of her father.

Mae's brow furrowed as she shook her head. "Those poor babies," she said. "They're still so small. Noah in particular."

"It's not Noah I worry about."

Mae waited for him to elaborate.

Jared scraped a hand over the five-o'clock whiskers on his chin. "Will," he admitted. "He's old enough to remember, old enough to be angry, old enough to…" His voice trailed off.

Old enough to want revenge…

Rogue cleared his throat. "That's all of it though, Princess. The whole tale."

"That's not all of it," she said, refusing to let the subject drop.

He turned back toward her. She was watching him with an intense curiosity in her bright-green eyes, as if he were a puzzle she was trying to solve.

What she didn't realize was that she'd solved the mystery of him years ago. When she'd been a girl, a sweet, young girl who'd seen something in him, even when no one else had. She'd always been his answer, the key to what softened him, completed him, made him whole. Maybe that was why he'd never been able to let her go after all those years, because deep down, he knew he would never be whole again without her.

What agony to know the one thing that would complete him, revitalize and restore him, would never, *could never* be his. Not unless he wished to destroy her.

"It's more than that," she persisted.

He brushed her comments aside. "I don't know what you mean."

"You're powerful beyond measure, richer than Midas, more influential than Caesar among your kind. You said yourself that for a wolf like you, impossible deals and situations are easy. You could have found someone to take the children in, to care for them as their own, but you didn't. Instead, *you* chose to bring them here to Black Hollow to live with you, for you to keep a watchful eye on them, practically like a surrogate father."

He failed to see how that mattered. "And your point?"

"Why?" she asked. "Why would a hardened criminal want to care for three young orphans? Unless…" Her voice trailed off, but her meaning was clear.

He'd already told her he had no family. "Unless I was an orphan myself," he finished for her. The statement was met with silence. He turned back toward the window where the clouds eclipsed the moon until the little light that remained was smothered. "You're right," he said. "Though I was much older than them. Far better equipped to handle the cruelty of our world, but still…" He left the rest unspoken. The weight of his secrets filled the room, even as he hid the full truth of his past. Leave it to Mae to flay open the dark, shriveled excuse for a heart he possessed.

"Tell me," she whispered.

Her plea hung heavy in the air between them.

Initially, he resisted, but the more he contemplated it, the more he wanted to.

Why couldn't he tell her? If he muddled the details, glossed over the description, she'd never be the wiser.

No closer to seeing him than she was now.

"I was fifteen when I was cast from my pack," he said. "My father was cast out with me. He intended to protect me, as parents and guardians are wont to do, but he died before he ever had the chance to do that."

He could still hear the sound of his father's pleas, the pain as he cried out. Not the physical pain, but the pain of betrayal, of being kissed on the cheek by a Judas of a man who'd sworn to be his father's friend, his brother.

All because Jared had chosen to protect Mae.

That'd been the only moment he regretted his decision.

He'd never had the best relationship with his father. The man had always held Jared to such an impossible standard of alphahood that as a young, bullied boy, Jared had never felt he could live up to it, even though he'd secretly longed for his father's approval. Or not so secretly; at least Mae had known.

When it had become clear that the consequences for disobeying pack would affect more than him, he'd realized Thomas Grey's actions were merely an excuse to steal a throne rightfully meant for Jared. It didn't matter that Thomas was punishing a young boy to the letter of pack law for protecting the packmaster's own flesh and blood, that Jared's father was innocent in the whole charade. Jared, and by association his father, were simply pawns in Thomas's agenda—a means to an end.

That moment of realization had been the only time Jared had regretted what he'd given up for the love of Maeve Grey. But at that point, it had already been too late.

He'd long ago made peace with how his actions had destroyed his father. He knew now, without a doubt, that if it hadn't been his sacrifice for Mae, Thomas would have found another excuse to exploit.

Thomas Grey had been all too eager to preserve the power of his legacy by ensuring his only and eldest son was the continued heir to the Grey Wolf throne, not a wolf from the Black family, despite them being equally as Grey Wolf as they came. The ancestors of the Black family, Jared's ancestors, had been there centuries ago at the founding of the Grey Wolf Pack, just as the other two founding families had—the Cavanaughs and the Greys.

"My father was murdered by a packmaster who valued

little more than power, even over his own family," Rogue said. "And my critics, your brother included, say I have a hatred for pack wolves."

He didn't. Not really. He only resented what had been stolen from his family and the privileges that had been withheld from so many rogue wolves. "But what wolf wouldn't feel hatred for that?"

Not any wolf he cared for. That was for certain.

"I'm so sorry," Mae whispered.

"Don't disgrace me with your pity, Princess. I don't deserve pity. Not from an innocent like you." She'd been another victim in all this, though she didn't know it. She had no idea what her father had done, what her brother had later kept hidden from her.

"I'm not as innocent as you think," she countered.

"I don't think you're innocent. I know you are."

"I killed a man once."

The admission caused him to stiffen.

"I...killed him," she repeated. He held the impression it was the first time she'd admitted it out loud. "With my own two hands. With a knife."

"And does it haunt you?" he asked. He wasn't certain he wanted to know the answer.

"No. He was an abuser, a predator who'd hurt me in ways that still keep me up at night." Her lip curled into a shadow of a snarl as she thought of her disgusting excuse of an uncle. "No, I don't regret it. He deserved it." Her hands clenched into fists even though he could tell sadness plagued her. "But my best friend took the fall, and I've never forgiven myself, not in the twenty years since."

"I'm sure your friend wouldn't want you to feel that way.

He'd likely tell you to move on with your life, forget about him and the consequences of that damn incident once and for all."

"Maybe," she said. "But I'll never know. He's been dead for twenty years, and yet I…" She inhaled a sharp breath, and the regret he heard there cut through him. "…I still can't bring myself to forget him."

Rogue was certain someone had ripped his still-pulsing heart from his chest. It felt as if the organ lay there on the floor between them, still beating and causing him pain as the words she spoke acted like daggers and sliced it to shreds.

"You should," he urged. "Forget him, that is. The essence of grief is carrying love in your heart that has no place to go, and if you carry it for too long, it festers inside you, infecting your chest like a plague and eating you away until there's nothing left. At least, nothing that's worth saving."

Her fingertips brushed over his spine, tracing the lines where, beneath his shirt, the ink of his dragon tattoo lay. Not the dragon whose fate was to be slayed by the prince, but the dragon that spent its life guarding and protecting the princess inside her tower. Her touch was so gentle that he nearly crumbled beneath it.

He shook beneath her hands. It took everything in him not to turn toward her, to confess all his darkest sins, who he was both now and then. He'd tell her everything. His dreams, his hopes, his fears, his pain, because he wanted the absolution she offered, the loving look in her eye that she'd given him as she'd passed him that damn aloe plant and offered him friendship.

Even though he'd done nothing to deserve it.

But he didn't. Instead, he stood there, frozen beneath

her touch and unable to look at her, because if he did give in to his desires, he'd destroy the one true promise he'd sworn to keep. And what kind of monster would he be then?

The muscles of his shoulders writhed and tensed. "Go back to bed now, Princess." The graveled words were harsh and feral, filled with every ounce of the pain that ached in his chest. He could scarcely breathe as he choked on them. He couldn't take another moment of her gentle touch. Not if he wanted his sanity to remain intact.

"Why?" she asked. There was more hurt in her voice than he ever wanted to hear. "Every time we get close, why do you push me away?"

Hell if he knew the answer, because deep down, he wasn't certain keeping his promise to her was worth the fight anymore…

He cleared his throat, his next words coming on a growl as, thankfully, she stepped toward the door.

"Because there's not enough whiskey in this decanter to chase the demons away."

Chapter 13

MAE SPENT MORE TIME SEARCHING FOR HER WAYWARD teacup pig than was reasonable, and unfortunately even she recognized this. The following morning, she trekked through the pasture's green grass, heading out to the stables to find a horse to aid in her search. Tucker had taken to wandering out to the pigpens to visit his fellow piggies, and while Mae enjoyed a good walk, she wasn't about to risk the chance of getting stranded in the middle of the pasture again.

Since they'd arrived at Black Hollow, Tucker had taken his liberties to new bounds. At Wolf Pack Run, while he enjoyed free range over the ranchlands, he generally kept close to Mae. But since they'd arrived at Black Hollow, the little piglet had a newfound appreciation for exploration.

Exploration.

She supposed that was one word for it. Her thoughts turned to Rogue and how she'd wanted to *explore* with him last night. It had taken everything in her to leave him there, alone in the library, while she returned to bed. He was one of the most powerful wolves on the continent, a cowboy with a reputation forged of iron will and bloodshed, and yet she'd wanted to go to him, to hold him in her arms, to *be* with him in every sense of the word. She'd wanted to heal him.

And for the first time since they'd met, her feelings for him had been about more than desire or curious intrigue. He might be a devil, a monster of a wolf who'd do anything to get his way, but he was also a man who fiercely protected those he cared for, the vulnerable. Like hell if that didn't soften her opinion of him more than she'd bargained for.

She picked up her pace as she neared the stables. She was a cowgirl at heart, and a ride through the foothills with the summer breeze ruffling her short hair would do her good. Breathing in a long draw of mountain air, she paused as she reached the stable doors. The warmth of the summer sun beat down on her face and prickled over her skin, likely leaving additional freckles in its wake. Before tonight, she needed to clear her head. At least if she expected to make it through their intel meeting without her nervous heart pounding out of her chest.

Stepping into the stables, she stopped midstride, taking in the sight before her.

Rogue gripped the reins of a sable-colored mare as he led her toward a black-and-white Appaloosa stallion. The mare wore a chain of yellow daisies around her neck that, if Mae had to guess, had been picked and threaded together by the clapping five-year-old beside Rogue. Noah was also with them, holding his sister's hand with an equally excited grin on his lips, while Bee had taken to huffing cantankerously inside his stall gate. Will, however, was nowhere to be found.

Mae fell back into the shadows of the stable door as she watched.

"Oh, Martha's so beautiful," Hope squealed with delight.

"A woman is never so stunning as on her wedding day," Rogue said.

Hope shot him a chastising glare.

"Or a mare in this case," he amended.

Mae stifled a laugh. Who would have thought all it took to bring a wicked cowboy wolf like the Rogue to his knees was a precocious five-year-old girl?

"G-good boy, O-Ollie." Noah patted the Appaloosa through the stall gate.

"He looks so pleased!" Hope clutched her hands together over her heart.

"I think he looks oblivious to the whole thing," Rogue commented.

Ollie's large black eyes stared unfocused into the distance as he chewed a piece of straw caught in his mouth. It appeared that prior to the ceremony, he'd been rustling around in his stall. The horse looked as if he had as much intellect as a cow chewing its cud, and any rancher with half a brain would say cows were dumber than…

"Shit," Rogue swore, drawing Mae's attention back to him.

He'd apparently stepped in some and had announced it accordingly.

"Murtagh's told you not to say those words around us." Hope wagged a finger at him as Noah mimicked her.

"Murtagh isn't the one tasked with officiating a horse's wedding every other morning," Rogue grumbled as he scraped his boot off on the concrete. The grin on his lips softened the complaint considerably.

"It's time now," Hope announced, glancing at the horses.

Mae wasn't certain what indicated that, but Hope appeared convinced.

"Say the words. Say the words," Noah chanted.

Rogue finished scraping the manure off his boot before he thumped a fist hard against his chest and made a show of clearing his throat.

Mae struggled not to laugh.

"Dearly beloved," Rogue began, "we are gathered here today to join in holy matrimony, Ollie the oblivious Appaloosa"—he gestured to the stallion—"and Martha the matronly mare," he proclaimed.

"*Psst*," Hope hissed. "What's 'matronly' mean?" She lowered her voice to a whisper so as not to interrupt the ceremony.

Not struggling at all to cover up the fact that the phrase really meant the mare had no purpose but breeding, Rogue whispered back, "It means she's a…mature woman."

Hope shot him a glare.

"Er, a mature mare," he corrected.

This time, at the sight of a wolf like the Rogue kowtowing to the will of a five-year-old, Mae couldn't suppress a bark of laughter.

Without missing a beat or turning toward her, Rogue said, "I wondered when you were going to stop taking a leaf from my book and lurking over there."

The benign comment sent a chill down Mae's spine since it was clearly meant for her. Of course, a criminal cowboy as legendary as Rogue wouldn't be easy to sneak up on.

Now aware of her presence, Hope and Noah beckoned her over. "Come join us."

Mae crossed the stable and accepted Noah's outreached hand. She stood directly across from Rogue, who gave her a pointed look.

"Ollie appreciates older women," he said with a completely straight face.

Mae gathered the distinct impression he was trying to make her laugh again—and he was succeeding.

"Does he?" She chuckled. She couldn't have kept a straight face if she tried.

Rogue patted Ollie on his thick neck. "Unfortunately, it runs in the family. He comes from a long line of brainless studs who, when it comes to anything other than coitus, are too lacking in intelligence."

"I think I've met a few wolves of that sort in my lifetime," Mae joked.

"Murtagh insists on keeping him, only for sentiment—"

"What does 'stud' mean?" Noah asked.

"And 'coitus'?" Hope chimed in.

Rogue shook his head. "Nothing important," he answered. "Not until you're older." He faced the horses and cleared his throat again. "As I was saying, dearly beloved…"

While she held Noah's hand, Mae listened to Rogue officiate at the rest of the ceremony with a satisfied grin on her face. When she'd first arrived at Black Hollow, she'd thought he was a monster. Even then, she'd sensed something more in him, but he hid it so thoroughly behind his cynical exterior that, for a brief time, he convinced her that he didn't have the capability for kindness in his heart. Had she left him bleeding on that forest floor, she might have returned home, but she never would have known the truth.

He didn't have the mere capability for kindness in his heart. He didn't. He acted out of kindness and care in almost every action he took, even when he used dark and conniving means, and now that she'd seen he acted on that kindness, that he was more than just capable of it, it would never be able to be unseen.

He'd still be the Rogue, a dark, nefarious criminal with a list of enemies so long it could've stretched the length of the Yellowstone River—twice—but to her, he'd now also be the fierce yet gentle cowboy who officiated at horse weddings in his spare time, and now that she knew that, she'd never regret the decision she'd made.

It made Mae feel that the promises he'd made her—protecting her pack, granting her the freedom she longed for—were possible. And if a wolf like the Rogue could find kindness in his heart for small children, she trusted him, even if her brother didn't.

After finishing the ceremony, Rogue headed out to the pasture. He'd directed Murtagh and Sterling to set up the details of the meeting with his informant that evening, so he spent most of the day running the tedder, lost in thought as the sun beat down on his bare back and left a thick sheen of sweat from a hard day's work in its wake.

The sunset painted hues of orange and magenta over the blue-ridge mountain skyline as he rode in that night. He was used to working until past sundown, but considering he and Mae had a few hours of driving before they reached their destination, they needed to head out early.

Rogue quartered Bee in the stables before taking the truck back to the house. Once inside, he searched for Mae. She'd need to be ready to leave in less than an hour, and Rogue had a feeling she would want to rock Tucker to sleep or feed him a bottle or something else equally as endearing as it was odd, at least to a rancher.

As he passed the open doors of the library, out of the corner of his eye, he spotted Will perched in the windowsill.

The boy had been absent at his sister's scheduled horse wedding this morning, and while the eight-year-old was often quick to make his displeasure of such silliness known, he usually attended anyway. Will wasn't the type to do something simply to appease his little sister, and Rogue suspected the protests were only meant to save face and make him appear tougher. He had a sneaking suspicion that deep down, Will found the ceremonies as amusing as his siblings did—at least the parts where Rogue was forced to make a fool of himself.

Rogue moved to step inside to ask Will what had kept him preoccupied, but as Rogue stepped to where Will came farther into view, he realized the boy wasn't alone. Mae sat on the windowsill across from him, her legs tucked up to her chest and her arms wrapped around them as she mirrored Will's position.

Rogue stepped back, his wolf senses attuned as he listened in.

"You weren't at Martha and Ollie's wedding ceremony. Where were you?" Mae asked.

Will shook his head, refusing to look at her. "It doesn't matter."

Rogue recognized that dismissive statement all too well from his own childhood.

"It matters to me," Mae said. "I enjoyed it."

She smiled and a part of Rogue hoped it was at the thought of him.

A memory of the two of them together as children shook him. All the other Grey Wolf pups had decided to venture out into the woods to build a campfire, and when their mothers had heard, they'd packed them all a picnic with sandwiches and fruit, complete with bags full of marsh-mallows with graham crackers and little chocolate bits for dessert.

"Why didn't you come along?" Mae had asked him when she and the other kids had returned that evening.

"It doesn't matter," he answered.

"It matters to me," she said. "I wanted you to come."

In that moment, she'd made him feel as though he mattered—to her at least—and that had been more than enough. She'd seen past the hurt, the anger, to what had really been there: the pain of the fact that he was the only Grey Wolf child who didn't have a mother to dote on him. His mother had passed several months earlier. Cancer. An extreme rarity among those of their kind who had an imbalance in the human side of their DNA.

"As peacefully as she could have gone," the adults of the pack had loved to say.

As if that somehow made it easier for him, for his father.

"Don't be stupid. Why would it matter to you if I were there?" Will snapped. "You barely know me."

"True," Mae admitted. "But part of being friends is getting to know someone. So while I may not know you yet, I'd like to." She gave a soft smile as Will lifted his head from where it rested atop his knees.

Rogue turned his gaze from Mae to Will, and the pain he saw there was so familiar, it took everything in him not to collapse with the weight of his own grief. He knew that look. The look of a scared and angry little boy who pushed others away when all he wanted was for someone, anyone to draw him close. He knew that look, because in many ways, after twenty years apart from the girl who'd made him whole again, when he looked at his own reflection, he was still that same angry little boy, fighting for someone to see him.

She'd seen him. Years ago. She always had. Just as she saw Will now.

Maeve Grey might be a high-maintenance princess by birth, but in all the ways that counted, she was also an angel. An angel who cast out the darkness wherever she went, and though over the years, he might have thought he'd lost her to that privileged Grey Wolf princess identity, deep down, she was still the same sweet girl. She still had such a capacity for kindness and love, even for him.

She made him feel as if he deserved it.

And fuck, he knew with every fiber of his being that he didn't.

"You...you want to be my friend?" Will asked in disbelief. "But I was just mean to you. I called you stupid."

Mae nodded. "That's true too. But sometimes I find the wolves with the hardest exteriors have the softest insides."

"Not Rogue," Will countered.

Rogue stiffened.

"I'd have to disagree with you," Mae replied. "I think, like you, he works hard to push people away, but on the inside, he's really all soft and gushy."

Gushy?

Rogue struggled to reconcile the darkness of his past and present, the blood that had coated his hands hundreds of times over, with the softness of the word *gushy*, but he couldn't envision it. Had anyone else called him that, he would have shifted into wolf form and used his canines to tear them to shreds for daring to suggest he was weak.

But that was what Mae did to a man.

She could take even the meanest of feral alpha wolves and make them her friend.

Will stared out the window, gazing over the mountains in the distance so he didn't have to look at Mae. "I didn't come to Hope's ceremony, because…" His lower lip quivered in an unusual display of vulnerability. "Today would have been our mother's birthday, and I…I'm the only one of us old enough to remember it."

Tears poured down his small cheeks, despite how he fought to swipe them away.

"I didn't want to upset Hope and Noah. They don't remember the details like I do, so I…so I've been here, thinking about her. By myself. Wishing she were here," he sobbed.

He collapsed into Mae, and she caught him in her arms, drawing him against her as he shook with the weight of his grief.

Even Rogue had to swallow down the massive lump that now resided in his throat.

"I miss her. I miss her so much," Will sobbed as Mae gently stroked his hair.

Mae didn't bother to tell him it was okay, that it would be all right, or that she was sorry. She didn't do any number of things a typical person would do. But Rogue wasn't surprised, because that was one of the things about Maeve Grey—one of the many beautiful, wonderful, odd, exquisite things about her. She knew how to sit with someone else's pain. She took it on as her own without judgment, pity, or worthless platitudes that only added fresh salt to open wounds. She simply sat there with a man, with the horrible hurt that constricted his chest…

And understood.

She always understood, because she saw him. The real him. The one who existed beneath all the bullshit.

Rogue stood there for a long time, watching as Mae comforted Will until the boy had cried so thoroughly, he fell asleep in her arms as if he were a babe again.

When Rogue was certain he wasn't disturbing him and that he wouldn't rob the boy of what little dignity he had left, Rogue went to her. He lifted Will from where he was curled again Mae's chest and carried the boy up to his room. When he returned, Mae was still waiting there, her own eyes speckled with tears from absorbing the weight of the little boy's pain.

"It's time to go save your pack," Rogue said.

Mae stood and followed him out of the library, not bothering to reply—a fact for which Rogue was grateful because he knew that had she called him Rogue in that moment, he wouldn't have had the strength to keep up the lie.

Chapter 14

THE MIDNIGHT COYOTE SALOON REEKED OF SMOKE AND whiskey. The sounds of guitar-laden country music thumped through the surround system, crooning a tune about a long-lost pair of lovers as Rogue and Mae stepped inside. Dim drop-hat lights cloaked the bar in shadow, leaving plenty to the imagination, and peanut shells littered the floor, crunching beneath the heels of their boots. The open space showcased an array of booths and tables all centered around an old wooden bar top. From appearance, this was little more than a hole-in-the-wall western bar, but Rogue knew better.

The Midnight Coyote Saloon played host to some of the supernatural world's most dangerous clientele. The previous incarnation of the bar, which had resided in downtown Billings, had been raided nearly a year ago by the Execution Underground, leaving the bar and its owner out of business. Rogue had personally offered the proprietor, a notorious warlock known as Boss, an interest-free loan to reopen in a location of his choosing. In exchange for his generosity, Rogue expected information about the bar's patrons.

If there was anyone who kept tabs on the underbelly of the supernatural world, it was Boss, and thus far, the warlock bar owner's debt to Rogue had paid off in spades.

Rogue gripped Mae's arm as he nodded toward a darkened booth in the far corner of the bar where Boss would be waiting for them.

"Stay close," he warned. "And let me do the talking."

"What's the point of being partners then?" Mae whispered back.

He leaned in, careful none of the other clientele could hear them. Even beneath the heavy music, any shifter's ears could be attuned. "You're here, aren't you? Risking your life for some silly need for adventure. Isn't that what you wanted?"

She glared at him. "I *want* to save my pack."

"And you will," he nodded. "But in this case, you'll do so by keeping your mouth shut."

She scowled at him as they headed toward the booth.

But it wasn't Boss who waited for them. Instead, another cowboy sat in his place.

Rogue immediately bristled. "Where's Boss?" he asked the other man.

The cowboy tipped his Stetson. "Boss left me in charge of the bar for now. I'm his spokesman."

Rogue scowled. Which meant that the human hunters were on Boss's trail again, and he'd gone deep underground to avoid detection.

The human hunters were relentless in their pursuit of the warlock, since he was privy to even more supernatural secrets than Rogue himself. To get intel on *any* kind of supernatural—shifter or otherwise—Boss was the man to speak to.

Which also meant this young cowboy was no more than the bar manager standing in during Boss's absence. From the scent of him, he was a shifter, but not a wolf. Cougar perhaps? Rogue fought down a displeased grumble. He fucking hated dealing with the large cat shifters. They were always a pain in his ass—prideful and aloof pussies that they were.

"Boss gave me the intel you need," the cougar reassured him.

Reluctantly, Rogue slid into the booth and Mae followed suit.

"You brought a she-wolf with you." The cougar's purr rumbled from across the table.

Rogue refused to look toward Mae, hoping the cougar shifter would do the same. "She's none of your concern."

"Any little she-wolf who comes into Boss's bar with a wolf like you is my concern." The cougar leaned forward. The drop-hat light above the table and the neon-blue Coors sign next to him illuminated his face. He grinned, flashing cat eyes as he assessed them both. The thin catlike slits of his irises made his stare unsettling.

And Rogue didn't care for it one bit. His wolf stirred inside him, eager to react.

"Tell me. What's your name, little she-wolf?" The cougar searched her face.

Mae glanced toward Rogue but didn't answer. Whoever this cougar was, Rogue didn't care for his lack of deference. Clearly, Boss hadn't told him exactly who he'd be dealing with. All this shifter likely knew was that Rogue was powerful and wealthy, like all of Boss's clientele. Rogue didn't make it a habit to disclose his identity, so Boss had likely kept that information close, confidential and discreet, the behavior he was known for—and if Boss had in fact disclosed who Rogue was to this cougar shifter, well, it made this cat a fool with a death wish.

It'd been a mistake to bring Mae here, to indulge her need to be involved. This was no place for a princess like her. Rogue had known that from the start. While his and

Boss's relationship was complicated, he trusted the warlock. But he didn't trust this appointed lackey as far as he could throw him.

"Let's get to business," Rogue said, drawing the cougar's attention back toward him. "Boss tasked you with relaying to me."

The cougar leaned into the booth seat, giving a slow nod. "He did."

"And?" Rogue prompted.

The cowboy cougar shrugged a single shoulder. "Depends on what you're willing to pay for it."

Rogue's hands clenched into fists, the champion rings he wore flashing. It'd been years since he'd fought his way to the top, earning his reputation with the blood spilled by his bare knuckles, but he wouldn't allow this imbecile to forget it.

Beneath the shadows of the old western bar top, buried deep in the basement, the Midnight Coyote Saloon boasted an underground fighting ring that allowed its participants to deal in supernatural favors. The fights were often to the death and the rewards just as steep. There were no rules. Just bloodshed and gambling.

Years ago, it was in the Midnight Coyote's ring that Rogue had clawed his way out of hell, transforming himself from a nameless rogue wolf into the monster he was now. Stripped of his pack and with nothing to lose, rage had fueled him, making him more ruthless, more fearless than any other—a legend. It had been the beginning of cementing his reputation as he built his empire. One favor, one debt won at a time. Boss knew the monster Rogue was, because he'd witnessed Rogue's creation. It'd been

Boss who'd first paid him to fight in order to draw a crowd, though he'd been barely a man, and the warlock had never forgotten it.

Small price to pay, Rogue thought.

But apparently, the hired help didn't know he was sealing his own death wish. If Rogue didn't kill him first, Boss would in due time. The warlock didn't tolerate shenanigans, particularly when it came to his supernatural clientele.

Rogue leaned forward into the light of the table. "Need I remind you of my and your employer's current arrangement?" The threat that laced his tone was clear.

The cougar sneered. "I'm aware."

Rogue's jaw clenched. He didn't have time for this shifter's ill-timed games.

Rogue tried not to notice Mae in his peripheral vision, but he did. She was glancing between them, the rise and fall of her chest rapid. She sensed the underlying tension. Had she not been beside him, Rogue would have reached across the table and made good on his threats. But he'd keep this civil. For her.

"Give me the location, and I'll pay you whatever you want." Rogue forced his voice to remain level. There was no other choice. If not them, this idiot would find another buyer for Boss's information. If he didn't have one already, it would only be a matter of time before the whole of the supernatural world would be knocking down Boss's door, and with Boss underground, they'd be dealing with this imbecile. Any shifter in their right mind would want this information, and Rogue had more than enough resources, monetary or otherwise. All Boss's clientele did. He'd pay whatever it took.

And the cougar damn well knew it.

What he didn't know was he would also be buried six feet under by sunrise for ever daring to extort Rogue. Hearing about it from Rogue, Boss wouldn't blink twice over the transgression. All he'd need to do would be to put the word out on the street.

"Name your price," Rogue growled.

The cougar grinned. "I owe a debt to Boss. If I don't pay it, the old warlock will see me dead. I want my debt to Boss erased. Pay however much he asks for."

So that was this moron's motivation for this little extortion suicide venture? Rogue almost felt sorry for the bastard. He'd caught himself between two powerful supernatural entities, and apparently, his gamble was that he was less likely to die at Rogue's hands.

He'd bet wrong.

"Done." Rogue didn't so much as hesitate. He'd pay whatever price to see this scumbag gone.

The cougar shook his head. "I'm not finished."

Of course he wasn't. Rogue leaned back in his seat, waiting. "Go on."

"I want an open-ended favor." The cougar leaned into the light again, his eyes twinkling with greed.

Mae stiffened. An open-ended favor from a wolf like him was a hefty price tag. She placed a hand on Rogue's arm, shaking her head. "It's not worth it," she whispered. "We'll find another way."

But she didn't understand. It *was* worth it. To him, *any* price was worth it. This was for rogue wolves everywhere if he played his cards right and, most importantly, for her. She might have been a spitfire who reveled in throwing

wrenches into his plans, but he would do anything, pay anything, say anything, if only it kept her safe.

Not to mention, he didn't intend to allow this fool to live
long enough to make good on his promises.

Rogue turned away from Mae, meeting the cougar's
unsettling gaze. "You'll have your favor. Now, I want mine."

The cowboy's grin widened. He clapped his hands
together, more than a little bit pleased with himself. He
ought to be, considering he'd erased what was likely over a
million dollars in debt and now had a wolf like Rogue in his
pocket in a single sitting—or so he thought.

Rogue almost felt sorry for the bastard.

Almost.

The cougar laced his fingers together as he propped his
elbows on the tabletop. "Boss searched for your information,
Rogue, and there's only one wolf who can give it to you."

Rogue nodded. "Tell me."

"Walker Solomon."

Rogue stiffened.

Walker Solomon was likely the only rogue wolf on the
North American continent who Rogue *didn't* have under
his thumb—and the one wolf he refused to deal with. The
owner and proprietor of a supernatural casino near Amarillo,
Texas, Solomon was a rogue werewolf and businessman.
Aside from being Rogue's only rival, Solomon was the crazi-
est bastard Rogue had ever had the misfortune to encounter.

If you asked Rogue, the rogue wolf was verifiably insane.
Rogue had heard it rumored more than once that Solomon
had been nearly poisoned one too many times over the
years, and the rogue wolf had the reputation to show it. He
was powerful, bloodthirsty, and an unpredictable son of a

bitch if there ever was one, and Rogue refused to deal with that unpredictability. Solomon wasn't a man of his word. He wagered the vast majority of his business dealings on card games—fucking card games—and at the Gold Tooth casino, the house always won…

…and the losers left in body bags.

Mae gripped Rogue's knee beneath the table. "We can't strike up a deal with Walker Solomon. He's a criminal."

The cougar gave a dark chuckle. "Apparently you're not aware of the company you keep."

Mae ignored him, lowering her voice to a near whisper. "He once killed one of the Grey Wolves driving the cattle to market, all because he said he wanted a fresh steak."

That sounded like Solomon all right. He shed blood without rhyme, reason, or remorse. Rogue might have had blood on his hands, but at least he chose his enemies wisely. His decisions were strategic, deliberate. Solomon didn't give a shit about logic as long as there was blood.

Rogue knew that firsthand.

"The Grey Wolves?" A dark fire sparked in the cougar's eyes.

Mae opened her mouth to answer, but Rogue gripped her hand and squeezed—hard—the surprise of which stopped her short.

"Excuse us for a moment," he said.

The cougar glanced between them, his eyes narrowed. "Of course," he ground out. Slowly, he slid from the booth.

Once the cat shifter was out of earshot, Rogue rounded on Mae. "What the hell are you thinking?"

Mae glanced between him and where the cougar now stood at the bar. "What did I do?"

"What did you do?" Rogue gaped at her. "How about giving away your identity?"

Mae's eyes widened. "I thought Boss was in your pocket, one of your guys."

Rogue growled. "In case you weren't following, Boss is. But his lackey has a death wish."

Mae shrugged. "But you're more powerful than him."

"You're right, and he'll be dead soon. That's for certain." Rogue leaned into her. "But secrets around here are bought and sold faster than a head of cattle. He may be no more than the hired help, but if he passes your whereabouts on before I smack him down like the fly he is, that will fail to matter." Rogue inhaled a deep breath, forcing himself to remain calm.

Between this and the news of Solomon, they were shit out of luck.

He cleared his throat. "After that little raid your Grey Wolf second-in-command, Wes Calhoun, orchestrated on the original Midnight Coyote, many of Boss's clientele have a bone to pick with the Grey Wolves. Not to mention most rogues are no fan of your brother. Now that this weasel knows who you are, if he can find a way to profit off that information, he will."

"You can't know that he knows who I am. He didn't say—"

"I know from the way he's been watching you ever since he left the table."

Mae glanced over her shoulder.

The unnamed cougar lingered at the bar, a bottle of Sierra Nevada in his hand as he whispered to the barmaid, Trixie, and another one of the female servers. His eyes were glued to Mae like a hawk scouting its prey.

The color drained from Mae's face. "Why didn't you warn me?"

Rogue gripped her shoulder, forcing her to face him. "I warned you to stay quiet, and rule number one of life as a criminal is fairly obvious: *never* give away your identity."

Mae gritted her teeth. "I thought he'd be smart enough not to cross a wolf like you."

"The more powerful you are, the more imbeciles emerge from the woodwork hoping to gain that power for themselves. He'll be taken care of, but maybe not fast enough and not without causing a scene." Rogue shook his head. "*This. This* is exactly the reason why bringing you with me was not a good idea." He leaned back in his seat, nodding toward the exit. "Go wait in the truck."

"But—"

He didn't want her to bear witness to what he was about to do. Rogue's eyes flashed to his wolf's. "Go to the truck, Mae," he growled. "You'll be safe. My men are watching."

Chapter 15

MAE SHOVED HER WAY OUT OF THE BOOTH. HE WAS right. It *was* her fault. She'd come with the intention of helping her pack, but so far, she'd failed miserably. As Mae beat feet out of the bar, "Someday You'll Want Me to Want You" by Patsy Cline played from the jukebox, the sounds of Patsy's sweet voice ringing in her ears. Mae shook her head, still seething with anger. The woman had sure known how to sing those sweet hurt songs.

Clutching the keys to the truck in her hand, Mae headed toward the back entrance.

She had almost reached the exit when the blond barmaid drew her attention. "Hey, sugar." The barmaid waved her bar towel to flag Mae down, calling out to her over the music.

Mae paused, glancing over her shoulder to make sure she wasn't mistaken, but the woman's attention was clearly on her. Mae hesitated. But from where Rogue and the cougar were now seated again, she was out of eyesight.

Someday you'll want me to want you, When I'm strong for somebody else, Patsy crooned over the loudspeakers.

Slowly, Mae made her way to the bar top, curiosity getting the better of her. The fiery scent of whiskey mixed with dish soap from the bar sink thickened the closer she eased to the bar. The barmaid wiped the inside of a tulip beer glass with a microfiber towel as she gave Mae a once-over.

"Is it true?" the woman asked. "You're a Grey Wolf?"

From her scent, Mae could tell she was no shifter. But she had to be *something* if she was in a place like this. Mae's eyes flashed to her wolf. "What's it to you?"

The barmaid smiled, her grin as sweet as cherry pie and her southern accent just as sugary. "Just a word of advice, darlin'." She leaned over the bar top, an ample amount of cleavage tilting into view. "If you really are a Grey Wolf, I'd stay clear of the likes of that one." Her eyes flicked to the far corner of the bar.

Mae followed her gaze, expecting to see the cougar shifter, but the barmaid's sights weren't fixed on the cougar. They were focused on Rogue.

The hairs on the back of Mae's neck rose on end. "And why would I trust some barmaid in this godforsaken place?" she snapped.

She didn't know who the hell this woman was, but she didn't have time for games.

The blond's brown eyes turned toward her. In the dim bar lighting, they glowed a bright shade of amber. "Because this *barmaid* has seen a thing or two." The woman set down the glass on the bar top with a small thud.

"Bully for you." Mae moved to walk away, but the other woman stepped from behind the bar, coming to stand in front of Mae as if they were old friends exchanging whispers.

"He's hard to resist. All that dark charm, the bad boy persona. It'll draw you in, make you want him. You'll think you can change him, but you can't."

"I don't know what you're talking about." Mae stepped past the woman. "We're done here."

"He's already in love with someone else."

Mae stopped short. She chanced a look over her

shoulder. "And would that someone else happen to be you?" She'd suspected Rogue still held a flame for someone from his past. He'd practically confessed as much to her in the library. She supposed they shared that trait.

The blond smiled. "Not me, sugar, but whoever she is, it doesn't matter how sweet you are." She gave Mae another quick once-over. "In his mind, you won't hold a candle to her." The barmaid eased back behind the bar top. "Just consider it a word from a friend."

Mae moved to step away again.

"Oh, and sugar?"

Mae paused, looking over her shoulder one last time.

The barmaid flashed her a coy grin. "When you get back home, tell Wes and Naomi that Trixie says howdy."

The name drop caught Mae off guard. She stared at the woman, wondering what her connection was to her friend and the Grey Wolf second-in-command, but she didn't dare ask. Considering Wes's dark past, she wasn't sure she *wanted* to know. Without another glance, Mae walked away, headed toward the back entrance again. Her mind reeled as she replayed the brief exchange in her head. The barmaid's warning echoed through her.

He's in love with someone else.

It shouldn't have mattered to her. She wasn't in love with Rogue—she barely knew him—but still the warning shook her. She'd been trying to push the thought of kissing him, of their night together from her mind, but the exchange only brought those feelings to the forefront. Every time she closed her eyes, she still felt the electricity that had passed between them tingling on her lips. He'd lit a fire in her, igniting something deep she hadn't realized existed.

Though it pained her to admit it, Mae wanted the stubborn bastard—badly. She had from the start. She didn't have to like it, but the attraction between them was undeniably magnetic, and deep down, part of her had hoped he would kiss her again.

So much for that...

Perhaps it was better this way. Even if there had been something between them, there wouldn't have been a future in it. Even if he managed to eliminate her pack obligations as he'd promised, if her brother found out she was literally sleeping with the enemy, she would never hear the end of it.

Mae pushed through the back entrance. When she stepped outside, she headed straight for the truck. The Midnight Coyote was nestled in a small western town in the middle of who-knew-where that reminded Mae of a modernized set of an Old West shoot-out film. They'd parked only a short walk away from the bar. Still lost in her own thoughts, she stepped in and out of the dim orange glow of the streetlights.

As she did so, the hairs on the back of her neck slowly rose on end. She could feel a pair of eyes on her, maybe even more than one. Rogue had said his men would be watching, but this felt *different*...

Her wolf instincts rose in red alert. She glanced over her shoulder. A pair of large alpha wolves flanked her several paces back.

Mae picked up speed, transitioning into a power walk. As she did so, the alpha wolves did too. Her breath caught. Whoever they were, they were following her. Mae's heart kicked into overdrive, and she burst into a full-on run. Rounding several nearby corners, she disappeared into a back alley, trying to outrun them. Finally, she slowed, lifting a hand to her chest in order to catch her breath when a large hand clamped down on her shoulder.

"Hey there, gorgeous." The alpha wolf stepped in front of her. His partner emerged from the darkness, shadowing him as backup.

"Excuse me." Mae moved to step around him, but the first wolf blocked her path.

A sleazy grin twisted his lips. "Hey now, I paid you a compliment. Aren't you going to say thank you?" He shot a glance toward his friend. "A Grey Wolf like you should know how to say thank you, don't you think, Jack?"

The friend nodded in agreement.

Mae stiffened at the Grey Wolf comment. Though they were wolves, these guys had to be with the cougar shifter. In the absence of pack loyalty, rogues of different species occasionally banded together. They had to have followed her out of the bar, but she'd been too caught up in thinking of Rogue to notice at first. *Damn it.* She tried to push past the first wolf, but he blocked her again. She growled, allowing her eyes to flash to her wolf's. "Move out of my way."

Jack snickered. "Looks like you've caught a live one, Clint."

"That's okay," Clint shot back. "I like 'em with a little bit of fight."

Fine. If they wouldn't move, Mae would head back in the direction from which she'd come. The last thing she needed was an altercation. These idiots weren't worth it. She turned to walk away, but the bastard gripped her by the wrist—hard.

"Where you going so fast, sweetheart?"

"Fuck off." Mae snarled, fighting to tear her hand away, but he overpowered her. She was strong, but no match for an alpha male.

Wrenching her toward him, he used his other hand to grip her by her hair. Pain shot through Mae's scalp as he slammed her against the alley wall. He pinned her with an arm across her chest, his other hand still fisting her hair so hard her scalp ached. Mae's stomach churned. She would have shifted, tried to show this bastard what was what, but a silver blade pressed against her throat.

Clint leaned in. His pungent cologne filled her nose, and his breath reeked of cheap beer. Mae's stomach churned.

"No little she-bitch is going to talk to me like that, especially not a little Grey Wolf whore," he growled. "I paid you a compliment. Now I expect something in return." He yanked her hair, which he still held by the fistful.

A sharp cry of pain tore from Mae's lips. Fear gripped her.

"How about a kiss, sweetheart?" Clint leaned into her, his mouth nearly shoving against hers, but Mae turned her head at the last second, his wet, smacking lips slobbering over her cheek.

"I bet your lips will taste like candy," Clint sneered. A humiliating chuckle tore from his throat, and his partner laughed too. The sound of their laughter at her expense slithered through Mae. It made her feel small, powerless. Memories of her disgusting uncle Buck and everything he'd done to her bubbled to the surface, bringing bile to her throat. He'd laughed too.

"Are you going to play nice now?" Clint pushed the knife harder against her throat.

Mae opened her mouth to cry out, but the sound of cracking knuckles suddenly cut through the night. Instantly, her attacker stilled. A feral snarl sent a shiver down Mae's spine as Rogue stepped into view, his wolf eyes flashing golden. His Stetson cast a shadow over his face, revealing only the gnarled, scarred skin of the left side. The scars streaked white, barely containing the intensity of his rage, a sharp contrast against the darkness. As he stepped toward them, the rings on his knuckles glinted in the moonlight, lethal and threatening. His hands and those rings were a weapon in their own right. She had no doubt of that. She'd seen as much when he'd taken down the vampires.

Rogue eased forward toward her attackers.

One look at him, and her attackers blanched.

Immediately, Clint released her, lifting both hands in surrender, still clutching the blade he'd held against her throat in his right one. "I didn't know. I didn't know she was yours, Rogue. I swear it."

Rogue didn't answer. He came to stand in front of the rogue wolf, watching him with eyes so cold his face looked like it had been chiseled of iron and stone. Rogue lashed out, his strike so sudden and quick, it reminded Mae of the lethal piercing jaws of a viper. One boot to her attacker's front kneecap was all it took. The crunch of broken bone echoed. Clint crumpled to the ground, howling. Mae gasped with immediate relief as her attacker lay at her feet, gripping the back of his knee and cursing.

Rogue advanced past her, his eyes focused on the wolf howling at his feet. He was so absorbed in his task that it was as if he didn't even see her. From the look in his eyes, she had no doubt he would easily bleed the other wolf dry. His foot bashed into the bastard's chest. A crack of ribs beneath his boot pierced the quiet night air. Rogue dug his heel in, forcing the man down like the dog that he was. The sleaze-bag was howling, clutching his now-broken ribs and plead-ing like the spineless trash he was. All previous bravado had escaped him.

Rogue released him with a rough shove of his foot. He picked up the silver blade that had skidded across the ground. "Get up."

Mae's breath caught. From the look in Rogue's eyes, he wouldn't hesitate to use the man's blade to kill him.

Clint cried. "Rogue, please. My ribs. I can't—"

"I said, get up," Rogue growled. The cold anger in his eyes flared.

Clint's friend stepped forward to help him, but Rogue's eyes barely flicked toward him before the wolf stopped in his tracks. "Don't play the hero," he warned. "Heroes die violent deaths around these parts."

The friend blanched. With a pathetic-sounding *eep*, he scampered away, running off into the night without a back-ward glance toward his comrade.

Coward.

But no more cowardly than the wolf rolling in pain at Rogue's feet.

Slowly, Clint managed to drag himself to his knees, still clutching his ribs.

Rogue wrenched him up by the front of his shirt and slammed him into the brick wall he'd pinned Mae against. He pressed her attacker's own blade against his throat. "What's your name?" Rogue snarled.

The coward refused to look at him. His eyes were

squeezed shut, and his head was turned as if he couldn't meet Rogue's eyes, lest he find death there. "Clint, sir. Clint."

Rogue snarled. "And who am I, Clint?"

Clint whimpered. "King. You're king," he cried. "King of the Misfit Wolves."

"That's right." Rogue traced the dull edge of the blade over the other wolf's throat. "And whose kindness allows you to live?"

"Yours. Your kindness." Tears streamed down Clint's face now. His features scrunched as he let out an ugly cry. Mae almost felt sorry for him.

"And do you know the rules?" Rogue asked. His voice was so cold and calculated, it wrapped a chill around her despite the humid summer air.

Clint struggled to form a sentence. "A-anyone who l-l-lays a hand on a child or a woman…is…is…."

"…is no servant of mine," Rogue finished. "You exist solely because I allow it."

"Please have mercy," Clint pleaded.

Rogue lifted the knife, prepared to drag the sharp end across this coward's throat. "I'm not feeling very forgiving."

Rogue drew back the blade, prepared to strike.

"Wait!" Mae clutched his arm, stopping him short. If she'd thought he'd been made of stone before, her touch turned him into immovable steel. He hardened like titanium beneath her hands. Slowly, he turned, looking toward her for the first time since he'd arrived. The cold fury in his eyes shook her, urging her to release him, but she knew it wasn't meant for her. She refused to let him go.

"Don't kill him," she murmured.

Something dark flared in Rogue's eyes. Clearly, he

begged to differ. One look told her he could and would kill the other wolf. "I've killed worthier opponents for less."

"He's not worth it," Mae said.

Rogue lifted a brow. "Are you asking me to spare him?"

"As much as I'd like him to pay…" Mae glanced to the blubbering coward clutched in Rogue's threatening hands. "Yes, I'm asking you to spare him."

"Please. Please," Clint pleaded.

Rogue fixed his gaze on her attacker again. "That means you owe your life to the woman you assaulted." Slowly, Rogue lowered the blade before he shoved Clint to the ground again. Dry dirt and gravel clouded where the bastard fell. Rogue pointed toward Mae. "I want to hear you grovel at her feet."

Within seconds, Clint was sprawled across Mae's leather boots. "Thank you. Thank you." He clutched at her shoes as if they were made of gold.

Mae wrinkled her nose in disgust. She wished with all her might that she were cruel enough to laugh at him the way he had at her, that she could take pleasure at his expense, but she couldn't.

"That's enough," Rogue growled.

Immediately, Clint released her.

Rogue stepped forward. The silver of the blade in his hand glinted. "Do you remember the rules, Clint? How does a rogue wolf like you stay in my good graces?"

Clint was nodding. "No women. No kids. Those are your rules, sir."

"That's right." Rogue stood next to Clint, towering over him as he pocketed the rogue wolf's blade. He cracked his knuckles once again with a menacing crunch. The sound sent a visible shiver running through the other wolf. "And if I *ever* see you lay a hand on a woman again, next time, your queen won't be here to save you," Rogue growled. "I don't want to see you near the Midnight Coyote ever again." Rogue stared down at her attacker, his face full of pure contempt. "Now run, coward."

Clint scrambled from the ground, clutching his broken ribs as he hobbled away into the darkness. Rogue stared after him, watching as his silhouette faded into blackness. Mae watched his chest heave in and out, holding in the rage he'd been prepared to unleash. He looked every bit as lethal as he had when he'd stood, bloodied stake in hand, over the vampires. Adrenaline coursed through Mae's veins. But she was safe. Alive.

Once again, thanks to him.

"Thank you," Mae whispered. When he didn't respond, she stepped toward him. "Would you really have killed him?"

He looked toward her, his golden wolf eyes masked in a mixture of fury and confusion, but he didn't say a word.

She nodded toward the darkness. "Clint," she clarified.

He watched her, steeled eyes searing into her. "In a heartbeat," he answered.

Just when she'd started to think she understood him, he threw her for a loop. He was wild, unpredictable, feral. "Why?" she breathed. "Why kill for me?" A vampire was one thing. They were the mortal enemies of the wolves' species. They'd killed the brother of one of his beloved friends, and a bear was inconsequential, but another rogue wolf, one of his own kind…

There was significance in that.

Your queen…

His words echoed in her head. She didn't know what he'd meant by that, but it stirred something deep inside her, something that made her feel strong, invincible.

He stepped toward her, his gait the prowling, lithe movement of a predator. Then he gripped her hand in his. His hand was firm yet gentle, nothing like the hardened warrior she'd felt against her palm moments earlier.

"Come," he growled.

Her hand was in his, pulsing electricity through her at his touch as he led her through the darkness of the alley, out into the open and abandoned streets of the small western town. The dim, orange-tinted glow of the streetlights cast small pools of light in the dry mountain dirt. As they reached the middle of the abandoned road, he released her, rounding on her with such a fierce intensity it was staggering.

"When I saw him standing over you, that dark desire in his eyes and his lips lingering so close to yours as if he were about to kiss you…" Rogue stepped toward her as he brushed back a piece of her hair. He drew closer. Their bodies were so close together now, she felt the rise and fall of his breath. "…I couldn't bear it," he said. Slowly, he lifted a hand, brushing his knuckles, the instrument that had wounded so many, against her cheek.

She shivered.

"Why should he kiss you when I can't?" he growled.

When I kiss you and it means something, you'll know it, he'd said.

Mae's breath caught. "I didn't know you wanted to."

Something dark flared in his eyes. "Don't be foolish, Mae. That's like saying the sun doesn't set in the west." His hand trailed lower, curving along the bare skin of her neck. "I should have killed him for ever getting this close to you."

She had no doubt he would have, had she not been there to stop him.

His golden wolf eyes traced her every move. The rise and fall of her chest grew more ragged. This close to him, she could barely breathe.

The tension between them pressed in on her until she struggled to speak. "You could kiss me, you know," she said. "Make me forget." She drew in a small breath as his knuckles reached her clavicle. "It's only when you're this close that I feel like this. I feel dangerous." She eased closer, so close she could smell the scent of whiskey on him. "And I like it."

A wicked grin crossed his lips. Slowly, he reached around the nape of her neck, gripping her there. "And what would you do if you were a dangerous rogue, Mae?"

Even in the darkness surrounding them, she knew he saw the blush that colored her cheeks. "I wouldn't ask for a kiss. I'd steal it."

"Wise words," Rogue muttered. He pulled her in toward him, rough and close. "Go on then." His voice was a dark, rumbling purr. "Claim your prize," he challenged.

And she did. Before Mae could stop herself, she pressed her lips against his and lost herself. She wasn't Maeve Grey, younger sister to the Grey Wolf packmaster. A woman who was bound by the rules and restrictive conventions of her pack. A woman who did not kiss mysterious men because she was undesirable to all her packmates, because no one dared touch the packmaster's sister. Instead, she was Mae. Just Mae. In all her full glory, claiming a kiss from a wild, dangerous cowboy.

Not because she'd been told to, but because she
wanted to.

Her lips crashed against his, and immediately her hands
gripped his belt. As if he weren't the reason her world had
turned sideways to begin with. He drew her in closer,
anchoring her to him in the wild heat of the moment.
His tongue parted her lips, exploring and claiming her
mouth with raw, unbridled passion. His teeth nipped at
the swollen sensitive skin, causing a small moan to escape
her mouth. He devoured that moan, teasing and licking
and claiming until all Mae could feel, see, touch was him.
When he finally released her, Mae was gasping for air—for
him, for another breath of him pressed against her just-
kissed lips.

Slowly, he eased away from her, facing outward toward
the abandoned night. The crack of his knuckles pierced the
night, and even the sound of the summer cicadas stilled. He
released a long, echoing howl before he called out into the
darkness. "Whoever lays a hand on her answers to me," he
snarled into the darkness. "She's mine."

Mae stilled as dozens upon dozens of golden wolf eyes
appeared in the shadows. On the rooftops, in buildings, all
staring down at them. She hadn't even realized they were
there. They blended into the darkness, an army of rogue
wolves, lingering in the shadows, waiting for their king's
beck and call. A chorus of howls filled the night, echoing
against the buildings and calling up to the moon above.
Goose bumps prickled over her skin.

Rogue snapped his fingers, and at the end of the street,
one of his wolves emerged from the darkness. Rogue
plucked the still-dangling truck keys from Mae's hand and

passed them toward the rogue wolf who joined his side. The wolf nodded.

Rogue turned his wicked gaze toward her again, his Stetson dipping low over his brow. The weight of his power washed over her. With one declaration, he'd given her the keys to his dark kingdom.

Your queen, he'd said.

The lingering feeling of his kiss, the prickled scratch of the stubble hair on his chin still haunted her, a ghost of the desire she felt.

His words were a deep, hungry purr as he spoke to her. "Go back to the ranch now, Princess. No harm will come to you tonight. You've never been safer than you are right now."

She didn't doubt it for a second. He stepped aside as his rogue wolf beckoned her forward. She eased past him, feeling the weight of hundreds of eyes on her, but it was his gaze that pierced through her, stripping her bare as the weight of it followed her all the way to the truck. As they rode back to the ranch, she watched the dark mountain landscape out the window as night faded into early-morning twilight. Mae didn't breathe evenly again until she was back on the ranch inside the mansion. As she pressed the door shut, a sharp breath fell from her lips and a tremble shook her.

Rogue had been right. She'd never felt safer or more powerful in her life.

Chapter 16

TWO DAYS. FOR TWO DAYS ROGUE HAD AVOIDED BEING alone with her. Yet as he descended the mansion staircase, heading out to load the square bales into the hayloft, she cornered him.

"Hold on a second," Mae called after him.

Rogue froze. Between his days on the ranch and his evenings searching for a new lead, it'd been easy to avoid her. He'd used Murtagh to update her on their progress, but he'd given the ranch hands an evening off. It was only the two of them inside the house, so he couldn't pretend he didn't hear her.

She stood at the top of the staircase in that godforsaken nightgown, the one that reminded him of her moans as she'd pleasured herself.

She was gorgeous—breathtaking, really—and Rogue wasn't the kind of sentimental yeehaw who used words like *breathtaking*. But even from the bottom of the stairs, the electricity between them struck him harder than a bolt of lightning. She was everything he'd imagined in his boyhood and more— heart-shaped face, warm smile, the spattering of freckles across her cheeks. She was strong, graceful, and so damn delectable.

His wolf wanted to devour every inch of her.

But he couldn't.

"What?" he grumbled, hoping his tone would put her off.

From the eager way she descended the stairs toward him, it didn't seem to. "Can you take me out to the pigpen to pick up Tucker?"

Rogue nearly growled. Of course, this was about the damn pig. According to Murtagh, she'd taken to leaving him out in the pen for short stints because she'd decided *socializing* with the other hogs was good for him.

Rogue shook his head. "No. I'm headed out to the barn to put the square bales in the loft. There's only enough light left for that."

"The pigpen is on your way," she protested. "It won't take more than a minute."

He flicked his gaze over the thin nightclothes she wore. "You're wearing a nightgown." It was a ridiculous excuse, but he was desperate enough to use it.

Outside the Midnight Coyote, when she'd leaned in toward him, he'd wanted to kiss every freckle across her body—to lick and tease and suck any inch of bare skin he could find. If knowing how she tasted had been torture, then *her* kissing *him*—grabbing him and stealing a kiss beneath the stars and streetlights as if he were the prize—well, it had flayed him open.

And he couldn't take it. Not for another fucking second. Not if he expected to keep his damn sanity intact. He was the villain in all this, and when all was said and done, she'd hate him for it. Of that, he was certain.

But if she kept looking at him like that, like she was remembering exactly how it'd felt to be in his arms, he wouldn't be able to control himself.

Which meant he needed to stay far away from her.

She was holding the sketchbook and pencils he left her in her room, and she drew them to her chest. "I'll get Tucker and sit in the truck with him while you finish with the hay. I don't mind waiting. You won't even know I'm there."

He doubted that. He was acutely aware of her. Even when he'd been out working in the pastures, his mind had wandered to her as if he were a lovesick puppy rather than the hardened criminal he really was.

She made him forget himself...

"Fine," he relented. He didn't see any way to escape her without wasting the remaining daylight.

The last rays of the sunset peeked over the mountains as Rogue pulled the truck out into the pasture. The skyline cast a pale-blue shadow over the landscape, leaving the ranch cloaked in quiet stillness.

"Murtagh said you're still looking for alternative leads to Walker Solomon," Mae said.

Rogue white-knuckled the steering wheel. Aside from the kiss they'd shared, the last thing he wanted to discuss with her was the current status of the antidote search—and definitely not his sordid past with the likes of Walker Solomon. With each passing day, their alternatives thinned, but Rogue wasn't prepared to admit defeat. Not yet. Not when everything he had ever worked for depended on it.

He grumbled in response as he steered the truck toward the pigpen. She must have gathered he wasn't in the conversing mood, because she didn't press further. When they reached the pen, he shifted into park. Immediately, he slid out of the truck. He slammed the door shut as Mae exited the vehicle and tossed her the keys.

She caught them with two hands, eyes wide with surprise as he mumbled, "You can take the truck back." He'd walk to the stables and ride Bee out to one of the older utility trucks parked farther out on the property. Anything to keep her away from him in this moment. But when he glanced toward the pigpen, all thoughts of escaping her came to a halt. One small nursery pig in the corner caught his eye.

"Shit," he swore.

The nursery pig used one hoof to pivot around in circles. A few others wandered around aimlessly, and another kept bumping into the side of the pen. Rogue hopped over the fence, heading straight to the water lines. The pigs' water supply was fed through a nipple attached to the water lines through the pump, ensuring water was readily available at all hours. The hydration of pigs was key to their health and thus a major part of the ranch's profit margin.

Rogue checked several of the lines. No water. He swore again.

If the water pump had broken, the pigs had been without water in the hot summer sun all day. The feeder pigs, finishing pigs, and nursing sows were likely still fine, considering it hadn't been long, but from the look of the small nursery pigs, salt poisoning was already setting in. Pigs needed two and a half times more water than feed, and without it, even their normal food contained too high a salt concentration. Rogue checked several other lines. It wasn't likely they were all clogged, which meant the pump was broken.

It'd be midafternoon tomorrow before he'd be able to get the necessary parts to fix it.

"What's wrong?" Mae asked. She'd entered the pen through the gate and was cradling Tucker in her arms. He'd only been in the pen a few hours and was likely still well hydrated, but the last time O'Brien had been out to check the pen and slop the hogs had been earlier that morning.

"The pump's broken," Rogue replied. "And from the looks of the little ones, they've been without water too long."

Mae's eyes grew wide. She'd recognized what that meant.

Though salt poisoning was a common problem, the mortality rate for pigs was high.

"Where's the nearest working pump?" she asked.

"In the stables." Several miles out.

Mae set Tucker down. "And do you have a trough and some buckets?"

He nodded. "Yeah, in the shed around back. Take Tucker, and I'll drop you back off at the house while I take care of this."

He'd need to trek back and forth gathering water for the pigs for well over an hour. Their rehydration needed to be gradual and controlled. The only thing worse for the pigs' immediate health than dealing with salt poisoning was reintroducing water too quickly and in an unlimited supply, which only increased the mortality rate.

"If you think I'll sit by while Tucker's piggy brethren suffer, you don't know me at all."

Piggy brethren? He shook his head. The woman was the worst kind of bleeding heart.

Rogue headed toward the truck. "I thought you said he wasn't a hog. He's a teacup pig."

She waved a hand in dismissal. "Well, they're cousins, distantly related at least."

"Says the vegetarian rancher." He shook his head.

"I'm no rancher. I just live with them, and you'll thank me later," she said. "Now hand me those buckets while you set up the trough."

Two hours and several trips out to the stable's water pump later, both Rogue and Mae were covered in sweat and caked with a layer of dry dirt as they climbed into the truck.

From the thick layer of humidity hanging in the air, they'd have rain before night's end. All the more reason Rogue needed to hurry to the barn and get the square bales from the truck bed into the hayloft.

Mae wiped a layer of sweat from her brow as he started the engine. "I don't think I've done that much ranching work since I was a teen," she said.

"I'll send someone out here to keep them watered," he said, leaving the conversation at that. She'd been a quick and efficient worker, helping alongside him, but the last thing she needed from him was encouragement.

An awkward silence passed between them as they rode out to the barn. He'd left it open in anticipation of loading the bales, but he'd need to close it since it wouldn't be long before he lost sunlight.

"This won't take long," he mumbled as he hightailed it from the truck. He was almost inside the barn when he heard the passenger door slam behind him.

Shit.

"Did I do something wrong?" Mae called after him.

Her words froze him in place. He released a long breath through his nose, trying to calm himself as he turned toward her.

She stood next to the truck, still in that godforsaken nightgown, a look of total innocence on her face as she cradled the damn pig in her arms. Everything about the situation, about her, should have struck him as ridiculous, but it didn't. She didn't. During every second he spent with her, she only proved herself less of a princess and more of a strong, resilient, passionate, creative woman any man in his goddamn right mind would want.

Even a man like him.

That thought only fueled his frustration. "How about the part where you revealed your identity to that piece-of-work cougar?" He picked the first thing that came to mind. Sure, the consequences of that had yet to bring any issues forth, but he knew it would rile her all the same.

Mae gaped at him. "Last I checked, I didn't reveal anything to him. He came to that conclusion on his own."

"You're conveniently forgetting the part where you brought up your pack as if we were having a casual conversation."

"But I never said I was a Grey Wolf!"

Rogue adjusted his Stetson as he turned away from her. "You might as well have."

"You're only mad because your plan didn't go your way."

The words stopped him in his tracks. "If you'd listened to me in the first place and stayed out of it, it *would* have gone my way."

Mae shook her head. "Not a chance. We'd still be in the same situation with no lead except a sociopath like Walker Solomon."

"You're right, but at least then we wouldn't be facing your pack with the vampires on our tails."

She set Tucker down. The piglet gave a muffled grunt before he wandered a few paces away, sniffing the ground in search of acorns. "What do you mean?" she asked.

"You think that cougar kept such valuable information to himself? Think again. He'd likely already passed it on before you left the bar. Any advantage we had of no one knowing your location will soon be gone. Every supernatural in their right mind will be after us."

"And you're suggesting that's my fault?"

"If the shoe fits, Princess."

Mae's hands clenched into fists. "You're insufferable! I don't see why you're complaining. *I'm* the one they're after, and *I'm* the only one who will be forced to spend several more days with a criminal."

He sneered. "You didn't seem to be singing that same tune outside the bar."

Mae's jaw dropped. "You're a pig."

"Well, we both know you have no problem keeping pigs in your bed."

Mae gasped. Her face flamed red in a look of pure fury. Good, let her be angry. Let her see what a beast he was. Maybe then she would stay away.

Without a backward glance, Rogue headed into the barn, but from the sound of Mae's footsteps scuffling behind him, she wasn't letting him go that easily. He flicked on the overhead lamps, illuminating the darkness that crept in with the setting sun. He shook his head. Mae never made anything easy. Murtagh would have said that should remind him of someone, but he squashed that thought as quickly as it came. Sure, he was stubborn, but she made everything difficult.

Not even ranching, the one thing that allowed him to lose track of time and escape, had been easy since she'd come crashing back into his life. His thoughts were too consumed with her, with the salty-sweet taste of her lips.

They were nothing alike. They couldn't be more different.

She was perfect. A beautiful, privileged princess who lived a life of leisure and luxury. And him? He was the monster hiding in the shadows, the scarred hideous beast who'd clawed his way out of the pits of hell, his only weapons fury and rage.

The sharp soprano of her voice cut through his thoughts. "That's what this is about, isn't it?" she demanded. "How I kissed you outside the Midnight Coyote?"

Rogue ignored her. If he refused to give in, she'd eventually tire and leave him in peace. He climbed the ladder to the hayloft to lower the pulley, but she followed him, clamoring into the loft as if she weren't wearing only her nightclothes.

As he reached the pulley, the loud sound of her stomping her foot echoed throughout the barn. "Answer me, damn it," she swore. "You can't kiss me until I'm weak in the knees and then expect me to forget it."

Weak in the knees?

No. Rogue gripped the pulley rope, crushing it beneath his fist. He couldn't look at her. Not now. Not if he expected to hold himself together.

"God knows I've tried to forget, but I can't," she confessed. "I can't even be in the same room with you without hoping you'll have mercy on me and kiss me again."

He stiffened, the muscles of his back writhing as he fought to hold himself in place. The knowledge she was just as affected by what was between them threatened to rip him in two.

But it's not you she wants. Not Jared. It's the Rogue, his mind taunted. *The lie, the persona.* The darkened part of himself he showed to the world, not his true self.

"You said when you kissed me and it meant something, I'd know it." Her voice broke as she spoke, tearing him to shreds. "Well, I'm sorry, but I *know* that I mean something to you. I…I know I sound ridiculous. It's just…when I'm with you, I feel strong, powerful, and I…" Her voice cracked again as if she were fighting back tears. "I know I'm not the most desirable woman out there, but—"

He rounded on her. He was about to tell her exactly how ludicrous that was. Whoever had put that ridiculous thought in her head deserved to be drawn and quartered for their lies. But as he faced her, Rogue found his boots were suddenly frozen in place. His cock stiffened even as the rest of him proved immobile. The way the overhead lights were positioned, her nightgown was illuminated underneath the hem, making the material see-through. She was naked underneath, open and bare. Her nude silhouette cast a tantalizing shadow, but he could see every inch of her. The fleshy peach color of her taut nipples, the delicate curve of her slender hips, and the smooth cleft between her legs.

He wanted to bury himself there, to drown in the taste of her against his tongue as she screamed for him. In an instant, he no longer gave two flying fucks that he was the villain. If she wanted the Rogue, he'd give that side of himself to her. Let her hate him when all was said and done. But for now, if he wanted her, he'd have her.

"And what do you want me to say, Princess?" His voice thickened, turning into a low, purring growl. "That I'm haunted by the thought of your lips pressed against mine?" Slowly, he prowled toward her, unable to hold himself a second longer. "That the thought of your tight little body pressed against me keeps me awake at night?" He stood next to her now, close enough to see the rapid rise and fall of her chest, the way those peach nipples puckered. She stared at him with those wide, innocent green eyes that he could drown in.

Rogue reached out and fingered the edge of her nightgown just above her breast. He would suck and tease those taut nipples until she was bucking against him. His eyes flashed to his wolf's. "Do you want me to tell you that not even my own hand can satisfy the ache?" he whispered.

Mae drew in a sharp breath as his hand dipped to her breast, his fingers rolling her nipple between his fingers. A small moan escaped her lips.

He released her, putting her in control. "Take your pleasure."

Her eyes grew wide at the offer. She hesitated, and for a moment, he thought she might not be daring enough until slowly she eased toward him. Her small hands pressed against the planes of his chest, and she leaned in toward him. Her lips brushed and hovered near his, featherlight and tentative.

He gripped the nape of her neck. "Like you mean it," he growled.

She threw herself at him then, arms wrapping around his neck with a force that knocked his Stetson from his head. Her lips slammed against his, hungry, desperate—wild. This was a woman who knew what she wanted and exactly how to take it. Rogue smirked against her lips. She'd said she felt dangerous in his arms, and she was right. This was a woman made dangerous with freedom, with desire.

And he reveled in it.

Rogue gripped her by her neck with one hand, his fingers knotting in the base of her hair as the other hand settled onto the tight curve of her ass. He lifted her into his arms. Her legs wrapped around him, locking behind his lower back. She tasted like berries, deliciously sweet and tart as his tongue crashed against hers. They were all hands, both of them grabbing, stroking, touching as he pulled the hem of her nightgown over her head.

He cast the damn thing aside and gripped her bare ass cheeks in his hands. A small moan escaped her mouth, and he growled in response. He'd spread her wide open, leave her bucking and screaming for him until the sounds of her pleasure echoed throughout the barn.

One of the already loaded bales had fallen open, leaving a scattering of hay covering the hard wooden floor of the loft. He laid her out there, positioning himself over her as she tore his shirt over his head. Her hands explored the skin of his chest, exploring, feeling.

"Tell me what you need, Mae," he growled.

He ran a hand up her thigh as he parted her legs. She was gorgeous, pink and bare. She was wet for him, already glistening with desire. Fuck.

"Do you want me to pin you against this floor and fuck you till you're screaming my name?" It would be the name of the monster he'd become, not his true name, but Rogue couldn't bring himself to care. He gripped one of her hands in his, leading it down until he pressed it against the rockhard length of him. He was straining against his jeans. She bit her lower lip, running her hand over the bulge of his cock.

"Or is it my mouth you want?" He lowered his head until he dipped down between her legs, his lips brushing over her bare cleft. "Pick your poison," he growled against her pussy.

"I…" Her voice was a breathy, panting moan. "I want…" She bucked her hips forward, brushing against the heat of his mouth. He'd wanted to taste the sweet heat between her thighs from the moment he'd heard her moaning at the feel of her own hand.

She released a frustrated sigh that was part need, part amused anger. Her eyes flashed golden. "I want your mouth on me."

A wicked grin crossed Rogue's lips. "Good girl."

Chapter 17

HEAT. WHITE-HOT AND BLINDING. MAE FELT IT FROM THE top of her head to the tips of her toes, and she couldn't get enough. She bucked her hips forward as Rogue drew her clit into his mouth. His tongue fanned over her, scorching her from the inside out. He'd lit a fire inside her, leaving her helpless with pleasure, and all she could do was enjoy the burn.

If she'd thought kissing him had made her wild and dangerous, that was nothing compared to the feel of his mouth between her legs. She buried her hands in his hair. The shaved sides contrasted with the dark, silky locks at his crown. To bring a man like this—a dark, powerful wolf—to his knees…

It made her feel alive, powerful.

Free.

His tongue circled and massaged her clit as his hand ran up the inside of her thigh. He eased two fingers inside her cleft, still refusing to release her from his mouth. The tip of one of his canines gently grazed her most sensitive flesh, and a gasp tore from her lips. The sweet push of his fingers as his tongue licked, teased, and sucked was almost too much. A familiar pressure built inside her.

Her eyes widened. Pleasure built inside her, but she wasn't certain she could take it. She was on the brink of losing herself.

He raised his head from between her legs, releasing her with a feral growl. "Is it fucking with a wolf like me you want, Princess, or plain vanilla sex with the lights off?" The vulgarity of the question thrilled her. His tongue flicked over his chin to lick what remained of her sex away. As if he not only tolerated the taste of her but *enjoyed* it.

Mae could scarcely breathe. "You," she whispered. "I want you."

He cast her a dark grin from between her thighs, the mischief in his wolf eyes sparking like liquid fire. "Then I won't be denied, Mae."

He pushed into a plank position before he stood.

"What are you doing?" Mae panted.

He walked over to the black pulley rope for the hayloft and gripped it in his hands. His eyes darkened with mischief.

Mae's eyes darted between him and the rope. A thrill of shock and excitement shot through her. "You can't be serious," she said.

"Can't I?"

Mae felt herself slicken as she bit her lower lip. Her hand trailed to her own breast as she kneaded the tip of her nipple. A hungry growl tore from his lips. She wanted him, all of him. The dark and the light. Slowly, she stood, crossing the hayloft toward him. There was something more vulnerable about standing in front of him fully nude that caused her breath to hitch.

"Good girl," he purred.

Within seconds, he had her in his arms, wrapping the cords of the pulley rope around her wrists until her hands were secured above her head. He dropped to his knees, gripping her bare ass with both hands until he'd spread her wide.

"Any last words, Princess?" he teased. A devious grin crossed his lips.

She shook her head. She couldn't believe she was doing this. "You're wicked," she said.

His eyes filled with dark promise. "You'll be glad about it." His mouth was on her again in seconds, his tongue licking and teasing—and this time, she had no escape.

He released her. The heat of his breath danced over her sensitive skin. "Fuck," he swore. "You taste sweeter than honey."

As the sweet pressure built again, she trembled until her toes curled. He slipped his fingers inside, curling them forward and pushing against a spot inside her she hadn't realized existed.

"Rogue!" she cried out.

Wave after wave of pleasure washed over her as she climaxed against his tongue.

As the last of her orgasm raked through her, she slumped against her hangings. Immediately, he stood, releasing the knot at her wrists. She sank against him.

He cradled her in his arms. As his eyes faded from his wolf's to that icy blue, she cupped her hand over his cheek, her fingertips brushing over the rough skin of his scars. There was longing in his eyes, a look so pained, but it was gone within an instant, replaced with the hardened look of a dark, feral wolf.

He released her, leaving her standing in the hayloft again, weak-kneed and sated.

She stared up at him before she sighed and closed her eyes. "That was—"

She started to tell him exactly how amazing that had been, how she'd never climaxed so hard in her life, but then her balled-up nightgown landed across her stomach. She caught it, and her eyes shot open.

He was standing on the other side of the hayloft, tugging his shirt back on.

"Rogue?" she said.

He didn't look at her, but she watched as his shoulders tensed. "Please don't call me that. Not now."

Mae blinked. "Where are you going?"

He picked his Stetson up off the floor and tipped it back onto his head. "I told you, Princess. I don't do romance."

"I know, but I thought—"

He faced her then. She wasn't sure what emotion she'd expected to see from him, but certainly not the hurt that was there.

"You thought what?" he asked. "That another taste of you would change things?"

Heat flamed in her cheeks. She clutched her nightgown to her chest, suddenly feeling far too naked. "That's not it at all."

"Isn't it? You've had your fun. A walk on the wild side with a dark, mysterious rogue. That's what you wanted, isn't it? An escape from the dull life you live."

Mae stiffened.

He stepped even closer, the sound of his boots hitting hard against the wooden flooring. "Tell me, Princess, do you intend to take a wolf like me back to Wolf Pack Run with you? What would your packmates think as you parade me around your little ranch home? What would your brother say when he finds out that the man he calls his enemy is now fucking his sister?"

Mae didn't know how to answer.

"Would you tell him?"

Mae struggled to find the answer. "No," she finally managed. "No, I wouldn't it. But that doesn't mean I'm ashamed of—"

"Doesn't it?" The question wasn't accusatory or angry. Instead, it was tinged with disappointment.

Mae struggled to breathe as he stared down at her. The anger in his eyes should have terrified her, but she knew it was only a mask, hiding wounds far deeper than the scars that marred his face.

"Please," she pleaded. He had to understand, to let her explain.

He shook his head. "You Grey Wolves are all the same. A rogue's only good enough as long as they're useful to you. The rest of the time, we're no better than the dirt beneath your boots." He turned away from her.

"Rogue—"

She reached for him.

He growled in warning. "Don't." He stepped away from her. "You've had your pleasure, Princess. Let's not pretend it will ever be more than that."

Was he right? Did she think he was beneath her? She'd never thought about it like that until he'd said it. He climbed down the hayloft stairs, leaving her standing there, naked and full of anger—at him, at herself.

Because deep down, she feared he might be right...

Rogue tore from the hayloft like a bat out of hell, only pausing long enough to leave the truck keys sitting on the hood. Forget the bales of hay. He didn't care if the rains soaked them to the point of ruin. If needed, he'd purchase hay come winter. At the moment, he needed to get the hell away from the loft, away from the scent of berries on her skin, the taste of her sweet sex against his tongue, and the memories that threatened to destroy him.

He'd known bringing her here would conjure up memories he'd rather keep buried, but he'd been willing to make that sacrifice. Yet he'd never expected it to be like this. He'd never anticipated being near her would hurt so much he could barely stand it. Every waking moment, he ached for her, wishing for what had once been. Even in his dreams, he couldn't escape her. She came to him each night, the ghost of their past, and in his dreams, he didn't need to lie, to pretend he was only the dark wolf that the world had shaped him to be. He could just be with her—scars, broken past, and all—and that would be enough.

But in the waking hours, when she still didn't know who he was, it was never enough. Having her in his arms, kissing her, making her writhe beneath him. None of it would ever be enough.

Rogue shifted into his wolf, running back toward the house until his legs burned with the exertion. When he arrived, he went straight to his room and showered, hoping to wash the scent of her from his skin, but it was no use. Once he was clean and clothed again, he made his way down to his personal bar in the library. He'd forgo the cup in favor of the bottle. It was in his armchair, legs slung over the armrest as he gripped the bottle neck, that Murtagh found him.

"What the bloody hell happened to you?"

Without casting a glance toward Murtagh, Rogue turned away. He gripped the neck of the bottle, tilting it to his lips. The fiery liquid burned down his throat.

"Ach, Christ. Doona tell me she *still* doesna know. I thought ye might 'ave told her."

"No, she doesn't and she won't."

"She's far tougher than ye think. I can say that fer certain now that I know the lass. She can handle it."

Rogue shook his head. Mae was one of the strongest women he knew. She was resilient, intelligent, kind beyond reason, but even *she* had her limits. "No. It would destroy her."

Murtagh growled. "And ye think yer betrayal won't?"

Rogue refused to answer. They wouldn't agree on this.

"When she finds out who ye really are, that ye've been using 'er to get yer revenge, that'll do her in, ye ken?"

Rogue sloshed the amber whiskey around in the bottle, watching its surface quiver. He was quickly losing patience with Murtagh. "She's already lost me once. What's a second time?"

"And ye would put her through that again?"

"What choice do I have?" Rogue slammed the whiskey bottle down on the table beside him. Glass echoed against wood with a resounding thud. "She's already been taken advantage of by her family. Her uncle should have loved her, protected her, but instead he used her as he pleased. Now, twenty years later, you expect me to tell her how her father betrayed her? How he used her pain as an excuse to cast my family from the pack and steal the throne, all for her beast of a brother?" Rogue stood. He was shaking his head. "I might as well tell her that her whole life is a lie. I won't violate her like that. I won't take away her remaining happiness."

Not even as the lie destroyed him...

"And when ye have the antidote? When ye announce yerself and ye force her to turn against her own brother in exchange fer her pack's safety? Ye think that willna destroy her? She'll realize the truth then, about you and the lies her family told."

Rogue stepped around Murtagh, heading to his desk where he kept the ranch's files, the ledger. "The responsibility for that will land solely on my shoulders. She may be angry with her brother for his role, but it's me she'll hate. His misguided transgressions will pale in comparison. Then at least the truth won't cause her to become estranged from the only member of her family she has left."

Murtagh was shaking his head at him. "Nae, she'll only lose the man she loves."

"The boy she *loved*," Rogue corrected. "And she already lost him a long time ago." He started to shuffle the papers on his desk, hoping Murtagh took that as a dismissal, but he didn't. The Highlander wasn't going to give this up.

Rogue braced himself against the desk, staring down at the paper there as he refused to look at Murtagh. "I have a chance to regain my father's legacy, make life for our kind better, and avenge Cassidy's death all at once. I can't miss out on this chance. Not when everything we've worked for is at stake."

Not when the promise he'd made her hung in the balance.

"And when this is all said and done? When the dust settles?" In his peripheral vision, Rogue saw his friend draw closer. Murtagh's voice softened. "Ye may not be my blood, Jared, but I've come to know a wee bit about ye. And losin' that woman again will ruin ye."

Rogue had no doubt Murtagh was right.

"If that's what it takes, so be it."

Murtagh waved a hand as if Rogue were a hopeless cause. "Yer as stubborn as a damn mule and twice as ornery," he grumbled. He turned to leave, but he paused by the doorway. He drew in a sharp breath. "Cassidy would hate to see it, ye ken? He knew ye loved that girl more than the very air in yer lungs."

Rogue released a heavy sigh. "I don't know what love is anymore, Murtagh. I haven't for a long time."

Murtagh shook his head. "Tell that to some toff who'll believe ye, because I doona think that to be true fer a second." He gripped the doorframe. "Yer a fool. A damn lovesick fool, and it's no one's doing but yer own." Murtagh started to leave but was nearly mowed down by a frantic female rancher.

Rogue glanced up. Daisy stood in the doorway, ruddy in the face and struggling for breath as if she'd just run a marathon. Daisy's eyes turned toward him. "Vampires," she panted. "On the ranch. They got through the guards."

Every muscle in Rogue's body tensed. He'd known the cougar had sold them out, but he hadn't anticipated the information would spread this soon.

"The children?" he and Murtagh asked in unison.

Daisy placed a hand to her chest. "Everyone's here, safe in the house, except—"

Rogue darted from the desk, knocking over the side table and the whiskey bottle in his path. The glass shattered across the marble floor, liquid gushing from the remains, but Rogue paid no attention. The next thing he knew, he was running.

Mae.

His pulse pounded in his ears as he raced toward the barn. He had to get to her, had to find her.

Before they do…

He was wrong. Mae knew that now without a doubt. She'd sat in the hayloft for the past two hours with her sketchbook, working on her graphite rendering and listening to the gentle whooshing sounds of the evening rain. Night had long since fallen, yet she drew by the dim light of the barn lamps. The dark gray of the graphite pencils stained her fingers from where she'd smudged and shaded sections of the image. Aside from the rain, the occasional rustling of hay, or a long moo from the cows, silence was her only company. Tucker had taken up residence in one of the empty stalls below and fallen asleep.

May glanced out the cracked barn doors to the truck. She'd considered heading back to the house more than once, but she wasn't ready to face Rogue yet. The pain in his eyes haunted her, but now that she'd mulled it over, she recognized how wrong he was. She wasn't ashamed of him. No more than he was of her, and it wasn't her fault that they came from different worlds. Sure, her initial attraction to him had been to his dark persona, but that had changed the moment he'd risked his life to save her, and now that she knew the kindness in so many of his actions, it only further cemented how she felt. There was more to him than his rough image. She knew that now, and she wanted to know more.

If only he would let her in...

She needed to find a way to show him that. She contemplated this, her pencil scratching across the paper like a form of meditation until the sound of the barn door creaked open. She was about to call out to see who was there when the sickly sweet smell of death hit her nose.

Mae froze. Her whole body tensed as the scent of vampire carried to her on the breeze.

They'd come for her.

With tentative movements, Mae lowered herself flat against the hayloft floor. From where she was sitting, they likely couldn't see her above them, and the longer she stayed hidden, the better. She'd need to formulate an escape plan. The sounds of two voices drifted from the stall row below.

"She's got to be in here. I smelled her scent in the truck cab."

The sound of one of the stalls slamming open caused several of the cattle to moo. The vampire released a menacing hiss.

"I don't smell wet dog," another answered. "Just cow shit."

The first hissed. "Trust me. She's here."

Mae stiffened. Their exchange was followed by the sound of more stall gates being kicked open. Supplies from shelves hit the floor. The cows started mooing in distress at the racket, and Mae heard a disgruntled oink from Tucker. Thank God the little teacup pig couldn't climb ladders, or she had a feeling he would have given her away by now.

Lowering herself onto her belly, she army crawled to the loft edge. The vampires were tearing apart the barn below in search of her. Shelves of bottles and milk replacer for calving season were scattered across the floor along with shovels and pitchforks. Black Hollow's barn was a sizable space, but it wouldn't be long before they ran out of options and checked the loft.

Easing away from the edge, Mae shifted into wolf form. Fur sprouted, and muscles and limbs twisted until her gray wolf emerged. The nasty scent of the bloodsuckers hit her nose twice as strong in wolf form, and she covered her muzzle with her paw. She'd need to catch them by surprise. If she could do that, she could fight her way free and make a run for it.

Mae crept on her belly toward the edge of the hayloft again, golden wolf eyes peering down. In wolf form, her senses heightened, making her aware of the vamps' every move.

"She's not here," one of the bloodsuckers grumbled.

"Check the hayloft," the other ordered, red eyes flashing.

The hairs on Mae's haunches rose on end as she pulled away from the edge. Her fur prickled, and adrenaline coursed through her. She'd missed her chance. Footsteps clapped toward the hayloft ladder, but a sharp pop of gunfire rang in the distance, cutting the sound short.

"What the fuck was that?" one of the bloodsuckers growled, distracted.

It was now or never.

Mae launched herself from the edge of the hayloft with a menacing growl, landing on top of one of the vamps. Her jaws snapped, teeth ripping and tearing into deadened vamp flesh. The vampire let out a shrieking hiss. But with surprise on her side, Mae sank her canines into the vampire's jugular, filling her mouth with a nasty iron taste. She ripped her muzzle back, taking out the vampire by its throat.

Blood dripped from her muzzle as she faced her other enemy.

One down, one to go. Maverick's voice echoed in her head, making her brave, giving her strength. But Mae didn't have more than a second to take pride in her kill before several other bloodsuckers rushed into the barn.

She snarled, warning them back, but it was no use. A whole army of them had flooded the ranch. All with one goal: to kill her.

She was surrounded on all sides. The vampires closed in, their circle around her shrinking by the second.

One near the entrance, likely one of the eldest, bared its sharp fangs and hissed. "You'll pay for that, you mangy bit—"

The vampire choked on its words, red eyes darting toward its chest, where a stake had pierced it from behind. It crumpled to the ground, exploding in a heap of blood.

Rogue stood where the bloodsucker had been seconds before. Blood dripped from his face, his expression so calm it was chilling. He clutched a lacquered wooden stake in his hand as his men stood beside him, marking him as the leader of the drove of wolves at his back. The tension in the air crackled as his icy blue gaze met Mae's.

"Run," he growled.

All hell broke loose. The inside of the barn erupted in battle fury. Several vamps dove for Mae at once, but they were met by Boone and Yuri. Rogue's men shifted into wolf form, meeting the vampires blow for blow as they stood guard over her. They protected her as if she were one of their own, fighting the vampires without hesitation.

With her back covered, Mae turned tail to run, but in her peripheral, she caught sight of Rogue. He was battling two bloodsuckers, looking as feral and lethal as that first night in her bedroom. He didn't need to shift into wolf form; his fists were a weapon all their own. The obsidian of his rings glinted in the dim overhead lights as he drove his stake into one of the bloodsuckers' hearts, but that was when Mae saw another emerge from the other side of the barn, headed straight for Rogue's turned back.

Mae didn't think. She darted through the melee, diving under and over the raging battles as she headed straight for the bloodsucker. She leaped. Her paws connected with the bloodsucker's chest, knocking it backward, but it lashed out, fangs sinking into the flesh of her shoulder.

A yelp tore from her throat.

She fell to the ground. Upon impact, she shifted into human form. Pain seared through her. It wasn't enough to maim, but blood poured down her bare shoulder all the same. It still hurt.

At the sight of her, Rogue moved on the offending vampire. In an instant, he caught the bloodsucker by the throat, lifting it with a single arm. His biceps strained and several veins on his forearm pulsed. The rage in his face shook her.

"No one lays a hand on her," he snarled. His arm shook with exertion as he slowly crushed the vampire's trachea with his bare hands.

Mae could barely handle the sight. With blood spattered across his scarred face and fury burning in his eyes, he looked every bit the lethal monster his reputation painted him to be.

But he'd killed *for her*.

Once again.

The vampire crumpled to the ground. It hadn't met its true death. Vampires could only be killed by a stake or decapitation, but the bloodsucker was close to it—helpless and maimed. If left alone, it would take days to heal. Rogue stabbed his stake into its chest, finishing it off once and for all. Howls from Boone and Yuri drew their attention. Another onslaught of vamps had arrived. Even with Rogue's men who guarded the ranch, they were outnumbered five to one.

Rogue's gaze flicked toward her, his golden wolf eyes taking in her wound. His nostrils flared. "Protect her," he growled. "With your life." He turned back toward the melee, shifting into wolf form.

Mae wasn't sure whom he'd spoken to until a large hand gripped her by the arm. She snarled, prepared to shift again, only to realize it was Sterling tugging her out of the barn.

His dark features were deadly serious. "Come with me." The deep timbre of his voice rumbled through her. Without warning, he scooped her in his arms.

Mae shook her head, struggling against him. "No. I can't leave him. He—"

"You can and you will, Mae," Sterling ordered. He carried her through the darkness with swift, predatory speed. The sounds of battle echoed throughout the ranch. When they reached the cover of the trees, Murtagh waited for them, perched in Bee's saddle.

Despite her protests, Sterling lifted Mae onto the horse.

"Murtagh," she pleaded. "They have him outnumbered. I have to go back. I have to—"

The Scot shook his head. "Nae, lass." He wrapped a blanket around her shoulders. She'd been so focused on the battle that she hadn't thought twice about her nudity after shifting. "The only thing worse to him than death would be seeing ye hurt."

She wasn't certain she believed that, but she didn't have time to protest. Murtagh kicked Bee into motion. The horse shot forward, carrying them into the cover of the mountains. The battle sounds of the vampires attacking her newfound friends and the man who'd risked his life for her—more than once—raged in the distance. Pain throbbed through Mae's shoulder. She held on to the horn of Bee's saddle as she gripped the blanket around her shoulders.

All she could do now was hope they made it out alive.

Chapter 18

Rogue's limbs ached and his temple throbbed as he rode through the darkened mountain paths. The moon shone overhead as his horse climbed the beaten trail, heading to where he knew Murtagh would have set up camp and guarded the children.

He and his men had managed to hold off the bloodsuckers long enough to give Mae, Murtagh, and the ranch's smallest shifters a head start. They'd been so outnumbered they hadn't managed to kill all the vamps, but they'd taken out their fair share before they made their escapes. Each wolf had taken a different escape route—a tactic meant to confuse their enemies. The bloodsuckers likely wouldn't catch up with them before daylight.

Still, now that they'd been sold out and the vampires knew Rogue had her, that would limit the rogues' movements. To complicate matters further, the knowledge would spread and her packmates wouldn't be far behind. With the additional challenge of their sole lead being Walker Solomon, they were up shit creek without a paddle. Even Rogue wasn't certain he could work himself out of this. They'd need to reevaluate if they expected to move forward with the plan.

His horse picked up speed, alerting him that they were drawing close. The Arabian wasn't as fast as Bee, but he was less ornery, adequate. They cut through a dense band of trees, revealing the campsite located just outside a hidden cove of volcanic hot springs. A small fire flickered, burning down to embers. The children lay sleeping in their camping sacks as Mae, Murtagh, his men, and Daisy gathered around the fire, having all abandoned the mansion during the raid. Most of the other ranch hands had made it out and scattered in various directions. They'd likely lie low for the few hours till morning. They knew what to do.

The crew that sat around the fire was eating some game that Murtagh had likely caught. From the sound of it, Mae was in the middle of delivering the final punch line of a joke. The ranch hands burst into another round of roaring laughter, grinning like a bunch of fools. Boone even had the nerve to clap her heartily on the back.

Of course, they were taken with her. Everyone was…

Rogue cleared his throat. At his approach, the group glanced up, relief etched across their faces. Save for Mae, who was staring down at…

Rogue glared at the sleeping pig in her arms. *Of course*, the little bacon monster had made it out unharmed. No wonder Bee was lying in the dirt on the other side of the camp, away from the rest of the group, looking as if he'd eaten a sour apple. Bee let out a pissed-off whinny, whether at the sight of Rogue riding another steed or the presence of Tucker the demon pig, Rogue wasn't certain.

"Ye made it out in one piece then," Murtagh said as Rogue dismounted.

"Barely," he grumbled.

They'd need to reassess their plans to find the vanished bloodsucker and retrieve the antidote, prepare a different course of action. They were running out of options faster than he'd anticipated.

"The bloodsuckers are desperate. We may have been out-numbered, but that raid was poorly planned," Boone said. He sank his teeth into a bite of whatever game he was eating.

From the scent, Rogue guessed rabbit. He and the other men nodded in agreement.

"It may have been poorly planned, but it was still ter-rifying," Daisy added. "No one was as unexpected as Mae though. I heard she took a vamp out by the throat." Her face beamed with pride for her fellow she-wolf's accomplishments.

Sterling nodded in agreement. "She was damn brave."

"Could've gotten herself hurt a lot worse than she did," Boone added, a hint of concern in his voice.

Rogue hadn't forgotten. The sight of her bleeding for the sake of guarding him would keep him awake for days. He glanced toward Mae. She was still staring down at the piglet in her arms. From the looks of it, there was a bandage on her shoulder. She hadn't bothered to look at him since he'd arrived.

"I see the hog made it out alive," he said.

Yuri grumbled. "Bit me several times on the way here, but I got him out."

Rogue had given Yuri express instructions to save the ridiculous little beast.

Mae huffed. "We've been through this already. He's a teacup pig, not a hog."

Rogue eyed the beast in her arms. The piglet looked as if he'd grown to twice his size overnight. "Has he gotten bigger?" he asked.

Mae finally looked at him, her eyes narrowed. "Don't you start. He's a *teacup* pig." She stressed the word *teacup*.

Rogue wasn't in the mood, not after several rounds with the bloodsuckers. "I hate to break it to you, Princess, but there's no such thing as a teacup pig. He will not stay small and adorable. That's what conniving breeders call potbelly piglets to convince bleeding hearts to buy them as pets."

Mae glared at him. Her lips puckered as if she were angry, but he saw the hurt on her face as clear as day. In an instant, he felt like that small, mean little boy again, mud covering her purple dress as she'd nearly burst into tears.

"You're insufferable." She shoved off the rock she was sitting on, still clutching the pig in her arms as she stomped off toward the caves.

The silence left in her wake was deafening.

Murtagh was shaking his head as he crossed his arms over his large chest. "Go after the lass. She was worried about ye, ye daft ninny!" He glared up at Rogue. "Thought ye might 'ave been dead. It was all we could do to keep the woman from burstin' into tears, ye ken?"

Rogue didn't need to hear any more. For once, Murtagh was right. He'd been cruel and she hadn't deserved it. He swept past his fellow rogues and followed Mae. He found her a short walk away from the campsite, perched near the pools of the volcanic hot springs. The rising heat and humidity from the water hit his face. The waning half-moon cast a dim glow over the watery depths. Mae sat on the edge of a rock near the spring's edge, the ever-growing Tucker still cradled in her arms. Rogue lingered there, watching her.

She was the first to speak. "You were right."

He shoved his hands into his pockets. "Look," he said, choosing his words carefully. "Teacup pig or not, I suppose... *Tucker*"—he practically had to choke out the name—"is used to a certain...standard of care." He couldn't believe he was about to say this. "So I suppose I'll have to get used to him, but unless you want Murtagh to put him on a roasting spit, don't bring him into—"

"That's not what I'm talking about," she said.

Rogue raised a brow. If not the damn pig, he wasn't sure what they *were* discussing. Crossing the rock, he sat down beside her. That was when he noticed the tears streaming down her face. He stilled.

"You were right," she repeated. "What you said in the hayloft about how my pack uses rogues. You were right." Her voice broke. Tears poured down her cheeks, leaving thin lines that in the reflection of the spring's pools appeared to glisten in the moonlight. "I've lived in an ivory tower my whole life, let my packmates and my brother use rogue wolves as scapegoats, as stepping-stones whenever we needed, and never once did I think of how we'd used them...how I'd used *people*, wolves like you." She sniffled.

The sound tore at whatever shriveled mess he had left for a heart.

"A few days ago, the others told me about what happened to Murtagh's brother," she confessed. "I can't stand the thought of him not getting justice."

After his father died, Rogue had had no one. But when Murtagh and Cassidy had found him half-dead and beaten in the snow, his face freshly scarred from where the Grey Wolf packmaster had maimed him, they'd nursed him back to life. Murtagh had been almost eighteen, a man in all the ways that counted, yet still a child himself and already caring for his younger brother. Still, he had taken Rogue in as if he were one of them. Murtagh and Cassidy's had been the only kindness he'd known as a rogue wolf.

"I won't let Cassidy's death go unavenged," he said quietly.

Which was one of many reasons why he was determined to find the antidote—to protect Mae, to avenge Cassidy for both himself and Murtagh, to give the rogues the rights they deserved, to make the vampires be the ones to bleed—even if that meant betraying the only Grey Wolf he'd ever cared for. Even though her pack would be protected, she wouldn't thank him in the end, but everything he did was—at least in part—for her.

"What if you weren't around?" she asked.

"Murtagh can more than fend for himself. He's—"

"It's not just Murtagh. It's all of them." Mae was shaking her head. "Boone told me he was barred from joining a pack because of petty theft charges from his early teens, living on the streets and stealing *food*—food of all things, even though he would have starved otherwise—and Daisy was disqualified when she applied for Grey Wolf membership because she attacked a man at her job in self-defense when he tried to *assault* her. They didn't do anything I wouldn't have done myself, yet they'll never have a pack because of it. How is that fair?" She searched his face for reassurance.

But he had none to give her.

"You're right," he said. "It's not fair."

Life wasn't fair. All those years ago, that'd been the first lesson he'd learned. Life as a rogue wolf was harsh, cruel. There was no forgiveness, no second chances for their kind. There was only survival. It had twisted him into the monster he was. To survive, he'd needed to be crueler, darker, more bloodthirsty than any other. He'd clawed his way out of the pits of hell with nothing more than his bare hands, and now that he was at the top, if he had to break the laws of the pack that cast him out, the pack that had stolen his birthright from him, then so fucking be it.

"That's why you do what you do, isn't it?" she asked.

He raised a brow.

"The theft, the extortion, the backroom deals my brother goes on about. That's why you do it, isn't it? To champion the vulnerable."

"You make it sound more virtuous than it is."

"Do I?" She swiped some of her tears away. "And here I am, whining about my pack obligations while I'm trying to protect them. No wonder you think I'm a princess."

"You may be a princess, but you're more tolerable than most Grey Wolves."

"More tolerable?" Mae let out a harsh laugh. "First you say I'm not unattractive. Now we've moved to tolerable. Aren't you a romantic?"

"Do you want me to be romantic?" He asked the question before he could stop himself.

She shook her head at him before she glanced away. He could have sworn he saw a blush darken her cheeks, but with the evening shadows, he wasn't certain.

"I think they like you a bit more than 'tolerable.'" He nodded in the direction of the campsite.

"And what about you?" she asked.

He smirked. "You mean do I like stubborn, spitfire she-wolves who complain at every turn and think livestock belongs inside the house?" he teased.

"You're one to talk about complaining," she grumbled.

He couldn't help the chuckle that escaped his lips at that. "Yes, Mae. I do like you, even with that damn pig in your arms," he admitted.

Too much for his own good.

She smiled slightly. "Good," she said. "I can almost forgive you for *abducting* me then." She joked. "*Almost.*"

They fell silent. The sounds of the rogue wolves nearby drifted out to them. Rogue was surprised they weren't hiding in the trees eavesdropping. They were meddlers, the whole lot of them, and they loved nothing more than to see him get his just deserts every now and then.

Mae glanced over her shoulder, listening to the sounds of the group that drifted to them. Her smile softened and an air of sadness visibly weighed down her shoulders.

"It isn't too late to change things, you know." He wasn't certain why he was reassuring her. It would only make things worse in the end. "You're helping the rogue wolves now, more than most."

"By finding the antidote?" she asked.

"Yes," he answered. If she knew the extent to which she would be *helping* rogue wolves like him, she might not be so keen on the idea. The thought soured Rogue's stomach. He didn't want to use her like this, a means to an end, but he had no other choice.

Not unless he wanted to sacrifice everything he'd worked for…

A moment of silence passed between them. They lingered there, on the edge of the hot spring pools, allowing the quiet sounds of the forest to stretch between them. The hoot of an occasional owl. The rustling of leaves. The rushing movement of the hot spring water.

Mae cleared her throat. "That's not the only reason I was upset, you know," she said, glancing in his direction.

There was a spark in her eyes. A watery quality to the pale green of her irises. Some emotion he'd never seen from her before. Not the nostalgia of someone who held fond memories, or even a sadness that longed for the past.

This was grief. Plain and raw.

And it ruined him.

"I lost a friend once. Years ago, and tonight, I was scared I was about to lose another."

"Mae," he breathed. "Please don't say that." He was pleading with her as much as a wolf like him could. He couldn't bear to hear her call him her friend, not with the guilt of his true intentions lingering just beneath the surface of their every interaction. Twenty years ago, she'd been his only friend. She'd always be his friend, but now...

Now he dreaded hearing the word cross her lips.

He couldn't be a true friend to her. Not in the way he wanted to be.

"Why? Why can't you admit that we're friends?"

"Please, Mae." He turned away from her. "Don't ask this of me. Not this. Not now."

Not twenty years too late...

He watched her reflection in the pool of the hot spring.

"We *are* friends," she said to his back, "and I'm not ashamed of you, Rogue. I care about you. I want you. And even if I'm nothing more, we *are* friends. We've been vulnerable with each other. Shared secrets. We've—" She reached out to touch his shoulder.

He couldn't take it anymore.

"Enough." He spoke the word with quiet force. He

rounded on her, gathering her into his arms with all the strength of his longing for her. "Will you spare me a single shred of mercy, woman?" he pleaded.

Placing one hand on her lower back as the other gripped the base of her short hair, he drew her flush to him. He had her pinned against the volcanic rock wall surrounding the hot spring within seconds. The length of his erection pressed against her, grinding into her center as he kissed her as if he loved her, as if she meant something to him.

Because she always had.

As he pulled away from her, his mouth still lingering near hers, he felt the warmth of her tears spilling down her cheeks. Joy. Relief.

"Isn't it obvious?" he whispered against her lips. "Don't you realize I've wanted you from the start?" He brushed his fingers over her cheek. "I've offered you everything you've asked of me. What else is there left to give?"

"You," she whispered.

Rogue had faced death hundreds of times. But that single word was the only dagger that had ever truly pierced him.

"I want you. Not the Rogue. Not the dark, devilish persona, but the man who lies beneath, whoever the hell he happens to be." She gently cupped his cheek. "I want all of you. Heart and soul, because I...I think I'm falling in love with you," she confessed.

Rogue struggled to breathe around the emotion that blocked his airway.

No. She couldn't. He'd longed so many times over the years for her to say those very words to him, but not here. Not now.

Not now that they no longer stood a chance.

He smiled through the pain before he laid a gentle kiss on her forehead. "Don't you see?" The pain in his voice was palpable. Capturing her chin in his hand, he forced her to meet his gaze, his touch as tender and gentle as a monster of a man like him could manage. "You're already my past, my present, my future. There's nothing else left for me to give."

At those words, a torrent of desire washed over them, making them both lose themselves. Before he could even comprehend the weight of his actions, they were both naked and he was making love to her as reverently as he'd always dreamed of doing.

As he filled her core with the thick length of him, she cried out. He caught that cry with his lips as he kissed her—thoroughly and completely—without holding any of himself back. He poured himself into the moment, refusing to feel the regret that he knew would plague him come sunrise, because for right now, it didn't matter that she still didn't recognize him, that she had no clue who he was. He couldn't bring himself to care. He wanted this woman, loved this woman—plain and simple—and if there was one thing becoming the Rogue had taught him, it was that when he wanted something, nothing else mattered.

He would claw himself from the pits of hell all the way to the pearly gates of St. Peter himself, if only she were the prize that waited there.

He made love to her all night, using the walls, the floor, and inside and out of the hot water pools, their bodies steaming with the heat as they made the caves their own adult playground. As the sun rose over the horizon and lit the mouth of the cave, Mae lay in his arms, her eyes heavy with sleep as she ran a hand over the corded muscles of his arms and pectorals. As her eyelids began to flicker closed, she traced the intricate tattoos there with her fingers. His naked body cradled hers. He felt full, sated and satisfied in a way he hadn't known he could as he held her against him.

Rogue lay there for a long time, counting the spattering of freckles across her cheeks.

But just before she drifted into slumber, she cupped the scarred side of his face in her hand, and as she did, Rogue felt himself die a little, because he knew he'd never feel more alive than he did in that moment.

Chapter 19

WHEN MAE WOKE AND EMERGED FROM THE CAVE THE following afternoon, Rogue was nowhere to be found. It was nearly nightfall by the time he returned to the campsite. The sun hung low in the sky, quickly disappearing beneath the mountain pines. The smell of burning wood and smoked meat filled the campsite. Fortunately for Mae, she and Daisy had spent the afternoon foraging, and they'd found a few raspberry and blackberry bushes not far from the camp. Murtagh had also given her a handful of granola and protein bars from the ones he kept in his pack for the children.

Mae was biting into one of the protein bars as Boone dealt out another hand of blackjack when Rogue made his appearance. He tore into the campsite, wearing little more than a pair of jeans, which hung so low on his hips that the bones and sinew muscle were visible leading down to…

She tore her gaze away.

Even after everything they'd done last night, she *still* wanted him, and she'd meant what she said.

She wanted all of him, heart and soul.

The prospect of that terrified her. She turned her attention back to the game. Rogue lingered nearby, leaning against a towering tree. Boone finished dealing the round. She watched as Sterling beckoned for another card.

"Hit me."

Boone dealt the next card, a king of hearts on top of a four of diamonds. It was Yuri's turn.

"Stay," he said.

The card facing up in front of him was a ten of spades. Mae watched as the other players stayed or passed, taking note of their cards as she ran calculations in her head. When it reached her turn, she accepted two more cards before stopping at exactly twenty-one.

A collective round of groans sounded.

"That's the fifth damn time in a row," Sterling howled.

Boone slammed the deck down on top of the rock. "You're cheating," he grumbled, pointing at Mae.

"So what if she is? You cheat all the time," Daisy shot back.

Mae cast Boone a coy grin. "I wasn't aware cheating was frowned upon by criminals."

"We may be criminals, lass, but even a lot like us has morals," Murtagh said as he gathered the cards. "Gamblin' is sacred among our kind, y'ken?" he teased.

"How are you doing it?" Yuri asked.

Boone growled at him. The young wolf was high-spirited and kind but a sore loser. "How do you think she's doing it? She's counting the cards!"

"Where'd you learn that trick?" Daisy asked.

"It's not a trick." Mae shrugged a shoulder. "It's math."

The response led Boone into another round of curses while Mae and Daisy exchanged grins.

As Murtagh finished gathering the cards, he noticed Rogue watching them from the edge of the clearing. "'Bout damn time yeh joined us."

Rogue grumbled something unintelligible in response.

Whatever it was, Murtagh didn't seem to care for it. "While you were out gallivanting 'bout the woods, we were discussin' a plan."

Rogue quirked a brow, but from the scowl on his lips and the quick dart of his eyes toward Mae, he didn't seem pleased that she'd been part of the discussion.

But if she hadn't been intimidated by him before, last night had made any prospect of that out of the question.

"We need to face Walker Solomon," she said, inserting herself into the conversation.

"No." Rogue said the word with such cold finality that it caused Mae to stiffen.

"It's the only way," she said. "We have no other leads, and you said yourself that now that the vampires know where we are, any progress we make will be extremely difficult."

"The lass is right," Murtagh added.

Rogue was shaking his head.

"You made a promise. You swore to me that if I came with you, you'd find the antidote, save me, my pack, the rogues—everyone."

"And I will," he shot back, "but that doesn't mean Walker Solomon is the way to do it."

"We're running out of time." Mae felt that in her bones. After all the events of last night, everything felt more urgent. She needed to save her pack, herself, before the vampires struck again and destroyed them all.

Rogue shook his head. "No, I won't get mixed up with Walker Solomon." He shoved off the tree he was leaning against and made his way over to the campfire.

"What other choice do we have?"

"Anything that doesn't involve getting fucked by the likes of that crazy bastard," Rogue growled. He moved to follow after Bee, who carried his saddlebag and its contents. She wasn't foolish. He was brushing her aside.

Mae knew Solomon's reputation and knew it well. The rogue wolf was bloodthirsty, brutal, and he answered to no one. Not even Rogue. He was as close to a villainous rival as Rogue would likely ever get.

But this was the right choice, and she knew it.

"I wouldn't have taken you for a coward," she said.

Rogue froze in his tracks.

"Oh shit," Sterling mumbled.

"Is she trying to get us all killed?" Yuri whispered to Boone.

Boone nodded. "I think so," he whispered back.

Slowly, Rogue turned. The heels of his cowboy boots dug into the ground as he prowled toward her. He didn't stop until they were practically nose to nose.

The gold of his wolf eyes blazed. "If you want to sacrifice yourself, then so be it, Princess, but I won't give my blessing for it. I won't ask my men to go on a death mission."

"You don't have to," Mae challenged. "Solomon's a casino owner. Murtagh says he makes all his deals over games of cards. I can play him. Count the cards. Beat him. Only you and I would have to be—"

Rogue's eyes narrowed as he looked toward Murtagh, and that one look alone was enough to cut Mae short.

"This was your idea?" he asked Murtagh.

If looks could kill...

"Actually, it was mine." The brave voice came from Will, who had been using a spare deck of cards to teach his sister how to play blackjack while Noah attempted—and repeatedly failed—to build a house of cards. The children had been listening throughout the conversation.

Rogue let out a short staccato laugh underscoring that

he didn't find this situation amusing at all. "Wonderful," he said. "Now we're taking battle advice from an eight-year-old."

"I'm almost nine," Will corrected, as if that made it any better. "And by the way, Murtagh, learning long division sounds good if I can count cards like Mae."

Mae almost laughed. She had to admit, she admired his bravery.

"Whatever plan you all made, forget it," Rogue said. He turned back toward her, gripping her hand and pulling her in close enough so only she could hear him. "If you think that after last night I'm going to let you come within a hundred miles of Walker Solomon, think again." His eyes held hers with a feral intensity. "I won't put you in that kind of danger. Not now. Not ever. You can challenge me on a lot things, Mae, but the question of your safety isn't one of them."

With that last word, he stormed off into the forest again, leaving Mae standing in his wake.

"Well, that didn't go according to plan," Daisy commented.

After a few comments from the rogue peanut gallery, the other wolves continued with their various activities, but Murtagh continued to watch Mae.

She released a long sigh. "He's wrong on this."

"Aye." The Scot shuffled the deck of cards in his hand. "But at least he's wrong for the right reasons."

Mae's brow furrowed.

"He's tryin' to protect ye, lass."

"Says the man who helped him plot to kidnap me."

Murtagh chuckled. "I dinna say he didn't have a right daft way of showin' it." The giant Scot rose from where he was seated. He crossed the clearing toward Mae and passed her the deck. "I'll speak to him. Make him see this is the only way."

Mae clutched the deck of cards in her hand. "I don't know what has him so worried about me."

"I think ye ken that ye do." Murtagh cast her a knowing smile, which caused Mae to blush. Of course, they would realize what had passed between her and Rogue.

The Scot made to step after Rogue, but he paused before he twisted back toward her. "He's had a hard life, y'know. Cast from his pack as a boy, maimed by the packmaster himself. That's how he earned the scars on his face." Murtagh gestured to his own features, mirroring where Rogue's scarring lay. "The only way the three of us survived was by fighting in the pits of the Midnight Coyote, winning bets, money, favors."

"The Midnight Coyote?" The bar he'd taken her to for information. Mae's breath grew short. What dark memories had it cost him to have to go back there? Yet he'd done it, to save her and those he cared for.

"Aye, the same," Murtagh acknowledged. "It's how he started to amass power. But it was in Billings then."

Billings? Just outside Wolf Pack Run? Rogue had never mentioned he'd lived anywhere near there. Though she supposed she still wasn't exactly certain where he lived *now*. She'd long since guessed Black Hollow was located somewhere in Idaho, based on the flora and fauna, but she couldn't be certain.

But still, Rogue residing in Billings seemed...significant.

"Almost recruited us to the Wild Eight in those days," Murtagh continued, being unusually chatty, "but Rogue had different ideas, ye ken? He's always been righteous about the treatment of rogues. Even in the beginning. I wager it was difficult for him to fall so hard from grace like that."

Murtagh raised a brow. He seemed to be trying to tell her something he wasn't saying aloud, but Mae wasn't catching his meaning. When she didn't respond, he smiled and gave a shake of his head. "I'll speak with him. Make him see."

"Thank you, Murtagh," Mae said softly.

The Scot moved to step away and then paused. "Mae," he said, "it'd be a favor to me if ye remember that everything he does is for the love of ye."

Mae wasn't certain what he meant by that. But before she could ask, the Scot shifted into his wolf—a giant grey beast with tufts of reddish fur on his paws—and then he was gone.

Chapter 20

DRY DESERT DUST COATED ROGUE'S BOOTS AS HE AND Mae approached the Gold Tooth's entrance. Flashing neon signage illuminated the hard Texas ground, and the loud sounds of country music mixed with dinging slot machines filtered through the front doors. He couldn't believe he'd allowed Murtagh to talk him into this. When the Scottish wolf had tracked him down in the middle of the Salmon Challis National Forest, he'd gone on a rant so long, Rogue had nearly fallen asleep halfway through—something about feminism and bodily autonomy and how he needed to allow Mae to make her own choices, even if those choices involved putting herself in a dangerous situation beside Walker Solomon. It had all sounded very reasonable at the time.

Rogue gripped Mae's shoulder, stopping her short. "Are you sure you want do this?"

"You have a reputation to uphold. Ask me that once more, and I might think you care about me." She smiled as she reached for the door handle. Beating him to the punch, she stepped inside.

Rogue adjusted his Stetson and blazed after her. He didn't like this plan one bit, but even he had to admit that if there was any she-wolf tenacious and smart enough to hold her own against an alpha like Walker Solomon, it was Maeve Grey. She held her own against him after all. She wasn't faint of heart.

It was whether Solomon would be a graceful loser that unsettled Rogue.

His only reassurance was that if things got sticky—which he anticipated—he would bleed Solomon so fast, the bastard wouldn't have time to so much as glance sideways at Mae.

He didn't want to consider the implications of killing a wolf like Walker Solomon. A man with followers, loyalists who might not see the error of their ways. But it'd be worth it.

Rogue joined Mae inside, hooking his arm through hers and leading her across the casino toward the bar in the private high-rollers room—supernatural clientele only. She leaned in toward him, the sweet smell of berries in her hair mixing with the acrid cigar smoke lingering throughout the casino.

"Where will we find him?" she whispered.

"You should know from dealing with me, that isn't how it works." They reached the bar top. "You don't go looking for a wolf like Walker Solomon, Mae." Rogue pegged her with a hard stare. "He finds you." Rogue turned toward the bartender. "Jack Daniel's neat." He glanced toward Mae.

"The same," she said.

The bartender set two rocks glasses on the bar top and poured the amber drink into each. Rogue brought the fiery liquid to his lips, watching as Mae did the same. She looked stunning in a slinky little black dress they'd bought on a supply stop along the way. They'd regrouped at a safe house as they'd laid their plans, gathering equipment and additional weapons as needed. Slender curves and dark heels made Mae appear long and lean despite her petite height. A small sparkling earring dangled from each ear, highlighting the smooth angles of her pretty face. She was dressed for the part. She would draw attention.

"I wouldn't have pegged you for a whiskey drinker," he commented.

"Back at Wolf Pack Run, I wasn't."

His brow furrowed.

She smiled at him before she sipped from her glass. "I've developed a taste for it lately." Her large green eyes darted to his lips and lingered momentarily.

Rogue fought down a hungry growl. Had they been in any other place, he would have found the nearest dark room and made certain the hem of that dress never fell past her hips.

He pushed the thought aside as he drew a sip from his own drink. "For a Grey Wolf about to meet a monstrous rogue like Walker Solomon, you're calm."

"I'm focused," she replied. "And you underestimate how far I'd go to save my pack."

"I don't underestimate you, Mae. Not a chance."

He'd done so the very first time they'd met, when he'd thought he could scare her away in the woods. He'd never make that mistake again.

"It's just math. I'll be fine."

"Good." Rogue threw back his drink before he clapped it on the bar top. He glanced over Mae's shoulder as he pushed the glass toward the bartender. "Because here comes trouble now."

Mae followed Rogue's gaze to the casino's proprietor, who was headed toward them. Mae's eyes widened, and Rogue knew in an instant Solomon wasn't what she'd expected.

For starters, the bastard may have been as crazy a motherfucker as they came, but he was handsome nonetheless—the kind of man women looked twice at, the kind of man Rogue would be if half his face hadn't been mauled and maimed beyond recognition by her father.

Tall and lean-muscled with light-brown hair slicked back to his head, a thin blade of a nose, and a trimmed, sandy blond beard two shades lighter than his hair, only Solomon's dark grin ruined his image. The ol' Brit had never bothered to have his teeth fixed, and a nasty chewing habit he'd taken up as a teen had left his teeth yellowed around the edges.

Hideous or not, it was a grin Rogue knew from experience a man didn't want to see.

Not unless he had a death wish…

Solomon opened his arms toward Rogue, pulling him into a stiff hug. "Well, old boy," the wolf grumbled in his heavy Brummie accent. He still sounded as if he'd been plucked straight from the streets of jolly old Birmingham. "Didn't think I'd ever see you darkening my barstool again."

Mae glanced back and forth between them, her eyes wide with horror. "You know each other?"

"Know 'im?" Solomon's brow crinkled. "I saved this bastard's life on several occasions." Solomon raked his gaze over Mae, lingering a little too long for Rogue's liking. "Who the 'ell are you?"

Rogue's jaw clenched. "It was once. We were seventeen. That was a long time ago."

Solomon grinned at him, dark teeth flashing before he glanced toward Mae again. "Don' let 'im fool you. Long time ago that, but he's not daft enough to forget it."

"How exactly *did* you save him?" Mae asked. Her eyes refused to leave Rogue's. From the tight draw of her mouth, she was hurt he hadn't told her.

She might have wanted him, thought there was something between them, but she'd think him enough of a monster when all was said and done. He hadn't wanted to add to that by putting himself in league with a known sociopath.

"It was a long time ago," Rogue reiterated.

He didn't want Mae to believe there was any loyalty between him and Solomon, because there wasn't. There never would be. Even an outlaw like him had to draw a line in the sand somewhere, and Walker Solomon was his line. They might both be rogues, their power born from the same shitty gambling fights that'd allowed them enough of a platform to make a name for themselves, to amass power and loyalty from the other rogues among them, followed by wealth. But they were never, would never be anything but rivals.

Rogue fought to convey that to Mae in a single look.

Solomon signaled to the bartender, who poured him a full glass of whiskey. Solomon chugged it down in several gulps as if it were water.

Mae's eyes grew wide as she shot Rogue an uneasy glare.

He understood immediately.

The only thing more terrifying than an unhinged killer like Walker Solomon was the prospect of that same wolf angry and slightly inebriated.

Rogue cut Mae a look. There was no backing out now. He'd warned her.

Solomon banged his glass back on the bar top, so hard the glass cracked. But the wolf didn't seem to notice, or at least he didn't care. "Dragged 'im off the street half-frozen and naked, and got 'im a job at the Midnight Coyote, I did."

Mae quirked a brow.

"Murtagh was the bloke who nursed his pansy arse back to health, he did. Gave 'im a place to stay and a warm bed. All them niceties and all that. *I* was the one who got 'im a job. Made 'im what he is."

Mae glanced at Rogue. "Is this true?"

Rogue grabbed his own glass off the bar top, giving it a

slight shake as he brushed off Mae's question. "Details," he mumbled.

"Details, my arse," Solomon said. He signaled the bartender for another round. The bartender made to grab him another glass, but Solomon waved him away. "I don' need another cup that's damn fine china, you fool." The bartender mumbled his apologies while he fetched the bottle again.

Solomon eyed the bartender, refusing to look away. "'E was like an alley cat back then. All snarly and feral. Just look at 'im now." He grinned at Rogue again. The dark color of his teeth was made even more questionable in the casino lights. "Was covered in blood when I found 'im, since this was still fresh." Solomon tapped Rogue twice on the scarred side of his face.

Rogue's hand clenched into a fist at his side as Solomon eased back to look at him.

The alpha wolf wrinkled his nose. "Pity the other side's so pretty, isn't it?" he said to Mae.

Rogue growled, but Solomon paid no mind.

"Well, you didn't come 'ere just to look at my 'andsome mug now, so what game will it be then?" Solomon clapped his hands together, rubbing them back and forth eagerly.

"Lady's choice." Rogue nodded toward Mae. He was thankful for them to finally be getting down to business. As much as he would ever feel good about doing any kind of business with Solomon.

Mae glanced around the casino, feigning an inability to decide, though Rogue knew she already had a plan in store. "I like blackjack."

Solomon grinned. He clapped his hands together again. "Poker it is then," he roared. Within seconds, he was headed off toward the poker tables, cracked glass of whiskey in hand. He mumbled something unintelligible as he went, which might have been about hating blackjack.

Mae gaped after him. "He's…"

"Mad as a fucking loon," Rogue growled. "I tried to warn you. Don't let him fool you, though. The only thing more dangerous than a sociopath like him is a stark, raving mad one."

"I guess I'll be playing cards with a murderer then." She turned to walk toward the poker tables, but Rogue caught her by the hand.

"He changed the stakes. You can't count cards in poker."

"I know that, but I'm more than decent," Mae challenged. "It's still game theory."

"I don't doubt that," Jared said. "But we can back out now. No one would blame you."

"And risk the lives of the only wolves we both call family? Allow the vampires to destroy either me or our kind before we finally find the antidote?" She quirked a brow. "Not a chance. It's my blood the vampires want for their serum, no one else's, so I plan to see this through. I came here to play, and I intend to win. It's more than just the fate of my own pack riding on this. I'm no coward." She eased away from him, striding toward the poker tables in heels that would have made some women less graceful.

But on her, they didn't.

Rogue growled as he stormed after her. His resolve in his own plans only hardened with each stubborn step she took. Murtagh was wrong. Mae would be fine once all was said and done. She was built of stronger stuff than she let on. She was brave, resilient. Rogue knew her, perhaps better than anyone, and she was cut from far tougher cloth than most.

Princess indeed…

Chapter 21

POKER. THE MURDEROUS BASTARD WANTED TO PLAY poker. Mae strode toward the poker tables, drink in hand, her heels jabbing into the plush carpet with each angry step. She hadn't expected to feel so much hatred and anger toward Walker Solomon, but the moment he'd sauntered up to the bar, she'd been hit with the full force of her rage.

Not only had he killed one of her pack members in cold blood, but he was the sole wolf standing between her and the fate of their species. If he had even an ounce of loyalty to his kind, she and Rogue wouldn't have to work for the information. The antidote would save the lives of thousands of pack and rogue wolves alike, but Solomon didn't give one flying fuck. He only cared about how he could benefit.

And that meant he was not only a cold-hearted killer but also a selfish, disloyal bastard.

Mae slid into the seat across from Solomon at the poker table. The casino owner was babbling at the dealer— something about cutting the deck wrong—in between gulps of whiskey. A woman stood behind him, one arm draped over Solomon's shoulders.

She was curvy and dark and more feminine than Mae could ever dream to be. Her hands massaged Solomon's shoulders, long, red nails digging in. Her deep-brown eyes followed Mae until adrenaline coursed through her, but it eased when she felt Rogue's dark presence guarding her back. She might have been frustrated with him—hurt that he hadn't told her about his familiarity with Solomon—but she knew without a doubt he'd protect her.

He had before.

The dealer laid down a row of cards.

"What are the stakes?" Mae asked. She wanted the terms spelled out ahead of time. No way would she let Solomon back out.

Solomon grinned, crooked, stained teeth undercutting his handsome features. "We both know why you're here, don't we, Roguey old boy?"

Mae felt Rogue tense behind her. His large hand squeezed her shoulder.

When Rogue didn't respond, Solomon leaned back in his chair, sweeping his arms wide until all the cards fluttered off the table. "Fifty-two pickup." He smiled. "Next time, cut the cards right," he said, forcing the dealer to collect them and deal the round again. Solomon's features hardened as he turned back toward them. "Come now, Roguey. You going to stand there all night or tell your bitch to move?" Solomon gestured toward Mae.

Rogue snarled, but Mae placed her hand over his. "You'll be playing against me."

Solomon laughed, long and loud. Long enough to make the moment even more uncomfortable. When he finally quieted, he was shaking his head with that putrid grin across his lips. "Like 'ell I will. It behooves me to play against Roguey 'ere. He's shit for poker. Always has been. That's why I chose it, and you may be a pretty little piece, but there'll be no Grey Wolves sitting at my table."

Mae's heart stopped. She had to fight to keep her face straight. Rogue had warned her that Solomon wasn't an easy man to pull one over on. That with his reputation, he might recognize her, but she hadn't realized how much that would unnerve her. If they failed against Solomon, the blowback might come against her packmates.

Solomon chuckled. He glanced over his shoulder toward the she-wolf at his back. "Did ye see that, Sophia? She didn't think I'd know she's a Grey Wolf, did she?" He laughed.

Sophia forced a smile as she nodded.

Solomon glanced at Mae as he continued to speak to the woman behind him. "Spitting image of her brother. Same eyes—less 'airy though—and she thinks I'm daft enough not to realize." His laughter faded into a moment of calm.

Without warning, Solomon knocked over his chair, diving for Sophia. He gripped her by the face and throat, fingers digging in so hard they would leave bruises.

Mae jumped from her chair, surging forward.

"No." Rogue caught her by the arms, hauling her backward. "React and he'll kill her and you too," he hissed into Mae's ear. When that failed to calm her, he snarled. "She's not his true target, Mae."

Sophia held Mae's gaze, dark eyes wide with fear. It took everything in Mae not to go to her, to try to save her. It didn't matter that she didn't know her. She could have been a killer herself or Mae's most hated ex-friend—it didn't matter. She would have tried to save her.

But the trembling fear deep inside her gut told her Rogue was right.

Solomon's voice remained calm, eerily so, despite the rage blazing in his eyes. "What do I think of she-wolves who think I'm daft, Sophia?" he asked.

Sophia swallowed hard, unable to answer.

Mae couldn't take it. She shook with the weight of the other woman's fear.

When Sophia didn't answer, Solomon gave her a rough shake, tightening the hand around her throat until the veins in his arm strained.

Sophia whimpered as her face began to turn red.

Mae shook with rage, held back only by Rogue's strength.

Releasing the woman's throat enough that she could speak, Solomon growled. "What do I think of that, Sophia?"

Sophia's lip quivered as she gasped for air. "You think those she-wolves end up dead," she whispered. She stared straight into Mae's eyes, making the threat clear.

It wasn't Sophia who would die at Solomon's hands.

Rogue gripped Mae's shoulders, fortifying her, giving her strength.

"Right," Solomon said, his tone suddenly upbeat again, as if they were talking about the weather. He gave Sophia a gentle tap on the cheek before he released her.

Sophia stumbled back, clutching her throat.

Mae opened her mouth to tell Solomon exactly where he could shove it when Rogue pulled her into his arms, clutching her against him in a way that stopped her breath short. "I think I need another drink before we start," he announced out of nowhere. "You don't mind, do you, Solomon?" It was less of a question and more of a statement.

Considering the violent display they'd just seen, Mae admired the bravery in that.

"If you'll excuse us." Rogue gripped Mae to his side, ushering her toward the bar again.

Once they were out of earshot, Mae rounded on him. "How could you stand there like that while he manhandled her?"

"One wrong move and he would've killed her without even blinking—and you too."

Mae growled. She knew that, but she didn't have to like it. For once, she'd wanted him to be the dark, nefarious Rogue. She wouldn't have blinked twice if he'd chosen to end Solomon then and there—preferably with his bare hands.

"And what now?" She shook her head. "You're shit at poker. Solomon said so."

Rogue frowned. "I may be shit at poker, but I'm a damn fine cheat."

Mae was still shaking her head. "Even if I could count cards for you, it wouldn't help. In poker, you can't—"

"Mae," Rogue interrupted. His eyes flicked behind the bar top, where a backsplash mirror reflected the view of the casino.

And Solomon's back.

Mae's eyes widened. If she positioned herself correctly, she'd be able to see directly into Solomon's hand.

Mae grinned. "You really are a wicked criminal, aren't you?"

"I may not be as bloodthirsty as Solomon," Rogue smirked. "But I'm as wicked as they come."

A few minutes later, after they'd devised a code and a plan, Mae sat at the bar top, watching Rogue make his way back to the poker tables. It was just him and Solomon now. Sophia had disappeared. Mae hoped she'd scurried off to safety somewhere.

Mae watched the two rogue wolves in the backsplash mirror as they laid down their blinds. She clutched another glass of whiskey in her hand, her finger poised on the side to tap or circle the rim in a specific pattern accordingly. Rogue could see her hands reflected in the mirror edge from where she was positioned behind Solomon, and she had a straight view into the bloodthirsty casino owner's hands.

The two rogue wolves picked up their cards. Solomon's first hand wasn't impressive. Only a pair of twos. Mae tapped the result out on her glass.

Adrenaline gripped her stomach into knots. This hadn't been their original plan, but if it worked, they'd finally be able to move forward. Mae held her breath as the two wolves bet their chips. Rogue laid down a pair of fives. He'd won the first round.

Mae continued to tap out Solomon's hand onto her glass, her confidence increasing with each consecutive round. Occasionally, Rogue threw a hand to make it realistic. Each round won brought them one step closer to the antidote, one step closer to saving her pack, her family, the rogue wolves.

One step closer to freedom.

Until a smooth, purring voice pulled her from her thoughts. "You're making a mistake."

Mae twisted on her barstool to find Sophia staring back at her. The other woman held a martini glass in her hand filled with pink liquid, something fruity like a cosmo.

Mae's eyes darted to her neck, where the bruises left by Solomon's rough hands had already begun to form. It undermined Sophia's image as a well-kept beauty.

"I'm not sure what you mean." Mae trained her eyes on the other woman, forcing herself not to glance toward the backsplash mirror. Rogue would likely lose this hand without her guidance, and it might take them a few more rounds to regain composure, but it'd be worth it in the long run if she could get Sophia off their trail.

She may have been a victim of Solomon's violence, but

Mae knew enough about abusers to know that Sophia might be loyal to Solomon all the same. Mae knew from experience that until Buck attacked Jared, she never would have told anyone all the ways in which her uncle had hurt her. She'd been too scared of disappointing her parents, ruining and destroying her family, and she'd been so young that her pedophilic asshole of an uncle had done a damn fine job of convincing her that his abuse was her fault.

She knew better now.

Sophia shook her head before she drew a long sip of her drink. From the fire in her eyes, she wasn't buying Mae's denial for a second. "You think you're the first wolf to come in here and try to cheat against him?"

Mae schooled her features, forcing herself to remain calm. She wouldn't allow her body language to give her away. "I don't know what you're talking about. I'm just enjoying my drink." She lifted her glass toward the other woman before she sipped the fiery liquid.

"I'm no fool." Sophia shook her head. "You've been sitting here for the past hour signaling his cards."

Mae set her whiskey down on the bar top with more force than she intended. "Are you sure you don't need to see a doctor, Sophia? Those bruises on your neck might just be the beginning of your injuries." She didn't like referencing the other woman's abuse, but she needed to catch her off guard, and Mae had no doubt that what Solomon had done to Sophia earlier was only the tip of the iceberg.

There was pain in Sophia's face that Mae recognized all too well. She'd seen it on her own face every night as a preteen, after her uncle would leave her bedroom.

Before Jared had given her the strength to save herself...

If only she'd known in that moment what it would cost him.

A pang of sadness filled her chest for the boy who'd sacrificed everything for her, who'd given his life to protect her and ensure her happiness.

Sleeping with the enemy or not, Mae hoped Sophia would either find a Jared—or a Rogue—of her own to save her or find the courage to leave. She empathized with the other woman, loyal to Solomon or not. She really did.

Seemingly unfazed by the comment, Sophia set her drink down on the bar top beside Mae's. She eased closer, lowering her voice to barely above a whisper. "Even if you win, he'll still kill you."

Mae shook her head. "Solomon can make his own threats. He doesn't need you to do it for him."

"No, he doesn't," Sophia agreed. "But you're still making a mistake." She picked up her drink again. "I can't allow this to happen. Not on my watch." She turned to head toward the poker table.

Adrenaline coursed through Mae's veins, sending her into a panic. As the other woman started to walk away, she struggled to find something, anything to stop her.

"He won't stop, you know." They were the first words out of her mouth.

Sophia paused.

"You can beg him, plead with him to stop hurting you, but he won't," Mae said. "Not while you're still within his reach." She knew that. Her uncle never would have stopped hurting her, at least not until she was old enough that she no longer interested him.

Monsters like that didn't know the meaning of the word

stop, didn't care about a woman's pain. They thrived on it. As far as Mae was concerned, they were less redeemable than a cold-blooded killer would ever be, because they didn't just cause others pain; they enjoyed it.

Sophia's shoulders tensed. Her back was still turned toward Mae, as she refused to turn and look at her.

"You don't owe him any loyalty," Mae challenged. "There're people who can help you. *I* can help you. Rogue can too."

Sophia inhaled a deep breath. Mae thought the other woman might not answer, that she might walk away without another word. But she didn't.

She cast Mae a glance over her shoulder. "There's a Grey Wolf. He's half coyote. His name's Austin. Do you know him?"

The question caught Mae off guard. Austin was one of the Grey Wolves' eight elite warriors. Before her long-lost cousin Dr. Belle Beaumont had come into the picture, Austin had served as the Grey Wolves' only medic. Like all the elite warriors, he was practically a brother to her.

Tentatively, Mae nodded. She wasn't certain how to answer since she didn't know where Sophia was going with this. "Yeah, I know him. Why?"

From the way she said it, the question seemed to carry more meaning than Sophia was letting on, but Mae couldn't decipher what that meaning was.

Sophia must have recognized this, because she released a long sigh. "Tell him I said hello then. From an old *friend*," she said, stressing that final word.

Mae quirked a brow.

Friend?

Sophia moved to step away, but Mae dove and caught her by the wrist.

"Please," she pleaded. "Don't do this."

For the sake of our species. For yourself.

"I can get you out. I can help," Mae offered.

"No one can help me but myself. I learned that before I ever came here." Sophia gently pulled her wrist away. "You'll thank me for this later." Without another word, Sophia turned and headed straight toward Solomon.

Mae swore under her breath, uncertain whether the other woman was friend or foe. "Damn it." Mae trailed after her, making a beeline straight for Rogue. He was watching her as she approached. From the dark look in his eyes, he already suspected something was amiss.

Mae gave him a pointed stare. They needed to get out of here—and fast.

Immediately, Rogue pushed back his chair. "This has all been lots of fun, Solomon, but I'm needed back at Black Hollow." The ranch name was the code word Rogue had given Murtagh in case things went south. Mae had had the idea to put a wiretap in one of Rogue's boots. It was a move that was more in line with what the Grey Wolf warriors would do during a raid, rather than Rogue and his men, but Rogue had been open to it.

Sophia was already bent over and whispering in Solomon's ear. "Now hold on just a second there, Roguey boy." The casino owner held up a finger.

Rogue and Mae moved to step away from the table, but within seconds, several of Solomon's men had surrounded them, the threatening looks in their eyes and their intentions clear. If Mae or Rogue took so much as another step, they'd be in for a fight. At that moment, Murtagh, Sterling, Boone, and Yuri appeared, slipping in from the depths of one of the back entrances, so quiet and stealthy that Mae wouldn't have noticed them had it not been for the flash of the blade in Murtagh's grip as he passed one of the slot machines.

"Sophia here just told me something very interesting." Solomon's eyes took on a dark, wild look, the same look they'd held when he'd threatened Sophia earlier. "I don't like to be taken for a fool." He trained his gaze on Rogue. "Wouldn't have pegged you for a cheat, old boy, but luckily, there's still honor in this world—loyalists—like Sophia here."

"I'm not loyal to you." The words were spoken so quietly, Mae almost didn't hear them over the sound of the country music thumping throughout the casino's speakers.

Solomon's features crinkled into a look of confusion. He glanced over his shoulder toward Sophia. From the look on his face, he looked more alarmed that she'd spoken at all than at her words. He growled, low and foreboding. "Come now, Sophia. Can you not see I'm speaking, love?" The words dripped with underlying violence and threat.

"I said, I'm not loyal to you," Sophia repeated, her voice louder and more confident this time. "I didn't do this for you."

She held Solomon's full attention now. Every eye was on her.

Sophia swallowed—hard. "I did it for me."

Mae sucked in a harsh breath. It was at that moment that she saw the small penknife clutched in the other woman's fist. Without warning, Sophia lunged toward Solomon, stabbing the penknife into his spine and allowing all hell to break loose.

Solomon's guards lunged for her.

Mae froze. She didn't know what to do. She'd only experienced this kind of violence once before. As the melee raged, she was back there again. She was the terrified little girl who'd suffered far too much abuse at the hands of an uncle who was supposed to care for her and love her but who instead had taken advantage of that trust and used it to silence and abuse her... And then there was Jared, diving from the closet, attacking Buck as he tried to rape her yet again. Buck's hands were quickly around Jared's throat. She was screaming.

Jared's blue eyes had bulged as he'd struggled for air.

And then she was standing there. Buck lying bloody on the floor as she held the knife.

From a distance, someone was shouting her name. The shouting ripped her from the horrible nightmare her traumatic stress trapped her in.

"Mae!" A pair of strong hands gripped her, hauling her sideways and into a pair of arms until they were hidden behind the bar top.

She was vaguely aware of a flying chair hitting the wall somewhere beside them. Piercing cerulean eyes came into focus. Not Jared's but Rogue's, except that the fog of her memory made them one and the same.

She traced over his features. The scarred side of his face, while not deformed as he said it was, had been badly injured enough that it made some of his features hard to recognize. The sharp, cutting cheekbones of the intact side were too masculine and harsh to remind her of the soft face of a young teen boy, but now that she thought of it, the color of his eyes and the hue of his fur when he was in wolf form were so familiar that when she accounted for the passage of twenty years, she could almost convince herself that...

No, it couldn't be. Her father had told her himself. She'd never understood why the Grey Wolf's elite warriors of the time had chosen to hold a boy as young as fifteen to such strict standards of their law—and for saving the packmaster's daughter from a man who'd abused her. But Buck had been her father's brother, a respected alpha and warrior among the pack. She'd always assumed none of the other alpha warriors had believed her or her father—or at least they hadn't wanted to admit it—because Buck had been their friend, someone they'd trusted, better liked than her father himself, a man who'd ruled the pack with an iron fist. She knew alphas didn't often want to admit they were wrong, but she'd always secretly suspected her father hadn't believed her either, even though he'd said he did.

But he'd told her the other alphas of the pack had voted on it. He might have been packmaster, but he'd been outnumbered. At least, that'd been the story.

But Maverick had confirmed it. Jared was dead.

Wasn't he?

She focused on Rogue's gaze. There was understanding in his eyes, a knowledge of exactly what she was seeing that confused her. She couldn't possibly be seeing straight.

"Don't allow yourself to go back there, Mae. Not now," he growled. His features were twisted with battle-worn rage, but his gaze was filled with an odd depth of understanding. As if he'd been there. As if he knew.

But he couldn't.

Jared was dead.

"Run," he growled, giving a slight shake to her shoulders to bring her to her senses. The fighting continued around them. He must have engaged in it at some point, because there was a trickle of blood running from the scarred side of his lip.

"Escape through the emergency door down the back hall and wait for Murtagh around the back entrance," he hissed.

Mae was still too caught up in the fog of her own head that was making her see things in his eyes, hear things in his voice that weren't there. "You can't leave her," she answered, thinking of Sophia. The question about Austin had significance. She knew it. "I think she might be on our side."

Rogue's words were rushed with adrenaline. "You heard me outside the Midnight Coyote. No women or children. That's my rule." He shot a glance over his shoulder as a loud crash sounded, followed by a sharp yelp of someone injured while in wolf form.

Whether his men or Solomon's, he likely didn't know.

He turned back toward her. "Our side or not, I won't stand by and allow Solomon or his cronies to tear any woman to shreds. Now, go." Shoving her toward the emergency exit door, he rushed into the melee.

This time, she listened. Mae shifted into her wolf form and raced toward the exit, barreling around the thick of the fighting. She darted under tables and dodged flying debris as she ran. She ran, because she knew if she didn't, she'd start seeing things that weren't there again, thinking there was a possibility that a dark criminal like the Rogue was somehow Jared, her childhood love, risen from the dead, and she couldn't allow herself to go down that line of thinking.

It isn't true, she told herself as she burst through the casino's back exit and into the night. She didn't stop until she was safely hidden in the darkness of the alley.

It can't be true, she repeated to herself again.

Chapter 22

WITH MAE FINALLY HEADED TOWARD SAFETY, ROGUE dove back into the melee. Sterling, Boone, Daisy, and Yuri had managed to hold off Solomon's men as Murtagh extricated Sophia from the wolf's clutches. She was still alive, thanks to the Scot.

Rogue couldn't say the same for Solomon. At least not for long.

Not with what Rogue was about to do to him.

Rogue prowled toward Solomon's office. He had watched the bastard escape there, bloodied and wounded, after his men had joined the brawl.

It'd take more than a penknife to kill a wolf like him, and Rogue wouldn't hesitate.

Rogue prowled into the office. As he entered, Solomon's back was turned toward him, his massive shoulders heaving with the excitement of battle. Blood trickled from his neck, but it was a second knife wound at his side that Solomon clutched. A pool of blood grew beneath his hand. But not enough to kill the bastard. From the look of it, Murtagh had left his mark but unfortunately just missed the other rogue wolf's vital organs. Solomon was like a damn cockroach, impossible to kill.

Upon Rogue's entrance, Solomon cast a glance over his shoulder and stiffened. For a tension-filled beat, they held each other's gaze. The scuffle of metal against leather holster broke the silence. Solomon turned toward Rogue, each man cocking back the hammer on his revolver simultaneously.

"You were always a fast draw, but never faster than me." Solomon chuckled, flashing his disgusting rotting teeth. "Come now, Roguey. You don't want the secrets you came for to die with ol' Sully now, do you? And all over that worthless, fecking bitch of yours?"

Rogue didn't bother to react. The repeated and less-than-subtle use of his old nickname brought back too many memories Rogue would rather forget. Solomon had been taunting him with it all night. He'd trusted Sully. Like so many others had. And while he might not have been the sole reason Rogue had become who he was—a monster no longer worthy of a Grey Wolf princess like Maeve Grey— Solomon was still an unfortunate part of that.

Another scar on Rogue's already deformed soul.

Murtagh slipped into the room behind Solomon, his blade in hand. But from the flick of Solomon's gaze, he was all too aware of Murtagh's presence, and he wouldn't allow Murtagh to draw close enough to use his dagger. Murtagh snarled. The Scot had always hated Solomon, even though they'd fought in the same ring together. Long before Solomon had become their rival, Murtagh had seen right through him. He'd hated the psychotic bastard from the start. He'd told Rogue as much after he'd taken Rogue in, but Rogue had been too young and naive to listen, too hell-bent on earning enough petty change to help himself, Murtagh, and Cassidy survive while he worked to earn his revenge against the Grey Wolves.

One ruthless battle at a time.

Solomon wasn't a friend, but he hadn't always been

Rogue's enemy either. Thomas Grey might have maimed him and betrayed him and his family, but the wolf had died years ago. Rogue had never been able to seek retribution there, and he wasn't even certain he could have—for Mae's sake—but Solomon had destroyed him too. It'd been killing other wolves for sport, all for the sake of survival, for the money and power he earned from the bets he won and the adrenaline of winning that'd made him addicted to it, even as it'd torn him to pieces. It allowed the rage inside him for all he'd been through to become infected and fester, slowly turning him into a monster with each drop of blood that dripped from his fists, each champion ring he still wore.

And it'd been Solomon who had convinced him to do it.

Only to become even more of a monster than Rogue was himself.

Rogue leveled the barrel of his revolver at Solomon's head. "You know my rules. No women. No children. The rogue wolves are my kingdom, and I've let you exist in it long enough." His voice was calm, collected, because he'd been here dozens of times before—staring down another man he intended to kill.

His identity as the Rogue had been born of it.

"Tell me where to find the antidote, and I'll let you live," he threatened.

It was a lie, and Solomon knew it.

The Birmingham cowboy laughed. "We both know that ain't true, old boy. That's not how I taught you, is it?"

"Ye didn't teach him anything," Murtagh snarled. "He was brutal all on his own."

Rogue frowned. "I appreciate the vote of confidence, Murtagh."

Murtagh's wolf eyes blazed as he assessed Solomon with disgust. "He's a right lavvy-heided wankstain is all he is."

Solomon laughed, long and hearty. "I like that one. I like that one a real lot, Murtagh."

"Appreciate it." Murtagh nodded.

"How 'bout we try this one on for size, shall we?" Solomon said. "Go diddle yerself, ye cock-thumping trolly."

Murtagh wrinkled his nose as he shook his head. "We Scots do it better," he said.

"Bugger off," Solomon scoffed, his gun still trained on Rogue. "We Brits should've done in all you bloody Highlanders when we 'ad the chance."

Murtagh growled. "Ye daft—"

"Would you two idiots swear like some fucking *American* cowboys for once? Christ," Rogue swore.

He had their attention again now. Solomon's finger was already on the trigger, as was Rogue's. Rogue's grip tightened in threat. "Last chance," he warned.

"Your ol' antidote will die with me, Roguey."

At the moment, Rogue couldn't bring himself to care. He'd originally intended to do this without Solomon, so why the hell did it matter? He'd protect Mae for as long as it took and find another way. He'd made a mistake coming here.

As Murtagh closed in on Solomon from the side, Rogue came at him from the front, backing the casino owner into a corner. Rogue sensed the tension mounting. They all did.

"I was always faster in the ring, Jared," Solomon hissed, using Rogue's real name to throw him off, to try to make him remember the days when they'd been boys together, street urchins without a name or purpose.

Rogue shook his head. "We're not in the ring, Sully."

Solomon's trigger finger twitched, but not fast enough. Rogue shot him in the forehead point-blank. Blood spattered as Solomon crumpled to the floor.

Murtagh didn't so much as blink. He was used to the cleanup routine by now. He gestured to Solomon's limp body. "It's unlike you to shoot straight fer the head. I thought ye would have savored that more."

Rogue holstered his gun. He crossed the room to where Solomon lay. He didn't even bother to nudge the bastard with his foot. No one survived a bullet to the head. "He deserved to be put down like the damn dog that he was," he growled. He glanced back up at Murtagh. "Plus, I didn't feel like washing his blood off my boots."

Daisy appeared in the doorway to interrupt. "There's a brawl going on with Solomon's men outside, and when they find out he's dead and his power is up for grabs, all hell is going to break loose."

Rogue didn't hesitate. He strode out into the melee, firing shots into the casino's ceiling. The gunfire quieted the brawling wolves immediately.

"Solomon's dead." Rogue looked out over the crowd of rogue wolves. "You answer to me now, and you'll obey my rules." Without warning, he turned and shot one of Solomon's men in the leg, the one who'd tried to aid Solomon in hurting Sophia.

The wolf crumpled to the ground, howling in pain as he clutched his leg.

"What the fuck did you shoot him for?" one of the other wolves growled.

Rogue snarled. "Because I'm just as mean a bastard as the man you used to answer to." He gave a nonchalant shrug. "And

I felt like it." He tipped the brim of his hat toward the men who now answered to him. "Behave yourselves," he warned.

As Rogue strode toward the exit, he signaled for his men and Daisy to follow him as they left the building. The ragtag group shifted into their wolf forms as they ran to where the truck was parked a short way away.

The desert dust blew, coating their fur as they passed several large cacti.

It was a little too western, even for Rogue's taste. He much preferred the mountains of Idaho or the big sky in Montana.

They found Mae and Sophia next to the truck, Mae in wolf form. She raised her hackles, prepared to fight if necessary, but when she saw it was them, she shifted back into her human flesh. Rogue's men averted their gaze as Daisy helped her quickly grab a blanket from the truck bed and wrap it around herself. Nudity was a way of life for shifters, and most of the time, none of them paid any mind, but Rogue's men knew if their eyes lingered on Mae for even a second too long while she was naked, they wouldn't be pleased with the consequences.

She fell into him, holding on to him like a vise. "Tell me you got the location from Solomon."

"He didn't," Murtagh said as he climbed into the truck bed. "He killed the damn bastard."

Mae's eyes widened as she looked toward him. "You what?"

"Th-the scientist?" Sophia sputtered. "That's what you all were here about?"

"Of course," Murtagh answered. "What else would we be here for? Didn't ye just hear those two 'bout the antidote?"

"I was a little busy, trying not to get killed." Sophia's eyes were full of tears, but her voice was full of fire and sass. "Your scientist is holed up in a hostel down in Tijuana."

"Tijuana?" the Scot barked in confusion.

Rogue had to agree. Whoever heard of a vampire vacationing in Tijuana? Everyone knew that bloodsuckers became few and far between anywhere south of Cleveland. Though he guessed that was likely why the vamps had chosen such a location.

"Yes," she said. "I overheard Solomon talking about it a few days ago."

Rogue growled. "If you knew where he was, why not just tell Mae and be done with it?"

"Until this exchange, I thought you were here about the children," Sophia said.

"The children? What children?" Sterling asked.

Sterling and Daisy had joined them, while Boone and Yuri dragged behind.

"Sarah's children," Sophia answered.

"Who's Sarah?" Daisy questioned.

"The mother of Will, Hope, and Noah," Sterling replied.

"How do you know about them?" Rogue leveled the question at Sophia. He didn't like the idea of Walker Solomon, or whoever Sophia was to him, knowing about the rogue orphans' presence—dead or not.

"She was a friend," Sophia said. She wrapped her arms around herself in an attempt to calm the shaking. "She told me if anything ever happened to her, to make sure the Rogue found out. She knew you had a reputation for helping rogue children and women. She trusted you would protect them from their father."

"Their father?" Mae asked.

"Solomon," Sophia answered.

"Christ," Rogue swore. Will, Hope, and Noah were Solomon's bastard children?

He didn't want to consider what the repercussions of that information might be.

Mae gaped at Sophia. "If you were friends with the mother of Solomon's children, then why were you ever with him?"

"I've never been with Solomon. Not *really*. I was trying to get close to him, gain his trust, in order to kill him myself. Even if I'd known that was what you'd come for, I couldn't just give you the information. He has eyes everywhere. I was trying to keep my cover. But now that they know I was after him…" She shrugged a shoulder as her voice trailed off. "Long story. For another time."

From the sound of it, Sophia would likely need protection.

"There'll be plenty of time on the ride to the airport," Yuri said. He and Boone had joined them now.

Boone hopped into the truck bed. "Tijuana, here we come." The young wolf let out a hollering whoop of excitement as he tossed his cowboy hat.

The rest of Rogue's crew followed suit as Rogue rounded to the driver's side and Mae headed to the passenger's seat.

Mae was shaking her head. "It's just like with the Grey Wolf warriors. Where these raids lead us never ceases to amaze me."

Rogue tipped back his Stetson as he climbed into the truck. Considering she'd spent her whole life on that god-forsaken ranch and the last raid she'd participated in with the Grey Wolves had led to her being locked in a cell beside him of all unsavory people—a situation which by proxy had led to all this—he had no doubt about that.

———————

Mae stood on the balcony of Rogue's Southern California mansion. The hacienda-style architecture overlooked the Pacific Ocean. She leaned out over the balcony ledge, staring at the sea. The gentle rush of the tide rolling over the sand, coupled with the occasional squawk of seagulls in the distance, put her at ease. The sunset painted the soon-to-be night sky in various shades of orange, blue, and yellow as a cool saltwater breeze coated her face. She closed her eyes and took it all in. She'd never been to the ocean before. Hell, she could count the number of times she'd left Montana on one hand.

A pair of footsteps approached. The sound of cowboy boots clopping against marble.

Mae glanced over her shoulder as Rogue slid next to her. He leaned over the balcony beside her, resting his weight atop the ledge. She was surprised he was still here. She'd thought she was alone.

"I thought you were headed down to Tijuana with Murtagh and your crew," she said. She hadn't expected them back until morning.

"Boone has never been south of the U.S. border and was eager to head down there, so I took him off guard duty and sent him with Murtagh and the other wolves instead," he answered. "I think he had it in his head that once they had what we needed, Murtagh was going to allow him to drown himself in tequila shots, but we both know Murtagh runs a tighter ship than that."

Mae chuckled. "Yeah, Boone doesn't have a chance." Murtagh wasn't likely to let the young wolf get away with anything.

Mae turned back toward the ocean, watching the roll of the crashing waves.

Rogue adjusted the brim of his Stetson to sit higher so it would no longer darken his eyes. Silence passed between them as the quiet serenity of the seaside washed over them.

"Where are you?" he asked her, training those icy irises in her direction.

"What do you mean?" She turned toward him.

"When you look toward the ocean like that, I can tell you're thinking of something. You're here, but it's not the waves you're looking at. Not really." He touched the brim of his Stetson again. "You don't fool me, Princess."

"You're right," she admitted. "It's kind of ridiculous how easy it is for you to read me."

"It's kind of ridiculous how easy you are to read," he teased. He faced the mansion again, leaning his back against the balcony.

She smiled. The sunset illuminated the smooth side of his face, but as the remaining rays shifted slightly, the puckered scars were bathed in the orange glow too. The lighting reminded her. "I have something for you."

He raised a brow. "You do?"

She nodded. "Let me go get it." She disappeared into the mansion, returning a few minutes later with a piece of paper clutched in her hand. "Here." She extended it toward him.

He accepted the gift and glanced down.

It was the portrait she'd been drawing of him, with the sketch pad and graphite pencils he'd bought her, the portrait she'd told him she'd wanted to draw that night together in his bedroom.

She thought she might have rendered him speechless. She considered it a compliment that she could do that to a man like Rogue with little more than a pencil and some paper. She'd never been more proud.

"Mae, it's…" He struggled to find the word.

"Breathtaking?" she finished with a small smile. "Just like I said it'd be." She drew in close to him, pointing over his shoulder. "It's the contrast. Light and dark. Scarred and unscarred. You made a great subject. I've been working on it since you left the sketch pad on the bed for me, but I wanted to make sure to finish it before…"

The Adam's apple in his throat gave a knowing jerk. "Before tomorrow."

Mae bit her lip as tears started to well in her eyes. She wouldn't cry now. She wouldn't.

"What's on your mind, Princess?"

The tears continued to threaten. "Tomorrow," she said softly.

They both knew what lay ahead of them. Once they had the antidote, they could return to Wolf Pack Run. She'd long since gathered he intended to strike some sort of deal with her brother, something that provided the antidote for both her pack and the rogue wolves, but Rogue had been vague about the details. That was his way though. She was coming to realize that. Even now that she was close to him, an air of mystery still kept him hidden from her—always slightly distant and just out of full reach.

But with the antidote secured, it'd be more than his mysterious ways that separated them. He'd go back to his life and she'd return to hers. Sure, she missed her family and packmates, and she knew they'd be worried about her—and Tucker would likely be glad for Murtagh to stop looking at him as if he belonged on a roasting spit, that was for certain—but she wasn't eager for the other aspects of their adventure to end yet. If she was honest with herself, she'd enjoyed the escape of being away from Wolf Pack Run.

And more importantly, she didn't want to end things with *him* yet.

"I know what you're thinking, Princess, but don't you remember what I told you? What I warned you about?"

She shook her head.

The edges of his lips turned up slightly, but the smile didn't reach his eyes. Not by a long shot. He wasn't ready for what was between them to end either. She sensed it.

"All great romances end tragically," he'd said.

At the time he said it, she'd sighed at how swoony and romantic it had seemed, coming from a hardened cowboy like him, but now it didn't. Now, it just made her angry with the constraints of her life, her circumstance.

Mae crossed her arms over her chest in an attempt to hold herself together. "If it ends tragically, it's not a romance. It's a love story, and a poor excuse for one at that."

She glanced toward the ocean again. The blue of the water was quickly fading to black as night approached. "When we were in the caves, you asked me if I wanted romance, and I didn't answer." She leaned in toward him, and he drew her into his arms, pressing her into him in a way that was both wicked and sinful but also belied a new gentleness in his touch. "The answer is yes," she said. "I do want romance, true romance, and I don't want us to end tragically."

He traced his knuckles over her cheek until he cupped her chin in his hand. "If there's one thing I've learned from life, it's that no matter how much we want something, we don't always get it. I've had to learn that the hard way." His eyes flashed to his wolf's. "But we can make what we have worth it."

He kissed her then. Fully and completely. Without holding anything back. He poured himself into her, and she allowed him to. The love, the pain, and the pleasure. Every ounce of it.

When she eased away, her lips were swollen from the intensity of him, and she felt the prickle of the stubble on his jaw brush over the smooth skin of her cheek.

"There's one other thing on my mind."

"Mm-hmm." He had moved on from her lips and was trailing his lips down the curve of her throat. The brush of his canines as he nipped at the base of her neck, the lobe of her ear, sent a delicious chill down her spine. Her nipples stiffened.

"I know it sounds crazy," she murmured, her words starting to sound more like pants as he continued.

He inhaled the scent of her before his hands dove beneath her shirt. His large hands cupped her breasts, the callused pads of his thumbs, hardened from years of working on a ranch, tickling sensations across the sensitive skin there.

"But when we were at the Gold Tooth and I had my..." She didn't know what to call that little all-consuming flash of memory, and with what his hands were doing, she was struggling to think straight. "...episode," she finally settled on, "you said for me not to go back there, but you seemed to have an idea of where *there* was."

"We've already concluded you're easy for me to read," he purred. Using his thumb and forefinger, he rolled one of her nipples, and she stifled a gasp.

"So there wasn't any deeper meaning to it?"

He didn't answer. Instead, he hoisted her onto the balcony, pushing her thighs open as he started to strip off her pants. Once she was bare, he dropped to his knees in front of her, his intentions clear.

She was learning that an alpha wolf like him was a man of insatiable appetites, and his hunger was solely focused on *her*, the most intimate parts anyway.

"Enough thinking for now, Princess." He clamped onto her thighs, spreading her wide as he flashed that wicked grin up at her from where he'd settled between her legs. "There are more important tasks at hand."

His mouth was on her within seconds, his tongue circling her clit in a way that was so delicious she struggled to hold herself upright on the balcony ledge. But she knew he wouldn't let her fall. Not by a long shot.

Because if there was one thing she'd learned about this wicked cowboy wolf, it was that he might have been a damn good villain, but when it came to protecting her, nothing would stand in his way.

Chapter 23

To say Rogue had dreaded this day for the past twenty years was an understatement. He'd always known he would return to Wolf Pack Run to claim his rightful place, but he'd expected to feel triumphant, righteous. And he couldn't.

Not when it felt like losing her all over again.

He never should have involved her in this plan, but when he'd heard about the antidote, he'd seized the opportunity as a means to an end but also because deep down, he'd wanted to protect her, be close to her again, and that had been his mistake. He never should have tempted himself. He'd thought he could resist her, but he'd been a goddamn fool to ever think that he could. But now that he was here, it was already too late.

And the dread that consumed him left him sick to his stomach.

No. Not dread.

Dread failed to capture the intensity of the vise grip that constricted and strangled his insides until he found it hard to speak. Since they'd left the SoCal mansion this morning with the scientist in tow, his captured presence promising a fresh round of antidote injections in the near future, and the formula to create them on a widespread scale in his pack, he'd barely spoken. Mae was equally silent throughout the private flight, and when they'd finally touched down in Billings, the mood among the crew could only be described

as morose. It wasn't until they were just outside the borders
of Wolf Pack Run that the weight of what he was about to
do floored him.

How would it feel to lose her again? Not like the first time.
He knew that now. The first time, he'd given everything up
for the love of her, and this time, he was losing the only thing
that ever truly mattered to him—her. Even if it meant giving
her everything she'd ever hoped for. That'd always been the
true intent of his plan, even in the beginning.

She's not for you, and she never will be.

Somehow, that didn't seem to matter now.

He was riding atop Bee. Mae rode behind him, saddled
atop a white Arabian, as they neared the border of the Grey
Wolf packlands. His crew flanked them, and Mae even had
hold of Tucker in a carrier bag tucked beneath her arm.

As soon as they drew close, the Grey Wolf warriors
emerged from the trees. Of course they'd know the rogues
were coming. Maverick might be sitting atop the throne to
an empire that *should* have been Jared's, but he was more
than deserving of the role—formidable, fierce, cunning.
He would have figured out by now who'd taken Mae, and it
was likely only by the grace of the dozens of homes Rogue
kept throughout the country that the Grey Wolf packmaster
hadn't managed to find them yet. It was like trying to find a
needle in a haystack.

But Rogue had no doubt that had they taken longer,
Maverick Grey would have searched every one of his
homes. Hell, every place he'd ever rested his head at night.
Maverick loved his sister, even if he had a fucked-up way of
showing it, and he'd always been fiercely protective of Mae.
Unfortunately, it was to a near fault. In adulthood, it had led

him to keep her in a cage, trapped like a little songbird who wanted to fly free. Just as their father had.

That was what Rogue had to offer her that her pack didn't. Freedom. To go where she wanted, to be who she wanted, to *love* who she wanted.

Even if that wasn't him.

Maverick Grey stepped forth from beneath the pines. His Stetson shadowed his face as the sun drew low beneath the clouds. He was a massive wall of a man, nearly identical in size to Rogue. Long, mangy brown hair peeked from beneath his hat, making him look far more wolf than man, but unlike Rogue, his face wasn't crippled and deformed. Only one thin, jagged scar cut through his eyebrow and stopped just before the lid.

The single shot Rogue had taken at the bastard twenty years earlier.

But it was the pair of striking green eyes peering at them that unsettled Rogue. They were so similar to Mae's. It was damn near eerie.

Rogue had always hated that. It had seemed like a cruel twist of fate that one of his most fearsome rivals had the same pair of eyes as the only girl who could heal him and make him forget.

"Maverick." Mae's voice held a hint of affection as she dismounted. She was likely relieved to see him.

Maverick's warriors emerged from the trees, their weapons drawn. Rogue's men responded in kind. His rogues didn't outnumber the Grey Wolf elite warriors, but considering what they'd come for, it didn't matter.

Rogue recognized most of the Grey Wolves immediately. The faces that in his childhood memories remained boys instantly changed into those of the grown men who stared back at him. Grey Wolf elite alpha warriors. They all were.

Except for Rogue.

Maverick. Colt Cavanaugh. Malcolm, Dean, even that damn goofy idiot Blaze, who'd run off to Caltech to study computer science when they were fourteen. Hell, Rogue even recognized Wes Calhoun, former packmaster of the Wild Eight, though he'd never known him in his boyhood.

There were a few new faces he didn't recognize, but it didn't matter. He wasn't one of them anymore, and he never would be.

"Are you all right?" Maverick stepped toward his sister.

But Rogue's men raised their weapons higher, warding him off.

Maverick snarled.

He would need to wait for Mae to come to him. She'd made her choice. She was standing on their side of the border. With Rogue.

Good girl, Mae-day.

He'd always known she had more of a heart for the underdog than her brother did. Her love for that damn pig was evidence enough, as much as the little bacon monster irked him.

"I'm fine." She dismounted from her horse, setting Tucker's carrier on the ground as she met her brother's gaze. "I *chose* to go with him."

The stoic packmaster didn't so much as blink at the admission. Of course, what Mae thought would be a revelation wouldn't be for Maverick. He had known Jared was still alive all along, knew he'd become the Rogue, and he had also known how Mae had felt about him. Her brother perhaps understood why Mae was drawn to him better than she did.

But she'd understand soon enough.

Mae released her horse's reins, crossing the chasm between the two groups in order to stand on the border between them. One side of Rogue's lips pulled into a satisfied smirk. It was the perfect image of who she'd become over the past few days. She'd changed, for the better. Anyone with eyes could see it. She was still a Grey Wolf princess but was also a woman who cared about those less privileged than her, whose kindness could stretch to the ends of the earth and back.

Rogue had never been more proud.

"There's an antidote to the vampire's serum. We have the scientist who can create the formula to make it available to all wolves." She gestured to him and his men, as if she were one of them, instead of a pack wolf. "I made a deal with Rogue to save our pack. I knew time was running out before the vampires waged a full attack, and Alexander kept dragging his feet on the alliance. But you and I both know that even with Alexander's help, the Grey Wolves would have been slaughtered. I couldn't sit by and watch everyone we love, and so many other shifters, die. It was just a matter of time, and I—"

Maverick held up a hand as if he'd heard enough. "You trusted this criminal?"

Mae's eyes darted toward Rogue, and the confidence he saw there cut so deep his chest ached.

Confidence he was about to betray.

"Yes, I did," she said without hesitation, and as if that didn't make the faces of the Grey Wolf alpha warriors appear stunned enough, she added, "And I'd do it again in an instant."

The rage in Maverick's eyes as he looked toward Rogue lived up to every bit of the hatred Rogue had witnessed in the eyes of Maverick's father's that night so many years before. Thomas had sported the same look the night he'd chosen to beat Jared, maim him to the point of scarring and deforming his face permanently, then leave him for dead in the cold Montana snow. All this after he murdered Jared's father.

It hadn't been personal. In fact, the sick bastard had thanked Jared for saving Mae and for killing his disgusting pedophilic brother, but that single action had given him the excuse he'd needed to ensure that the Grey Wolf throne didn't pass to the Black family as the other pack wolves had voted. If there were no longer any heirs to the Black family, the title of packmaster remained with the Greys. In a single night, Thomas had committed murder to ensure the ascension of his only son, Maverick, to take his place.

Before Thomas had left Jared bloodied on the mountainside, he'd summoned Maverick. The young Grey Wolf had been ordered by his father to see the deed through, to kill Jared. As far as Maverick had known, Jared was his uncle's murderer. It should have been his very first kill in a long line of lives the Grey Wolf packmaster had taken since.

But Maverick had shown Jared mercy. Or what the young wolf had *thought* was mercy.

To this day, Rogue still wasn't certain why. Perhaps he'd known that someday he'd have to confess the sin to Mae.

As Jared had lain there bleeding, dying in the snow, he'd pleaded with Maverick, tried to tell Maverick the truth about his father, but the young wolf had refused to listen, calling him a liar. They'd even gotten in a tussle about that very detail, the result of which had left Maverick with a single scar over his eye and had only made Jared bleed even quicker.

Rogue had known the truth about Maverick Grey since that night. The Grey Wolf packmaster might be a valiant warrior, but underneath it, there was darkness in him, a streak for vengeance that was all too familiar each time Rogue looked in the mirror.

Maverick hadn't killed Jared, but the fate the misguided boy had sentenced Jared to had been far worse.

A long life knowing the woman he loved would never be his.

Rogue could still hear the echoing sound of Maverick's teenage voice damning him.

She's not for you, and she never will be, Maverick had hissed at him.

Maverick started to prowl toward Mae, his concern and frustration with her evident with each step he took.

"Maverick," Colt warned.

The Grey Wolf high commander reached for him, but Wes Calhoun, who stood directly to Maverick's side, interceded.

"Let him go, brother," Wes growled. The former Wild Eight packmaster lowered his voice, but with Rogue's wolf senses attuned, he still heard him. "Mae's more than capable of handling him."

At least he and Calhoun were in agreement.

Maverick stalked toward her, meeting her on the border as they stood nose to nose. "You made a deal on behalf of the pack without my permission?"

Mae stared down her brother without an ounce of fear

in her eyes. Older brother or not, a lesser wolf would have crumbled beneath the fury of Maverick Grey, but she didn't. Mae was no fighter when it came to battle, but she wielded power in a different way. She could be told what to do by no one. Not even the most powerful packmaster in the world.

Not even a rebellious Rogue.

She was her own woman. She always had been. She'd simply needed a reminder of that.

"I don't need your permission."

Maverick snarled. His eyes flashing to his wolf's. "I'm your packmaster. Your brother—"

Mae wasn't having one second of it. "You may be the packmaster of the Grey Wolves, but you're no *master* of mine." Her eyes transitioned to her wolf's. The golden hue blazed. "Need I remind you, brother, that the only reason you're packmaster and I'm not is because you happened to have the fortune of being born male," she hissed.

"You tell 'em, Mae." Daisy let out an encouraging whoop of girl power.

"Not now, Daisy," Rogue said, despite his grin. He remained cool, calm, collected.

The ice to Maverick's fire.

Mae continued with her righteous tirade. "Our pack laws are outdated, and you know it. I may not be a warrior, but the same blood runs through my veins as yours. As far as I'm concerned, you have no more right to make decisions for this pack than I do."

"Is that this bastard putting ideas in your head or—?"

"They're *my* ideas," she shot back. "If you'd paid atten-tion, you'd know I've felt that way for a long time. I'm tired of you thinking you can control me, just like Dad did."

"Mae, I've only tried to protect you. If you had told me, I—"

"You wouldn't have listened," she said. "Not without me doing something drastic."

"She's likely right. You're a horrible listener," Wes mumbled.

"Can it, Calhoun," Maverick snarled.

Rogue liked this Wes Calhoun character more with each passing second.

"And you picked *this* as your drastic measure?" Maverick gestured around them. He was shaking his head. "You have no idea what you've done, Mae."

"He's not what you think," she defended him. "He's loyal and kind and—"

"Your brother's right, Mae," Rogue said. He couldn't take another second of her defending him, not with what he had to do.

Mae turned toward him. "What are you talking about?"

In a single look, he tried to convey everything he needed to tell her. Everything he knew he wouldn't get the chance to say.

I did this for you. I wish you could understand, but I know you won't. It's okay if you hate me, but I had to...

Maverick took the liberty of answering for him. "It's not that he's not *what* you think, Mae. But he's not *who* you think, that's for certain." Maverick faced him, a snarl curling over his upper lip. "You always did know how to make an entrance."

Mae's brow furrowed in confusion. "You two have met before?" She looked confused but not hurt or angry. She still didn't realize. Her mind wouldn't let her. She was too convinced of his death, of her father's and brother's honesty to believe it. But deep down, she had to have had the inclination, even if it'd been tucked away in her subconscious.

Rogue liked to think that was why she'd been drawn to him from the start.

"No, we've never met before," Maverick answered, beating him to the punch. "At least, not as adults. Not for the past twenty years."

"Twenty years?" Mae glanced between them.

And there it was. Finally, out there in the open.

The realization played out on Mae's face within a matter of seconds, and it killed Jared.

What was left of that boy anyway...

Denial. Confusion. Incredulity. Then as the realization settled in, a brief flash of joy, happiness, relief. It was all there. But it flickered away just as quickly, replaced instead by the one emotion Rogue knew he couldn't take.

Her disappointment.

In him. In what he'd done.

Mae was shaking her head as tears poured down her cheeks in streams. "No. No," she whispered. Slowly, she walked toward Rogue, looking at him as if she'd never seen him before, as if he were a ghost risen from the dead.

Rogue didn't move. He couldn't.

When she reached him, she lifted a hand and traced it over the scarred side of his cheek. She'd felt it before, but the scars held a new meaning for her now. Proof of everything that'd happened. Everything that'd been hidden from her.

If Rogue had thought the pain in her eyes on the night she'd killed Buck would haunt him for an eternity, it was nothing compared to the pain and sorrow in her features now.

He wanted to hold her, to comfort her, to touch her. But his hands remained frozen at his sides.

"Jared," she whispered.

He didn't nod in answer. He knew he didn't have to.

She turned away from him, rounding on Maverick with a silent fury the likes of which he'd never seen from her before. "You knew," she whispered at him.

As her eyes raked over her brother, her nose wrinkled in disgust. She looked at him as if he were nothing more than the dirt beneath her boot.

"I didn't at first," Maverick said. "I knew he wasn't dead, but I didn't know he was the Rogue until—"

"You knew!" Mae shrieked. Her chin trembled. "And you lied to me!" She cast a glance in Rogue's direction. "You both did."

"Mae, I can explain," Maverick said. "I did it to protect you. I—"

Mae lifted a hand to silence him. "No," she said. "Save it." She was shaking her head. "I can't do this. I can't do this. Not now. Maybe not ever."

She started to walk away. Not in Rogue's direction or Maverick's but following the boundary line further up the mountain. Rogue wanted to let her go. He really did.

But he couldn't.

"We're not through here, Princess," he said. "Not yet."

His voice sounded disembodied to his own ears. It was the voice of the Rogue, the cold, calculating villain he'd become, not Jared, the future Grey Wolf cowboy who'd given his whole life for the love of a girl, a teenage girl who would only have broken his heart.

Even though for all intents and purposes, his birth

identity was dead, Rogue had always felt deep down that he wasn't the Rogue. He was still that same boy in love with a girl who'd meant everything for him.

But now, as he turned toward Mae, he wasn't certain he could tell himself and the Rogue apart.

Mae twisted toward him. Rogue. Jared. Whoever he was to her.

Past. Present.

But not future as he'd said. Not now.

He was watching her. Everyone was. Him, his men, her brother, the entire Grey Wolf Pack. They were waiting to see what her reaction would be, to see what she was made of, if she would crumble like the princess they all thought she was. She'd never liked the nickname he'd given her, but now her feelings for it bordered on hatred—and those feelings grew more intense with each second.

She was no princess, and she'd show them that.

"What do you mean, we're not through?" she asked. She didn't bother to swipe her tears away, but she wouldn't allow any more to fall. Not in front of everyone. Not for him.

"There's still the matter of our deal."

She stepped several paces back toward them all. "What could you possibly ask of me?"

"I told you I would collect my payment when it was due." Rogue stepped forward and drew his dagger from a holster nestled on the belt of his chaps. He hadn't unsheathed it in the time she'd known him as the Rogue. If he had, she would have recognized him immediately.

Because it was the same blade she'd killed her uncle with.

He stepped forward. She almost expected him to throw the blade at Maverick, but instead, he staked it in the ground just across the Grey Wolf border line, no more than a few paces away from Maverick's feet. As he rose from his task, he pegged her with a hard stare.

In that moment, even though she now knew who she was, she didn't recognize him, and it wasn't the scarring on his face that caused the confusion. It was the cold, piercing look in his eye. The look of a man who wanted revenge.

Oh, Jared.

"I'm only asking you to help me reclaim what was supposed to be mine." He faced Maverick. "I challenge your bid as packmaster."

A collective round of gasps and murmurs sounded through the forest, coming from the Grey Wolf packmembers who'd gathered behind the elite warriors.

"Can he do that?" The inane question had, of course, come from none other than Blaze, who at the moment was sporting a strange T-shirt that said "I'm nacho daddy," of all things.

"I can and I will," Rogue answered.

He was right. Mae knew it. Pack law dictated that any male heir of the founding families could challenge the current packmaster to battle for the right to rule the pack. All he needed was a fellow Grey Wolf packmember to sponsor his bid.

And he'd already secured himself one to do it.

Mae's stomach twisted.

Rogue addressed his next words to Maverick. "I'm the

sole heir to the Black family, one of the three founding families of the Grey Wolf Pack. I have just as much right to be packmaster as you do, and when I am, the Grey Wolves will no longer live on the bloodied backs of the rogue wolves."

Murtagh and the other rogues let out a victorious roar. Mae didn't blame them. Regardless of her opinion of Rogue—she couldn't bring herself to call him Jared now, not with what he was doing—she understood their argument, and had it not been her brother they were trying to defeat, she might have even supported their plight.

"I need a sponsor," Rogue said. His gaze turned toward her. Cerulean eyes and cheekbones so sharp they could cut.

He was still handsome, but now that thought only made her heart hurt.

That was where she came in. She stalked toward him. As she drew close to Rogue, several of the Grey Wolf warriors made to grab her.

"Mae," Maverick warned.

"I won't hurt her," Rogue assured them.

Mae stood in front of him. "You already have." It took everything in her not to fall into his arms, to ask him why he would do this to her, to her pack, to herself. But deep down, she didn't need to ask. She knew.

He wanted revenge.

More than he wanted her…

"Our deal was open-ended," he reminded her.

"I'm aware." Mae wasn't aware that she'd chosen to slap him until her hand had already connected with the side of his face.

Rogue didn't bother to move or defend himself. "I deserved that."

"You did." She nodded. "But you also deserve this." She gripped him by the collar and pulled him in to her, kissing him senseless. She poured everything she felt for him into that kiss, urging him to feel it all with her. The elation that he was still alive. Her gratitude for what he'd done for her. The hurt over how he'd lied to her. And the pain and sorrow she felt that he'd destroyed any chance she had to be with him.

Several whoops of approval at the public display sounded from some of the rogue wolves, while a few of the Grey Wolves snarled.

When she released him, she could see in his eyes that he'd felt every emotion she'd gifted him with. "Thank you," she whispered, low enough that only he could hear her. "For saving me from Buck." He ran her hand over the puckered scars of his cheek. "I just wish doing so hadn't destroyed the boy I loved so thoroughly."

She stepped back from him then.

"My packmembers will be safe and receive the antidote regardless of the outcome?" she asked.

He nodded.

She glanced between him and Maverick. "Unlike the two of you, I keep my promises and I never lie." She faced Rogue again. "I owe you a debt for the antidote, and I intend to keep it." She bent and pulled the dagger from the ground as was custom. She extended the blade toward him. "But that's the last bit of kindness from me you'll ever get."

"I wouldn't dream of asking for anything else." There was a sadness in his eyes, but she didn't allow herself to trust it was real. She was still too desperate for him to be who she wanted him to be. Her Jared or the secretly kindhearted Rogue. Maybe both? She wasn't certain anymore.

"I warned you I was no hero."

"You were," she said. "You were once, for me, but not now. You failed to tell me that you weren't just a villain. You're worse." She struggled to hold back her tears. "You're a monster," she whispered. "What a shame I was too in love with you to see it."

"You wouldn't have gone through with it if I hadn't lied to you. Not to save them," he gestured to the rogue wolves behind him. "Not even to save your pack."

She nodded. "You're right. I wouldn't betray my brother. Not willingly anyway. But if it saves the Grey Wolves' lives, I'll do anything. Not that you've given me a choice." It was this or have their whole journey result in nothing. She swallowed the lump in her throat. "I sponsor his bid as packmaster."

There were no gasps and murmurs. The forest surrounding them seemed to respond to the tension between them, growing so silent that she could hear the flow of the nearby river.

The river where she'd found him all those years ago, where she'd forced him to be her friend despite how he'd been mean to her to mask his pain.

She still didn't regret it.

She shot an angry glare toward her brother. "You lied to me as much as he did. Don't expect me to be there cheering you on come morning." She strode onto the Grey Wolf territory. The crowd of packmembers parted for her as if she were a live wire and if they touched her, she might spark.

"Mae," Maverick tried to stop her.

Colt held him back. "Let her go, Maverick."

Mae paused, glancing back toward where her brother

and Rogue still stood. "For what it's worth, I hope neither of you win." She snarled at both of them. "I hope you tear each other to pieces."

Mae shifted into wolf form and ran. She ran back to Wolf Pack Run, a place that now felt as foreign and unlike home to her as the opulent walls of Rogue's mansions. She didn't stop until she'd reached the private safety of her bedroom. She locked herself inside, closing all the doors and windows to keep them out, all of them, before she allowed herself to cry.

She didn't want to let them see her crumble.

But now that she had allowed herself to fall to pieces, she didn't know if she could pick herself back up.

Chapter 24

THAT NIGHT, AS ROGUE WAS SUPPOSED TO BE SLEEPING, he lay awake, staring up at the explosion of stars that stretched for eternity across the forests of Big Sky Country, recollecting every subtle detail of Mae's kiss. The slap he'd expected. He'd anticipated it even. He deserved it. He knew that, but the kiss she'd gifted him with had been unexpected.

And the pain he'd felt from her during that kiss was slowly eating away at his insides.

He was sprawled across the forest floor outside the small camp they'd erected just across the border of the Grey Wolf territory. He was supposed to be resting. Come sunset tomorrow, he was supposed to bring himself to fight the battle of his life, to reclaim his place as packmaster, a role that had been stolen from him, and when he won the battle, to change the lives of rogue wolves everywhere.

But none of that seemed to matter anymore.

Not without her.

"Ye've finally realized it, haven't ye, ye daft ijit?" Murtagh approached him, sitting down on a large rock beside Rogue.

"Realized what?" Rogue mumbled in between sips of whiskey. He'd downed enough Jack Daniel's that any human would be drunk as a skunk, but with his wolf metabolism, he was just getting started. There wasn't enough liquor in the world to numb the pain in his chest.

He'd thought his black heart gone, a shriveled hole in his chest.

He'd been horribly, terribly wrong.

"Ye finally realized I was right. That the loss of that lass will be the death of ye."

"I'm not dead yet."

"Ye will be soon if ye drown yerself in any more whiskey." Murtagh snatched the bottle from Rogue's hand.

Rogue growled, but Murtagh ignored him.

Gripping it by the neck, the Scot drew a long swig himself. "Is the revenge worth it?"

"I don't know. I haven't beaten him yet." He was lying through his teeth, and Murtagh knew it.

"We both know ye could beat her brother any day with both hands tied. There's no question. So how does it feel?"

"Like I've drunk too much whiskey?"

Murtagh snarled.

"What do you want me to say, Murtagh?" Rogue snarled back. "That I've royally fucked over the only good thing I've ever had in my life? Because if that's what you want to hear, I'll say it. You were right. It wasn't worth it. Not by a long shot. Losing her again will be the death of me, and it's death that I've chosen by my own hand." Rogue ran his fingers through his hair. "But you have to know, it really wasn't about the revenge. It was justice for the rogue wolves, and more importantly, it was for her. It always has been."

"If ye really mean that, you have a right dumb way of showin' it." Murtagh shook his head.

"I'm not sure where I went wrong. When all this is through, she'll have everything she ever wanted."

"Except for you." Murtagh mumbled several colorful curses as he stood. "The moment ye went wrong was when ye chose to bury the past, Jared."

Murtagh wandered away, heading back to where the other rogue wolves were still celebrating near the campfire. Something in Murtagh's words resonated, but not in the way the rogue wolf meant. Rogue didn't hesitate.

Within an hour, he found his way into Maverick's office. Slipping the locks proved far easier than expected, and it was there he waited. It was just before sunrise when the door finally opened and the packmaster eased inside.

To Maverick's credit, he sensed Rogue's presence immediately. Maverick's gaze never faltered from the dark corner where Rogue stood veiled in shadow. It was as if the packmaster were anticipating the next move of a coiled snake ready to strike.

After several prolonged moments, something in the fire of Maverick's gaze shifted, as though he'd found his resolution. Finally, he prowled across the room toward Rogue. The heavy sound of his leather boots as he approached held all the forceful promise of the blade clutched in his hand.

But Rogue was ready for the onslaught. He didn't fear death; he never had, and he'd experienced far crueler fates than a valiant death at the hands of a true warrior, a man who took his kills with swift and unrelenting justice. As Maverick stood over him, a deep snarl ripped from Rogue's throat, and he held his opponent's gaze. But the sharp, fatal brunt of the other man's blade would never come.

He knew Maverick too well, and they'd been down this path once before.

Suddenly, Maverick thrust his knife straight against Rogue's throat. "I should kill you. Right here. Right now," the packmaster snarled. A deep growl tore from his lips. "What makes you think I'll spare your life again?"

Rogue had taken a chance and played his cards well, because he had been right. Maverick had a streak for mercy, which meant it was as he'd always suspected. He was the fiercer wolf, but her brother was the better man. A twisted laugh rumbled in Rogue's chest. "Because you spared me for her sake. You won't kill me unprovoked, and we both know it. You've always been too heroic for your own damn good."

A twisted smirk curved over Rogue's lips. "You know I can't say the same." His irises narrowed, and his eyes flashed to the gold of his wolf's. One last challenge for old times' sake. "Because if it were me holding that blade"—he locked eyes on the Grey Wolf warrior—"my enemy would be dead already."

Maverick snarled. "Say your piece and be gone, Rogue."

Rogue intended to do exactly that. Murtagh's words had made him realize the truth. It wasn't him or even Maverick that Mae needed, and it wasn't hiding his identity to protect her that had been truly wrong, nor had his drive to protect the rogues been ill advised. None of those instincts had been fully wrong. He'd just gone about it entirely the wrong way. He'd done it the Rogue's way. Not Jared's.

But now that he realized, he still had time to set things right.

It wouldn't bring her back to him, but it was the right thing to do.

For once, he didn't have to question that.

"We both love Mae," Rogue said. "So I'm here to make one final deal. This time, for her."

The following afternoon not long before sunset, Mae stumbled from her bedroom, her eyes still swollen and puffy. She'd cried more tears than she'd ever known a person could cry in a lifetime, and she still wasn't certain she was done crying.

She wasn't certain she'd ever be done crying over him.

But she had a bone to pick with Maverick and questions she needed answered if she was supposed to find a way to heal, and she needed those questions answered *now*.

She found him in his office inside the main compound at the center of Wolf Pack Run, the compound that housed all the elite warriors. The same one that as a child, she'd assumed Jared would live in.

When she entered, Maverick glanced up from what he was doing and immediately froze. He was looking at her as if she were a bomb about to go off right there in the middle of his office.

"Mae, I'm—"

She shook her head. "Don't," she warned him.

She knew her older brother, and she knew that voice. It was the same tone he'd had every time he'd apologized to her over the years, but she didn't want his apology. Not this time.

"Save your apology for someone who wants it. I don't forgive you, and I don't know if I will for a long time. Maybe not ever."

Maverick nodded. "That's fair."

Mae wrung her hands, trying to decide if she really wanted to know the answer to the question she was about to ask. "Why?" she finally managed. "I've gathered that you and Father lied about Jared's death, but I…I don't understand why."

"Because Father told me to kill him and I didn't. I let

him live, for your sake and yours alone. For all intents and purposes, he *was* dead. At least for you, at least then. I'd planned to tell you one day, to let you make your own decision, but then he became the Rogue. You know his reputation. I chose to protect you. I chose—"

"For me," she finished. "You chose *for me*. Packmaster or not, you had no right to." She was shaking her head. "And you followed Father? You allowed him to order a boy's death? You were supposed to do the right thing." She'd always trusted him to before. He may have been overprotective of her, sometimes misguided, but she'd always thought his heart was in the right place. Now she wasn't so certain.

"What else would you have had me do? I didn't know what the right thing was, Mae. I was fifteen!"

"So was he!" Her hands clenched into fists at her sides as she tried to stop herself from shaking. "So was he," she breathed.

"Jared may have been your friend, but he chose his fate. He knew our laws, but he still killed Buck. Our father was a good man. A fierce warrior who was loyal to his pack. A kind cowboy who…"

"Our father was a murderer! He killed Jared's father and nearly him too. Do you not understand? He nearly murdered the boy who saved me from our beast of an uncle. The same uncle who spent night after night raping me!"

Maverick's features went completely slack, and he dropped the pen he'd been holding in his hand. "What?"

"He didn't tell you?" Mae shook her head. "Of course he didn't. Dad was truly a manipulative, evil bastard, wasn't he?"

"Mae, what are you talking about?" Maverick rounded his desk to come to her side, but she stepped away from him.

"Buck had been hurting me, assaulting me for months, Maverick."

For once, her brother's reaction wasn't rage, anger, or disappointment. It was grief. "Mae, I didn't know. I swear it. You have to believe me. I—"

"I don't have to do anything, Maverick. Not for you or Father. Not anymore." She released a long exhale through her nose. She'd kept her own secrets buried too long. "Jared was in my room that night, telling me how his father had gifted him with his blade. But then Buck came down the hall. There wasn't time for Jared to leave. I told him to get in my closet and close his eyes, but he must not have listened. As he hid, he must have seen what Buck was about to do, because, all of a sudden, he burst out the door and was on top of Buck. It didn't take much for Buck to overpower him, and then he was choking Jared, and I...I grabbed the dagger on the bed and I...I made him stop."

The silence between her and Maverick was deafening.

"Don't you see?" she said. "*I* killed Buck. It was never Jared. But when Father came in, Jared took the fall for it. He grabbed the knife and declared it was him. He confessed to protect me from the repercussions, and by the time I realized Jared wouldn't receive any mercy from the pack alphas, it was too late." She shook her head. "I suppose Father didn't bother to tell them about what Buck had done. They must have thought Jared killed Buck in cold blood, and he wasn't even the one to do it."

"You never told me."

She pointed an accusing finger at him. "*You* told me he was dead, yet you expected me to be honest with you? To tell you that I was too scared to come forward, to tell the truth about Buck, about the decisions I'd made that had supposedly led to the death of the only boy, the only man I ever…"

Loved. She was going to say loved. She did love him. Still.

I've already given you my past, my present, my future, he'd said, and she felt the same.

Oh, Jared.

She loved him then and she loved him now, despite the position he'd put her in.

Which meant she had a choice to make.

But how could she forgive him? He'd chosen his revenge over her.

"Love," Maverick finished for her. "You love him still?"

She nodded. "I always have. I've never stopped. I'm fairly certain I fell in love with him the day we jumped from that tree together as children. The day he started calling me Mae-day. He was my best friend, and for the past twenty years, I've never been able to forget him." She released a long sigh. "Please don't kill him. I'm not sure I could bear it."

"There will be no battle between us."

"So you'll surrender to him?"

"Never," he growled. The fiery drive of a warrior who'd never known defeat flashed in Maverick's wolf eyes. "I never surrender. I live and die by this pack. You know that."

Mae had no doubt of that. Her brother was a fierce warrior, loyal to his pack no matter the personal cost. "If you're not surrendering, then did you already—?" She couldn't bear the thought.

"Don't think so little of me, Sister. I wouldn't kill him. Not knowing what he means to you. I love you too much for that. Why do you think I let him live all those years ago? Father ordered me to kill him. I thought he'd murdered our uncle, and still I didn't—for you." Maverick slid open one of his desk drawers and reached inside. "He showed up in my office this morning. Before sunrise. He was just sitting here in my desk chair. I have no idea how he got in."

Mae shrugged. "He does that."

"But he called the whole thing off, although not without making some negotiating demands first."

"Negotiating demands?"

"He said he didn't want to be packmaster. Not really. He said all he wanted was rights for the rogues."

"So the rogues have their justice?"

At least there was that.

"Yes." Maverick nodded. "But you have to know, Mae, not all of them are like Jared."

"I know that." She thought of Walker Solomon.

Good riddance.

"But some of them *are* like Jared, and they're worth saving," she added. "I know they're not pack wolves, but—"

"It was *never* about pack status, Mae. With all our subpacks, pack shifters outnumber rogues. I had a choice to make, and I couldn't allow the pack to be the constant target of human hunters. Too many lives would have been lost. The human hunters were out for someone, and the rogue wolves were their choice. Turning a blind eye may not have been fair, but it was for the greater good. Fewer lives were lost because of it. This new arrangement with the rogues may be beneficial to *them*, but the Seven Range Pact will have to terminate our agreement with the Execution Underground. We won't have the immunity from their hunters that we've enjoyed for so long. It will bring hellfire down on all of us, lives *will* be lost, but it was that or allow the vampires to destroy our whole species before we got the antidote."

For once, her brother looked tired, wary, as if he wasn't sure of himself or anything anymore. She knew the revelation of her father's character would take a toll on him, more than the alpha wolf would ever admit. Maverick had always aspired to rule in the way he thought their father had, but now with the truth of their father's transgressions out in the open, Maverick would have to grapple with the fact that his singular role model hadn't been the man he'd thought him to be.

The weight of that would shake her brother to his core. She knew that.

Moving forward, Maverick would have to forge his own path. And she had no doubt he would. There was still a fire in his eyes, a will to fight. He'd do whatever it took to keep their friends and family safe. He'd even sacrifice his own life if necessary.

"Well," she said. "Better to die with honor while protecting *all* of our kind, and I'm not worried, Brother. I know you'll be able to handle whatever challenges are ahead. *You'll* lead us through. With or without Father's example."

Of that, she had little doubt. Her brother might have angered her, but he was a formidable warrior—unrivaled in his skill—and when he needed to be, he was a just and fair packmaster who even, on occasion, had a penchant for mercy. She thought of Maverick's treatment of Wes Calhoun, and his brother, Colt Cavanaugh, and now Jared as well. Other packmasters would have cast them out, killed them even, for their disobedience, but Maverick was stronger than that. His critics had called his mercy reckless, but he was too brave and courageous to care. He'd done what was just. What was right. He might have been misguided when it came to the rogues and to her, but his intention—protecting the Grey Wolves no matter the cost, protecting her—was honorable.

"You know I'll do whatever it takes." Maverick cast her a half-hearted smile. "But there was one more thing, Mae. Before they left this morning, he asked that you be freed from all your obligations as a Grey."

Mae blinked. She wasn't certain she had heard him right. "What?" she murmured.

"He told me to give you this." Maverick extended a bundle of something toward her. "He left this for you. I was going to give it to you when you came in, but you didn't let me get a word out at first."

"You deserved it," she said, reaching out to accept the gift.

"You're right. I do. I deserve a lot of things, Mae, and your forgiveness isn't one of them. But I do want it, and I promise I'll earn it. In time."

There was a note tucked on the outside, scrawled with a familiar script. Jared's writing.

Twenty years ago, this lay between us as I swore a promise to you, Maeve Grey. I'm sorry it took me so long to deliver that promise. I hope someday you can forgive me.

Carefully, she unwrapped the cloth from around the item. As she stared down at Jared's dagger in her hand, the dagger his father had given him, she stifled a gasp. The memory of the night he'd sacrificed everything for her gripped her. The words he'd whispered to her echoed in her ear as fresh as if he were standing right there beside her.

"If you want freedom, I'll give it to you. Someday I'll take you away from here, Mae. As far as you want to go."

And he had. He'd kept his promise. He'd not only given her the taste of freedom she'd always wanted, but he'd given up his hard-earned revenge, the revenge he rightfully deserved, to do it. Her only regret was that it'd taken her so long to realize his intent, that she'd doubted him.

Mae breathed out a breath she hadn't realized she'd been holding.

He *was* a hero.

She'd suspected it, but it'd been hidden so far beneath the dark outer shell of a villain that there'd been moments when she doubted it. But she'd been right.

The Rogue. The Dark Devil. The King of the Misfit Wolves.

He was all those nicknames and more.

But he was also the defender of the vulnerable, protector of abused women and orphaned children…hell, any underdog too weak to fight for themselves.

And more importantly…

He was *her* Rogue.

A man she loved, whether he was or wasn't Jared, her dearest childhood friend.

Because as hard as she'd fallen for Rogue, theirs was a tragic love. She didn't think that out of pity. In fact, she counted herself lucky that she'd experienced two great loves in her life, even if unfortunate circumstance forced her not to keep them. Like Orpheus and Eurydice, her and Rogue's time had been limited, but she'd allowed herself to fall for him anyway. Parting ways with him without looking back would be painful, but even though she didn't want to live that pain, she knew she could, because she was prepared for it.

She had been from the start.

The only thing more painful than losing Rogue, the man she loved, would be to resurrect Jared, her best friend, from the dead, only to lose him again…

She couldn't finish this conversation with Maverick. "I have to go."

"What do you mean, you have to go, Mae? You just arrived back home. You—"

"And I'm not coming back," she interrupted as she rushed toward his office door. "Not for a long time."

"You're going to go to him?"

"Of course I am," she said. "I love him, despite everything. Maybe even because of it."

"And you'd leave your pack, your family for it?"

"Yes," she said without hesitation. "If that's the choice I'm forced to make, then yes. I'd give up everything for him. He's already given everything in his life for me. It's only fair I return the favor."

Maverick looked stricken, but he didn't protest. "Then go," he said. "You'll still be a Grey Wolf when you come back."

Mae smiled. "I don't forgive you for lying, Brother, not yet. Honestly, I'm not sure I'll ever forgive you. But I'll forget, that I can promise you, and that might well be the same."

Maverick nodded. "I'll take what I can get."

"I love you."

Maverick smiled, but it didn't quite reach his eyes. "I love you too."

Mae turned to leave, but his next words stopped her.

"Just promise me you're not going to have little rogue children running around. The thought makes me sick to my stomach."

"There are already rogue children running around," she said.

His eyes grew wide. "Good Lord, you're not pregnant. Are—?"

"No." She laughed. Though she supposed there was a hint of possibility, all things considered. "No, they're not mine. They're orphans. He took them in."

Maverick scoffed. "Of course he did. A criminal who cares for orphans. You were doomed from the start." He swore.

Mae couldn't help but chuckle. "You're right. I was doomed, but only because I wanted to be." She moved to leave again. "I'll see you around, Brother."

"Stay safe, Sister." Maverick waved a hand in dismissal. "But, Mae," he said, causing her to pause again. "One last thing."

She quirked a brow. "What's that?"

"Tell Rogue, or Jared, or fuck, whatever his name is now, that he wins." Maverick's eyes flashed to his wolf's. "This time."

Mae smiled. "I love you, Brother. But when Rogue sets his mind to something, you wouldn't stand a chance against him."

She ran from her brother's office, not bothering to look back.

Chapter 25

IT'D BEEN NEARLY TWO WEEKS SINCE ROGUE AND HIS MEN had left Wolf Pack Run with the reassurance that Maverick would work to widely distribute the antidote among all shifters of their kind—pack wolves or not. The antidote would prevent shifter blood from having any effect on the vampires, regardless of whether the vamps had received their dose of the serum. Additionally, once Maverick had agreed to loosen the restrictions the Grey Wolves had on allowing rogue wolves to join their pack, Rogue and his men had made their way back to Black Hollow. After the vampire raid, the barn had needed a significant amount of rebuilding, and they had been working on it ever since.

The summer days were still long. In the past, he'd been grateful for that. It'd allowed him to escape himself and his identity as the Rogue as he buried himself in ranch work. Now, every time he headed out to replace one of the boards in the barn and glanced toward the hayloft, or especially any time he had the misfortune to be tasked with slopping and caring for the pigs, he couldn't escape thoughts of a certain Grey Wolf princess who thought the little pink beasts were appropriate pets.

He was aware that thinking of Mae in relation to pigs wasn't the most romantic of notions, but he couldn't help himself. She'd dragged that little, pink hell beast along the entire time she'd been with him. But most frequently, he thought of her at night. As he sat in the library, attempting to read. Every time his eyes scanned over the page, he'd have to force himself to reread it, because instead of the words before him, all he saw was her face. Her kind smile. The freckles across her cheeks, and those gorgeous green eyes, so beautiful and stunning they stole his breath, despite how they resembled her brother's.

Rogue knew the nature of deep pain. It never lessened over time. It was only something a man learned to live with. But for a cowboy like him, a criminal in every sense of the word, he had no doubt he'd live through it. He was made of far tougher stuff than to allow the loss of a woman to break him, even a woman he would always love.

He could live without her. He had for twenty years.

But he'd never want to.

Not by a long shot.

Rogue tilted his Stetson off his head, swiping at the sweat on his brow with a handkerchief he kept tucked in his back pocket. It was hotter than Hades inside the barn, and considering he'd been hammering away at these boards for the past two hours, the summer heat wouldn't allow him to forget it.

He grabbed the hammer to set to work again, but as he did, he heard a distressed-sounding whinny from where Bee was tied up just outside the barn. He followed the sound, taking the hammer with him as he went to investigate.

When he found Bee where he'd left him tied, the mustang was stomping and fussing at a small squealing animal on the ground. Rogue raised a brow.

No. That couldn't possibly be Tucker, could it?

If it was, he'd grown to nearly twice his size in just as many weeks.

"Put down the hammer and step away from the pig."

Mae's voice sounded from behind him as she approached from the other side of the barn.

She'd come for him. He'd known there was a possibility. After the way he'd hurt her, he hadn't anticipated it. But she was here.

Which meant she'd chosen him.

He'd gifted her with all the freedom the world had to offer. She had it all: a pack to love her, yet the freedom to do whatever she chose. No restrictions. And she'd used that freedom to come back to him.

"You mean the hog?" he drawled without turning around. The question was playful, intended to tease.

"You know what I mean, Jared."

The sound of his real name on her lips and not said with contempt shook him to his core. He dropped the hammer into the grass and turned toward her.

She was leaning against the barn, cloaked in the building's shadows. Her cowgirl hat was tipped low over her eyes and her boots crossed at the ankles, mirroring the same position he'd been in when he'd shown up unexpectedly in her bedroom.

"Evenin', Prince," she greeted.

He chuckled. "Mae, it's not evening."

"Obviously," she said with a shrug. "Just go with it."

He didn't have it in him to protest.

"What are you doing here?" he asked.

"Observing," she said, mimicking him again. "I've found I have a taste for shirtless cowboys." Her gaze raked over his bare chest suggestively.

An amused smirk crossed his lips. "Do you now?" he said.

She shrugged again. "It's to be expected. I did grow up surrounded by them—mostly gorgeous ones at that."

"Of course," he replied. "The Grey Wolf warriors." Any woman would have to be blind not to think such. He'd at least give the bastards that.

She removed her hat from her head, casting it onto the grass. "But there's only one Grey Wolf I've ever had eyes for." Pushing off from the barn where she leaned, she eased toward him.

Rogue shook his head. "Mae, you don't have to do this. I hurt you. I know I did, and fuck if I don't regret it, but when I negotiated your freedom with Maverick, it was no strings attached. I want you to be happy, with whoever it is who will give you happiness. You don't have to choose me. You—"

She was standing in front of him now. She gripped the buckle of his chaps with one hand and pulled him toward her as she used the other to press a single finger to his lips. "Hush," she shushed him. "It's my turn to talk."

When she looked at him with that sultry gleam to her eyes as she bit her lower lip, he would have listened to her for hours—days—if she'd let him.

"I'm here to make a deal with you."

Rogue shook his head. "I've done enough deal making for a lifetime."

She shook her head at him. "I told you to go with it."

"All right. All right." He shook his head. "What kind of deal?"

"The kind of deal that gives you my love, past, present, and future." She wrapped her arms around his neck, dropping the charade in favor of seriousness. "I don't forgive you for how you hurt me, but I know that you lost so much of yourself over the years to being the Rogue, to fighting to survive, that I'm willing to forget it. I'm not even sure you know how to love."

Rogue's stomach dropped. So she wasn't here for him after all. But then why was she—?

"But the deal is, I'm going to teach you how," she said, drawing in close enough that her lips brushed against his. "As long as you promise to try to love me back."

Rogue kissed her with all the weight of everything he felt for her. He kissed her like she meant something to him, because she did. She had all along, and he'd never allow himself to forget it.

He deepened the intensity. Drawing her toward him, he hoisted her in his arms and carried her toward the barn, pressing her against the outside wall. He didn't care that they were out in the middle of the pasture; he'd take her right then and there.

A hungry growl rumbled in his throat. He intended to take her in so many ways before the sun set that night that she'd be riding sidesaddle for weeks. But first he had one last deal to make.

"You have yourself a deal, Princess. But I need you to understand something," he said.

She traced her knuckles gently over his scars before she cradled his cheek in her hand. He'd never consider himself deformed again. Not if she kept touching him there like that.

"And what's that?" she asked.

"There's no *try* about it, Mae-day." He smiled at her as he shook his head. "I've loved you for the past twenty years. Longer even. But I promise I'll find better ways to show it."

At the sound of her childhood nickname on his lips, she grinned. The wholehearted smile she gifted him with filled the dark, cavernous hole that had consumed his chest for so many years, bringing in light, casting out the dark. As she always had done for him.

With a single look, she made him whole.

"You better," she warned, but the censure was belied by an amused grin. "Though there's something else I need to understand before we seal this deal," she said.

Rogue prepared himself for any number of questions—about his dark past, the men he'd killed, any number of horrible things that might scare her away from a wicked cowboy like him. "And what's that?"

She gestured to where Tucker was now nipping ferociously at Bee's ankles. The horse was stomping furiously at the little monster as his teeth bared in a growl.

"Why do you dislike Tucker so much?"

She had to ask?

"He's a good little pig."

Tucker released an angry-sounding grunt as he dove for Bee's back ankle.

Rogue frowned as Mae forced a smile. "Okay, so he's more than a bit territorial—"

"Territorial? He's attacking Bee," Rogue countered. "On *my* land."

"*Our* land, if you'll allow me to stay here with you," she corrected. "But be serious."

"Be serious while discussing my feelings toward your pet pig?" Rogue laughed.

But she wasn't going to kiss him again, or allow him to do anything *else* for that matter, until he gave her an answer. He could see that. "Mae, the only reason I don't like Tucker is because he interrupted our first kiss. It was a kiss I'd waited twenty years to steal from you"—he cast her a devilish smirk—"and no criminal like me can forgive that."

About the Author

Kait Ballenger hated reading when she was a child, because she was horrible at it. Then by chance, she picked up the Harry Potter series, magically fell in love with reading, and never looked back. When she realized shortly after that she could tell her own stories and they could be about falling in love, her fate was sealed.

She earned her BA in English from Stetson University—like the Stetson cowboy hat—followed by an MFA in writing from Spalding University. After stints working as a real vampire—a.k.a. a phlebotomist—a bingo caller, a professional belly dancer, and an adjunct English professor (which she still dabbles in on occasion), Kait finally decided that her eight-year-old self knew best: she was meant to be a romance writer.

When Kait is not preoccupied with writing captivating paranormal romance, page-turning suspense, or love scenes that make even seasoned romance readers blush, she can usually be found spending time with her family, being an accidental crazy cat lady (she has four now—don't ask), or with her nose buried in a good book. She loves to travel—especially abroad—and experience new places. She lives in Florida with her doting librarian husband, her two adorable sons, a lovable, mangy mutt of a dog, and four conniving felines.

And yes, she can still belly dance with the best of them.

THE LEGEND OF ALL WOLVES

For three days out of thirty, when the moon is full and her law is iron, the Great North Pack must be wild...

The Last Wolf

Silver Nilsdottir is at the bottom of her Pack's social order, with little chance for a decent mate and a better life. Until the day she meets a stranger and decides to risk everything...

A Wolf Apart

Only Thea Villalobos can see that Elijah Sorensson is Alpha of his generation of the Great North Pack, and that the wolf inside him will no longer be restrained...

Forever Wolf

With old and new enemies threatening the Great North, Varya knows that she must keep Eyulf hidden away from the superstitious wolves who would doom them both...